NINE MONTHS TO
CHANGE HIS LIFE

BY
MARION LENNOX

Marion Lennox is a country girl, born on an Australian dairy farm. She moved on—mostly because the cows just weren't interested in her stories! Married to a 'very special doctor', Marion writes for the Mills & Boon Medical Romance and Mills & Boon Cherish lines. (She used a different name for each category for a while—readers looking for her past romance titles should search for author Trisha David as well). She's now had more than seventy-five romance novels accepted for publication.

In her non-writing life Marion cares for kids, cats, dogs, chooks and goldfish. She travels, she fights her rampant garden (she's losing) and her house dust (she's lost). Having spun in circles for the first part of her life, she's now stepped back from her 'other' career, which was teaching statistics at her local university. Finally she's reprioritised her life, figured out what's important and discovered the joys of deep baths, romance and chocolate. Preferably all at the same time!

CHAPTER ONE

FROM THE MOMENT they were born, the Logan boys were trouble.

They were dark-haired, dark-eyed and full of mischief. Usually ignored by their wealthy, emotionally distant parents, they ran their nannies ragged and they ran themselves ragged. There wasn't a lot they wouldn't dare each other to do.

As they grew to men, tall, tough and ripped, their risks escalated. Some of those risks turned out to be foolish, Ben conceded. Joining the army and going to Afghanistan had been foolish. Back in civvies, attempting to get on with their careers, the trauma was still with them.

Sailing round the world to distract Jake from his failed marriage had also turned out to be stupid. Especially now, as Cyclone Lila bore down on their frail life raft, as one harness hung free from the chopper overhead.

'Take Ben first,' Jake yelled to the paramedic who'd been lowered with the harness, but Ben wasn't buying it.

'I'm the eldest,' Ben snapped. He was only older by twenty minutes but the responsibility of that twenty minutes had weighed on him all his life. 'Go.'

Jake refused, but the woman swinging from the chopper was risking all to save them. The weather was crazy—no one should be on the sea in such conditions. Arguing had to be done hard and fast.

He did what he had to do. The things he said to get Jake to go first were unforgivable—but he got the harness on.

'The chopper's full,' the paramedic yelled at Ben as she signalled for the chopper to pull them free. 'We'll come back for you as soon as we can.'

Or not. They all knew how unlikely another rescue was. The cyclone had veered erratically from its predicted path, catching the whole yachting fleet unprepared. The speed at which it was travelling was breathtaking, and there was no escape. Massive waves had smashed their boat, and they were still on the edge of the cyclone. The worst was yet to come.

At least Jake was safe—he hoped. The wind was making the rope from the chopper swing wildly, hurling Jake and the paramedic through the cresting waves. *Get up there,* he pleaded silently. *Move.*

Then the next wave bore down, a monster of breaking foam. He saw it coming, slammed down the hatch of the life raft and held on for dear life as the sea tossed his flimsy craft like a beach ball in surf.

We'll come back for you as soon as we can.

When the cyclone was over?

The wave passed and he dared open the hatch a little. The chopper was higher, but Jake and his rescuer were still swinging.

'Stay safe, brother,' he whispered. 'Stay safe until I see you again.'

A cyclone was heading straight for him. *Until I see you again...* What a bitter joke.

This was no mere storm. This was a cyclone, and in a cyclone there could surely be few worse places to be than on Hideaway Island.

Hideaway Island was tiny, a dot on the outer edge of the Bay of Islands off New Zealand's north coast. Two of Mary's friends, a surgeon and his lawyer wife, had bought it for a song years ago. They'd built a hut in the centre of the island and bought a serviceable boat to ferry themselves back and forth to the mainland. They'd decided it was paradise.

But Henry and Barbara now had impressive professional lives and three children. They hardly ever made it out here. It'd been on the market for a year, but with the global financial crisis no one was buying.

Right now, Henry and Barbara were in New York, but before they'd left, Henry had tossed Mary the keys to the hut and boat.

'You might use some solitude until this fuss dies down,' Henry told her with rough kindness. 'Could you check on the place while we're away? Stay if you like; we'd be grateful. It might be what you need.'

It was what she needed. Henry was one of the few who didn't blame her. Hideaway had seemed a reasonable place to run.

Until today. Heinz, her terrier-size, fifty-seven-or-more-variety dog, was looking at her as if he was worried, and his worry was justified. The wind was escalating by the minute. Outside the trees were bending and groaning with its force, and the roughly built hut felt distinctly unstable.

'We could end up in Texas,' Mary muttered, shaking her useless radio. Had a transmission tower fallen in the wind? Her phone was dead and there was no radio reception.

At six this morning the radio had said Cyclone Lila was five hundred miles off the coast, veering north-east instead of in its predicted northern trajectory. There was concern for a major international yacht race, but there'd been no hint that it might turn south and hit the Bay of Islands. Residents of New Zealand's north had merely been advised that the outside edges could cause heavy winds.

'Tie down outside furniture,' the broadcast had said. 'Don't park under trees.'

That was a normal storm warning—nothing to worry about. Mary had thought briefly of taking the boat and heading for the mainland, but the wind was rising and the usually placid sea around the islands was rough. It'd be safer to sit it out.

Or it had seemed safer, until about an hour ago.

Another gust slammed into the hut. A sheet of iron ripped from the roof and sleet swept inside.

The foundations creaked and the pictures on the wall swayed.

Uh-oh.

'I think we might head for the cave,' she told Heinz uneasily. 'You want a walk?'

The little terrier-cum-beagle-cum-a-lot-of-other-things cocked his head and looked even more worried. Right now a walk didn't appeal even to Heinz.

But the cave was appealing. Mary and Heinz had explored it a couple of days ago. It was wide and deep, set in the cliffs above the only beach where swimming was possible. Best of all, it faced west. It'd protect them from the worst of the gale.

Now that the roof was open, there didn't seem to be a choice. She had to go, and go now before it got worse. But what to take? The cave was only two or three hundred yards away. There was a flattish track and she had a trolley, the one Barbara and Henry used to lug supplies from boat to hut.

The boat. There was a sickening thought. The tiny natural harbour on the east of the island should protect the boat in all but the worst conditions—but these were the worst conditions.

She had no communications. No boat. She was on her own.

So what else was new? She'd been on her own now for as long as she could remember. Like it or not, she'd learned to depend entirely on herself, and she could do it now.

Concentrate on practicalities.

She grabbed plastic garbage bags and started stuffing things inside. Provisions, dog food, firestarters, kindling, bedding. Her manuscript. That was a joke, but she was taking it anyway.

Water containers. What else? What would Barbara and Henry want her to save?

Barbara's patchwork quilt? The lovely cushions embroidered by Barbara's grandmother? They went into plastic bags, too.

Another sheet of roofing iron went flying. The cottage was now totally open to the weather.

She had to stop. This was starting to be seriously scary and she had to pull the trolley.

'Why couldn't you be a sled dog?' she demanded of Heinz as she hauled open the door and faced the weather. 'You could help me pull.'

In answer, Heinz stared up at the wildly swaying trees, jumped onto the trolley and wriggled down among the plastic bags.

He was terrified. So was Mary, but she made herself pause. She made herself think. What else might be important?

'First-aid kit,' she muttered, and headed back into the already soaking cottage to find her medical bag. As a district nurse she still had it with her, and she'd brought it to the island just in case.

In case of splinters. In case of colds in the head. Not in case of cyclones.

She could hear branches splintering from the trees. There was no time for more.

And then the rest of the roof peeled off, with a shriek of tin against tin.

'Go,' she muttered, and started pulling. Heavy didn't begin to describe it. Sleet was stinging her eyes, her face, every part of her.

What to discard? Everything but essentials? Nothing Barbara and Henry cherished?

'Don't be a wuss,' she told herself. 'They entrusted you with their island. The least you can do is save their stuff. The path's reasonably flat. Come on, muscles, pull.'

She tugged and the trolley moved.

'I can do this,' she said through gritted teeth, and put her head down into the wind and pulled.

The life raft was in freefall. Ben was falling over and over. It felt like one of those crazy fairground rides, only he'd forgotten to buckle his seat belt. Who had designed this thing? It'd be safe enough on a calm sea but who got shipwrecked on a calm sea?

He could find nothing to anchor himself to. He was flailing, bashing against the sides of the raft with every bounce.

He felt ill but he didn't have time to be ill.

At least Jake was safe. It was a mantra, and he said it over and over. He had to believe the chopper had pulled his twin to safety. Thinking anything else was the way of madness.

The raft crashed again, but this time it was different. It was smashing against something solid.

They'd been miles from land when the yacht had started taking on water. Ben knew what this must be and his nausea increased. The raft would be bashing against what remained of the yacht's hull. Caught in the same currents, with no way to get himself clear, he'd be hurled against timber at every turn.

The second crash ripped the side of the life raft. Another wave hurled over him, and the life raft practically turned itself inside out.

Tossing its human cargo out with it.

He grabbed one of the ropes around the outside of the raft. The bulk of the craft should stay upright. If he could just hold…

Another wave hit, a massive breaker of surging foam. No man could hold against such force.

And then there was nothing. Only the open, smashing sea. The GPS was in the life raft. Chances of being found now? Zip.

It was no use swimming. There was no use doing anything but hope his lifejacket wouldn't be torn from him. He could only hope he could still keep on breathing. Hope… Hope…

There was nothing but hope. He was fighting to breathe. He was fighting to live.

There was no help. There was nothing but the endless sea.

She had to round the headland to get to the cave. It meant putting her head down and pulling almost directly into the wind. She had no idea how she was doing it, but the trolley was moving.

Tourists came to this place in summer, beaching their kayaks and exploring. The cliff path had therefore been trodden almost flat. It was possible, and she had terror driving her on. 'This is mad,' she muttered, but her words were lost in the gale.

She was at the point where the path veered away from the headland and turned towards the safety of the cave. Five more steps. Four…

She reached the turn and glanced down towards the beach,

beyond the headland where the storm was at its worst. And stopped.

Was that a figure in the water, just beyond the shallows? A body? A crimson lifejacket?

She was surely imagining things, but, dear God, if she wasn't...

Triage. Her medical training kicked in. Get the provisions safe, she told herself. She was no use to herself or anyone else without dry gear.

She had to haul the trolley upwards for the last few yards but she hardly noticed. In seconds she'd shoved the trolley deep inside the cave. At least the cave was in the lee of the storm, and so was the beach below.

It was wild enough even on the safe side of the island.

'Stay,' she told Heinz, and Heinz stuck his head out from the plastic bags and promptly buried himself again. Stay? He was in total agreement. It was dry and safe in the cave but outside the scream of wind and ocean was terrifying.

She had to face it. She wasn't sure what she'd seen was... someone, but she had to find out.

The path down to the beach was steep but manageable. Running along the beach on the lee side of the island was almost easy as well. Thankfully the tide was out so she was running on wet sand.

She could do this.

And then she rounded the headland and the force of the storm hit head on.

She could hardly see. Wind and sand were blasting her face, blinding her.

Was it all her imagination? Was she risking herself for a bit of floating debris? The tide was coming in—fast.

She'd come this far. There were rocks at the water's edge. She was pushing her way along the rocks, frantically searching, trying to see out into the waves. Where...?

He was falling and falling and falling. He had no idea how long he'd been in the water, how far he'd drifted, how desperate his position was. All he knew was that every few seconds he had to find the will to breathe. It was as easy and as impossible as that.

His body was no longer his own. The sea was doing what it willed. Waves were crashing over and around him. The chance to breathe often stretched to twenty, even thirty seconds.

He could think of nothing but breathing.

But then something sharp was crashing against his leg. And then his shoulder. Something hard, immoveable…

Solid. Rocks?

The water washed out and for a blessed moment he felt himself free of the water.

Another wave and it must have been twenty seconds before he could breathe. Whatever he was lying on seemed to be holding him down.

Another wash of water and he was free, hurled away from the sharpness, tossed high.

Onto sand?

He was barely conscious but he got it. His face was buried in sand.

Until the next wave.

Somehow he lifted his head. Sand. Rocks. Cliff.

The water came again but he was ready for it. He dug down, clung like a limpet.

The wave swept out again and somehow miraculously he stayed.

He couldn't resist the water's force again, though. He had to crawl out of the reach of the waves' power. Somehow…somehow… The world was an aching, hurting blur. The sand was the only thing he could cling to.

He clung and clung.

And through it all was the mantra. Make Jake safe. Dear God, make Jake be okay.

Another wave. Somehow he managed to claw himself higher, but at what cost? The pain in his leg…in his head…

He could close his eyes, he thought. Just for a moment.

If Jake was safe he could close his eyes and forget.

* * *

And then she found it. Him.

Dear God, this was no detritus washed up in the storm. This was a dark-haired, strongly built man, wearing yachting gear and a lifejacket.

He was face down in the sand. He'd lost a shoe. His pants were ripped. Lifeless?

As she reached him she could see a thin line of blood seeping down his face. Fresh blood. He'd been alive when he'd been washed up.

His hands were sprawled out on the sand. She knelt and touched one and flinched with the cold. His skin was white and clammy—how long had he been in the water?

She touched his neck.

A pulse! Alive!

She hauled him over—no mean feat by itself—so he lay on his side rather than face down. She was frantically trying to clear sand from mouth and nostrils. She had her ear against his mouth.

He was breathing. She could hear it. She unclipped his lifejacket and she could see the faint rise and fall of his chest.

There was so much sand. His face was impossibly caked. Wiping was never going to get rid of that sand.

He'd be sucking it into his lungs.

She hauled off her raincoat and headed into the waves, stooping to scoop water into the plastic. That was a risk by itself because the waves were fierce. She backed up fast, up the beach to where he lay, then placed her back to the wind and oozed the water carefully around his face. She was trying to rid him of the caked sand. How much had he already breathed?

Why was he unconscious? That hit on the head? Near drowning? With his mouth clear, she put her mouth against his and breathed for him. It wouldn't hurt to help him, to get more oxygen in, to keep that raspy breathing going.

His chest rose and fell, rose and fell, more surely now that she was breathing with him.

She kept on breathing while the sleet slashed from all sides, while the wind howled and while wet sand cut into her face and hands, every part of her that was exposed.

What to do? The tide was coming in. In an hour, probably less, this beach would be under water.

She thought of the trolley, but to pull it on a sandy beach was impossible. This man must be six foot three or four and strongly built. She was five foot six and no wimp, but she was no match for this guy's size.

How to move him? She couldn't.

'Please,' she pleaded out loud, and she didn't even know what she was pleading for.

But as if he'd heard, his body shifted. He opened his eyes and stared up at her.

Deep, grey eyes. Wounded eyes. She'd seen pain before and this man had it in spades.

'You're safe,' she said, keeping her voice low and calm. Nurse reassuring patient. Nurse telling lies? 'You're okay. Relax.'

'Jake…' he muttered.

'Is that your name?'

'No, Ben. But Jake…'

'I'm Mary and we can worry about Jake when we're off the beach,' she said, still in the reassuring tone she'd honed with years of district nursing. 'I'm here to help. Ben, the tide's coming in and we need to move. Can you wiggle your toes?'

She could see him think about it. Concentrate.

His feet moved. Praise be. She wasn't coping with paraplegia—or worse.

She should be factoring in risks. She should have him on a rigid board with a neck brace in case of spinal injury.

There wasn't time. Survival meant they had to move.

'Now your legs,' she said, and one leg moved. The other shifted a little and then didn't. She could see pain wash over his face.

'That's great,' she said, even though it wasn't. 'We have one good leg and one that's sore. Now fingers and arms.'

'I can't feel 'em.'

'That's because you're cold. Try.'

He tried and they moved.

'Good. Take a breather now. We have a little time.' Like five minutes. Waves were already reaching his feet.

He had a slash across his face. The bleeding had slowed to an ooze but it looked like it had bled profusely.

Head injury. He needed X-rays. If he had intracranial bleeding...

Don't even go there.

Priorities. She had a patient with an injured leg and blood loss and shock. The tide was coming in. There was time for nothing but getting him off the beach.

The sand and sleet were slapping her face, making her gasp. She was having trouble breathing herself.

Think.

Injured leg. She had no time—or sight—to assess it. The slashing sand was blinding.

Splint.

Walking-stick.

She made to rise but his hand came out and caught her. He held her arm, with surprising strength.

'Don't leave me.' It was a gasp.

She understood. She looked at the ripped lifejacket and then she looked out at the mountainous sea.

This guy must be one of the yachties they'd been talking about on the radio this morning. A yacht race—the Ultraswift Round the World Challenge—had been caught unprepared. The cyclone warning had had the fleet running for cover to Auckland but the storm had veered unexpectedly, catching them in its midst.

At dawn the broadcasters had already been talking about capsizes and deaths. Heroic rescues. Tragedy.

Now the storm had turned towards her island. It must have swept Ben before it. He'd somehow been swept onto Hideaway, but to safety?

Would this be as bad as the storm got, or would the cyclone

hit them square on? With no radio contact she had to assume the worst.

She had to get him off this beach.

'I'm not leaving you,' she said, and heaven only knew the effort it cost to keep the panic from her voice. 'I'm walking up the beach to find you a walking-stick. Then I'm coming back to help you to safety. I know you can't see me clearly right now but I'm five feet six inches tall and even though I play roller derby like a champion, I can't carry you. You need a stick.'

'Roller derby,' he said faintly.

'My team name is Smash 'em Mary,' she said. 'You don't want to mess with me.'

'Smash 'em Mary?' It was a ragged whisper but she was satisfied. She'd done what she'd intended. She'd made him think of something apart from drama and tragedy.

'I'll invite you to a game some time,' she told him. 'But not today. Bite on a bullet, big boy, while I fetch you a walking-stick.'

'I don't need a walking-stick.'

'Yeah, you can get up and hike right up the beach without even a wince,' she said. 'I don't think so. Lie still and think of nothing at all while I go and find what I need. Do what the lady tells you. Stay.'

Stay. He had no choice.

'Smash 'em Mary.' The name echoed in his head, weirdly reassuring.

The last few hours had been a nightmare. In the end he'd decided it was a dream. He'd been drifting in and out of consciousness or that was how it'd seemed. The past was mixing with the future. He and Jake as kids in that great, ostentatious mansion their parents called home. Their father yelling at them. 'You moronic imbeciles, you're your mother's spawn. You've inherited nothing from me. Stupid, stupid, stupid.'

That's how he felt now. Stupid.

Jake, flying through the air with the blast from the roadside bomb. Stupid, stupid, stupid.

Jake on a rope, smashing through the waves.

'Ben, look after your brother.' That was their mother. Rita Marlene. Beautiful, fragile, fatally flawed. 'Promise me.'

She was here now. *Promise me.*

Where was Jake?

This was all a dream.

His mother?

Smash 'em Mary.

There was no way a dream could conjure a Smash 'em Mary. The name hauled him out of his stupor as nothing else could.

Stay.

He had no choice but to obey. The nightmare was still there. If he moved, it might slam back.

He'd lie still and submit. To Smash 'em Mary?

She'd been so close he'd seen her face. She had an elfin hair-cut, with wet, short-cropped curls plastering her forehead. She had a finely boned face, brown eyes and freckles.

She had shadows under her eyes. Exhaustion?

Because of him? Had she been searching for him—or some-one else?

How many yachts had gone down?

Memory was surging back, and he groaned and tried to rise. But then she was back, pushing him down onto the sand.

'Disobedience means no elephant stamp,' she told him. 'I said lie still and I meant lie still.' Then she faltered a little, and the assurance faded. 'Ben, I can't sugar-coat this. Your leg might be broken and there's no way I can assess it here.

'In normal circumstances I'd call an ambulance, we'd fill you full of nice woozy drugs, put you on a stretcher and cart you off to a hospital, but right now all you have is me. So I've found a couple of decent sticks. I'll tie one to your leg to keep it still. The other's a walking-stick. You're going to hold onto me and we'll get you off this beach.'

He tried to think about it. It was hard to think about anything but closing his eyes and going to sleep.

'Ben,' Mary snapped. 'Don't even think about closing your eyes. You're cold to the marrow. The tide's coming in. You go to sleep and you won't wake up.'

'What's wrong with that?' It was a slur. It was so hard to make his voice work.

'Because Jake needs you,' Mary snapped again. 'You pull yourself together and help me, and then we'll both help Jake. Just do it.'

And put like that, of course he'd do it. He had no choice.

Afterwards she could never figure out how they managed. She'd read somewhere of mothers lifting cars off children, superhuman feats made possible by the adrenalin of terror. There was something about a cyclone bearing down that provided the same sort of impetus.

She was facing sleet and sand and the blasting of leaves and branches from the storm-swept trees of Hideaway Island and beyond. She had to get this man two hundred yards up a rocky cliff to the safety of the cave. The sheer effort of hauling him was making her feel faint, but there was no way she was letting him go.

'If I had to find a drowned rat of a sailor, why couldn't I have found a little one?' she gasped. They were halfway up the path, seemingly a million miles from the top. Ben was grim-faced with pain. He was leaning on his stick but his left leg was useless and he was forced to lean on her heavily. His weight was almost unbearable.

'Leave me and come back when the storm's done,' he gasped.

'No way,' she said, and then, as he propped himself up on the walking-stick, turning stubborn, she hauled out the big guns. 'Keep going. Jake needs you even if I don't.' She didn't have a clue who Jake was but it shut him up. He went back to concentrating on one ghastly step at a time, and so did she.

His leg seemed useless. He was totally dependent on one leg, his stick and her support. Compound fracture? Blocked blood supply? There hadn't been the time or visibility on the beach to see. She'd simply ripped her coat into strips and tied the stick on his leg to keep it as steady as she could.

But it was bad. He was dragging it behind him and she could feel that every step took him to the edge.

She felt close to the edge herself. How much worse must it be for him?

'If I were you, I'd be screaming in agony,' she managed, and she felt him stiffen. She could feel his tension, his fear—and now his shock.

'Smash…Smash 'em Mary screams in agony?'

'I'm good at it,' she confessed. 'It's great for getting free points from the referee.'

'You're…kidding me.'

'Nope.' She was trying desperately to sound normal, to keep the exhaustion from her voice as they hauled themselves one appalling step after another. Dizziness was washing over her in waves, but she wouldn't succumb. 'I've watched wrestlers on the telly. I swear their agony is pretend but they make millions. Some day I might.'

'As a wrestler, or with roller derby?'

'I might need to work on my muscles a bit for wrestling. I should have done it earlier. Muscles'd be helping now.'

They surely would. He was doing his best but she was practically dragging him.

Left to his own devices, he'd have lain where he was until the storm passed. Or not. This diminutive woman was giving him no choice.

'Mary—'

'Shut up and keep going.'

'You don't have to—'

'Lie down and we lie down together,' she muttered, grim with determination. 'I don't give up. I might get it horribly wrong, but I don't give up. Ever.'

He had no clue what that meant. All he knew was that she

was iron. She wasn't faltering. No matter how steep the ground grew, she wasn't slowing.

But she stopped talking. She must be as close to the edge as he was, he thought. If he could only help…

And then suddenly, blessedly, the ground flattened. His leg jolted with the shock of a change of levels but she didn't pause.

'Heinz… Heinz's waiting just round this corner.' She was gasping for breath, not bothering to disguise her distress now they were on level ground.

'Heinz?'

'My…my guard dog.'

Somehow she hauled him another few steps, around a bluff that instantly, magically chopped off the screaming wind. Ten more steps took them towards darkness…the mouth of a cave? Five more steps and they were inside. The rain ceased. The light dimmed.

'Welcome to my lair,' Mary managed, and that was all she could get out.

'I can't…' she muttered—and she folded into a crumpled heap.

What the…?

Somehow he dropped beside her, fumbling to lift her head, to clear her face from the sandy ground. Was this a faint? Please, God, let this just be exhaustion. To have hauled him so far…

This woman had put her own life on the line to save his. She'd given her all and more. Her faint had to be from sheer exhaustion, he told himself fiercely. It had to be. If it was worse, he'd carry the guilt for the rest of his life.

Her eyes were open, dazed, confused.

'Hey,' he managed. 'It's okay. We're safe now. You've saved me, now it's your turn to relax.'

He was so close to the edge himself. He could do so little but he did his best. Somehow he got his arm under her shoulders. He lifted her head so her face was resting on his chest instead of the rock and sand. He felt her heartbeat against his.

Somehow he hauled her deeper into the cave, tugging her

along with him. His leg jabbed like a red-hot poker smashing down.

They were out of the wind. They were out of danger.

He held her but he could do no more. The darkness was closing in. The pain in his leg… He couldn't think past it.

Exhaustion held sway. He closed his eyes and the dim light became dark.

CHAPTER TWO

SOMETHING WARM AND rough was washing his face.

Someone was hauling away his clothes.

How long had he let darkness enfold him? Too long, it seemed. Things were happening that were out of his control.

Who was he kidding? He'd been out of control ever since the yacht's mast had snapped. Or ever since the cyclone had turned and headed straight for them.

His sodden jacket and sweater were off. There was a towel around his chest.

His pants were coming off. He grabbed at them but too late— they were down past his knees and further.

The face washer was working faster.

'Heinz, leave the man alone. He's all sandy,' a voice said. 'He'll taste disgusting.'

His rescuing angel was alive and bossy again, and for a moment relief threatened to overwhelm him. She'd survived. They both had.

He opened his eyes. There was a light to his left, a flame, a crackling of wood catching fire.

A dog was between him and the flame. A scruffy-looking terrier-type dog, knee-high, tongue dangling for future use and his tail waving hopefully, like adventure was just around the corner.

His pants disappeared. He had what seemed like a towel around his torso. Nothing else?

A blanket was lowered over his chest on top of the towel. Fuzzy. Dry. Bliss!

Not over his legs.

'Now let's see the damage.' The bossy, prosaic voice was becoming almost a part of him. He wanted to hold on to that voice. It seemed all that stood between him and the abyss. 'But first let me wriggle a blanket under you. I need to get you warm.'

Two hands held him, hip and chest. They rolled, slowly but firmly, just enough to haul him on his side. His leg responded with even more pain, but her body held him close enough to her to stop his leg flopping. The rolled blanket slipped under, unrolling so he had a base that wasn't sand. Her hands rolled him the other way and he was on a makeshift bed.

It had been a professional move.

She was a roller-derbying medic?

'Who…who are you?'

'I told you. Mary to my friends. Smash 'em Mary to those who get in my way.' She hauled something else over the top of him, some kind of quilt. Soft and deep.

He was naked? How had that happened?

He wasn't asking questions. The blanket was under him. The quilt was on top. The beginnings of warmth…

If it wasn't for his leg he could give in to it but his leg was reminding him of damage with one vicious jolt after another. The fearsome throbbing left room for little else, pushing him back to the abyss.

She had a torch and was playing its beam down on the source of pain. He felt light fingers touching, not adding to the pain, just feather-light exploring.

'I want an X-ray,' she said fretfully.

'I'd assumed you'd have the equipment,' he managed, trying desperately to get his words to sound normal. 'X-ray equipment in the next room.' What else did she have in this cave? That he was lying on a blanket under a quilt with a fire beside him was amazing all by itself. The pain eased off for a moment but then…

Jake.

Jake was suddenly front and centre, his body dangling precariously from the chopper.

'Who's Jake?' she asked. Had he said his name aloud? Who knew? His head was doing strange things. His body was no longer under his control.

'My...my brother,' he managed. Hell, Jake... 'My twin.'

'I'm guessing he was on the boat with you.'

'Yes.'

'Idiots,' she said, bitterly. 'Off you go, great macho men, pitting yourselves against the elements, leaving your womenfolk lighting candles against your return.' She was still examining his leg. 'I remember my dad singing that song, *"Men must work and women must weep...and the harbour bar be moaning..."* I bet you didn't even have to work. I bet you did it just to prove you're he-men.'

It was so close to the truth he couldn't answer. He and Jake, pushing the boundaries for as long as he could remember.

'No...no womenfolk,' he managed.

'Except me,' she said bitterly. 'Lucky me. Was Jake with you? Could he be down on the beach as well?'

And he knew, he just knew that, no matter how warm and safe this refuge was, if he said yes she'd be out there again, scouring the beach for drowned sailors. She'd passed out from exhaustion and yet she was ready to go again. This wasn't a woman for weeping. This was a woman for doing.

'No,' he managed.

'You got separated?'

'We were well clear of the rest of the fleet, making a run for the Bay of Islands.'

'Which is where you are.'

'Great,' he managed. 'But I hadn't planned on floating the last few miles.'

'And Jake?'

'They tried to take him off.' He was having real trouble getting his voice to work. 'The last run of the rescue chopper.'

'Tried?'

'They lowered a woman with a harness. The last I saw he was hanging on to the rescue rope off the chopper.'

'Was he in the harness?'

'Y-yes.' Hell, it was hard to think. 'They both were.'

'Well, there you go, then,' she said, in such a prosaic way that it broke through his terror. 'So the last time you saw him he was being raised into a rescue chopper. I know those teams. They never lose their man. They'll bring him all the way to Auckland dangling from his harness if they have to, and he'll get the best view of the storm of anyone in the country. So now I can stop fretting about idiot Jake and focus on idiot Ben. Ben, I reckon your kneecap is dislocated, not broken.'

'Dislocated?' What did it matter? Broken, dislocated, if he had his druthers he'd have it removed. But there was an over-riding shift in the lead around his heart. Jake was safe? What was it about her words that had him believing her?

But she was now focused on his leg. 'You've figured I'm a nurse?' she demanded. 'I spent two years in an orthopaedic ward and I think I recognise this injury. Given normal circumstances, I wouldn't touch this with a barge pole. If it's broken then I stand to do more damage. But we're on the edge of a cyclone. The island you've been washed up on is the smallest and farthest out of the group and I have no radio reception. There's no way we can get help, maybe for a couple of days. If I leave this much longer you might be facing permanent disability. So how do you feel about me trying to put it back?'

He didn't feel anything but his leg.

'Ben, I'm asking for a bit more of that he-man courage,' she said, her voice gentling. 'Will you trust me to do this?'

Did he trust her?

His world was fuzzy with pain. He'd spent hours with the sea tossing him where it willed. He'd convinced himself Jake was dead.

Right now this sprite had hauled him from the sea, almost killing herself in the process. She'd put him on something soft. She'd given him Jake back. Now she was offering to fix…

'It'll hurt more while I'm doing it,' she said, and he thought, Okay, possibly not fix.

'And if it's broken I might do more damage—but, honestly, Ben, it does look dislocated.'

And he heard her worry. For the first time he heard her fear.

She was making a call, he thought, but she wasn't sure. If his leg was broken, she could hurt him more.

But her instincts said fix, and right now all he had in the world were her instincts.

'Go for it.'

'You won't sue if you end up walking backwards?'

'I'll think of you every time I do.'

She choked on laughter that sounded almost hysterical. Then she took a deep breath and he felt her settle.

'Okay. I'm going to wedge pillows behind you so you're half sitting and your hip is bent. That should loosen the quadriceps holding everything tight. Then I'm going to slowly straighten your knee, applying gentle pressure to the side of the kneecap until I can tease it back into place. I can't do it fast, because force could make any broken bone worse, so you'll just have to grit anything you have to grit while I work. Can you do that, Ben?'

'If you can, I can,' he said simply. 'Do it.'

To say it was an uncomfortable few minutes was putting it mildly. There was nothing mild about what happened next. When finally Mary grunted in satisfaction he felt sick.

'Don't you dare vomit in my nice clean cave,' she said, and her tremor revealed the strain he'd put her through. She was tucking the great soft quilt around him again. 'Not now it's over. I've done it, Ben. You can relax. If you promise not to vomit, I'll give you some water.'

'Whisky?'

'And don't we both need that? Sorry, my cellar doesn't run to fancy. Water it is.'

She held a bottle to his lips, and he hadn't realised how thirsty he was. How much salt water had he swallowed?

He tried a grunt of thanks that didn't quite come off.

'Stop now,' he managed. 'Rest…rest yourself.'

He couldn't say anything else. The blackness was waiting to receive him.

Rest? She'd love to but she daren't. She was back in control.

What had she been about, fainting? She'd never done such a thing. Probably if she had no one would have noticed, she conceded, but now, regaining consciousness sprawled on this man's chest had scared her almost into fainting again.

She had no intention of doing so. She was in control now, as she always was. To lose control was terrifying.

So she hauled herself back into efficiency. She cleaned his face, noting the blood had come from a jagged scratch from his hairline to behind his ear. Not too deep. She washed it and applied antiseptic and he didn't stir.

He looked tough, she thought. Weathered. A true sailor? There were lines around his eyes that looked wrong. What was he, thirty-five or so? Those lines said he was older. Those lines said life had been tough.

Who was he?

What was she supposed to do with him?

Nothing. Outside the wind was doing crazy things. The way the cave was facing, the sleet with the wind behind it seemed almost a veranda by itself. The ground swept down and away, which meant they were never going to be wet.

So now it was like being in front of a television, with the entrance to the cave showing terror. Trees had been slashed over, bent almost double. The sea through the rain was a churning maelstrom.

They'd only just made it in time, she thought. If this guy was still on the beach now…

She shuddered and she couldn't stop. She was so very cold. Her raincoat was in tatters and she was soaked.

Heinz whined and crept close. She hugged him.

Control, she told herself. Keep a hold of yourself.

The wind outside was screaming.

She stoked up the fire with as much wood as she dared. There was driftwood at the cave entrance—she should drag more inside, but she didn't want to go near that wind.

She couldn't stop the tremors.

'Rest yourself,' he'd said, and the urge to do so was suddenly urgent.

Ben was lying on her blanket. He was covered by her friend's gorgeous quilt. Queen-sized.

He looked deeply asleep. Exhausted.

She might just accept that she was exhausted as well.

She should stay alert and keep watch.

For what? What more could she do? If the wind swung round they were in trouble, but there was nothing she could do to prevent it.

If her sailor stirred she needed to know.

She was so cold.

She touched his skin under the quilt and he was cold, too. Colder than she was, despite the quilt.

What would a sensible woman do?

What a sensible woman had to do. She hauled off her outer clothes. She left her bra and knickers on—a woman had to preserve some decency.

She arranged her wet clothes and Ben's on the trolley, using it as a clothes horse by the fire.

She hugged Heinz close and gently wriggled them both onto the blanket.

Under the quilt.

She'd hauled off Ben's soggy clothes but she winced as she felt his skin. He was so cold. How long had he been in the water?

There should be procedures for this sort of situation. Some way she could use her body to warm him without...without what? Catching something?

Catching cold. This was crazy.

'Men must work and women must weep...'

Not this woman. This woman put her arms around her frigid

sailor, curled her body so as much skin as possible was touching, tried not to think she was taking as much comfort as she was giving…

And tried to sleep.

CHAPTER THREE

HE WOKE AND he was warm.

How cold had he been and for how long? There was a nightmare somewhere in the dark, the pain in his leg, his terror for Jake. They were waiting to enclose him again, but the nightmare was all about cold and noise and motion, and right now he was enclosed in a cloud of warmth and softness, and he was holding a woman.

Or she was holding him. He was on his back, his head on cushions. She was curved by his side, lying on her front, her head in the crook of his shoulder, her arm over his chest, as if she would cover as much of his body as she could.

Which was fine by him. The warmth and the comfort of skin against skin was unbelievable.

There was a bit of fur there as well. A dog? On the other side of him.

Well, why wouldn't there be, for on that side was a fire.

He was enfolded by dog and woman and hearth.

Words came back to him...

'Men must work and women must weep'?

Had she said that to him, this woman? Some time in the past?

This woman wasn't weeping. This woman was all about giving herself to him, feeding him warmth, feeding him safety.

He didn't move. Why move? He remembered a wall of pain and he wasn't going there. If he shifted an inch, it might return.

Who was she, this woman? She was soundly asleep, her body

folded against his. Some time during the darkness he must have moved to hold her. One of his arms held her loosely against him.

Mine.

It was a thought as primeval as time itself. Claiming a woman.

Claiming a need.

His body was responding.

Um…not. Not even in your dreams, he told himself, but the instinctive stirring brought reality back. Or as much reality as he could remember.

The yacht, the *Rita Marlene.*

The storm.

Jake, hanging from that rope.

'Want to tell me about it?'

Her voice was slurred with sleep. She didn't move. She didn't pull away. This position, it seemed, was working for them both.

It was the deepest of intimacies and he knew nothing about her. Nothing except she'd saved his life.

She must have felt him stiffen. Something had woken her but she wasn't pulling away. She seemed totally relaxed, part of the dark.

Outside he could still hear the screaming of the storm. Here there was only them.

'You already told me I'm a dumb male. What else is there to tell?'

He felt her smile. How could he do that? How did he feel like he knew this woman?

Something about skin against skin?

Something about her raw courage?

'There's variations of dumb,' she said. 'So you were in the yacht race.'

'We were.'

'You and Jake-on-the-Rope.'

'Yep.' There was even reassurance there, too. She'd said Jake-on-the-Rope like it was completely normal that his brother should be swinging on a rope from a chopper somewhere out over the Southern Ocean.

'You're from the States.'

'A woman of intuition.'

'Not dumb at all. How many on the boat?'

'Two.'

'So you're both rescued,' she said with satisfaction, and he settled even further. Pain was edging back now. Actually, it was quite severe pain. His leg throbbed. His head hurt. Lots of him hurt.

It was as if once he was reassured about Jake he could feel something else.

Actually, he could feel a lot else. He could feel this woman. He could feel this woman in the most intimate way in the world.

'So tell me about the boat?' she asked.

Rita Marlene.

'Pretty name.'

'After my mother.'

'She's pretty?'

'She was.'

'Was,' she said. 'Sorry.'

'A long time ago now.' This was almost dream-speaking, he thought. Not real. Dark. Warm. Hauled from death. Nothing mattered but the warmth and this woman draped over him.

'You sailed all the way from the States?'

'It's an around-the-world challenge, only we were stopping here. Jake's an actor. He's due to start work on a set in Auckland.'

'Would I have heard of…Jake?'

'Jake Logan.'

'Ooh, I have.' The words were excited but not the tone. The tone was sleepy, part of the dream. 'He was in *Stitch in Time*, and *ER*. A sexy French surgeon. So not French?'

'No.'

'My stepsister will be gutted. He's her favourite Hollywood hunk.'

'Not yours?'

'I have enough to worry about without pretend heroes.'

'Like antiheroes washed up on your beach?'

'You said it.' But he heard her smile.

There was silence for a while. The fire was dying down. The pain in his knee was growing worse, but he didn't want to move from this comfort and it seemed neither did she.

But finally she did, sighing and stirring, and as her body slid from his he felt an almost gut-wrenching sense of loss.

His Mary...

His Mary? What sort of concept was that? A crazy one?

She slipped from under the quilt and shifted around to the fire. He could see her then, a faint, lit outline.

Slight. Short, cropped curls. Finely boned, her face a little like Audrey Hepburn's.

She was wearing only knickers and bra, slivers of lace that hid hardly anything.

His Mary?

Get over it.

'Heinz, you're blocking the heat from our guest,' she said reprovingly, but the dog didn't stir.

'I'm warm.'

'Thanks to Barbara's quilt,' she said. 'Her great-grandmother made that quilt. It's been used as a wall hanging for a hundred years. If we've wrecked it we're dead meat.'

He thought about it. He'd more than likely bled on it. No matter. He held it a little tighter.

'I'll give her a million for it.'

'A million!'

'Two.'

'Right,' she said dryly. 'So you're a famous actor, too?'

'A financier.'

'Someone who makes serious money?'

'Maybe.'

'You mean Heinz and I could hold you for ransom?'

'You could hold me any way you want.'

Um…no. Wrong thing to say. This might be a dream-like situation but reality got a toehold fast.

'I'm sure I told you my rollerball name,' she said, quite lightly. 'Smash 'em Mary. Some things aren't worth thinking about.'

She was five foot five or five foot six. He was six four. Ex-commando.

He smiled.

'Laugh all you want, big boy,' she said. 'But I hold the pain-killers. Speaking of which, do you want some?'

'Painkillers,' he said, and he couldn't get the edge out of his voice fast enough.

'Bad, huh?' She'd loaded wood onto the fire, and now she turned back to him, lifted Heinz away—much to the little dog's disgust—and checked his face. She put her hand on his neck and felt his pulse, and then tucked the quilt tighter.

'What hurts most?

There was a question. He must have hit rocks, he thought, but, then, he'd been hurled about the lifeboat a few times, too.

'Leg mostly,' he managed. 'Head a bit.'

'Could I ask you not to do any internal bleeding?' She flicked on her torch and examined his head, running her fingers carefully through his hair. The hair must be stiff with salt and blood, and her fingers had a job getting through.

Hell, his body was responding again…

'Bumps and scrapes but nothing seemingly major apart from the scratch on your face,' she said. 'But I would like an X-ray.'

'There's no ferry due to take us to the mainland?'

'You reckon a ferry would run in this?' She gestured to the almost surreal vision of storm against the mouth of the cave. 'I do have a boat,' she said. 'Sadly it's moored in a natural harbour on the east of the island. East. That would be where you came from. Where the storm comes from. Any minute I'm expecting my boat to fly past the cave on its way to Australia. But, Ben, I do have codeine tablets. Are you allergic to anything?'

'You really are a nurse?'

'I was. Luckily for you, no one's taken my bag off me yet. Allergies?'

'No.'

'Codeine it is, then, plus an antinauseant. I don't fancy scrubbing this cave. You want to use the bathroom?'

'No!'

'It's possible,' she said, and once again he fancied he could feel her grinning behind the torch beam. 'The ledge outside the cave is sheltered and there's bushland in the lee of the cliff. I could help.'

'I'll thank you, no.'

'You want an en suite? A nice fancy flush or nothing?'

'Lady, I've been in Afghanistan,' he said, goaded, before he could stop himself.

'As a soldier?'

'Yes.' No point lying.

'That explains your face,' she said prosaically. 'And the toughness. Thank God for Afghanistan. I'm thinking it may well have saved your life. But even if we don't have an en suite, you can forget tough here, Ben. Not when I'm looking after you. Just take my nice little pills and settle down again. Let the pain go away.'

Her clothes were dry on one side and not the other. She rearranged them, wrapped a towel around herself and headed out to the ledge to look out over the island.

If there wasn't an overhang on the cliff she wouldn't be out here. The flying debris was terrifying.

It was almost dark, but in truth it had been almost dark for the last few hours. She checked her watch—it had been four hours since she'd hauled her soldier/sailor/financier up here.

The storm was getting worse.

She had so much to think about but for some reason she found herself thinking of the unknown Jake. Twin to Ben.

She only had a hazy recollection of the shows he'd been on, but she did know who he was. One of her stepsisters had raved about how sexy Jake Logan was. Mary remembered because it had been yet another appalling night of family infighting. Her stepsister had been trying to make her boyfriend jealous and he'd been rising to the bait. Her stepmother had been taking her sister's side. Her father had, as usual, been saying nothing.

She'd only arrived because she'd tried one last-ditch time to say how sorry she was. To make things right.

It had been useless. Her family wouldn't interrupt their fighting to listen. It was her fault.

Her fault, her fault, her fault.

Terrific. She was surrounded by a cyclone, she had a badly injured guy stuck in her cave—and she was dwelling on past nightmares.

Think of current nightmares.

Think of Jake.

She'd given some fast reassurance to Ben, but, in truth, the last radio report she'd heard before communications had been cut had been appalling. The cyclone had decimated the yachting fleet, and the reporter she'd heard had been talking of multiple deaths.

There'd been an interview with the head of the chopper service and he'd been choked with emotion.

'The last guy…we came so close… We thought we had him but, hell, the wind… It just slammed everything. The whole crew's gutted.'

The last guy…

Was that Ben's Jake?

She had no way of knowing, and there was no way she was passing on such a gut-wrenching supposition to Ben.

She felt…useless.

'But I did save him,' she told herself, and Heinz nosed out to see what was going on; whether it might be safe enough for a dog to find a tree.

Not. A gust blasted across the cliff in front of them; he whimpered and backed inside.

'You and Ben,' Mary muttered. 'Wussy males.'

She glanced back into the cave. All was dark. All was well.

She hoped. She still had no way of telling whether Ben's leg was fractured or, worse, if that crack on his head had been severe enough to cause subdural haemorrhaging. What if she walked back in and he was dead?

She walked back in and he was asleep, breathing deeply and evenly, with Heinz nuzzling back down against him.

What to do?

What was there to do? Sit by the fire and imagine subdural bleeding or twins falling from ropes into a cyclone-ravaged sea? Think of home, her family, the past that had driven her here?

Or do what she'd been doing for the last few weeks?

She lit a fat candle. Between it and the fire she could sort of see.

She shoved a couple of cushions behind her, she tucked a blanket over her legs, she put her manuscript on her knees and she started to write.

The door to the bar swung open.

She glanced at the sleeping guy not six feet from her.

He was six foot three or four, lean, mean, dangerous. His deep grey eyes raked every corner of the room.
Could he tell she was a werewolf?

She grinned. Hero or villain? She hadn't figured which but it didn't matter. There was a nice meaty murder about to happen in the room upstairs. A little blood was about to drip on people's heads. Maybe a lot of blood. She wasn't sure where Ben Logan would fit but he'd surely add drama.

'Call me Logan,' he drawled...

She thought maybe she'd have to do a search and replace when she reached the end. Maybe calling a character after her wounded sailor wasn't such a good idea.

But for now it helped. For now her villain/hero Logan could keep the storm at bay.

There was nothing like a bit of fantasy when a woman needed it most.

He woke, and she was heating something on the fire.

That's what had woken him, he thought. The smell was unbelievable. Homey, spicy, the smell of meat and herbs filled the cave.

He stirred and winced and she turned from the fire and smiled at him. Outside was black. No light was getting in now. Her face was lit by flickering firelight and one candle.

'Hey,' she said. 'Dinner?'

He thought about it for a nanosecond or less. 'Yes, please.'

'You can have the bowl. I'll use the frying pan. I wasn't anticipating guests. Would you like to sit up a little?'

'Um…'

She grinned. 'Yeah, I'm guessing what you need before food. Are you ready to admit I might be a nurse and therefore useful? If I'd known I'd have brought a bedpan.'

He sighed. 'Mary…'

'Mmm?'

'Can you hand me my clothes?'

'Knickers is all,' she said. 'The rest are still wet.' She handed him his boxers—and then had second thoughts. She tugged back the quilt and slid his boxers over his feet before he realised what she intended.

'Lift,' she ordered, and he did, and he felt about five years old.

She was still scantily dressed, too, in knickers, bra and T-shirt.

Her T-shirt was damp. He shouldn't notice.

He noticed.

'So it's okay for you to stay cold but not me?' he managed.

'That's the one.' She was helping him to stand, levering herself under his shoulder, taking his weight.

'Mary?'

'Mmm?'

'Hand me my stick. I can do this.'

'In your dreams.'

'Not in my dreams,' he said. 'For real. I won't take your help.'

'This is Smash 'em Mary you're talking to. I'm tough.'

'This is a five-feet-five-inch runt I'm talking to. Let me be.'

'You want to sign an indemnity form so if you fall down the cliff it's not my fault?'

'It's not your fault. How could it be your fault?'

'Of course it could be,' she said, and there was a sudden and unexpected note of bitterness beneath her words. 'Somehow it always is.'

He managed. He got outside and in again. He almost made it back to his makeshift bed but he had to accept help for the last couple of yards.

He felt like he'd been hit by rocks. Maybe he had been hit by rocks.

Propped up on pillows again, he was handed beef casserole. Excellent casserole.

There were worse places for a man to recuperate.

'How did you manage this?' he demanded, intrigued.

'There's a solar-powered freezer in the cabin,' she told him. 'The solar panels were one of the first victims of the storm so I packed a pile of food and brought it here. I loaded whatever was on top of the freezer so who knows what the plastic boxes hold. This time we got lucky but we might be eating bait for breakfast.'

'The storm came up fast, then?'

'The radio said storm, tie down your outdoor furniture. They didn't say cyclone, tie down your house.'

'This isn't a cyclone,' he told her. 'Or not yet. I've been in one before. This is wild but a full-scale cyclone hits with noise that's unbelievable. We're on the fringe.'

'So it's still to hit?'

'Or miss.'

'That'd be good,' she said, but he heard worry.

'Is there someone else you're scared about?' he demanded. He hadn't thought...all the worrying he'd done up until now had been about Jake.

'You,' she said. 'You need X-rays.'

'I'm tough.'

'Yeah, and you still need X-rays.'

'I promise I won't die.' He said it lightly but he somehow had the feeling that this woman was used to expecting the worst.

Well, she was a nurse.

Nurses didn't always expect the worst.

'I'd prefer that you didn't,' she said, striving to match his lightness. 'I have a pile of freezer contents that'll be fine for up to two days but then they'll decompose. If you're decomposing too, I might be forced to evacuate my cave.'

He choked. Only a nurse could make such a joke, he thought. He remembered the tough medics who'd been there in Afghanistan and he thought...Mary could be one of those.

The nurses had saved Jake's life when he'd been hit by a roadside bomb. Not the doctors, they had been too few in the field and they'd been stretched to the limit. Nurses had managed to stop the bleeding, get fluids into his brother, keep him stable until the surgeons had time to do their thing.

He kind of liked nurses.

He kind of liked this one.

He ate the casserole and drank the tea she made—he'd never tasted tea so good—and thought about her some more.

'So no one's worrying about you?' he asked, lightly, he thought, but she looked at him with a shrewdness he was starting to expect.

'I've left a note in a bottle saying where I am and who I'm with, so watch it, mate.'

He grinned. She really was...extraordinary.

'But there is no one?'

'If you're asking if I'm single, then I'm single.'

'Parents?'

That brought a shadow. She shook her head and started clearing.

She was so slight.

She was so alone.

'You want to share a bed again?' He shifted sideways so there was room under the quilt for her.

She must be cold. The temperature wasn't all that bad—this was a summer storm—but the cave was earth-cool, and the humidity meant their clothes were taking an age to dry.

She was wearing a T-shirt but he'd felt it as she'd helped him back into bed and it was clammy.

She needed to take it off. This bed was the only place to be.

She was looking doubtful.

'It'll be like we're flatmates, watching telly on the sofa,' he said, pushing the covers back.

'I forgot to bring the telly.'

'That's professional negligence if ever I heard it.' Then he frowned at the look on her face. 'What? What did I say?'

'Nothing.' Her face shuttered, but she hauled off her T-shirt and slid under the covers—as if the action might distract him.

It did distract him. A woman like this in his bed? Watching telly? Ha!

He pushed away the thought—or the sensation—and managed to push himself far enough away so there was at last an inch between their bodies.

The temptation to move closer was almost irresistible.

Resist.

'So tell me why you're here?' he asked. If she could hear the strain in his voice he couldn't help it. He was hauling his body under control and it didn't leave a lot of energy for small talk.

Mary was an inch away.

No.

'Here. Island. Why?' he said, but the look on her face stayed. Defensive.

'You. Yacht in middle of cyclone. Why?' she snapped back.

And he thought, Yeah, this lady has shadows.

'I'm distracting my brother from a failed marriage,' he told her. He didn't do personal. The Logan brothers' private life was their own business but there was something about this woman that told him anything he exposed would go no further.

Armour on his part seemed inappropriate. Somehow it was Mary who seemed wounded. She wasn't battered like he was, not beaten by rocks and sea, but in some intensely personal way she seemed just as wounded.

So he didn't do personal but they were sharing a bed in the middle of a cyclone and personal seemed the only way to go.

'So Jake needed to be distracted?' she said cautiously.

And he thought, Yep, he'd done it. He'd taken that look off her face. The look that said she was expecting to be slapped.

Smash 'em Mary? Maybe not so tough, then.

'Jake's a bit of a target,' he said. 'He came back from Afghanistan wounded, and I suspect there are nightmares. He threw himself into acting, his career took off and suddenly there were women everywhere. He found himself with a starlet with dollars in her eyes but he couldn't see it. She used him to push her career and he was left…'

'Scarred?'

'Jake doesn't do scarred.'

'How about you?' she asked. 'Do you do scarred?'

'No!'

'How did you feel when your brother was wounded?'

The question was so unexpected that it left him stranded.

The question took him back to the dust and grit of an Afghan roadside.

They hadn't even been on duty. They'd been in different battalions and the two groups had met as Ben's battalion had been redeployed. Ben hadn't seen his brother for six months.

'I know a place with fine dining,' Jake had joked. 'Practically five-star.'

Yeah, right. Jake always knew the weird and wonderful; he was always pushing the rules. Eating in the army mess didn't fit with his vision of life.

The army didn't fit with Jake's vision of life. It was a good fit for neither of them. They'd joined to get away from their father and their family notoriety, as far as they could.

Fail. *'Logan Brothers Blasted by Roadside Bomb. Heirs to Logan Fortune Airlifted Out.'* They couldn't get much more notorious than that.

'Earth to Ben?' Mary said. 'You were saying? How did you feel when Jake was injured?'

'How do you think I felt?' He didn't talk about it, he never had, but suddenly it was all around him and the need to talk was just there. 'One minute we were walking back to base on an almost deserted road, catching up on home talk. The next moment a bus full of locals pulled up. And then an explosion.'

'Oh, Ben…'

'Schoolkids,' he said, and he was there again, surrounded by terror, death, chaos. 'They targeted kids for maximum impact. Twelve kids were killed and Jake was collateral damage.'

'No wonder he has nightmares.'

'Yeah.'

'Did he lose consciousness?'

What sort of question was that? What difference did it make?

But it did make a difference. He'd thought, among all that carnage, at least Jake was unaware.

'Until we reached the field hospital, yes.'

'You were uninjured?'

'Minor stuff. Jake was between me and the bus.'

'Then I'm guessing,' she said gently, 'that your nightmares will be worse than his.'

'I'm fine.'

'He's your younger brother.'

'By twenty minutes.'

'You'll still feel responsible.'

'He's okay.' He flinched at the thought of where he might be now. Put it away, fast. 'He has to be okay. But tell me about you. Why are you here?'

And the question was neatly turned. She had nowhere to go,

he thought as he watched her face. He'd answered her questions. He'd let down his guard. Now he was demanding entry to places he instinctively knew she kept protected.

They were two of a kind, he thought, and how he knew it he couldn't guess. But they kept their secrets well.

He was asking for hers.

'I'm escaping from my family,' she said, and she was silent for a while. 'I'm escaping from my community as well.'

'As bad as that?'

'Worse,' she said. 'Baby killer, that's me.'

It was said lightly. It was said with all the pain in the world.

'You want to tell me about it?'

'No.'

'You expect me to stay in the same bed as a baby killer?'

She turned and stared and he met her gaze. Straight and true. If this woman was a baby killer he was King Kong.

He smiled and she tried to smile back. It didn't come off.

'I've exonerated you,' he told her. 'Found you innocent. Evidence? If you really were a baby killer you'd be on a more secure island. Alcatraz, for instance. Want to tell me about it?'

'No.'

'I told you mine.' He lifted the quilt so it reached her shoulders. 'If you lie back, there are cushions. Very comfy cushions. You can stare into the dark and pretend I'm your therapist.'

'I don't need a therapist.'

'Neither do I.'

'You have nightmares.'

'And you don't?' He put gentle pressure on her shoulder. She resisted for a moment. Heinz snuffled beside her. The wind raised its howl a notch.

She slumped back on the pillows and felt the fight go out of her.

'Tell Dr Ben,' Ben said.

'Doctor?'

'I'm playing psychoanalyst. I've failed the army. I'm a long way from the New York Stock Exchange. My yacht's a hundred fathoms deep. A man has to have some sort of career. Shoot.'

'Shoot?'

'What would an analyst say? So, Ms Smash 'em Mary, you're confessing to baby killing.'

And she smiled. He heard it and he almost whooped.

What was it about this woman that made it so important to make her smile?

Shoot, he'd said, and she did.

CHAPTER FOUR

SHE GAVE IN.

She told him.

'Okay,' she said, and he heard weariness now, the weariness of a long, long battle. 'I've told you that I'm a district nurse?'

'Hence the drugs,' he said. 'Nice nurse.'

She smiled again, but briefly. 'I'm currently suspended from work and a bit…on the outer with my family,' she told him. She took a deep breath. 'Okay, potted history. My mum died when I was eight. She'd been ill for a year and at the end Dad was empty. It was like most of him had died, too.

'Then he met Barbie. Barbie's some kind of faith-healer and self-declared clairvoyant. She offered to channel Mum, using Ouija boards, that kind of thing, and Dad was so desperate he fell for it. But Barbie has three daughters of her own and was in a financial mess. She was blatantly after Dad's money. Dad's well off. He has financial interests in most of the businesses in Taikohe where we live, and Barbie simply moved in and took control. She got rid of every trace of my mother. She still wants to get rid of me.'

'Cinderella with the wicked stepmother?'

'She's never mistreated me. Not overtly. She just somehow stopped Dad showing interest in me. With Barbie he seemed to die even more, if that makes sense, and she derided the things I had left to cling to.'

'There are worse ways to mistreat a child than beat them,' he said softly, and she was quiet for a while, as the wind rose and the sounds of the storm escalated.

He thought she'd stopped then, and was trying to figure how to prod her to go further when she started again, all by herself.

'School was my escape,' she told him. I liked school and I was good at it. I liked…rules.'

'Rules make sense when you're lost,' he agreed. 'Sometimes they're the only thing to cling to.' Was that why he and Jake had joined the army? he wondered. To find some limits?

'Anyway, I studied nursing. I became Taikohe's district nurse. I now have my own cottage…'

'With a cat?' he demanded. 'Uh-oh. This is starting to sound like cat territory.'

And she got it. He heard her grin. 'Only Heinz, who'll eat me when I die a spinster, alone and unloved.' She poked him—hard, in the ribs.

'Ow!'

'Serves you right. Of all the stereotyping males…'

'Hey, you're the one with the wicked stepmother.'

'Do you want to hear this or not?'

'Yes,' he said promptly, because he did. 'Tell Dr Ben.'

'Your bedside manner needs improving.'

'My bedside manner is perfect,' he said, and put his arm around her shoulders and tugged her closer. 'I'd like some springs in this mattress but otherwise I can't think of a single improvement.'

'Ben…'

'Go on,' he said encouragingly. 'Tell me what happened next. Tell me about the baby.'

There was a long silence. She lay still. Seemingly unbidden, his fingers traced a pattern in her hair. It felt…right to do so. Half of him expected her to pull away, but she didn't.

Tell me, he willed her silently, and wondered why it seemed so important that she did.

Finally it came.

'So now I'm grown up, living in the same community as my stepmother and my stepsisters and my dad. My dad's still like a dried-up husk. The others ignore me. I'm the dreary local nurse who uses traditional medicine, which they despise. They put up with me when I drop in to visit my dad but that's as far as the relationship goes.

'But now they've started having babies—not my stepmum but the girls. Sapphire, Rainbow and Sunrise. Home births all. No hospitals or traditional medicine need apply. They've had six healthy babies between them, with my stepmother crowing that traditional medicine's responsible for all the evils of the world. And then…catastrophe.'

'Catastrophe?'

'One dead baby,' she said, drearily now. 'Sunrise, my youngest stepsister, is massively overweight. The pregnancy went two weeks over term but she still refused to be checked. Then she went into labour, and a day later she was still labouring. She was at home with my stepmother and one of her sisters to support her. And then I dropped in.'

'To help?'

'I hadn't even been told she was due,' she said. 'When I arrived I realised Dad was in Auckland on business but they'd taken over the house as a birthing centre. I walked in and Sunrise was out of her mind with pain and exhaustion. There was bleeding and the baby was in dire trouble. I guess I just took over. I rang the ambulance and the hospital and warned them but I knew already… I'd listened… The baby's heartbeat was so faint…'

'The baby died?'

'They called her Sunset. How corny's that for a dying baby? She was suffering from a hypoxic brain injury and she died when she was three days old. Sunrise was lucky to survive. She won't be able to have more children.'

'So that makes you a baby killer?'

'I didn't know,' she said drearily, 'how much my stepmother really resented me until then. Or make that hate. I have no idea why, but at the coroner's inquest she stood in the witness stand and swore I'd told Sunrise it was safe. She swore I'd said everything was fine. I'd been the chosen midwife, she said, and my stepsisters concurred. Of course they would have gone to the hospital, they said, but one after another they told the court that I'd said they didn't need to.

'And you know what? My dad believed them. The coroner believed them. They came out of the court and Sunrise was crying, but my stepmother actually smirked. She tucked her arm in Dad's arm and they turned their backs on me. She's had her way after all this time. I'm finally right out of her family.'

Silence. More silence.

He shouldn't have asked, he thought. How to respond to a tragedy like this?

'My roller-derby team has asked me to quit,' she said into the dark. 'My dad—or Barbie—employs two of the girls' partners. Some of my medical colleagues stand by me—they know what I would and wouldn't do—but the town's too small for me to stay. I'm on unpaid leave now but I know I'll have to go.'

'So you've come to the great metropolis of Hideaway.' His fingers remained on her hair, just touching. Just stroking. 'I can see the logic.'

'I needed time out.'

'What are you writing?'

'Writing?

'By the fire. While I was snoozing.'

'That's none of your business,' she said, shocked.

'Sorry. Diary? No, I won't ask.' He hesitated for all of two seconds. 'Did you put something nice about me in it?'

'Only how much you weigh. Like a ton.' The mood had changed again. Lightness had returned. Thankfully.

'That's not kind,' he said, wounded.

'It's what matters. My shoulder's sore.'

'My leg's worse.'

'Do you need more painkillers? We can double the dose.'

'Yes, please,' he said, even though a hero would have knocked them back. Actually, a hero would have put her aside, braved a cyclone or two, swum to the mainland and knocked the heads of her appalling family together. A hero might do that in the future but for now his leg did indeed hurt. Knocking heads together needed to take a back seat. But it wouldn't be forgotten, he promised himself. Just shelved.

'If I have hurt your shoulder...you can take painkillers too.'

'I'm on duty.'

'You're not on duty,' he told her, gentling again. 'You need to sleep.'

'In a cyclone?'

'This isn't a cyclone. This is an edge of a cyclone.'

'Then I don't want to see a centre.'

'Hopefully we won't,' he said. 'Hopefully when we wake it'll have blown out to sea.'

'Hope on,' she said, and sat up and found him a couple of pills.

'Mary?'

'Mmm?'

'Sleep with me.'

'I don't seem to have a choice,' she said, and settled down again, and when he tugged her to him and held her, she didn't pull away.

At dawn the cyclone hit square on, and even in the safety of the cave the world seemed like it was exploding.

Afterwards she read that winds had reached two hundred miles an hour or more. They couldn't measure precisely because the instruments had been blown from their exposed eyrie on a neighbouring island. All Mary knew was that when she woke it sounded like a hundred freight trains were thundering right over, under and into their cave.

The wind was blasting from behind the cave but with such ferocity that the cave entrance was a vortex, sucking things in. Sand, grit, leaves. Their makeshift bed was far back, out of harm's way, or she'd thought out of harm's way, but who could tell with such a force?

The noise was unbelievable. The pressure in the cave was

unbelievable. Heinz was under the quilt, as far down as he could get, whimpering in terror.

Mary felt like joining him.

'It's all noise and bluster.' Ben's arm was around her, holding her tight against him, and his voice was a deep rumble overriding terror. 'I don't think we're on the outside any more,' he said, his voice amazingly calm in her ear. 'Cyclone Lila's huffing and puffing and threatening to blow our house down, but she won't succeed. She won't because my heroine, the amazing Smash 'em Mary, found us a cave. We're surrounded by nice thick rock. We're safe, no matter what she hurls at us.'

She hurled a tree. Mary heard it crash against the cliffs. In the dim light at the cave entrance she saw the trunk slide sideways across the cave mouth, and Ben might have thought he was holding her but now she was holding him. Tight. Hard. She might be safe in her cave but this was something out of this world.

She clung. She clung and clung and clung.

The world was ending. Dawn might be breaking on a new day somewhere in the world but dawn was breaking here on catastrophe. She was expecting her cave to implode. She was expecting her island to pick up its roots and head for England.

So much for being nurse in charge. Ben had a head injury and a leg injury. She should be doing hourly obs, asking solicitous questions about his health.

All she could do was cling.

'You're safe,' he said into her ear, and when he was this close she believed him.

She clung. Skin against skin. His warmth and strength were the only things that mattered.

He was in boxers. She was in bra and panties. His body was rough against hers, and warm, and it was the only thing between her and catastrophe.

The noise was unbelievable. It felt like the entire world had been picked up and was blowing away. Even the ground under them seemed to be trembling, and their bodies were reacting accordingly.

She was no longer in charge of her body.

What were the needs on the Maslow scale? Food first and shelter, but sex was right up there.

If she buried herself in his body the noise would stop, but it seemed more than that. Much more.

If she'd been lying with a stranger, surely it wouldn't be like this, but Ben seemed no stranger. What was it between them? Danger, isolation, but more. She didn't know and she didn't have time to think it through. All she knew was that she was in this man's arms and she wanted him.

For this moment, this fragment of time, there was nothing but this man. There was no thought of the past or the future. For now, the only escape from the storm was Ben.

Less than twenty-four hours ago he'd thought he was going to die. He'd almost drowned. He was black with bruises. His leg was still giving him hell, but he was holding a woman in his arms and the pain and terror of the past couple of days was fading to nothing.

All that mattered was her.

Was this casual sex? Was this a fast mating because it was offered—for it *was* offered. He could feel her need.

The noise of the storm outside was unbelievable. She was holding him for comfort; she needed his strength, his warmth, his presence.

But this was more than that. She was holding him as if she'd merge with him.

This was more than casual sex.

Maybe he'd say that to himself, he thought, or he tried to think as his arms drew her closer, as her skin pressed against his skin. Her breasts were moulding to him, the slivers of her lace bra almost non-existent. She was the most beautiful creature he'd ever held.

The most beautiful woman...

Was that the storm talking? The adrenalin of the cyclone?

He pulled away and it nearly killed him. He put her at arm's length so he could look into those beautiful, wounded eyes.

This was a wounded creature hiding from the world.

This was a woman whose past resonated with his.

Nonsense. He was the indulged son of serious money. His family connections had always made life easy for him.

But her loneliness resonated with him in such a way...

But this wasn't loneliness. This was urgent physical need, and even if it killed him he would not take advantage of this woman.

'Mary, think,' he managed. 'I can't...stop. Mary, are you sure?'

'That I want your body?' Her voice was surprisingly calm. 'I'm as sure as I've ever been in my life.'

'I don't suppose...' His voice didn't match hers. It was ragged with want and there was no way he could disguise it. 'That you carry condoms in that nurse's bag?'

'You didn't pack some in your lifejacket pocket before you jumped overboard?' Her words might be light but the jagged need, the need that matched his, was unmistakeable.

'I can't think why not, but no.'

'So...so no diseases I should know about?'

'No, but—'

'Then I want you,' she said, as simply as that, and it took his breath away. 'Consequences can hang themselves.'

'Mary...'

'Mmm? She was holding him, her fingers touching his spine, her body pressing against him. Blocking out everything but the feel of her. 'How...how old is Heinz?'

She managed a chuckle. 'Old enough not to be shocked. And in case you hadn't noticed, it's pretty dark.'

'That's a relief,' he managed, and tugged her tighter still. 'Heinz, close your eyes. Your mistress and I are about to block one storm out with another.'

CHAPTER FIVE

THEY PRETTY MUCH clung to one another for twelve hours. That was how long it took for the cyclone to blast their slice of paradise to pieces.

It didn't matter, though, Ben thought in the moments he could surface to thinking. For now, for this time out of reality, he felt like he'd found his home.

Outside the cyclone shrieked across and around the island, doing its worst, while they made love and talked in whispers right against each other's ears because that was the only way they could be heard.

There was a couple of hours' eerie silence as the eye passed over. Mary suggested pulling apart then, checking the beach, thinking if something…someone else had been washed up… But Ben knew no one could have survived in a sea rougher than the pre-cyclonic conditions he'd been washed up in, and how did they know how long the eye would take to pass?

With his injured knee he couldn't move fast, and the thought of his Mary—*his Mary?*—being caught up in it was unbearable.

Then the darkness and the wind closed in on them once more and the quilt was their refuge again.

Their bodies were their refuge.

Heinz was there, too. Every now and then the little dog squirmed upwards as if to make sure his mistress was still there, head as well as toes. Then he'd retreat to the warmth of the nest their feet made—as if he knew they needed privacy.

Privacy? Ben had never felt so private.

He was a loner. His parents' appalling marriage, the family

wealth that set him and Jake apart, had turned him into himself. He'd moved into his father's financial world almost by default. There'd been no one else to take on his father's role as head of such a vast financial empire, but in the end he'd found it suited him.

He discovered he had a talent for finance, and the financial world was superficial enough to suit him. Emotion had no place. He moved in sophisticated circles, with women who were content to partner him for appearances. They knew not to intrude on his solitude.

And yet this slip of a girl had broken through. How? He didn't know, and for now he didn't care.

They talked and made love, talked again, then fell into a half-sleep where their bodies seemed to merge closer than he'd felt to anyone in his life. Closer than he'd imagined he could feel.

She asked questions and he answered, and vice versa. There seemed no boundaries. The storm had blasted them away.

He found himself talking of his childhood, of the isolation he and Jake had found themselves in, how one dare had led to another. He told her of an understanding nanny who'd said, 'Guys, you don't need to kill yourselves to get your parents to notice you.' And then she'd added, sadly, 'Your parents are so caught up in their own worlds, you mightn't manage it no matter what you do.'

Those words had been spoken when he was about twelve. They hadn't made one whit of difference to the risks he and Jake had taken, but thinking back...

His mother's demands that her children cheer her up, make her happy, pander to her emotions. Her eventual suicide when they'd failed. The appalling distant cruelty of his father. Their childhood behaviour made sense now, and here in this cocoon of passion and warmth and safety he could say it.

But he didn't need to say it. It was just one of the passing thoughts that went between them, and it was as if he was lying in the dark, totally isolated, talking to himself.

Or not.

Because she listened and she held him, and the words were absorbed and held. Somehow, within that cocoon, he felt the armour around his heart soften and crack.

Just for now. Just for this storm. They both knew there was no tomorrow. Was that part of the deal?

'Tell me about roller derby,' he said at one point, and he felt her body lighten. A frisson of laughter seemed to pass between them.

What was it with this woman? If she smiled, he seemed to smile with her. His body seemed to react to hers, no matter what she did.

They seemed…one.

It was the storm, he told himself. Shared danger. The emotion and peril of the last two days. It was nothing more.

But somehow, right now, it seemed much more.

'Roller derby's my home,' she said, and he blinked.

'Pardon?'

'You went into the army,' she said. 'I'm guessing roller derby's the same thing for me. Nice, little Mary, goody two shoes, knocked down whenever I do anything that might be noticed because I have a powerful stepmother and three overwhelming stepsisters. But when I put on my skates, I can be someone else. I can be the me I suspect I could have been if my mum had lived.'

'So when you put your skates on, you're Bad Ass Mary.'

'Smash 'em Mary,' she corrected him. 'I can do anything when I have my team around me. The power is unbelievable, but there are no roadside bombs for the unwary.'

'Only the odd broken leg.'

'I've never broken anything. I'm little and quick and smart.'

He could see that about her. It made him smile again.

'And rough?'

'You'd better believe it.'

'I'd love to watch you play.'

'That's not going to happen.' He heard her smile die.

'You'll find another team.'

'Another team, another town, another life?'

'Mary…' He rolled over and tugged her close.

'Mmm?'

'That's for tomorrow. Not now. Now is just…now.'

'I should stop thinking about it?'

'Yes.'

'I need distraction.'

'I'm good at distraction,' he said, and kissed her. He kissed her as she should be kissed, this wiry, tough, soft, vulnerable, yet ready-to-face-the-world warrior queen. 'I can provide distraction now. All you need to do is say yes.'

'Yes,' she whispered—and so he did.

She woke and there was silence.

Silence, silence and silence. It was so quiet it was almost loud.

She was cocooned against Ben's body, enfolded and protected, and for a couple of dreamy moments she found herself wishing she could stay. But the silence told her this time out was almost over.

Any minute now the world would break in. They'd be rescued, she could pick up the pieces and start again.

A consummation devoutly to be wished?

No. She didn't wish. All she wished was right here, right now. She closed her eyes and let herself savour Ben's body. Life was all about now, she told herself. She refused to think further.

'Mary?'

'Mmm?' Shut up, she was pleading beneath her breath. Don't you know that if we wake up it's over?

'It's over,' he said, and she kept her eyes closed for one last millisecond, gathering her resources, such as they were.

She could do this.

'We've survived,' she said, and she thought, I will survive. And then she thought, How dramatic is that? Woman who's just had a magnificent time out with a wounded warrior; celebrating survival? She felt like she should be celebrating much more.

She could put him in her book. Who was she kidding? He already *was* in her book.

And who was she kidding with her writing? Writing would give her an alternative career? That was fantasy.

Like now. But fantasy was over.

Ben was putting her gently away, kissing her with all the tenderness in the world but then setting her back, holding her shoulders so he could look into her eyes.

'That was a very nice way to spend the storm,' he said, and she managed a smile.

'Diversional therapy? They taught us that at nursing school. It works beautifully.'

'You never learned what we just did at nursing school.'

'I… No.'

'Mary, if there are consequences…'

'There won't be consequences.' She said it with more confidence than she felt. It was the wrong time of the month, she should be okay, but…but…

But there were things she could do. She just had to be practical.

'I'll always be here for you,' he said, and there was that in his voice that said he meant it. 'No matter where you are in the world, if you ever need me…'

'If ever I wash up on a beach…'

'I'm not joking,' he said, and touched her lips gently with his fingers. 'I'm yours for life.'

He meant he had a lifelong debt, she thought. Yours for life? No and no and no. Already she could see him moving on.

'We need a radio,' he said.

'There's been no transmission since before I found you. I suspect the mainland transmission towers have gone.'

'Phone?' he said without much hope.

'Same. But I turned mine off, conserving the battery so when it does come on again I can call.'

She saw his relief. 'You normally get reception?'

'From higher on the island, where the hut is.' She hauled

herself together, trying to ignore the feel of his hands on her shoulders, trying to ignore the part of her that was screaming that she didn't want to leave this place.

She had to leave.

'I'll do a recce,' she said. 'Heinz and me. It's time he got some exercise.'

'*We'll* do a recce.'

'Yeah, Commando Sir,' she said dryly. 'Have you seen the size of your knee?'

'It's better.'

'It's straight. It's not better. And there's no proof you don't have a broken bone. You want to be on the other side of the island and the bone shifts? What good would that do either of us?'

'I need to find out what's happened to Jake,' he said, and she knew his focus had gone out of this cave, back to the most important thing in the world.

His twin.

He'd moved on. She must, too.

She sat up and stared out into the bright morning light. The sky was clear, the wind had dropped to almost nothing, and she could see the turquoise blue of the bay. 'The tide looks like it's out,' she said. 'There'll be a couple of hours when I can access most parts of the beach. What if you stay here and tend the fire, and Heinz and I will do a circumnavigation of the island. We'll check and see what's left of the hut but we'll check the beach first.'

She very carefully didn't look at his face. She stared out to sea as if she wasn't thinking about anything at all except maybe finding the odd interesting shell. 'It'd be good to see what the storm's washed up,' she said in a voice that said she was hardly interested.

He wasn't fooled for a moment. 'Mary...'

She dropped the pretence. 'I know you're worried. You shouldn't be. He was in a harness. Those choppers don't drop anyone.'

'Thank you,' he said. He was trying to believe her but he

was also thinking of next worst-case scenarios. 'Mary, there were others…'

'I'll be looking. I'm not Jake-specific. Any more commando heroes washed overboard, I'll tug 'em home.'

'Isn't one enough?'

'One's more than enough,' she said, and then, because she couldn't help herself, she took his face between her hands and she kissed him. She kissed him strongly and surely, and he wasn't to know that for her it seemed like a goodbye.

'One's more than enough,' she said. 'One's given me strength that should keep me going for a long, long time.'

'How long?'

'I'd guess a few hours,' she said, forcing herself to put the kiss aside as it was too hard to think about. 'It normally takes two hours to walk the beach but with the debris it might take me four. Don't expect me home for lunch.'

'For better or worse but not for lunch?'

'That's right, dear,' she said, and grinned. 'I'll take an apple and a water bottle. Meanwhile, you keep the home fires burning and have my slippers warmed and ready. Bye.'

She left, taking Heinz with her, and he wanted to go with her so much it almost killed him. Only practicalities stopped him. His leg would impede them both. He did need her to go right round the island. He did need her to check the shore.

Just in case.

But she was right. Harnesses didn't fail. Jake would be safe. He was being paranoid.

And now, on top of his worry for Jake, another worry was superimposed. Mary, pushing her way through debris, navigating a cyclone-devastated island…

What if she fell?

She wouldn't. What had she said? She was little and quick and smart.

She was, too.

His warrior woman.

He smiled. Mary. He owed her so much. How could he ever repay her?

Do something about her appalling family?

What?

He threw a couple more logs on the fire and thought about the sequence of events leading to the coroner's verdict. Had she employed a lawyer? He bet she hadn't. A lawyer would have cross-examined, produced times and witnesses outside the family, talked about pre-existing family conflict.

Would Mary allow him to push for a rehearing? Would she allow him to do that for her?

He suspected not. He could hear the defeat in her voice, but also the loyalty. Somewhere there was a father she still loved, and these appalling women were his wife and daughters.

What else? He'd never felt so helpless.

She'd been gone for half an hour, far too early for her to return, yet already he was imagining worst-case scenarios. There'd been trees ripped, maybe landslides from so much rain. So many hazards…

Things on the beach.

Jake…

In desperation he picked up the papers she'd been writing on. He'd watched her, half asleep, and seen the intent look on her face. It had seemed like this was something that took her out of her current misery.

'None of your business.' She'd said it loud and clear.

It was none of his business. He owed her privacy but he was going out of his mind.

He hauled himself outside to sit in the sun, acknowledging as he did just how swollen his leg was; how impossible it was that he do anything useful.

He stared out over the storm-swept island, at the flattened trees, at the mountain of debris washed up on the beach.

Jake.

Mary.

It was too much. He hauled himself back inside to fetch the papers.

It was none of his business. He acknowledged it, but he started to read anyway.

Negotiating the beach was a nightmare. The cyclone had caused storm surges and the water had washed well up the cliff face. She looked at the new high-water mark and shuddered. If she hadn't found Ben when she had…

Don't go there, she told herself. It made her feel ill.

Surely no one else could have survived, but she had to check. The debris washed up was unbelievable—and some of it looked as if it had come from the yacht fleet.

Every time she saw a flash of something that shouldn't be there, a hint of colour, waterproof clothing, shattered fibreglass or ripped sails, her heart caught in her mouth. No bodies, she pleaded as she searched. No Jake? He had to have been rescued.

What sort of people manned those rescue helicopters? she wondered, thinking suddenly about the woman who'd been dangling in a harness with the unknown Jake. There was a prayer in her heart for both of them—indeed, for anyone who'd been out there.

But even before she'd found Ben, the radio had said people had died.

She searched on and stupidly, weirdly, she found herself crying. Why? Tears wouldn't help anyone. She was Mary, the practical one. Mary, who didn't do emotion.

Mary, who'd just spent twenty-four hours in a stranger's arms?

She didn't feel like Mary any more. Over the past months she'd been blasted out of her nice, safe existence, first by the death of her stepsister's baby, then by a storm—and now by a man holding her as if he cared.

He was shocked and frantic about his brother's safety. He'd been using her body to forget.

'And I was using him,' she told Heinz. She was sitting on a massive tree trunk washed up on the beach, retrieving her apple from her backpack.

But he'd held her as if he cared. No one did that. Even her father...

Don't go there. She'd loved her father as much as she'd loved her mother. Her mother's death had been unavoidable.

Her father's marriage to Barbie had meant desertion and she'd never truly trusted anyone since.

She stared down at her apple, but she didn't feel like eating. What was she doing, dredging up long-ago pain?

She wanted, quite desperately, to be back on the mainland, surrounded by her roller-derby team. She needed a fast, furious game where she could pit her wits and her strength against skills that matched hers—where she had no room to think of anything beyond the physical.

As she'd been when she'd lain in Ben's arms?

Only there'd been room for more than the physical with Ben. It had felt like there was far more.

And there wasn't. She didn't need anyone. Hadn't her whole life taught her that?

'So get over it. Get over him.' She crunched her apple with unnecessary force. Heinz looked at her with worry, and she bit off a piece and offered it.

He wasn't interested. He headed back into the kelp. Here be dead fish and stuff. Here be something better than apples.

'That's what I get for hauling your dog food to the cave,' she retorted. 'Some dogs would be grateful for apple.'

Her words caught her sense of the ridiculous and she managed a half-hearted smile. It was only half-hearted, though. She truly was discombobulated. In the last couple of months her world had been blasted apart, and the cyclone seemed the culmination.

Wrong. Ben seemed the culmination.

He was a fast reader but sometimes he slowed. Sometimes he wanted to soak in each word.

He'd desperately needed an escape from his worry about

Jake. Last night Mary had been that escape. Now the manuscript in his hands was giving him a lesser one.

His dark, shadowed eyes, grey and mysterious, seemed to bore into parts of her she hadn't even known existed. They seemed to see the wolf within.

He got it. He was grinning with delight as he recognised himself. She'd gone back and crossed a few things out in the backstory. His build, his eyes, his physique, were superimposed on…her hero?

This man was supposed to be a twin? Heaven help her if there were two of them. One was enough to make a werewolf run for cover.

He read on, entranced. Escape… That's what this woman was all about, he thought, and she was very, very good at it. Her writing was part of her. The whole was entrancing.

She rounded the entire island. She found storm-blasted birds, some dead but most simply stunned and battered, hunkering down while they recovered.

She—or rather Heinz—found dead fish. Heinz let the birds be but not the fish. How much fish could one dog eat? Mary was past caring.

Thank God, no bodies.

Finally she made her way inland to check on the hut. But what hut? The base of the fireplace was all that was left. The tin roof was scattered through the bushland. The timber walls had crumbled. Her friends' possessions were sodden and ruined. There seemed nothing left for her to save.

'And we've probably ruined the quilt as well,' she told Heinz. 'I'll fix it.'

Ben's voice in the stillness made her jump. She turned and

he was sitting on a fallen tree at the edge of the clearing, watching her.

'You shouldn't have come,' she said, shocked. 'You should be resting your knee.'

'You've been gone for four hours,' he said pointedly. 'A man's allowed to get worried. Two stout walking-sticks and I managed.'

'How did you know where to come?'

'There are two paths from the cave. One leads to the beach. I figured the other led here, and I figured this was where you'd end up. I'm up there with Einstein,' he said proudly.

She managed a smile. He looked astonishing. His face was battered, the shirt and pants he was wearing had the odd rip, he'd wrapped his one bare foot in a ripped towel to form a makeshift shoe, but he looked...healthy?

Maybe more than healthy, she conceded. He looked more tough, rugged and good-looking than any man had a right to look.

Especially when a woman had to be sensible.

Think about something else, she told herself desperately. *Focus.* She gazed around the clearing at the mess.

Nothing occurred. She just wanted to look at him.

'I'll have the quilt cleaned,' he told her. 'Restored if necessary. I'll have this cottage rebuilt if insurance doesn't pay for it. I'll do anything in my power to pay for what you've done for me. Starting with the quilt.'

'How did you know the quilt's important?'

'I've seen homes destroyed in Afghanistan. I've seen women who've lost all their possessions, and I've seen what a tiny thing can mean.' He smiled at her, but his smile had changed. All the compassion in the world was in that smile. 'After you left I had a chance to take a good look at that quilt. It's amazing.'

'Barbara's grandmother sewed it for her trousseau.'

Some time during the last twenty-four hours she'd told him about Barbara and Henry.

Some time in the last twenty-four hours she'd told him almost everything.

'There's not a lot here we can salvage,' he said, and she didn't reply. There wasn't any need.

'The boat?' he asked, without much hope.

'Smashed.'

'You didn't think to put it somewhere safe?'

She flashed him a look.

He grinned. 'Yeah, I know. Lack of forethought is everywhere. I should have put my yacht in dry dock in Manhattan.'

'The world's full of should-haves.'

'But on the other hand, I brought crackers, cheese and chocolate with me from the cave,' he said, and she looked up at his lopsided hopeful expression and she couldn't help smiling. He was playing the helpful Labrador.

And suddenly she thought... Cellar.

Henry had told her about the cellar, almost as an aside, when he'd been describing the house. 'There's a dugout under the washhouse,' he said. 'Accessed by a trapdoor. I keep a few bottles there if you're desperate.'

Did this qualify as desperate?

She left Ben and headed for where the washhouse had been. She hauled a few timbers aside and after a couple of moments Ben hobbled across to help.

'We're looking for?'

'Desperate measures,' she said.

'Sorry?'

'Desperate times call for desperate measures. I'll make it up to Henry somehow.' She hauled the last piece of timber aside and exposed a trapdoor with a brass ring.

Ben tugged it up. It was a hole, four feet wide, maybe three feet deep.

'You could have hidden in here during the storm,' he said.

'Yeah, right. Four feet by four feet, filled with a hundred or so bottles of wine.'

'After the first twenty you wouldn't have noticed you were

squashed.' He lifted out the first bottle and stared. 'Wow. Your friends have good taste.'

'It'll take me a month's salary to pay them back but this might be worth it.'

'I told you, I'm paying.' He lifted the next bottle out and eyed it with reverence. 'I've been trying to think of the perfect wine to go with crackers, cheese and chocolate. I think I've found it.'

'You think we dare?'

'I know we dare,' Ben said. 'My leg hurts. This is for medicinal purposes, if nothing else. And, Mary, I suspect you're hurting, too,' he said, and suddenly his voice gentled again. 'Carting me up that beach was no mean feat. You must be aching, and inside there's probably almost as much hurt as I'm carrying. I think we need this wine, Nurse Hammond. I think we both need all the help we can get.'

They sat on a sun-drenched log, looked out over the battered island, ate their crackers and cheese, and drank amazing wine.

The cheese was a bit dry and the glassware left a bit to be desired. Every glass in the cottage had been broken but a couple of ancient coffee mugs had survived the carnage.

It didn't matter. The food tasted wonderful. The wine—stunning even in different circumstances—couldn't have tasted better if it was drunk from exquisite crystal.

They didn't talk. There seemed no need.

They were perched on a ledge overlooking the entire west of the island. Every tree seemed to have been shattered or flattened. The beach was a massive mound of litter. The sea still looked fierce, an aftermath of the storm, but the sun was on their faces. The world around them had been destroyed but for now, for this moment, all was peace.

Heinz had been lying at Mary's feet. He suddenly stood, staggered a few feet away—and brought up half a fish.

'Nice,' Ben said.

'I reckon he ate about six,' Mary told him, grimacing. 'There may be more to come.'

'He might have chewed them before he swallowed.'

'He was a stray when I found him. He eats first and asks questions later. Even essential questions, like "Can I fit it in?" or "Is it edible?"'

'Really nice,' Ben said, and then, when Heinz looked wistfully down at his half-fish, he stirred, grabbed a stick, gouged a hole in the sodden earth and buried it.

Then, at the look on Heinz's face, he shoved the stick deep in the ground and tied a piece of ripped curtain at the top.

'*X* marks the spot,' he told Heinz. 'Come the revolution, you know where it's buried.'

'Nice,' Mary intoned back at him, and their eyes met and suddenly they were laughing.

It felt…amazing.

It felt free.

And Mary thought, for all the drama and tension of the last couple of days, she was feeling better than she'd felt for months.

Or years?

Because she'd made abandoned love to a guy she hardly knew?

But she did know him, she thought. She watched the laughter in his eyes, she watched the way he fondled Heinz's floppy ears, she saw the tension in his face that could never be resolved until he knew his brother was safe, and she thought…she did know this man.

Somehow in the last twenty-four hours he seemed to have become part of her.

And that was crazy, she told herself. Any minute now the world would break in, and part of her would disappear back to Manhattan.

Besides, she didn't do relationships. She'd trusted her father with her whole heart and he'd turned his back on her. His back was still turned. How did you walk away from something like that?

'I read your book,' he said, and she froze.

'You read…'

'Werewolves and dragons—and me.' He grinned. 'Entirely satisfactory.'

She was on her feet but feeling like the earth was opening under her. Her writing… It had always been her escape. This man had read it? 'You had no right…'

'I know,' he confessed. 'But I was bored. Do you mind?'

'I don't show my writing to anyone.' It was part of her, the part she disappeared into when life got too hard. That he'd seen it…

'You should. It's great.'

'It's fantasy.'

'I suspected that,' he said gravely. 'I haven't exactly learned how to handle a six-pronged sword in real life.'

She closed her eyes.

'Mary, I really am sorry,' he said. 'You look like… It seems important. I shouldn't have intruded. I shouldn't have looked.'

He shouldn't have looked into her? What was it about this man? He was seeing…all of her.

She opened her eyes again met his gaze. Straight and true. Where had that phrase come from?

He was a man to be trusted?

Maybe she had no choice. She'd already exposed so much.

Deep breath. What would a normal…writer…say if someone had read their work? 'You think it's over the top?' she tried, cautiously, and he seemed to relax.

'It is over the top and it's great.' He grinned. 'A few more thousand words and the publication world awaits.'

'Don't mock.'

'I'm not mocking,' he said, and there was that look again. Straight and true. 'Mary, it's awesome.' Then his face changed, to an expression she could hardly understand. 'I think you're awesome,' he added. 'I wish there were some dragons I could slay on your behalf in real life.'

This was doing her head in. Any minute now she'd step forward and take this man and hold him.

She didn't do relationships. She didn't trust.

She could trust this man?

'M-meanwhile, we need to figure how to get off this island,' she managed, and heaven only knew the effort it took to get the words out.

'We do,' he said ruefully. 'Fantasy's great, but the real world awaits us.'

'It does,' she agreed, and then she muttered an aside. 'I just need to keep remembering it.'

CHAPTER SIX

THE REAL WORLD broke in half an hour later.

Helicopters appeared in the distance, buzzing out over the islands but mostly out to sea.

'The yacht race was a disaster,' Ben said as they watched them. 'That's who they'll be looking for. The race was full of idiots like us, in expensive boats but not enough skills to cope.'

'How many sailors have the skills to cope with a cyclone?'

'We could have done better. I never questioned the seaworthiness of the life raft. The salesman told me it was state of the art. I knew how to set it up but it never occurred to me that it was little more than a giant beach ball. I just hope other yachts had better equipment.' He shaded his eyes, watching a couple of dots of helicopters flying out on the horizon. 'If they're still searching, I hope whoever they're looking for had a better life raft than ours.'

'They're probably looking for you.'

'Or Jake.'

'Let's face probabilities, shall we?' she said astringently. 'At last report, Jake was being winched to safety. You, on the other hand, were drifting in a beach ball. So they're looking for you. Driftwood. Matches, fire, smoke. Stat. We need to get smoke up there fast before the weather closes in again.'

'Is the weather closing in?'

'Who knows? I hope someone, somewhere is working frantically to restore a transmission tower but nothing's coming through on my radio. Or my phone.' She flicked her cellphone out of her pocket. 'Dead.'

'Is it charged?'

'You tell me to try turning it off and on again and I'll tell you where to put it, tech-head.' She tossed him the phone. 'Here. You play with the on and off buttons, then make your way back to the cave at your leisure. I'm off to try a less tech-heavy form of communication.'

'Mary…'

She'd started to turn away but she stopped and looked back at him. 'Yes?'

'Thank you,' he said simply, and they were a mere two words but all the power in the universe was behind them. He looked at her, just looked. Their gazes held for a long, long moment, and in the end it seemed to tear something when she had to turn away.

'My pleasure,' she managed, but as she headed back to the cave she felt those stupid tears slipping down her face again.

What was wrong with her? Smash 'em Mary was turning into a wuss.

There was a part of Smash 'em Mary that didn't even want the helicopter to come.

Only the helicopter did come. The fire took hold and she covered it with green leaves. Smoke billowed upwards, the chopper changed course and headed toward them.

Ben had made his way back by then, limping heavily, using his sticks for support. She should have moved slowly, staying to help him, but rescue had seemed more important.

Of course it was.

They stood in silence as the chopper approached. There seemed little to say, or maybe there was lots to say but neither of them could think what.

There was no way the chopper could land. The island was hilly, and the beach, normally a possible landing place, was a mess. The chopper came in low, assessing the situation, and then someone came down a rope.

A guy, Ben noted. Neither was it the chopper that had taken

Jake away. Why not? His stomach clenched, thinking of the chopper in that wild weather. Surely if it had survived…

'That's called catastrophising,' Mary said. 'Stop it.'

'How did you know…?'

'Your face is like an open book. Just because this isn't the chopper that took Jake, it doesn't mean Jake's at the bottom of the sea. I know you think New Zealand's tiny compared to the US, but we do run to more than one helicopter.'

He managed a smile and then the guy on the rope landed near them, and she headed forward to help.

Ben stayed where he was. He'd pushed too hard. His leg seemed like it was at the end of its useful life. He'd never felt so useless.

Jake…

'Take Ben first,' Mary was saying.

He roused himself and thought, *What?*

'She tells me you're injured, sir,' the paramedic said. 'Do we need to splint your leg before we move you? Any other injuries?'

'I don't think he wants to be stretchered up,' Mary said, and she was smiling.

He wasn't smiling.

'My brother…' he said, and the paramedic's face grew grim.

'You're one of the race crew?'

'Yes.'

'We're very pleased to see you,' he said. 'There are still crew members missing.' He turned to Mary, obviously forming a question, but she answered before he could ask.

'I've searched the beach and found no one.'

'Could someone have made their way inland?'

'If they were capable of getting inland they'd have found the remains of the hut. It's the obvious high point.'

'It's probably worth sending a team over to look more thoroughly,' the guy said, 'if this one's washed up.

This one. This victim.

Ben was going out of his mind.

'Do you know if my brother's safe?' he demanded. 'Jake Logan. He was pulled up on a chopper before the cyclone hit.'

'That'll have been a New Zealand crew,' the guy told him. 'We're Australian. I don't know who they did and didn't pull off.'

'The choppers are all safe?'

'I don't know that either,' he said apologetically. 'This is our first run. Please, our time's short.'

He didn't need to say more. Others were missing. He had to get back in the air.

'Put the harness on,' Mary said, and something inside him snapped.

'No,' he said. 'You go first and that's an order. I'll grab your manuscript and follow.'

'It's not important.'

'It is. Go!'

'Blimey,' the guy said, obviously astounded at the vehemence behind his words. 'Women and children first? The island's not sinking, mate.'

It wasn't, but the memory of Jake was all around him. He didn't know where Jake was. He wanted Mary safe.'

'You go first and I'll bring Heinz and the manuscript up with me,' he told Mary, and Mary looked at him as if he was out of his mind.

'You're the one with the bang on his head and the gammy leg. You're planning on holding my dog and my book while you air-swing? In your dreams, mister.'

The chopper guy sighed. 'Quiet dog?'

'He's eaten so many dead fish this morning he won't raise a wriggle,' Mary told him. 'But I wouldn't squeeze him.'

The guy grinned. 'Name?'

'Heinz.'

'I might have known. Okay, boys and girls, I'm taking the dog up while you sort the remaining order between you. No domestics while I'm away. Sheesh, the stuff we heroes have to put up with. Heinz, come with me while Mummy and Daddy sort out their rescue priorities.'

* * *

She went first, clutching the battered quilt. 'Because Barbara will forgive me everything but losing this.'

He came after, with her manuscript. He'd spent time in choppers in Afghanistan. He didn't like the memories.

He was hauled into the chopper and Mary was belted onto the bench. She was holding Heinz as if she needed him for comfort. She looked somehow... diminished?

Lost.

She'd come to the island to escape, he remembered. Now she was going home.

He sat beside her but she wouldn't look at him. She buried her face in Heinz's rough coat and he thought suddenly of the streams of refugees he'd seen leaving war zones.

Surely that was a dumb comparison—but the feeling was the same.

He touched her shoulder but she pulled away.

'Um, no,' she said, and she straightened and met his gaze full on. 'Thanks, Ben,' she said softly. 'But I'm on my own now.'

'You're not on your own.'

'This was a fairly dramatic time out,' she said. 'But it was just that. Time out. Now we both have stuff we need to face.' She shook herself then, and Smash 'em Mary took over. He saw the set of her chin, the flash of determination, the armour rebuilding. 'What I'm facing is nothing compared to you, but Jake will be okay. I'm sure of it.'

He had no room to respond.

In any other situation he would have...

Would have what? He didn't know.

For suddenly he was there again, in Afghanistan, watching a bloodied Jake being loaded onto the stretcher, knowing he couldn't go with the ambulance, knowing Jake's fate was out of his hands.

Loving brought gut-wrenching pain.

When he was fourteen years old his mother had suicided.

That day was etched into his mind so deeply he could never get rid of it.

Pain.

And here was this woman, sitting beside him, hurting herself. He'd forgotten his pain in her body. He'd used her.

He could love her.

Yeah, and expose him—and her—to more of the same? If he did…if he hurt her…

He hadn't been able to stop his mother's suicide. The emotional responsibility was too great.

Where was this going? He didn't have a clue. He only knew that he withdrew his hand from her shoulder, and when she inched slightly away he didn't stop her.

It was better to withdraw now. Kinder for both of them. He had relationships back in the US, of course he did, but the women he dated were strong, independent, never needy. They used him as an accessory and that was the way he liked it.

He never wanted a woman to need him.

'We're heading to Paihia,' the voice of the chopper pilot told them through their headphones. 'From there we'll have people help you, check you medically, find you somewhere to go.'

Mary nodded, a brisk little nod that told him more than anything else that she had herself contained again. She wasn't as strong as she made out, though, he thought. Strong, independent woman? Not so much.

It didn't matter, they were moving on.

It was what they both needed to do.

Paihia. A massive army clearing tent. People with clipboards, emergency personnel everywhere, reminding them both that they were bit-part players in a very big drama.

'Ben's hurt,' Mary managed, as a woman wearing medic insignia on her uniform met them off the chopper. 'I'm a nurse. He had a dislocated knee that I managed to put back in but it needs checking for possible fractures. He also had a bang on the head. I've pulled the cut together with steri-strips but it probably needs stitches.'

'We'll take it from here,' the medic said. 'And you?'

'I'm fine.'

'Can you come this way, sir? Would you like a wheelchair?'

'I don't need help,' he growled. 'I need to find my brother.'

'Your brother is?'

'Jake Logan. One of the yachties.'

'You're part of the round-the-world challenge?' Her face cleared. 'Thank God for that. They've lost so many, the organisers are frantic.'

That was a statement to make him feel better. Not.

'Jake...' he managed.

'The organisers have evacuated all survivors to Auckland,' she said. 'I don't have names.' She hesitated. 'We're sending a chopper with a couple of patients needing surgery in about ten minutes. If you let me do a fast check on your leg and head first, I can get you on that chopper.'

He turned and Mary was watching, still with that grave, contained face. The face that said she was moving on.

'Go, Ben,' she said. 'And good luck.'

'Where can I find you?'

'Sir...' the woman said.

The chopper was waiting.

'I need an address,' he told Mary. 'Now!'

'Email me if you like. I'm *MaryHammond400 at xmail dot com.*'

'*MaryHammond400?*'

'There's so many of us I got desperate.'

'There's only one of you.'

She smiled. 'It's nice of you to say so but there are millions of Marys in the world. Good luck with everything, Ben. Email me to let me know Jake's safe.'

'I will. And, Mary—'

'Just go.'

'Give me the quilt,' he told her, and she blinked, and he

thought bringing the quilt into the equation, a touch of practicality, threw her.

'You want it for a keepsake? You can't have it.'

'I'll have it restored for Barbara and send it back to you,' he told her. 'And I don't need keepsakes. Thank you, Mary 400. Smash 'em Mary. Mary in a million. I don't need keepsakes because I'll remember these last few days forever.'

She watched the chopper until it was out of sight. She hugged Heinz. She felt…weird.

She should feel gutted, she told herself. She felt like the man of her dreams was flying out of her life forever.

Only he wasn't. She even managed a wry smile. He'd been a dream, she decided, a break from the nightmare of the past. She was glad she'd made love with him. Abandoning herself in his body, she'd felt as if she'd shed a skin.

Was she now Mary 401?

'What can we do for you, Miss Hammond?' Another official with a clipboard was approaching, bustling and businesslike. 'Your American friends who own the island are frantic. We've fielded half a dozen calls. Would you like to ring and reassure them?'

'I'll do that,' she said, still feeling weird. 'I'll tell them their quilt's safe.'

'Is there someone else we can contact? You live in Taikohe. Can someone collect you?'

'Are the normal buses running?'

'Yes, but—'

'Then I'll take a bus.'

'I'm sure we can arrange someone to drive you. We have volunteers eager to help.'

'Thank you but no.' She took a deep breath. 'I need to put this behind me. Somehow life needs to get back to normal.'

CHAPTER SEVEN

New York

'MR LOGAN, THERE'S a Mary Hammond on the line, asking to see you. I told her you were fully booked but she says her business is personal. She's only in the country until Monday.'

Ben was knee deep in futures. The negotiations were complex and vital.

His secretary's words made the figures in front of him blur.

Mary Hammond.

Mary.

'Put her through.'

'She doesn't wish to speak to you on the phone,' Elspeth told him. 'She specifically said so. She's asking for a personal interview. Will I tell her no?'

His pen jabbed straight through a certificate with three wax seals on it. Three rather important seals, one of which was from a head of state. It didn't matter. 'I can see her now.'

There was a moment's silence while Elspeth returned to the outside line. His pen snapped.

'She can be here in an hour,' his secretary said, coming onto the line again. 'She's across town.'

'I'll send a car.'

'She's disconnected. Shall I delay the Howith negotiations?'

'Yes.'

'Will you need fifteen minutes? Half an hour?'

'I'll need the rest of the day,' Ben snapped. 'Cancel everything.'

His secretary disappeared, off to tell some of the world's top financiers that currency crises would have to wait. By the end of the day rumours would be flying. Ben Logan didn't miss appointments, not at this level.

But, then, Ben Logan had never been visited by the woman who'd saved his life.

He sat and stared at his desk and all he saw was Mary.

He should have flown back to the Bay of Islands to say goodbye, he conceded. He'd done all he could do, but still…

The days after the cyclone had been a blur. Getting off that chopper in Auckland. Walking over to that damned list.

Seeing Jake's name on the safe side.

Then he'd found Jake himself, in the admin office of the chopper company. He'd been shouting, offering to pay whatever it took, his entire fortune if necessary, to hire a chopper and head out to sea to personally look for Ben.

The look on his face when Ben walked in had been indescribable.

And then, of course, other things had superimposed themselves. Jake had insisted on doctors, on getting his knee checked.

Then a pub, late at night, and Jake saying quietly, 'Tell me about our mother.'

He'd remembered then the words he'd hurled at Jake as he'd forced his twin into being the one to leave the life raft. He'd finally thrown his mother's suicide into the equation.

'This is reality, Jake, not some stage play where you can play the hero. Face it now and move on. You're just like Mom. She couldn't face reality. Why do you think she killed herself?'

Until then it had been Ben's secret. Jake had been told she'd accidentally overdosed. Only Ben had known the truth, and twenty years on he hadn't enjoyed sharing.

They'd talked into the night, and drank, and things hadn't gotten easier. The pain of their mother's death was still bitter. Love… Ben didn't do it. He wouldn't. He never wanted that kind of pain again.

There was a reason the Logan boys walked alone. Jake had

tried and failed at marriage. The Logan men weren't meant for the soft side.

So even though he'd meant to go back and see Mary, in the end he'd decided it'd be better, kinder even, to make a clean break. The storm had only been that: a storm. It was over.

Except that the aftermath of that storm would be in his office in less than an hour.

Mary.

He hadn't quite managed to put her out of his head. On his laptop was a YouTube file, the final of the two top New Zealand roller-derby teams.

Smash 'em Mary was front and foremost, rolling for Taikohe. She was as she'd said, little, quick and smart, dodging girls twice her size, moving with lightning speed, taking her team to a win.

She'd played wearing fierce, warrior-woman make-up, black tights and purple socks, a tiny halterneck top and a short, short skirt.

The documents in front of him were important. He needed to concentrate.

He ended up watching the roller derby match, one more time.

If she didn't do this now, she never would.

It was crazy to come to the other side of the world just to talk to him. A telephone call would have worked, but it had taken courage to pick up the phone. Too much courage. She had to watch his face, she told herself, and in the end she'd decided it was the only way.

After all, it wasn't as if she hadn't had money for the fare, and that by itself needed personal thanks. Because three weeks after the storm a lawyer had appeared at the door of her cottage.

'Miss Hammond?'

'Yes?'

'Mr Ben Logan has sent me,' he told her. 'I'm Frank Blainey, QC, a lawyer specialising in defamation cases. Mr Logan has briefed me on a coroner's case that's put your career in jeopardy. He asked me to investigate. Miss Hammond, I've done some preliminary groundwork and frankly I'm appalled. Acting under Mr Logan's instructions, I've taken witness statements from individual members of your family, including your father, and from neighbours and colleagues.

'Because I've moved fast and interviewed in isolation, there's a clear case that we can take back to court. You have grounds for suing for perjury and defamation.'

She'd stood on the doorstep and forgotten to breathe. 'What… what…?'

'Take your time. It's big to take in, but I believe we've solved your problem.'

'Ben…Ben Logan?'

'He instructed me.'

'But I can't afford a QC.' It was a confused wail and the lawyer smiled.

'You have the Logan billions behind you. Whatever it takes, were Mr Logan's instructions, but in the end it's taken very little. You could have employed a lawyer yourself and got the same result.'

'But they're my family,' she whispered. 'My dad… I couldn't get up in court and call them liars.'

'Even when they are? Even though it has the potential to ruin your career?'

'I can't…'

'Well, I can,' he said, gently but firmly. 'And I have. Mr Logan seems to think you might not want to go to court again. If you don't wish it, I've arranged it another way. The witness statements are contradictory. I now have two colleagues' legal opinions that you have no case to answer.

'With your permission we'll present that to the nurses' registration body, together, if you wish, with your sworn statement that you don't wish your family to be put on trial for perjury. That will protect your job.

'As well as that, you've suffered significant financial and personal loss because of their perjury. Your stepmother has agreed to write this cheque on the grounds that you take it no further.'

He handed her the cheque. She looked at it and gasped.

'My father...' she managed.

The lawyer's tone gentled. 'I believe your father is appalled at the lies that have been told about you.' He hesitated. 'I don't believe he has the strength to stand up against your stepmother. He would wish to apologise but I doubt he will. He sees this cheque as an apology and he hopes you'll take it.'

It let them off the hook, she thought. She thought of all the lies, all the hurt.

Her father saw this cheque as an apology?

Standing there before the lawyer that Ben had sent, she thought suddenly that she'd never felt so alone.

Ben hadn't come to see her. He'd sent a lawyer.

Her father hadn't come to see her. He'd sent a cheque.

She was used to being alone, though. She could do this. She'd stood in the sun and forced herself to think of the ramifications of this money. Of the steps this lawyer—under Ben's instructions—had taken to help her.

'Ben asked you to do this?'

'He was aware you might think he has no right to interfere. I've done nothing except examine evidence in the public domain and present it to your family.'

'But on Ben's instructions.'

'On Mr Logan's instructions.'

It felt weird. It felt wrong. She was being paid off.

By Ben as well as her family?

It was a dumb thing to think. Unfair. But she stared at the cheque and thought of the difference it could make.

And she thought about a faint blue line—and she knew she needed to talk to Ben regardless.

'I'll tell Mr Logan you'll accept?' the lawyer asked.

'Thank you,' she said faintly. 'But I need to thank Mr Logan myself.

So a month later, here she was, in Manhattan, in Logan House, a building whose foyer looked as it it'd swallow half of Taikohe. To say it was intimidating was to put it mildly.

'Mr Logan's waiting.' An efficient-looking woman in a crisp grey suit was waiting to escort her upstairs. 'There's to be no interruptions under any circumstances,' the woman told the receptionist. 'Mr Logan's orders. He's out for the rest of the day.'

'If he's busy…' Mary faltered.

'He's not busy for you, dear,' the woman said, and led the way.

Dear…

Did she look like someone who needed TLC?

'I bet she doesn't address company moguls as *dear*,' she muttered under her breath.

She should have dressed up more. She should have…turned corporate?

She was wearing her weddings and funerals suit. It was a bit old. She should have worn more make-up. She should have bought new shoes.

It didn't matter. She didn't belong here, no matter what she wore, and she wasn't here for corporate reasons.

The lift stopped at the highest floor. The door slid open, and the woman put a gentle hand in the small of her back to guide her out.

Bet she didn't do that to company moguls either.

But maybe she needed it. 'I don't…' To say panic was setting in was an understatement. 'I shouldn't…'

'Mr Logan's waiting,' the woman told her. She swung open the inner doors—and Ben was rising from a massive desk, walking forward to greet her.

Ben?

The last time she'd seen this man he'd been battered and wounded. He'd been in pain and he hadn't been sure if his twin was dead or alive. She'd held him in the storm and they'd taken and given comfort to each other.

But now…

This guy was a suit plus. No one she'd ever met wore a suit like this. It was deepest black with a fine grey pinstripe, and it fitted him as if it was moulded onto his beautiful body. It screamed quality, as did his gorgeous blue tie and the crisp white linen beneath it. Even his shoes screamed quality.

He was clean-shaven. His dark hair was neatly cut and immaculately groomed.

His shadowed grey eyes surveyed her from the toes up and she was reminded suddenly of an eagle, his fierce, intelligent eyes capable of seeing things no man should see.

She was imagining things. He was scaring her.

She shouldn't have come.

And then he smiled, striding towards her with his hands held out, and with his smile suddenly he was the Ben she'd held. The Ben she'd made love to.

'Mary,' he said, with all the welcome in the world. 'Smash 'em Mary, here in my office. I'm honoured.'

He hugged her fiercely but briefly and then held her at arm's length to look at her. Once more she got that sensation that he could see far more than she wished to tell him.

Ben.

She wanted a longer hug but after that one brief hold he was back under control.

How could she think she knew this man?

'Thanks, Elspeth,' Ben said.

And she thought, *This guy really is a billionaire.* Those two words had been a dismissal to his secretary, mild and brief, but the authority behind them had been absolute.

He was a man in command of his world—and what a world!

In the last weeks she'd looked him up on the internet—of course she had. His brother Jake the actor was famous. Ben seemed to fly under the radar but his business credentials were so impressive they'd made her gasp.

She thought of the cheque her father and stepmother had given her and what a difference it was making in her life.

This guy's fortune was enough to make her eyes water.

How could she possibly tell him what she needed to tell him without him taking it the wrong way? And what was the wrong way anyway? She was in uncharted territory.

His secretary had disappeared. They were alone in his half-acre office, with the view that looked right out over the harbour to the Statue of Liberty. Mary had been in town for twenty-four hours, working up courage to come and see him. She'd queued to climb the Empire State Building to see all over New York.

She needn't have bothered. The view from Logan House was almost the same.

'To what do I owe the pleasure?' he said, and she struggled to get her words in order. She was here for a reason and she needed to get it right.

'I need to thank you.'

'I believe you've already thanked me,' he said gravely. 'Both through my lawyer and through the very nice card you sent me.'

'You make me sound like a ten-year-old writing thank-you notes.'

'I kept the card,' he said. 'I believe I'll always keep the card.'

There was a statement to take her breath away.

He was still holding her hands. Just holding…

'It's me who thanks you, though,' he said. 'You saved my life. I'll owe you forever.'

She gulped. The feel of his hands holding hers was doing strange things. She felt…she felt…

Stop it with the feeling, she told herself. Just say what she needed to say.

'I can't tell you how grateful I was to hear that Jake was safe,' she managed.

'You never doubted it.'

'I never admitted to you that I doubted it.'

He smiled, but his smile didn't reach his eyes. It was a smile that said there was trouble somewhere.

Trouble? What could be wrong in this man's perfect world?

'Is anything wrong?' she asked. 'With Jake, I mean?'

'What should be wrong? He's fine.'

'It's just…you look…'

'He's fine,' he said, almost roughly. But she knew there was something.

How did she know this man so well, this man in his billion-aire's office with his billionaire's suit? She thought, *He has the hawklike, all-seeing eyes but two can play at that game. Reading minds.*

She knew this guy. Inside he was just…Ben.

The thought settled her. It was okay. Underneath the glossy exterior he was still the man she'd held until the terror had faded.

She had been right to come.

'How's Heinz?' he asked.

'Probably bored. My next-door neighbour's looking after him. How's the knee?'

'You came half a world to ask about my knee?'

'No.' It was time. She released his hands and took a step back. She wanted to watch his face when she said what she had to say.

She was here for a purpose. Do it.

'Ben,' she said, and then she paused.

'Mary?'

Say it.

'I came to tell you I'm pregnant.'

CHAPTER EIGHT

HE DIDN'T GET his face right fast enough.

He didn't know how to.

Mary had stepped back so she was standing against the closed doors. She was pressing herself hard against the doors, her chin tilted, almost defiant.

That was an appalling suit she was wearing, he thought irrelevantly. She'd looked better in torn jeans.

Pregnant.

The word seemed to echo round and round the massive office. Deals were done in this room that affected the finances of the world. Yet nothing had ever been said in this office that seemed more important than this.

Pregnant.

'It's okay,' she said, hurriedly now as if she needed to clear whatever it was she saw on his face. 'I'm not here to sue you for half you own. I don't even want acknowledgement if you'd rather not. I just thought...I needed to tell you.'

'But I thought...' He was having trouble getting his voice to work. 'I thought...' But he hadn't thought. That was how it had happened—thought had been shelved. Their mating had been born of primeval need, with no thought of consequences.

The consequences now were blowing his mind.

'Maybe you thought there are morning-after options,' she said. 'There are. I just...didn't think of them until it was way after the morning after.'

And it was all there on her face. This wasn't a discussion about whether or not to go ahead with a pregnancy.

This woman was having his child.

He should walk forward, take her in his arms, hold her close and tell her this was joyful news.

He couldn't.

A baby.

Family.

His mother… The mess that was their family… He'd even messed it up with Jake. He couldn't hold anything together. Could a baby be tough and self-reliant? Not in a million years. But for him to be needed… For a child to rely on him…

'It's okay,' Mary said again, her tone gentling. 'This was a shock to me, too, believe it or not. Sense was blown away with the storm. But now I've decided that I want this baby and, Ben, what you've done for me makes it possible. Thanks to your lawyer I have the cheque from my family and I have my job back. My baby and I will be fine. It's just…I came here because I thought I owed you this much.'

'You owe me?'

'This is not a trap, Ben. I'm not here to ask you for anything. But for me, somehow this pregnancy seems right. I never imagined it but now it's happened it's wondrous. It seems amazing that something like this could come from…from what we had. So the more I thought about it, the more I decided I needed to tell you, face to face, in case for you this baby might help…'

'What on earth do you mean?'

'I mean this baby is bringing me joy, Ben,' she said gently. 'I know there'll be problems. I know it'll be tough, but the moment I realised I was pregnant all I felt was happiness. That something so wonderful could come from such a…'

'Chance coupling?' He said it harshly, cruelly even. She should flinch. Maybe she did, inside, but if she did she hid it well.

'It might have been a chance coupling for you,' she said, the chin tilting again, 'but for me it was like a dividing line. Before and after. I know that doesn't make sense to you but for me it's huge. I went to the island feeling defeated. I came home thinking I could cope with anything the world threw at me. I have the strength and happiness to raise this baby alone. Ben, you have no need to do anything. If you like, I won't even put your name on my baby's birth certificate. But I thought…I just had to tell you.'

He didn't answer. He didn't know what to say.

'I'll go now,' she said gently. 'Ben, there'll be no repercussions. For you it was a chance coupling, but for me it was magic. I believe our baby was conceived in love, and I'll remember that forever. Thank you, Ben. Thank you for my baby. Thank you for everything.'

And she turned and walked out the door.

She'd sounded sure, but her certainty faded the moment she closed the door behind her. Why had she come?

Back in New Zealand it had seemed like the only honourable thing to do. She'd meet him face to face. She'd explain that he was going to be a father.

Okay, a tiny part of her had been hoping for joy, but that was a tiny part. A dumb part.

Mostly she'd thought the conversation would be brief and businesslike, with her assuring him she didn't expect support. He needed to know he had a child but she didn't want more help.

What she hadn't expected was horror.

Maybe he had assumed she was here for a share in the Logan billions, but she didn't think so. The look on Ben's face had said this wasn't about money.

Why wouldn't the elevator come? She shoved the button again and thought maybe she'd hit the fire stairs.

She was a long way up.

She wanted to go home. Fiercely, she wanted to be home.

She never wanted to see that look on Ben's face again. She never wanted her child to see it.

'Mary…'

He was right behind her.

She jabbed the button again.

'I'm sorry,' he said, but she didn't turn around.

'You don't need to be sorry. I've said what I came to say. As far as you're concerned, this is over.'

'When did you arrive?'

'Yesterday.' Jab, jab.

'And when are you going home?'

'Monday.' Jab, jab, jab.

He leaned forward and covered her hand with his, stopping her touching the buttons. His touch seemed to burn.

What was wrong with the stupid elevator? 'You own this building,' she snapped. 'Put in more lifts.'

'Let me take you to lunch.'

'No.'

'That's not very gracious.'

'No!'

'Mary—'

'I've said what I came to say. Let me go.'

'Can I tell you why I reacted…as I did?'

And finally the elevator arrived. All she needed to do was step inside and head for the ground floor. Then catch a cab, collect her gear, head to the airport and go home.

'There's a reason,' he said.

The elevator door closed again and it slid silently away. He put his hands on her shoulders and turned her so she was facing him.

'Tell me.' She felt weary beyond belief. Jet-lag? Early pregnancy? She'd been feeling the effects of both these things but the look on Ben's face had made them ten times worse.

'I can't…' he said.

'Tell me,' she repeated, and she thought tears weren't far off. But why should she cry now? She'd had this sorted, or she'd thought she had.

Until she'd seen the fear.

'I don't do families,' he said.

This was a dumb place to have such a conversation, she thought inconsequentially. Outside the elevators. Public.

And then she glanced over Ben's shoulder and realised the palatial reception area was designed for one secretary and Elsbeth was nowhere to be seen. This whole floor was Ben's.

This was Ben's world and she had no place here. But…was this his refuge as Hideaway Island had been hers?

A storm had destroyed her refuge. Was she threatening his?

She wasn't. He didn't do families? She wasn't asking that of him.

But it seemed he intended to tell.

'Mary, my father, his father and his father before him practically owned Manhattan,' he said. 'My father was a womanising megalomaniac. My mother was a talented, beautiful, fragile screen star. Rita Marlene. You may have heard of her. She needed support and love and appreciation to thrive and with my father she got nothing.

'After Jake and I were born she retreated into her stage world, where her only reality was her acting. It reached the point where even when she was upset, we never knew what was real or make-believe. Ophelia, Lady Macbeth, Anna Karenina, Jake and I had them all. Plus isolation and nannies. The only time Jake and I were noticed by our parents was when we did something outrageous and, believe me, we made outrageous a life skill.

'I don't think we realised…how much worse it made everything. That every time we hit trouble our father blamed Rita. Rita.' He gave a harsh, short laugh. 'She was always Rita. Stage Rita. Never Mom. And my father was Sir.'

'Ben—'

'I know, this is self-indulgent history,' he said harshly. 'But hear me out. When we were fourteen Jake and I stole a car. Not just any car either,' he said, and once again there was an attempt at a smile. 'My father was trying to stitch up a deal with a spoiled brat son-of-a-sheikh. An oil magnate. He had him to stay in our family mansion and pulled out all stops to impress.

'You can imagine the scene. Servants everywhere, my mother dressed up in the most beautiful ballgown, almost ethereal, playing the subservient wife to a T. I believe…' He hesitated. 'I think now she was heavily into drugs. All the signs were there only, of course, no one wanted to see.'

'Oh, Ben…'

But he wasn't stopping. He knew she'd seen the horror, and maybe he had to explain.

'And so my father was barking orders, desperate to impress, bullying the servants, bullying Rita. And Jake and I were ordered to dress in suits we hated and present ourselves in the drawing room to be introduced as his sons. It did his street cred good,' he added. 'To have fine sons who obeyed every order.'

She didn't know where this was going. She thought she didn't want to.

'Only then my mother spilled her drink,' he said. 'She was sitting right beside the son-of-sheikh. He was looking at her in a way Jake and I hated, and she spilled it. And my father walked over, wrenched her to her feet and told her to get out. Apologies, apologies, apologies. And then I called him a….' And he said a word that made her cringe.

'Ben…'

'So that was it. We were propelled out, too. My father's pride was to be protected at all costs. The last thing we heard was my father apologising for his stupid family, and the son-of-a-sheikh agreeing that women and children were an eternal problem.'

She could hardly breathe. She didn't want to know, and yet… 'And so?' she managed.

'So Jake and I went out and hot-wired the son-of-a-sheikh's Lamborghini. Jake drove it all the way to Soho and then crashed it into the rear of a stationary bus. Jake swears the bus jumped out to greet us. Jake was concussed and taken to hospital and I spent the night in jail, not knowing if Jake was alive or dead. There was no way my father would bail me out that night. My father's assistant finally came to get me. I returned home the next morning to find my father apoplectic and my mother with a black eye and hysterical.'

'Oh, Ben…'

'His pride had been hurt—of course it had—so he'd taken it

out on her. And she kept crying and crying, and saying, "Sorry, Ben, sorry. My babies… Ben, you take care of Jake. He's your responsibility now." I thought she was talking about the crash, about Jake getting hurt. She was so melodramatic. To my never-ending regret I remember thinking, *Who are you playing now?*

'The hysterics went on and on. It was so real it terrified me but finally there was silence. My father went out. Jake was still in hospital. I was scared for Rita, but I was still scared for Jake. I lay in bed that night and told myself of course she was acting. I was angry, too. Jail had been shocking. I'd been terrified. Why hadn't Rita stood up to him? Why wasn't she stronger? Why wouldn't she tell me how Jake was? So I should have gone to her and I didn't. But she wasn't acting. She overdosed and was dead before morning.'

Mary didn't move. She couldn't. She thought of her own lonely childhood and she thought…how could it possibly compare? What had been placed on this man's shoulders… His mother's death.

'You were fourteen,' she said gently. 'You didn't know.'

'I should have.'

'And Jake…'

'You think I told him any of this? The black eye? The blame? He thought Mom died of an accidental overdose. How could I lay any more on him?'

'He still doesn't know?'

'The last minutes in the yacht,' he said heavily, 'I threw it at him. He was playing the martyr, telling me to go first. He has a weak leg, courtesy of the Afghanistan injury. I told him to get into the harness or he'd be suiciding, just like Rita. It shocked him enough to get into the harness, to get him to safety. But now…'

'He's holding it against you?'

'Who knows what Jake's thinking? He's certainly talking to me in words of one syllable. "Yes." "No." "I can't talk." "Bye."'

'And you?' she said gently. 'Where does that leave you?'

'Not with a family,' he said bluntly. 'Jake takes after Rita. He retreats into his acting world. Reality blurs. For me, though, try as I may, I'm my father's son. I enjoy running this company. I enjoy control. But all my life…' He took a deep breath. 'Ever since my mother died I've avoided the personal. One night, one vicious outburst and my father destroyed our family. Rita told me I was responsible for Jake. After she died I swore I'd never be responsible for anyone else.'

And she got it. She could read it on his face. 'You think you might end up like your father, too?'

'I'll never put myself in the position to find out.'

'No one's asking you to.'

'You're asking me to be a father.'

'No. I've given you the opt-out clause, remember?'

'How can I opt out?'

'Easy,' she said, and somehow she found the strength to drum up a smile. 'You can smile at me, say congratulations, wish me all the best and say goodbye.'

There was a long silence. He looked at her, he simply looked, and when he nodded she knew that somehow he'd moved on.

'I'll give you lunch first.'

'I'll accept lunch,' she said, still smiling determinedly. 'But nothing else. I'm no risk to your world, Ben, and neither is our baby. You're still free to be…as free as you wish. You're not responsible for our baby.'

Our baby.

The two words stayed with him as they left the building, but they weren't small. They echoed over and over in his head, like a drumbeat, like an off-rhythm metronome.

Like a nightmare.

He couldn't be a father. How could he risk…?

It'd been his stupid idea to steal the Lamborghini. The consequences had stayed with him all his life. His mother had died because of his stupidity.

His father had been a gross bully. He'd battered his wife but he hadn't killed her. *He* had done that by ignoring her, by not reading the difference between real and fantasy.

He'd spent his life trying not to tell Jake, trying to pretend it had never happened, being responsible. But one revelation from a slip of a girl and he'd told her everything.

Why? She wasn't asking him to commit to any part of this baby's life. There'd been no reason to spill his guts, and yet…the look on her face… To turn away from her was like slapping her.

He could do financial support. He decided that as they reached the ground floor. He'd be in the States. She'd be in New Zealand. There was no reason for him ever needing to see his…the child.

When…it…turned eighteen…it…might want to meet him. That could be okay.

'You're putting a note in your mental diary to have dinner when he turns twenty-one,' Mary said, and he turned and stared down at her. They were in the foyer. His colleagues, his staff were casting curious looks at the woman by his side.

The mother of his baby?

What was it with this woman? How could she read his mind?

'How did you know what I was thinking?'

'You're like an open book.'

'I'm not. And I wasn't thinking his twenty-first. It was his eighteenth.' Deep breath. 'Do we know if it's a he?'

'I don't have a clue,' she said cheerfully. 'Does it matter?'

'Of course not.

But then he thought, *A son.*

And then he thought, *A daughter.*

'You're getting that hunted look again,' she told him. 'You needn't worry. If you turn into your father, I'll be between you and our child with a blunderbuss.'

'I believe that,' he said. 'I've watched you playing roller derby.'

It was her turn to stare. 'Where?'

'YouTube.'

'You watched me?'

'Last year's finals. A woman who plays like that…who looks like that… I wouldn't get in her way for the world.'

'There you are, then. You don't have to worry about being like your father. I'll put on full make-up and intervene.'

'Don't,' he said, suddenly savage.

'Don't?'

'Put on make-up. Pretend. Jake does it all the time. My mother did it. They move into their acting world and disappear.'

'Is that what Jake's done now? Is that why you're hurting?'

'Can we quit it with the inquisition?' It was a savage demand but she didn't flinch.

'Sorry.' She sounded almost cheerful. They'd negotiated the revolving doors and were out in the weak spring sunshine. New York was doing its best to impress.

Where to take her for lunch?

Clive's was his normal business option, with comfortable seating, discreet booths, excellent food and an air of muted elegance. Clive himself always greeted him and no matter how busy, a booth was always assured.

He took Mary's arm and steered her Clive-wards, but she dug in her heels.

'The park's thataway, right?'

'Yes, but—'

'And it's Central Park. That's where the Imagine garden is. Strawberry Fields Forever. I loved John Lennon. Can we buy a sandwich and go there?'

'It'll be full of—'

'Kids and dogs,' she finished for him. 'Exactly. My kind of place.'

'I guess it will be if you have this baby.'

'It is anyway,' she said, her voice gentling, as if she needed to reassure him. 'I'm a district nurse. Kids and mums and oldies are what I do. Along with grass under my feet. Ben, I'm still jet-lagged. Fresh air will do me good.'

Now that she mentioned it, she was looking pale. He should have noticed before, but she was wearing drab clothes, she looked incredibly different from the last time he'd seen her and the news she'd brought had been shocking. Now he took the time to look more closely.

'You've been ill.'

'Morning sickness,' she said darkly. 'Only they lie. Morning… Ha!'

'But you decided to fly to New York, morning sickness and all.'

'It didn't seem right not to tell you.'

'Telephone?'

'I wanted to watch your face when I said it.'

'So you've said it. And I've been found wanting.'

'You haven't,' she said, and tucked her arm into his. 'You've explained why you're afraid of being a father. If I'd telephoned I'd never have got that. I'd have raised Gertrude or Archibald to think Dad doesn't care, rather than Dad cares too much. Where can we get a sandwich?'

Dad. The word did his head in.

'If we're having a sandwich we're having the very best sandwich,' he growled, fighting an emotion he didn't know how to handle.

'Excellent. Lead the way. We're right beside you.'

We.

Discombobulated didn't begin to describe how he felt.

CHAPTER NINE

HE HAD A diary packed with meetings.

He sat on the grass and ate sandwiches and drank soda with the mother of his child.

It seemed she'd done what she'd come to do. As far as Mary was concerned, the baby conversation was over. She chatted about the devastation caused by Cyclone Lila, about the rebuilding efforts, about Barbara and Henry's dejection at the possibility of selling a cyclone-ravaged island.

'Maybe I can buy it,' Ben found himself saying.

'Why on earth would you?' She'd hardly touched her sandwich, he noted. When she thought he wasn't watching she broke bits off and stuffed them into her bag.

Just how bad was the morning sickness?

'Because I can?'

'Just how rich are you?'

'Too rich for my own good,' he said, and grinned. 'It's a problem.'

'Where's your dad?'

'He died ten years ago. Heart attack. It couldn't have happened to a nicer man.'

'You really hated him.'

'Yes,' he said. 'I did. He was a total controller. Jake and I were supposed to go straight into the business. The power he wielded… We went into the army to get away from it. There was another dumb decision. It was only when he died that I took the first forays into commerce and found I loved it.'

'It doesn't mean you're like him.'

'No.' His voice told her not to go there, and she respected it. She abandoned her sandwich, lay back on the grass and looked up through the trees.

'It's the same here as in New Zealand,' she said in satisfaction. 'Trees. Grass. Sky. Nice.'

'You'd never want to live here.'

'No.'

He looked down at her. She'd come all the way from New Zealand to tell him something that could have been said over the phone. He'd reacted just about as badly as it was possible to react. She was in a strange country, she was jet-lagged and she was morning sick.

She looked happy?

'What?' she said, seeing his confusion.

'You could be a bit angry.'

'What's to be angry about?'

'If you had a half-decent dad he'd be here with a shotgun. I'd be being marched down the aisle and we'd be living happily ever after.'

'I don't see shotgun weddings leading to happy ever after.'

'But you're happy without it.'

'I'll have a job I love, my roller-derby team, a baby I think I'll adore to bits, enough money to exist on and trees, grass, sky. Oh, and Heinz. What more could a woman want?'

She was so…brave. He had so many emotions running through his head he didn't know how to handle them, but he looked down at her and he thought, involved or not, he wanted to help. Despite her protestations, he knew how hard the life she'd chosen would be, and the thought of this woman facing it alone was doing his head in.

'Mary, you won't have just enough money to exist,' he growled. 'You're having my child. I'll buy you a decent house; set you up with everything you need. You needn't go back to work.'

She thought about that for a bit.

He wanted to lie beside her. He was wearing an Armani suit. The grass…

'The grass is comfy,' she said.

And he thought, *What the hell,* and lay beside her.

She was gazing up through the treetops. The sky was amazingly blue. The tree was vast. He felt…small.

His body was touching hers. She was so close. He wanted…

'Just enough for the baby,' she said.

And he thought, *What?* What had they been talking about?

'The money,' she said, as if she'd heard his unspoken question. 'I don't want anything for me, but it'd be nice to think if he or she wants to go to university the choice won't be dictated by my finances. You're the dad. Our kid'll be smart.'

She said it like she was pleased. Like she'd made a good decision to choose him to father his child.

He sat up again. 'Mary…'

And once again she got what he was thinking. 'I did not plan this,' she said evenly.

'How do I know?'

'What, lie on an island and wait for a stud to be washed up? Hope to be pregnant? Why?'

'I have no idea.'

'You also have no idea how this pregnancy will affect my family,' she said, in that soft, even voice that he was growing to trust. 'They'll hate me. They've been forced to back down in their accusations. Now I'll turn up pregnant when my sister's just lost her baby. They'll tell me I'm rubbing their faces in it. It'll hurt. This isn't all roses, Ben.'

'But did you want it?'

'No,' she said, and she said it in such a way that he believed her. 'To be honest, I've avoided relationships. My father's…desertion gutted me, and I've always thought if I can't trust my dad, who can I trust? Like you, my family background doesn't leave me aching to copy it. But now…maybe you're right in one sense. Even though I didn't set you up, I'm welcoming this baby. Somehow the night of the storm changed things for me. I do want it.'

'Despite you not being in a position to afford it.'

'I can afford it. I didn't come here for money. Set up a trust or something for the baby if you want, but I want nothing.'

Nothing.

He thought of all he had here. A financial empire. An apartment overlooking Central Park. Any material thing he could possibly desire.

What would happen if he lost everything?

He'd have trees, grass, sky. Right now they felt okay.

It might get draughty in winter, he conceded, and he looked at Mary and he thought she'd just build a willow cabin or find a cave. She was a survivor and she didn't complain. She'd care for this baby.

And suddenly he felt…jealous? That was weird, he conceded, but there it was. He was jealous of an unborn child—because it'd have a mother like Mary.

'How's the book going?' he asked, feeling disoriented, trying to get things back on track, though he wasn't sure where the track was.

He saw her flinch.

'You don't have to tell me.'

She thought about it. 'That's okay,' she conceded. 'Maybe I have to open up a bit there, too. It's always been my private escape, my writing. If I'm to have this baby then I need to share.'

'So…share?' The request felt huge, he thought. It was only about a book, he reminded himself. Nothing else. 'Is it proceeding?' he asked.

'It is.' He could see her make a conscious effort to relax. 'In your fictional life you've been drinking weird, smoky cocktails with three slutty sisters, squeezing them for information, and all of a sudden they've transformed themselves into dragons. Very gruesome it is, and rather hot, but you're handling yourself nicely.'

'A true hero?'

'You'd better believe it.'

'Will you try for publication?'

'A million authors are striving for publication. What makes you think anyone would like my book?'

'I like it.'

'That's 'cos you're the hero. I'll send you a copy when I've worked out my happy ever after.'

'Happy ever after works in books?'

'You have to believe in it somewhere.'

A cloud drifted over the sun. A shadow crossed Mary's face and she shivered. Enough. He rose and put down a hand to help her up.

She stared at it for a moment as if she was considering whether to take it. Whether she should.

'You need to let me help a little,' he said gently. 'I'd like to.'

'I'd like to help, too,' she said. 'Where's Jake?'

'Still in New Zealand, winding up his movie.'

'Would you like me to talk to him?'

'No.'

'That's not very polite.'

'Families are complicated.

'You don't need to tell me that.' She ignored his hand and pushed herself to her feet, wincing a little as she did.

'You're hurt?' The tiny flash of pain did something to him. She was pregnant. What did he know about pregnancy? Surely she shouldn't have flown. What if there were complications? What if…?

'Twenty-four hours squashed in a tin can is enough to make anyone achy,' she said. 'So let's get that "Call the artillery and have me carted off to Emergency" look off your face.'

'Am I that obvious?'

'Yes.'

'You're sure you're okay?'

'Yes.'

'Where are you staying?'

She told him and he struggled to keep his face still. Not a salubrious district. Cheap.

This was the mother of his child.

No. This was Mary.

'I'll take you home,' he said.

'I've just figured out the subway.'

'Good for you but I'll still take you home.'

'You have a car?'

He hauled out his cellphone. 'James will be here in two minutes.'

'Wow,' she whispered. 'Wow, wow, wow. Bring on James.'

She sat in the back of a car that'd have everybody back home gathered round and staring. She sat beside Ben, and a chauffeur called James drove her back to her hotel.

It wasn't in a salubrious part of town. It wasn't a salubrious hotel.

The chauffeur pulled to a halt out the front of the less-than-five-star establishment and turned to Ben.

'Is this the right address, sir?'

'No,' Ben said. 'It's not.' He turned to Mary. 'When did you arrive?'

'The day before yesterday?'

'You've stayed here for two nights?' His tone was incredulous.

'It's clean,' she said. 'I checked it out on the internet before coming. It has everything I need and it's near the subway.'

'It doesn't have everything I need. This is a dodgy neighbourhood at the best of times. I bet you've been walking around alone, too. It's a miracle you weren't mugged.'

'I can look after myself.'

'Not if you're staying here you can't.' He sighed. 'James, stay with the car. Do not under any circumstances leave it alone in this district. We'll be as fast as possible.'

'We?' Mary pushed open the car door. 'There's no we. You've brought me home. Thank you very much. Goodbye.'

'You're not staying here.'

'Says you and whose army?'

'I am,' he said through gritted teeth, 'a trained commando. I'll take you by force if necessary.'

'Oooooh,' she said, pretending to cower. And then she sighed. 'Quit it with the dramatics. Bye, Ben.' She was out of the car and up the steps of the hotel—but he was right beside her.

'I said goodbye,' she hissed.

'I heard. Let me see inside.'

'No.'

'It's a public hotel.'

'No!'

'You're the mother of my baby,' he said, loudly, possessively, and she stopped and stared.

'My baby?'

'That's why you came all the way to New York. To tell me I have a share in this. I might not be able to dictate where you stay but I will have a say in how safe our child is.'

She stared at him.

She hadn't thought this through, she decided. Had she given him the right to dictate how she treated...his child?

What had she done?

'It's fine,' she said through gritted teeth, and he took her arm and smiled down at her, and she knew that smile. It was his *I'm in charge and you'd better come along quietly or I'll turn into a Logan* smile.

'Let's just see, shall we?'

Which explained why twenty minutes later she was standing on the doorstep of what must be one of the most awesome apartments in Manhattan, staring around with shocked amazement.

'I can't stay here!'

He hadn't quite picked her up and carried her but he might as well have. One look at her dreary hotel room, with its window that looked at a brick wall, with the smell of the downstairs hamburger joint drifting through the window and a bathroom with mould, and the father of her child had simply gathered her possessions and led her out. All the way to his place.

'I have plenty of room,' he said, dumping her decidedly downmarket duffel on the floor of his breathtaking apartment. She could see her face in the marble floor tiles. Her duffel was travel-stained and old. It looked ridiculous sitting against such opulence.

'My father bought this as his alternative to home when Rita's histrionics got too much,' he said briefly. 'Five bedrooms. My father never did things small.'

'N-no.' She crossed to the wall of French windows leading to the balcony. Leading to Central Park.

She needn't have bothered asking to have her picnic there. She could see the Lennon garden from here.

'It's convenient,' he told her. 'You'll be able to sightsee until you go home.'

'I should go home now.'

'But your flight isn't until Monday.'

'I… Yes.' Her last-minute decision to come here and tell him had meant last-minute tickets. Which meant not the week-end. Today was Friday. She'd have two days living in this… this…place.

'It's scary,' she said, staring around at the cool, grey and white marble, the kitchen that boasted four ovens, the massive leather lounge suites, the tinkling waterfall behind the living room wall. 'It scares me to death.'

'It beats the cave on Hideaway.'

'On Hideaway we had cushions and Barbara's quilt. Comfy. How do you get comfy here?'

'I'm not here much.'

'Social life?'

'I work.' He crossed to the kitchen, opened the massive fridge and stared into its interior as if he didn't know what the contents were but knew he'd find something.

'Soda? Cheese and crackers? Cold chicken?'

'I've just had lunch. Who fills your refrigerator?'

'A housekeeping service.'

'A housekeeper?'

'It's a service. More convenient than just the one employee. I don't need to worry about holidays.'

'So you don't even need to know your housekeeper.'

'They come and go when I'm not here.'

'That's awful.'

'What's awful about it?'

'You really are alone.'

'I don't need anyone,' he told her. 'I like my life.'

'You need Jake.'

A shadow crossed his face then. How had this woman guessed what was hurting him?

He didn't want to talk about it but then...this was Mary. Maybe he did.

'We fight to be independent,' he told her. 'But the twin thing makes it harder. When he was hurt in Afghanistan I damned near died myself. And when I didn't know whether that chopper had made it...it's not a sensation I'd like to repeat.'

'So you don't want to get close to anyone else?'

'I don't want the responsibility of loving like that—but I will do the right thing by your baby.'

'You just said it was our baby.'

'It is,' he said, and he sounded strained. 'So I will do what I can.'

'I hope he's grateful.' She gazed around with distaste. 'I can tell you one thing, though. If he's any child of mine, he won't want to inherit this place.'

Inherit. The word was a biggie. Why had she said it? It took things to a whole new level.

She watched Ben's face change again.

'I didn't mean...' She spoke too fast, trying to take things back. 'Ben, I'm not expecting anything, I told you. This baby... if you want, he can be brought up not even knowing he's your son. Or daughter for that matter. Inheritance is nonsense. We won't interfere with your life.'

'You already have interfered.'

'I shouldn't have told you?'

'Of course you should.' He raked his hair in that gesture she was starting to know. It softened him, she thought. It took away the image of businessman Ben and gave her back the image of Ben in a cave. The Ben she needed to care for.

'Ben, you like your isolation,' she said softly. 'We're not threatening that. I'll return to New Zealand and ask nothing of you. If you want, you can set up a trust for this child's education, but I'll not raise him expecting anything from you. You can walk away.'

'I can't walk away.'

'But I can,' she said. 'And I will. Come Monday. Meanwhile, which of these doors leads to a bedroom I can use?'

'The bedroom at the end of the hall's mine. Choose any other. They all have en suites.'

'Of course.'

'Mary?'

'Yes?'

'Have a nap,' he told her. 'Then I'll take you out to dinner.'

'I'm having a sleep, not a nap,' she told him. 'A really long one. I'm jet-lagged like you wouldn't believe and this pregnancy makes me want to sleep all the time. You can go back to whatever you were doing. You need to be independent and I'm not messing with that. Thank you, Ben, and goodnight.'

She slept. He headed for his study and stared out over the park.

He needed time to work out all that was inside him.

Maybe it wasn't possible for him to work it out.

Mary was carrying his child. He was going to be a father.

Coming, ready or not.

The old chant, sung by children for ages past in the game of hide and seek, was suddenly echoing around in his head, almost as a taunt.

A father.

Abortion? The word drifted through his consciousness but

when he tried to work out some way he could say it to her, something like a wall rose up.

He couldn't say it.

He didn't want to say it.

This would be Mary's baby and he didn't want her not to have a child. It was a convoluted thought but it was there as a certainty. And somehow... The time in the cave with her had been time out, like a watershed, where fear had laid all bare. That a child should come of it... It seemed okay.

Was that sentiment? Was it hope?

He couldn't get his head around it.

He didn't have to, he told himself. For some reason Mary had come halfway around the world to tell him, yet she was proposing leaving again on Monday. He never needed to see her again. He could pay into a trust account once a month. He could stop thinking about it.

How could he stop thinking about it? He slammed his fist down on the desk so hard it hurt, and suddenly he wished he could talk to Jake. Ring him. 'Jake, I've screwed up...'

In his present mood Jake could well say he should tell someone who cared.

In this position Jake might do better, he conceded. Jake would be able to play the caring dad. He was great at acting.

If he himself was better at acting, maybe he could pull this off.

Pull what off? Being a caring dad?

He couldn't do it. He didn't know how. He thought back to the rages and the coldness that had been his childhood. He tried to think how he could possibly relate to a child.

He could try, but he couldn't act, and if he felt nothing...

His father had felt nothing. His mother...she'd told them she'd loved them but in different ways all the time. Like she was playing different roles.

'I won't act,' he told himself. 'I can only do what I can do, and I won't put myself in a position of power.'

So what could he do? Send money? That felt so much

like what his father would do. Send money and get rid of the problem.

On impulse he hit the internet, heading for the site where Smash 'em Mary flew round the track, dodging and weaving, leading her team to victory.

It was a rough game, and that was putting it mildly.

Surely she wouldn't be able to play now she was pregnant.

The words of the lawyer he'd sent to help her echoed in his ears as well.

'We've won her monetary compensation, and she's been reinstated in her position as district nurse, but there is local antagonism,' he'd told him. 'Her father and stepmother are wealthy. They control much of the commerce in the town and people are afraid to upset them. Her stepmother is vindictive, more so now that we've forced this resolution. Life's not going to be easy for your Mary.'

Your Mary. The words had swept over him then, but they came back to haunt him now.

She wasn't His Mary. She was a woman he scarcely knew. He'd been stranded with her for two days. Two days was tiny.

She was a woman who'd come half a world to tell him she was pregnant because it was the right thing to do.

His fist slammed on the desk again. Lucky the walls were solid. Lucky Mary was sleeping three bedrooms away.

He needed to get away. Think. Go back to the office? Do something to stop him going mad.

He headed back to the living room. He'd carried Mary's duffel into her bedroom for her but her capacious purse was still on the bench. It looked shabby, worn, and it pricked his conscience as nothing else could.

A folder was edging out the top.

And suddenly he was back at the cave, waiting for Mary to come back from her interminable search of the island, hating himself that he couldn't be with her. Distracting himself by reading Mary's make-believe. He'd been the hero.

'I wonder what I've done now?' he said aloud, and looked at the purse again.

She knew he'd read the beginning. It was sitting on the bench, an open invitation. She'd said he was facing dragons.

He could just…read.

But not here. The proximity to Mary—to a woman he hardly knew, he reminded himself—was doing his head in.

He lifted the folder from her purse and put it in his briefcase.

He'd just go…somewhere and disappear into Mary's fictional world.

Maybe Jake was right. Maybe reality had too much to answer for.

CHAPTER TEN

SHE WOKE AT MIDNIGHT, thirsty beyond measure, and also hungry. She woke regretting those nibbled lunchtime sandwiches.

She headed out to the kitchen. The apartment was in darkness—or maybe not. Back in New Zealand the darkness at night was absolute. Here, the lights of the city glimmered through the drapes. Glamorous footlights were placed strategically around the skirting boards so no one could lose their way at night. There was a light on in the sitting room.

She was in New York. More, she was in Ben's fabulous apartment. Marble, glass, discreet lighting, floor-to-ceiling windows overlooking Central Park…

Money plus.

Her inheritance gaffe was still smarting. 'I never should have come,' she muttered to herself. 'Of course he'll think I'm after his money.'

But it had seemed wrong not to. She'd needed to tell him and for some reason she'd felt she had to do it soon. Before the time had come where she could terminate?

Not that she'd considered terminating. She wasn't sure why this little life was so precious, why she'd discovered she was pregnant and felt joy rather than dismay, but she had.

'And maybe I sort of wanted Ben to feel that way, too,' she muttered.

'Feel what way?'

He was on a window seat in the sitting room, working on his laptop. Wearing a bathrobe. Silk. She was in a T-shirt and jogging pants.

She felt like a poor relation.

He looked…hot.

Put it aside, she told herself, and somehow she stopped looking at him. It took an effort.

'I'm hungry,' she said, heading for the kitchen. She hauled open the massive refrigerator doors and thought, *Whoa*… 'How many people live here?'

'My housekeeper caters for every eventuality.'

Yep, money.

Get over it, she told herself. 'I just need toast.'

'I'll make it for you.'

'I can do it. Go back to bed.'

'I don't sleep much,' he said.

'It's a biggie.' She was staring into the refrigerator, thinking all sorts of things—like how hot he looked with his silk bathrobe open and…and forcing herself to think of condiments. Three types of jam. No, make that four. The raspberry looked good, but then there was quince…

'What's a biggie?'

Deep breath. The conversation couldn't all be about jam, and it surely couldn't be about silk bathrobes. 'Learning you're about to be a dad.'

He walked over and set about making toast while she went back to deciding on condiments. Tricky.

She was so aware of his body.

The island bench—approximately a mile long—gave her a couple of yards' clearance from Ben. She hauled herself up on the bench to watch toast-making.

'Most people sit on the stools,' Ben said mildly.

She peered behind the bench to see a row of fancy designer stools. Chrome and leather. Four different colours. Or make that shades. Designers did shades.

'How could I choose which one to sit on?' she demanded. 'I had enough trouble with jam.'

'You want tea?'

'No, thanks.' Actually, she would like tea but it'd mean she had to stay out here for longer. With this body.

Um…Ben. His name was Ben.

Maybe she should start calling him Mr Logan.

'I've been thinking I'm glad you don't want a termination,' he said.

She stilled. He was watching the toast. She was watching the breadth of his back. To all intents and purposes they were a couple talking cosy domestic things—like termination.

'Why?' she managed, and he abandoned the toast and turned to face her.

'It's been a shock,' he said softly. 'All afternoon…all to-night. Heaven knows how you slept but I couldn't. I wouldn't have wished for it but now it's happened…I do want this child.'

And he said it so fiercely that it was lucky she'd put the jam down.

There was a lot to think about in that statement. A lot to make her heart falter.

'One part of me's pleased to hear you say that,' she admit-ted at last. 'I was never going to terminate, not for a moment, but in a way I think that's why I came here so early in the preg-nancy. I needed to know your reaction. I wanted my choice to be your choice.'

'But the other part?'

Say it like it is, she decided. Just say it. 'Another part of me almost had a heart attack, just this minute,' she admitted. 'Do you want this child like you want another Logan? And how much do you want it? Enough to sue me for custody? I hadn't even thought about that.'

'I would never do that to you. And she's your baby.'

'She?'

'I thought tonight…' He looked at her for a long moment, his expression unreadable, but when he spoke, it was all ten-derness. 'I thought, what if she's a girl, just like her mother?'

What was there in that statement to take her breath away? What was there in that statement to make her forget toast and jam, to forget where she was, to forget everything except those words?

What if she's a girl, just like her mother?

She'd been terrific when she'd found out she was pregnant, she'd decided. She'd surprised herself by how calm she'd been. She'd set about making plans, figuring how she could manage.

She'd decided to tell Ben, rationally and coolly. She'd prided herself on her efficiency, getting a passport, deciding on flights, choosing the hotel Ben had so rudely rejected.

She'd told him calmly. Everything was going as planned.

But one little statement…

What if she's a girl, just like her mother?

She sat on the bench and stared, and suddenly the cool control she'd kept herself under for the last couple of months snapped.

She couldn't help it. Tears were rolling down her cheeks and there wasn't a thing she could do about it. She couldn't speak. She just sat there and cried like a baby.

Ben looked like he didn't have a clue how to handle it. That made two of them.

'Mary, I didn't mean…' He sounded appalled. 'Mary, stop.'

That'd be like asking the tide to turn. She gave her tears an angry swipe but nothing could stop these suckers.

She didn't have a tissue. She didn't have thirty tissues. Where were tissues in this über-rich mausoleum of a marble apartment?

One minute he was standing by the kitchen bench, talking to a woman he'd decided he hardly knew. The next moment the woman had turned into Mary. *His Mary.*

He knew this woman like he knew himself.

Tears were rolling down her cheeks and she was making no effort to check them. It was as if she didn't know what to do with them.

This was a woman who seldom cried. He knew that. What was happening now was shocking her—as well as shocking him.

She needed tissues, but his shoulder was closer. He stepped forward, gathered a sodden Mary into his arms and held her.

He should wear a towelling robe, he thought ruefully. Silk didn't cut it with tears.

Silk didn't cut it when the feel of her body was soaking through. But he held her and held her, until the shuddering eased, until she'd cried herself out, until he felt the imperceptible stiffening that told him she'd realised what she'd done, where she was.

He still held. He was cradling her like a child but this was no child. She'd slumped against him but the slump had turned to something more. Her face was buried in his shoulder but the rest of her... She was moulded to him. Her breasts were pressed to his chest. His face was in her hair.

'I can't...' It was a ragged whisper.

'I have it in hand,' he told her, and before she could make any objections he swung her into his arms and strode with her into his bedroom.

The woman needed tissues. There were tissues in his bedroom and that's where he was headed.

One minute she was cradled against Ben Logan, sobbing her heart out, releasing months of pent-up emotion and who knew what else besides. The next she was in his arms, being carried into his bedroom.

She should make some sort of protest, but who was protesting? She was making no protest at all.

They'd made love before as complete strangers. They weren't strangers now. Or maybe they were, she thought, dazed. How did she know this man?

She did.

He lived in a different world from her, a world he pretty much owned.

She felt she knew him inside out.

To the world this man was a hero, a rich, smart, controlling wheeler and dealer in the world's finances. But she'd seen what lay beneath. She'd seen the core that was pure need.

Who was she kidding? The need was entirely hers and she couldn't resist it for a minute.

She was catching her breath, finding control of a sort. The dumb weeping had stopped so when Ben set her on the bathroom bench and handed her a wad of tissues she could do something about it.

She blew her nose, hard, and Ben blinked.

'There's my romantic girl.'

She choked on something between a chuckle and a sob, but it was erring more towards the chuckle.

Something was happening inside her. She was in this man's bathroom. He was looking at her with such concern...

'Your face is puffy.'

'And there's a truly romantic statement,' she managed. 'I bet you say that to all the women in your life.'

'There are no women in my life.' He picked up a facecloth, wet it and gently wiped her eyes. Then her whole face. 'Just the mother of my child.'

What was it about that statement that took her breath away? That made her toes curl?

That made her drop her tissues into the neat designer trash slot and look up at him and smile.

'Ben...'

It was all she had to say. All the longing in the world was in that word. It was a question and an answer all by itself.

She put her arms up and looped her hands around his neck. He stopped and lifted her yet again.

'Your place or mine?' he asked huskily, managing to smile.

'I've only got a king-size bed,' she managed back. 'Puny. I bet yours is bigger.'

'You'd better believe it,' he said, and she did.

And that was practically the last thing she was capable of thinking for a very long time.

She woke and the morning sun was streaming over the luxurious white coverlet. She woke and the softness of the duvet enfolded her.

She woke and Ben was gone.

For a moment she refused to let herself think it. She lay and savoured the warmth, the feeling of sheer, unmitigated luxury, the knowledge that she'd been made love to with a passion that maybe she'd never feel again.

He'd made her feel alive. He'd made her feel a woman as she'd never believed she could feel.

He'd made her feel loved.

But he wasn't here now.

She'd slept, at last, cocooned in the strength and heat of his body. She'd slept thinking everything was right in her world. What could possibly be wrong?

She'd slept thinking she was being held by Ben and he'd never let her go.

She stirred, tentatively, like a caterpillar nervous of emerging from the safety of its dreamlike cocoon.

The clock on her bedside table said twelve.

Twelve? She'd slept how long? No wonder Ben had left her.

He'd left her.

Hey, she was still in his bed. Possession's nine tenths of the law, she decided, and stretched like a languorous cat.

Cat, caterpillar, whatever. She surely wasn't herself.

There was a note on his pillow.

A Dear John letter? She almost smiled. She was playing make-believe in her head. Scenario after scenario. All of them included Ben.

The note, however, was straightforward. Not a lot of room for fantasy here.

I need to go into work. I left loose ends yesterday and they're getting strident. Sleep as long as you want. It's Saturday, no cleaners come near the place so you have the apartment to yourself. I'll be home late but tomorrow is yours. Think of what you'd like to do with it.
Ben.

And then a postscript.

Last night was amazing. Please make yourself at home in my bed.

There was more stuff to think about.

She was interrupting his life, she thought. She really had pulled him out of his world yesterday. He'd need to pull it back together.

And then come back to her?

Just for tomorrow.

'But if that's all I can have, then that has to be enough,' she told herself. 'So think about it.'

Food first. What had happened to last night's toast? Who could remember? But she'd seen juice in the fridge, and croissants. And then…the bath in Ben's bathroom was big enough to hold a small whale.

'Which is what I'll be in six months…

'Don't think about it. Don't think about anything but tomorrow,' she said severely. 'Or maybe not even tomorrow. Let's just concentrate on right now.'

The office was chaos. One day out and the sky had fallen. Still, it had been worth it, he decided, making one apologetic phone call after another, trying to draw together the threads of the deal he'd abandoned the day before.

Mary was worth it.

She was with him all day, her image, the memory of her body against his, the warmth of her smile, the taste of her tears.

He was getting soft in his old age. He'd vowed never to feel this way about a woman.

About anyone.

He didn't want to feel responsible for anyone but somehow it had happened. Ready or not, he was responsible for Mary. The mother of his child.

His woman?

He wanted to phone Jake.

Why? To tell him he'd met someone? Jake's attitude to

women was the same as his. His brother had made one foray into marriage and it'd turned into a disaster. The woman had needed far more than Jake would—or could—give.

The Logan boys weren't the marrying kind.

But Mary...

No. He would not get emotionally involved.

Who was he kidding? He already was.

Which meant he had to help her, he thought as the long day wore on, as the deal finally reached its drawn-out conclusion, which meant the financial markets could relax for another week.

He thought of what the lawyer back in New Zealand had told him. 'She really is alone.'

If she was alone and in trouble...with his baby... There had to be a solution.

Finally at nine o'clock he signed the last document, left it on his secretary's desk and prepared to leave. But first one phone call.

Mathew Arden. Literary agent for some of the biggest names in the world.

'Well,' he said, as Mathew answered the phone. 'Am I right?'

She walked her legs off. She strolled down Fifth Avenue, she checked out Tiffany & Co., was awed by the jewellery and chuckled as the salespeople were lovely to her, even though they must know she could hardly afford to look at their wares.

She took the subway to Soho, just so she could say she'd been there, and spent time in its jumble of eclectic shops. She bought a pair of porcelain parrots for her next-door neighbour who was looking after Heinz.

She bought a truly awesome diamanté collar for Heinz. He'd show up every dog in the North Island.

She took the Staten Island ferry and checked out the Statue of Liberty from close quarters.

'You're just as beautiful as the pictures,' she told her lady-ship, and felt immeasurably pleased.

She ended up on Broadway and got a cheap ticket to see the last half of a musical she'd only ever seen on film.

She bought herself a hamburger, headed back on the subway to Ben's apartment—and was weirdly disappointed when he wasn't home.

She'd sort of wanted him to be impressed that she hadn't hung around all day waiting for him, but maybe she'd done too much trying to prove it. Her feet hurt.

She ran a bath and soaked, all the time waiting for his key in the lock.

'Just like I'm the little woman,' she told herself. 'Waiting for my man to come home.'

She let herself imagine it, just for a moment. If she and Ben were to take this further...

This'd be her life.

'Um, no,' she said, reaching out for a gorgeous-looking bottle of bath salts. Sprinkling it in. Lying back to soak some more. 'You know you never want to commit to some guy who'll turn out to be just like Dad. This is fantasy and nothing more.'

It was after ten when Ben reached home and he was feeling guilty.

This was what it'd be like if he ever tried marriage, he told himself. This was why Jake's marriage had foundered. The Logan boys' lives didn't centre round women. But still, the thoughts of the night before were with him. The memory of Mary in his bed was enough to make him turn the key with eagerness.

'Mary?'

No answer.

Her purse was on the counter. Her jacket was hanging on the chair. It felt good to see them. He liked it that Mary was in his apartment.

He checked his bedroom, half-hopeful that she'd be lying there as she'd lain last night.

'In your dreams,' he muttered. 'To have a woman wait for you…'

He checked her bedroom. She was curled in the centre of her bed, cocooned in pillows. She looked exhausted. She looked small and vulnerable and alone.

She looked…like Mary.

This woman was planning on returning to New Zealand to bear his child. With no support.

He didn't wake her. He headed to his study to think, and think he did. The idea that had been idling in the back of his mind all day was starting to coalesce into a plan.

It made sense—and Mary was a sensible woman.

He wasn't entirely sure how Heinz would fit in with the pedigree pooches who strutted round Central Park but he was pretty sure Heinz could hold his own.

Could Mary hold her own?

He was sure she could. In her own way she was as independent as he was.

He flicked open his laptop. There was work to be done, though not business. The financial world could manage without him tonight. Tonight Ben Logan was plotting a future for his child.

And his woman?

Be sensible, he told himself. There are levels of responsibility. You can take the practical route; just don't let the emotional side interfere.

CHAPTER ELEVEN

SHE WOKE AND FELT…lonely. This was crazy. How many mornings had she woken by herself in her life? Practically all of them, so what was different?

For a start, she was in Ben's apartment.

Yes, and tomorrow she was going home. Leaving.

Ben had inferred he wanted some input into their child's life. Did that mean he might visit? Or did it mean he might send for Ermintrude or whoever to visit him?

Worry about it when the time comes, she told herself.

He could have come to her when he got home last night.

He'd have been being kind. Letting her sleep.

'A pox on kindness,' she muttered.

She emerged and Ben was drinking coffee at the dining table. He had newspapers spread out before him but he wasn't reading. He was staring out over the park.

He turned and smiled and her heart did this crazy back flip with pike that she should be getting used to now. She wasn't.

'I didn't hear you come home. You should have woken me.' She sounded cross, she thought, and she tried to reel it in. She needed to be practical. She didn't need to admit that she wanted this man.

'You looked exhausted.'

She flushed, knowing she didn't look fantastic now either. Maybe she should have brought some hot lingerie for this trip. Maybe she should have at least brushed her hair before she'd emerged.

'You look great,' he said, and she thought again, *This man had some sort of telepathy going.*

'Says the man who didn't come to my bed last night. You could have, you know. You're hardly likely to get me pregnant.'

'Would you have wanted me to?'

And there was only one answer to that. Honesty. 'Yes,' she said. She managed a smile. 'Not…not that that's a come-on.'

'It's not taken as such,' he said, which flattened her because if he picked her up and carried her into his bedroom right now, she wouldn't object at all.

But he had no such intention. He looked…businesslike, she thought. He was wearing jeans and an open-necked shirt with the sleeves rolled up but he still managed to look sleek and clever. A man in control of his world.

A man not to be distracted by a woman in jogging pants.

'I promised you today,' he said. 'Coffee?'

'No, thanks, I've gone off it. A gallon of juice would be good. You don't need to do anything for me today.'

'What did you do yesterday?'

'Saw New York.'

'What, all of it?'

'As much as I could fit in. Statue of Liberty, Tiffany's, Fifth Avenue, Soho, Broadway, pastrami and rye sandwiches, bagels, New York cops being nice, wind coming up from under the pavements, markets, people, stuff.'

'Wow,' he said faintly. 'No wonder you slept.'

'My feet went to sleep first. Your pavements are hard.'

'Poor feet. So you don't want to walk today?'

'I might. With only one day left I won't waste it. But, Ben, you don't need to share.'

'I'm sharing,' he said brusquely. 'Four days to see America is ridiculous.'

'New York is enough.'

'It's not. What would you like to do?'

Go back to bed, she thought. *With you.*

She couldn't say it.

'I thought I might sit on a ferry,' she said. 'Just sit. I could see a heap and not walk at all.'

'So we're ruling out anywhere with pavements.'

'It's fine. Ben, you don't need to play travel escort.'

'No more city stuff?' he said, ignoring her.

'Ben…'

'Would you like to see my favourite place?' he asked. 'Somewhere I go to chill. When I have a business deal I need to clear my head from? Where I go to turn off?'

'That sounds like a bar.'

'It's not a bar,' he told her. 'Have you heard of the Adirondacks?'

'I… Yes,' she said. 'I mean…I guess I know it's a park of some kind.'

'A park,' he said, and snorted. He glanced out the window. 'Central Park's a park. I'll show you a park!'

'Isn't it…miles away?'

'You won't have to walk an inch, I promise. It's an amazing spring day, one out of the box. Let's take advantage of it. Okay, Mary Hammond, drink some juice and eat some toast while I do some phoning. Adirondacks, here we come.'

And two hours later, courtesy of a helicopter whose pilot greeted Ben like an old friend, Mary saw the Adirondacks.

First they flew over them.

'How can there be such a place so close to New York?' she breathed, looking down at what seemed endless mountains, rivers, lakes.

'It's our best-kept secret,' Ben told her through the headphones. 'It's bigger than almost all the country's national parks combined, enshrined in the constitution as a wilderness.'

At their landing place there were kayaks and a couple of burly men to help launch their craft. One kayak. One set of paddles.

'Because you're not paddling today,' Ben told her. 'This is your day of rest.'

'I can kayak.'

'It's pretty much floating. Give it a rest, Mary. Let me take charge.'

By which time she was flabbergasted. This was so far out of her league she was speechless.

'Just shut up and enjoy it,' he told her, so she did. This was another world. Ben's world. She wore one of Ben's big, warm jackets that smelled of him. She sat in the front of the kayak while Ben paddled behind and there was nothing to do but soak it in.

Ben paddled with the ease of a man who'd done this all his life. That made her feel…like she didn't know how to feel.

He took her along the Sacandaga River, into wilderness. There seemed to be no soul for miles, except for loons and ducks, and deer standing still and watchful on the river bank. When she saw a great bald eagle soaring in the thermals, even Ben seemed stunned.

'The eagles disappeared from here by the early sixties, but there's work to reintroduce them,' he told her. 'At last count we had twelve nesting pairs. It's a privilege to see them.'

She heard his awe and knew that for Ben this was indeed special.

'How often do you come here?'

'Often. Whenever I need to be alone.

You're almost always alone, she thought. *Surrounded by people, you're still alone.*

But she said nothing. This was not her business.

'I'm betting you help fund these wildlife projects,' she guessed.

'The company does fund wildlife projects,' he admitted, but he sounded brusque and she wondered why. Surely it wouldn't hurt to admit to being passionate about something.

But the more they paddled in this amazing place, the more the feeling of him as a loner intensified. What he'd told her of his family left her cold. Poor little rich boy.

He was a man in control. He was a financier, a commando, a billionaire.

Whatever, he seemed more alone than she was.

He paddled for miles, with strong, sweeping strokes that sped them along the calm surface of lakes and the streams that joined them. He must know where he was going. All she could do was trust him. All she could do was sit back and soak in the majestic mountains rising on either side of the banks, and the utter stillness, broken only by bird calls, the honking of geese and the weird calls of the stunningly marked loons.

The smell of the pine filled her senses. The sun was on her face and Ben was paddling with ease.

He did this often. Always alone? She guessed yes, and wondered if this was his only escape from the financial pressure he lived under.

Why did she keep coming back to his loneliness? Wasn't she the single mum? She should be worried about herself but, instead, the more she knew of this man the more her heart twisted for the isolation she sensed inside him.

She thought suddenly she'd vowed never to depend on a man. What if a man could be persuaded to depend on her?

It was a crazy thought but it shifted something inside. Something was changing. The defences she'd built up over so many years seemed to be cracking and she wasn't sure how to seal them again.

Ben was just…Ben. The man she'd held in her arms. A man she could hold in her heart?

It was a crazy thought, unthinkable, but against all reason the thought was there. What if…?

But the what-if stayed unspoken. Indeed, there seemed little need to speak at all. It was as if the wilderness itself was ordering them to be still.

Stop overthinking this, she told herself. Ben's a loner and he always will be. He's chosen his own course. Stop thinking and soak this in, because reality started tomorrow.

Alone for both of them.

* * *

This was make-believe. Time out.

Jake would approve, he thought. He was drifting through the most beautiful scenery in the world, with a beautiful woman…

Yep, it was playing make-believe, only it wasn't. She was a restful woman, his Mary. He could tell already that she loved this place. When he came here he could bring her…

Yeah, well, that was fantasy as well. His? She was a loner like himself. She wouldn't be his and he wouldn't be hers.

But they drifted on and the farther they went the more his plans came together.

This could work. He just needed Mary to think about it dispassionately, without emotion. There were two types of responsibility, he thought. One was tangible, the responsibility for keeping someone secure and protected. He could do that.

The other responsibility was emotional. His mother had demanded her children make her happy. He'd never ask that of anyone, neither would he expect the demand himself. Emotion needed to be set aside.

The problem was that for some reason, right now, emotion was everywhere.

The sun was on their faces. There was a rug stowed with a picnic hamper in the stowage area of the kayak. They could pull into shore, find a bed of pine needles and…

And not.

Today he had to be dispassionate. Today he needed to map out a sensible future for both of them.

Including a baby?

For all of them.

They ate lunch on the banks of the river, and the magnificence of the surroundings took her breath away.

Not enough, however, for her not to notice the lunch the guys at the landing place had handed them as they'd launched the kayak. Everything was in elegant, boxed containers, carefully labelled. Tiny bread rolls. Curls of golden butter. Crayfish, broken into bite-sized pieces. Tiny tomatoes, slivers of lettuce, radish, carrot, celery and a mouthwatering mayonnaise. Quiche in a container that had kept it warm.

éclairs filled with chocolate and creamy custard. Strawberries, watermelon, grapes.

Wine if she wanted, which she didn't. Two types of soda. Beer for Ben.

It should have been cold. They'd been drifting on fast-moving water from the spring thaw, but today...today it was summer.

Today was a day she'd remember for the rest of her life.

She ate the last éclair she could possibly fit in, stretched back on cushions—cushions!—and gazed up through the massive branches of a pine to the sun glinting through.

'This has been magic,' she whispered. 'Thank you so much for bringing me.'

'I could bring you once a month,' he said. 'Every time I come.'

It was said matter-of-factly, like a neighbour offering to share a shopping run. Once a month, take it or leave it.

'So you'd pop an airline ticket in the post for me once a month,' she managed when she got her breath back. This was fantasy. Maybe it was time they got out of here.

'I want you to stay.' He hesitated and then he said it. 'Mary, I want you to marry me.'

As a breathtaker it was right up there with the feeling she'd had when she'd looked at the blue line on her pregnancy-testing kit.

Maybe it was higher. She'd suspected she was pregnant. This had come from nowhere.

She'd been almost asleep, sated with the beauty of the morning, the food, the feeling of being with a man she felt instinctively would dive to her protection if a loon suddenly swooped to steal her éclair.

She wasn't asleep now.

I want you to marry me.

She glanced sharply at Ben, expecting to see him just as

dreamlike, making an idle joke that could be laughed off. Instead, she saw a man so tense there might be an army of loons lined up for attack.

'Wh-what?' She could barely get the word out. 'What do you mean?'

'I've spent twenty-four hours thinking about it,' he said. 'It's the only logical thing to do.'

She nodded, forcing herself to sound practical. Nurse humouring lunatic. 'Logical. I can see that.'

'Can you?'

'Um…no.'

'You won't be permitted to stay here unless we're married,' he told her. 'American immigration isn't welcoming to single mothers with no visible means of support.'

'Right.' She should sit up, she thought, but that'd mean taking his proposal seriously.

It didn't deserve it.

'I wasn't aware,' she said at last, 'that I wanted to live in America.' She glanced around and felt bound to add a rider. 'It's very nice,' she conceded. 'But it's not home.'

'Where's home?'

'In Taikohe, of course,' she said, astounded.

'Are you happy there?

'I have a job. I have neighbours. I have Heinz.'

'I've enquired about Heinz. We can get him over almost straight away.'

'To, what, live in your flash apartment?' This was the craziest conversation she'd ever had. 'Ben, what are you talking about?'

'I'm talking about us,' he said, and his voice said he wasn't crazy at all. His voice said this was a serious proposal. He'd put all the pieces of some weird jigsaw together and come up with a fully formulated plan. 'Mary, I've spent most of yesterday thinking this through. I would like to help you raise this child.'

Raise this child… That sounded mechanical, she thought. It sounded like following a recipe for making bread, or shifting a wreck off the ocean floor. *Raise this child*…

'How?' she managed, and apparently he really had thought about it.

'We're loners,' he told her. 'Both of us. We need our own space. That's a problem in that we need to raise this child together, but it's also good in that you have few ties to New Zealand. I've been trying to figure out how you could move to New York. I've run through the options, and the only one that'll work is marriage.'

'I…see,' she managed, but she didn't.

'You won't get a green card unless we do.'

'Why would I want a green card?'

'So you can stay here,' he said patiently. 'So I can have a say in raising this baby.'

'Will you stop saying "raising,"' she snapped, shock suddenly finding an expression. 'It's like building with Lego blocks. Producing something. A technical procedure. This is a baby we're talking about. A little person. You don't have to stand above and pull.'

'But it'll be work,' he said, refusing to be deflected. 'You can't want to bring it up by yourself.'

'I have Heinz—and my baby's not an *it*.'

'He—or she—will be my son or daughter, too.

'But you can't make me stay.' A niggle of fear suddenly grew much bigger. Had it been a mistake to tell him? He was a Logan. He had the world's resources behind him.

'I won't make you stay.' His voice gentled, as if he sensed her sudden terror and was backing off. 'How could I force you? But I want you to think about it. It could be good for both of us.'

'How would it be good?' she snapped. 'I know no one. I don't know if my nursing qualifications are acceptable. I have nowhere to live. I have nothing.'

'You could write,' he said, and shoved a hand into his pocket and produced a folded piece of paper. He handed it to her and then sat back and waited for her to read it.

She glared. She stared at the paper as if it contained explosives.

'Read it,' he said, gently, and she had no choice. And the letter took her breath away all over again.

Hey, Ben.
I'll admit I was pissed when you pushed me to read this so fast but now I'll admit to being impressed. This is raw talent and it's good. The story needs work but we could really take this places, especially if you're prepared to back us with publicity. It could be huge. Tell her to finish it and we'll go from there but if the end's as good as the beginning, we have a goer.

And then:

PS Her hero's sounding a lot like you, Ben, boy. Made me chuckle. She's good, your lady.

It was an email, dated late last night. From a publisher whose name was known throughout the world.

The words blurred into a black and white fuzz.

If the end's as good as the beginning, we have a goer.

She thought back to the cave, sitting writing what she loved. Using the time out. Writing Ben into her story.

He'd read it. He'd told her he'd read it.

Some time yesterday he must have copied it and given it to a publisher to read.

She should be thrilled, but…why did it feel such an invasion? Why did it feel he was almost taking over life?

'So here's my plan,' he said, before she could get her breath back. 'My apartment's huge. We won't need to stay this close long term but until you get your green card we need to live in the same premises to prove we're married. I'll get an architect in. We'll split the apartment so you have your quarters at one end, we'll put in a space for a nanny, and we can meet in the middle.

It'll need to be arranged so partitions can be set aside in case we have a visit from Immigration, but with a nanny, and me to take a role as well, you'll be free to write as much as you like.

'You can train Heinz to be an apartment dog—the park's just over the road. This could work.'

'You want me to live in your apartment.' She was having trouble speaking.

'You need help,' he said gently. 'I can't bear to think of you facing the future alone.'

'But marriage…'

'It's not exactly your standard proposal,' he said ruefully. 'We'll need a strong pre-nup agreement, but I'm trusting you.'

'Th-thank you?'

'I guess you'd be trusting me as well,' he said, smiling slightly. 'But I won't sue for half of Heinz.'

'You're thinking I'd sue?'

'It's not a real marriage but it'd work. It'd give you and the child security. It would mean I could keep in contact.'

'Why would you want to keep in contact?'

'Because this is my child.'

She was struggling to get her head around this. Struggling hard. He wanted to raise her child. He wanted to organise her writing. He wanted…what else?

'So you'd want to read bedtime stories and go to school plays? You'd want to change diapers and take sides when she faces school bullies?'

What was she gabbling about? she thought wildly. She was talking school plays? But the marriage thing was too big to consider. Marriage. Waking up beside this man, every day for the rest of her life.

But that wasn't what was on offer. What was on offer was assistance and control. This man didn't do close. Even the thought of the practicalities of child-rearing had him drawing back.

He'd really never thought of himself as a father? How lonely was he?

If the end's as good as the beginning…

The phrase from the publisher was suddenly front and centre.

She thought back to the cave, to holding each other, to mutual need. To the moment this baby had been conceived.

That had been the beginning. A joining of two people.

He was offering her an ending that was no such thing.

'The child-rearing would be over to you,' he said faintly. 'If you have a nanny, you should have time to cope with the odd diaper.'

'You don't want to share?'

'You keep your personal space and I'll keep mine.' He hesitated, then continued, but less sure, 'But, Mary, there is this attraction between us. Maybe we could keep that—if we both wanted.'

'With you living at one end of the apartment and me the other.'

'We could have visitation rights, to be decided as we go.'

He was joking?

He wasn't.

He'd plotted her future. She'd sit and write and care for their baby. Logan money would launch her book, which he'd organise to be published. *Her book.* Even her fantasy would be his. She'd be Mary Logan, author, promoted by the resources of the Logan empire. She'd live in New York and she'd have a nanny.

And she'd have a husband—*with visitation rights to be decided as we go.*

She was feeling just a little bit sick.

Actually, now she came to think about it, she felt a lot sick. Her body was taking over from her mind.

Ben must be able to see it. 'What's wrong?' he said sharply, but she waved him back.

'Just baby,' she said. 'Making its presence felt.' *It's telling me what it thinks of your stupid proposition,* she thought, but she didn't say it out loud. Her gorgeous day was spoiled.

He'd thrown her a sensible proposition to keep two loners staying as such. Why did it make her feel old and grey and ill? More and more ill.

'Leave me be for a moment,' she told him.

'Mary…'

'Leave me be.'

She had no choice. She could no longer face him.

She disappeared into the woods as fast as physical necessity dictated.

His first impulse was to follow. She was ill. She shouldn't be alone.

But, then, being alone was her right. Being alone was what his proposition was all about.

Except it wasn't. She'd be his wife. He'd be responsible for her—and for his child.

It freaked him out a bit, but he'd get used to the idea. He wouldn't get close enough to hurt them.

There was the rub. He'd been brought up in a household where sentimentality was exploited to ruthless effect. You protected yourself any way possible. You didn't get fond of nannies because they left—in fact, his father had come into his bedroom one night and found his nanny giving the twins a hug goodnight and the next day she was gone.

'I won't have any woman making my sons soft.'

There had been no softness in their house. His father had protected himself with his money and his power. His mother had manipulated him with emotion. She'd protected herself with her acting, and Jake had learned to do the same.

The one night his mother's acting had become reality, when he hadn't seen the difference, she'd died.

In time Ben had developed his own armour. He wasn't ruthless like his father. He didn't act. He simply held himself to himself.

The sight of Mary, shocked and ill, twisted something inside that hurt, but he knew that pushing to get closer wouldn't help. He'd help Mary practically but if she learned to rely on him emotionally he'd let her down.

He didn't know not to.

Raising a child… What had she said? You don't have to stand above and pull.

He didn't have a clue about child-raising. He only knew that he couldn't bear the thought of Mary going back to New Zealand.

Of Mary not having his resources available to her.

Of Mary being alone?

She was alone now.

She was ill. She wouldn't want him. She was a loner, just like he was.

So he forced himself to wait, packing the picnic gear, loading the kayak, making sure the site showed no traces of their stay. That's why he loved this place. He made no impression on it. It stood as it had stood for centuries, a place of solitude and peace.

It was a place where a man could be totally alone.

Except he wasn't alone now. Mary, was only yards away, being ill—because she was carrying his child.

Enough. The catering company who'd provided their lunch had provided napkins. He soaked a couple in the clear river water, and went to find her. He met her at the edge of the clearing. Whatever had happened was over. She looked wan and shaken and that same twist of his heart happened all over again.

He wanted to take her into his arms. He wanted to take her into his heart.

He didn't know how to.

For some reason he kept thinking of the night his nanny had been fired. Maggie was a loud, boisterous Australian. She'd bounced into their lives and she'd kept up with all the devilry he and Jake had thrown at her and more. For a while their lives had been fun.

Had he loved her? Maybe he'd started to, but one hug and she was gone.

He remembered his mother saying, 'Keep your emotions to yourselves, boys. I'm tired of interviewing nannies.' That was good, coming from his mother.

But if he fell for Mary…

Enough. He was putting neither of them at risk. Instead of hugging her, he proffered the napkins. Practical-R-Us.

'Thank you,' she said dully. 'And thank you for the proposal. It was well meant but I don't want it.'

'Why not?'

The question hung. She looked at him, just looked, and it was as if she was seeing everything he had to offer—and found it wanting.

'Because I'm not alone by choice,' she snapped. 'Because I love my community. I love my job and my roller-derby team and my dog. I love them. You don't get that, Ben, because you don't understand what love is, but I understand it. You're offering me a part of your world but that involves loneliness forever.'

She softened then, and the look she gave him was one of sympathy. Sympathy! No one offered Ben Logan sympathy but there it was.

'Ben, I know what love is,' she said, her voice bleak and flat. 'For a while I had my mum and my dad. I had my town and I had people who loved me. And it's precious. I know how precious is it, so I'll fight to get it back. Maybe I won't succeed but I'll try. Thank you for your offer. I understand how much it's taken to offer even so little of yourself but, Ben, I'm greedy. I want more and you aren't offering more. You can come and see us whenever you want. We'll work something out with our baby, but for now I want to go home.

Monday.

Her plane left at midday. She needed to be at the airport at ten. A cab might take an hour.

Therefore she stayed in her bedroom until nine. She hadn't slept all night but she was staying put. Ben knocked at seven, but she didn't answer. He'd knocked so lightly she could easily have been asleep—and how could she face him?

Marriage…staying here with Ben… In a way it was a siren call. She could stay here and hope. But hope was all she'd have, she thought. She'd be aching for him to want her. She'd be aching for him to be a part of her, and that wasn't what he was offering.

She'd be risking what had happened with her father. Loving a man and watching him turn away.

Nine o'clock. It was time to go. She needed to walk out without looking back.

Maybe Ben wouldn't even be here, she thought, not sure whether to hope or not. Maybe the knock on the door at seven had been to say goodbye.

Leaden hearted, she zipped her bag closed, gazed around the stupid cool grey room one last time, and walked out.

Ben was at the kitchen bench. A leather duffel was sitting by the door. A large duffel.

'H-hi,' she managed. Keep it simple, she told herself. Get it over with and ignore that bag. 'Could you call me a cab?'

'You need breakfast. You ate nothing last night and you lost your lunch.'

'I'll get something at the airport.'

'Eat here,' he growled.

'I don't have time.'

'Seeing the jet leaves when I say it leaves, you have all the time in the world.'

'R-right,' she managed. 'You'll ring the airline and say hold that plane?'

'I've organised our own jet.'

'You've…' She gasped. 'You've what?'

'Jake's in New Zealand, finishing up the movie he's working on. I'm therefore killing two birds with one stone. Seeing Jake. Taking you home.'

'In your dreams,' she said faintly.

He rose and headed to the other side of the bench. 'Toast?' he asked. 'One slice or two? No, make that two slices or three?'

She was hungry, she conceded. Morning sickness was a myth—it washed over her at any time it felt like it. Right now it was in abeyance and her stomach was telling her it was time to stock up.

But not at the expense of missing her plane.

'I'll have breakfast at the airport,' she told him, heading for the door. 'I'll hail my own cab.'

'So you'll sit in cattle class while I travel in luxury?'

'That's crazy. Flying your own jet all the way to New Zealand…just for one person.'

'Two if you come with me. That cuts our carbon footprint in half.'

'You have to be joking.'

'I'm not joking,' he said, and smiled at her, and, oh, that smile… She was wobbly anyway. That smile made her even more wobbly.

Maybe she needed to sit down.

'I'm…independent,' she managed.

'I know you are,' he agreed. 'That's one of the things I admire about you. But there's independent and there's pig stubborn. Come with me and you'll have your own bed, all the way to New Zealand.'

That caught her as nothing else could have. She still felt vaguely unwell. She'd flown over wedged between an overweight businessman and a harried mother who'd treated Mary as a free babysitter.

'My own…what?' she said cautiously.

'You heard. Full-size bed, with pillow menu.'

'You're kidding.'

He knew he had her. She could see it. His eyes got that twinkle she was starting to know, the one that said he was getting his own way. 'Pillows,' he said, like it was a siren call, and, oh, it was. 'I'd go for the double-size goosedown, with the neat Logan insignia on the pillowcase. Very classy.'

'It's a Logan plane?'

'Of course.' The toast popped. He flipped it onto a plate. 'Marmalade?'

She should get out of here. He'd clearly lost his mind.

Double-size goosedown…

'We provide pyjamas, too,' he added helpfully.

'It's not a double bed?' She was still trying to get her head around what he was offering, but her words came out as pure suspicion.

He grinned. 'You think I'd pay for a jet to fly to New Zealand just so I could get you back into bed?'

'I wouldn't put it past you.'

'The plane has full-size beds. One at either end of the plane.'

'How big's the plane?

'Big enough for you to jump me if you change your mind.' The twinkle grew.

'Ben…'

'I know.' His smile receded, but not far. 'You won't change, but, Mary, I can do so little. I respect your independence—of course I do—but allow me to make one last gesture. Let me take you home.'

And what was a girl to say? He stood there, smiling with that beguiling smile that would have caused harder hearts than hers to soften.

He didn't do the heart thing. She'd figured that. He was a man who kept himself apart and would continue to do so.

After he'd taken his private jet to New Zealand.

After she'd let him take her home.

CHAPTER TWELVE

HE THOUGHT SHE might talk to him during the flight. He thought he might even use the time to get her to change her mind.

Instead, she walked onto the plane, he showed her the bedroom set-up she could use and he lost her.

She looked at the piled pillows, the fluffy duvet, the magazines, the crystal glassware ready to be filled with anything she needed…

She yawned and smiled apologetically at Ben and the steward who accompanied them.

'Thank you so much,' she said. 'This is the stuff of dreams, and that's exactly where I'm going.'

So she slept, ensconced in privacy at her end of the plane. She didn't emerge.

Ben had also thought he might get some work done. He sat in front of his laptop and figures blurred.

He thought about independence and how much he valued it. He thought if he valued it, the least he could do was grant it to Mary.

He thought about Mary.

He'd arranged a car to be waiting at Auckland airport. Of course he had, Mary thought. It was a wonder it wasn't a limousine with chauffeur in attendance.

'I can catch a bus,' she said, but she was no longer in control.

'A four-hour bus journey? I don't think so. Why don't they have airports in Taikohe?'

'Because it's tiny. Ben, I'm fine. I'm nice and rested.'

'I'm not. Do you have a couch?'

'I…'

'I'll drive you home, stay overnight and head back tomorrow to see Jake.'

'You really do have it all planned.'

'I even have my international driving licence. Trust me?'

'No.'

'You want me to stay somewhere else?'

He'd paid for a jet to bring her all the way home. Maybe she could manage a sofa for the night. 'Fine.'

'Mary?

'Yes?'

'I'm not threatening your independence.'

'Believe it or not, that's not what this is about,' she told him. 'But it's okay, Ben. I accept your offer to drive me home and I won't threaten your independence either.'

To say Heinz was delighted to see her was an understatement. They arrived at her sparse little cottage and Mary had barely reached the front door before there was a hoy from the house next door and Heinz was tearing across the yard to meet her.

Mary fell to her knees, scooped him up and hugged him like she'd been away for months, letting him lick her. She even cried a little.

Over a dog?

But she meant it, Ben thought, remembering his mother's orchestrated emotion.

How did he know these tears were real?

He knew.

A middle-aged woman in farm-type overalls and mucky boots followed Heinz in. She enveloped Mary and dog in a bear hug and then turned to greet Ben. 'Hi,' she said, and stuck out her hand. 'I'm Mary's next-door neighbour, Kath. And you are?'

At least Mary had a neighbour, Ben thought. Mary's cottage was about a mile out of town but at least there was someone within calling distance. It should make him feel better, but it didn't.

'This is Ben, the guy I was stuck on the island with in the cyclone,' Mary said, emerging from Heinz's frenzied greeting. 'He's why I had to go overseas. I had to tell him I was pregnant.'

What followed was deep, uncompromising silence. Kath looked at him from the toes up, and then all the way down again.

'Pregnant,' she said at last.

'Yep.'

'Does your family know?'

'Not yet. You can spread it around if you want. They'll hear it in two minutes in this place.'

'You sure?'

'I'm sure I'm pregnant. The town might as well know.'

Ben was forgotten. Kath was staring at Mary, appalled. 'Mary, love, your stepmother and sisters will kill you. Sunrise's still blaming you for losing her baby. She'll say you've done it to spite her. You know your family. It's all about them. They'll have kittens.'

'I don't think it'll be that bad.'

'You know it will be.' But the woman checked Ben out again, and finally she began to smile. 'But you brought your guy home?'

'He brought me home.'

And the woman faced him square on. 'You staying? She'll need you.'

To say he was taken aback was an understatement. First, Mary hadn't told her next-door neighbour about her pregnancy before she'd left. Second, she was telling her now, and inviting her to share the news. She was telling the neighbourhood her business.

Why not? Did he want her to stay independent?

He wasn't sure what he wanted.

And, third, what the woman was saying was blunt and to the point.

She'll need you.

'He's not staying,' Mary said brusquely, pushing open the door. 'Or not more than a night. I don't need him. But thanks for caring for Heinz.'

'I have a casserole in the fridge. I'll bring it over.'

'I have stuff in the freezer. I'll be right on my own.'

'Mary, love…'

'Ben's staying tonight,' Mary told her. 'So I won't be eating baked beans by myself. And tomorrow I need to go back to work and get on with my life.'

He lay on her made-up-into-a-bed settee and stared into the night. The silence here was so deep it made him feel nervous. Somewhere outside a plover was making an occasional call to a distant mate, but there was nothing else. Nothing and nothing and nothing.

He was leaving her at the ends of the earth.

He thought the first time he'd seen her, on Hideaway Island, retreating even from this quiet place. She'd come back, though. She'd returned from her retreat and faced her world again. She was telling the world she was pregnant. She was facing them all down.

Her courage was breathtaking. He'd thought he was a loner but Mary had made it a life skill.

But still she needed…

Him?

Support, he thought. Someone to watch her back. Like him and Jake. For the last few years they'd gone their own ways, but they knew they were always there for each other.

Until now. He wasn't sure what Jake thought. The moments in the life raft had changed things.

They'd made him see how alone he really was.

But Mary needed him.

Three words kept blasting through his mind, refusing to let him sleep. She needs me.

How did she need him?

To face the community on her behalf? He suspected she had the courage to do that all by herself.

To whisk her off to New York and cosset her and keep her safe?

She wouldn't have it.

To just…be with her?

How could he do that? Where did he start? There was no common ground. He'd done all he could, asking her to stay in New York, yet she'd rejected it out of hand.

Maybe if he offered to knock a few walls down, share a bedroom…

Part of him wanted to. Part of him thought waking up next to this amazing woman for the rest of his life would be…

Terrifying. He'd hurt her.

Other people had successful marriages. He'd seen them; of course he had. Couples holding hands in public. Old men and women sitting peacefully at bus stations, their body language testament to a long life together.

He'd never trusted it.

Jake and his mother had learned to act to protect themselves, but he didn't have it—their ability to contain themselves while preserving an outer shell. That was why Jake had launched himself into his disastrous marriage while Ben knew he could do no such thing.

But he wanted Mary.

She was sleeping just through the door. The woman he wanted…

The fire was dying in the grate. Kath had set it so they'd just had to put a match to it as soon as they'd walked in. There was a small pile of chopped wood on the veranda and a mountain of logs out the back.

That was what he could do for her, he thought, and the idea gave him some peace. He'd spend another day here. He'd chop enough wood to last her through the winter.

Through her pregnancy?

He'd come back, he thought, when the baby arrived.

Before the baby came?

Okay, yes, because she couldn't have his baby alone.

She wanted to be alone.

There were too many thoughts playing in his head. He lay and watched the dying embers of the fire and thought about courage. He thought about one person's capacity to hurt another. He thought about independence.

'I'm better off getting out of her life now,' he told the darkness. 'I'll do what I can, but it has to be from a distance.'

The phone rang at five minutes past seven. Ben was already out on the veranda, checking out the wood situation.

Mary emerged in her nightie. She still looked pale, he thought. How long did morning sickness last? Had she been ill in the night?

'You're still here,' she said, and she sounded almost surprised.

'I'm staying for one more day,' he growled. 'I'll leave you with enough wood to keep you going through the pregnancy.'

'You don't need—'

'I do. Grant me that much, Mary.'

She looked at him for a long moment and then nodded. 'Thank you. But I need to go to work.'

'Already?'

'I'm on call, starting today. I took as much leave as I had, at Hideaway and then going to the States. I'm on call as of now and the phone's been switched through. Ross Scythe lives on the ridge with his wife, Ethel. Ross's had a fall but he's refusing to let Ethel call an ambulance. I need to go.'

He looked at her. She looked at her nightie.

She smiled but her smile was a bit wonky. She must still be feeling ill.

'I'll get dressed first,' she conceded.

'Very professional. And breakfast?'

'You're always pushing toast at me. I'll eat on the run. But, Ben, it means you'll be here by yourself.'

'I'm fine by myself.'

'Of course you are.' Her face changed, but before he could react she'd headed inside to get ready.

Only then her car wouldn't start. Flat battery.

'I use the district nursing car,' she said, frustrated. 'But I need to get down to the hospital to collect it.'

'We could use jump leads to start it. Do you have jump leads?'

'No,' she said crossly, and kicked a tyre in frustration. She looked cute, Ben thought. She was in her district nursing uniform, plain green pants and white blouse with nursing insignia on the breast. Her cropped curls were damp from her shower, framing her face beautifully.

If he lived in Taikohe he'd like a district nurse who looked like this, he thought. The way she looked, she was guaranteed to make a man feel better.

She was still pale.

'I'll drive you,' he said.

She looked worried, glancing at her watch. 'Thanks, but, Ben, timewise…I should get you to take me into town so I can get the work car, but Ross has been on the floor for half an hour already. His place is only a mile further out. Do you think you could drive me there first?'

So he drove her to see her patient. He sat in the car while she went inside. Then she called him.

'I think Ross has just twisted his knee,' she said. 'It might be broken but I doubt it, and he has someone coming to talk to him this morning about buying cows. Very important. I'll organise the ambulance to pick him up and take him down to the hospital for X-rays afterwards but meanwhile could you give me a hand to lift him off the floor?'

'You're not lifting anything,' he said, startled, and she gave him an exasperated stare.

'Ben, I know what I can and can't do and that's why I'm asking you for help now. It's one of the reasons I came to New York to tell you about the baby. I know when I need to share. Share or not, Ben Logan? Lift.'

So he helped Mary get the elderly farmer into a fireside chair and followed instructions while Mary got him dressed in respectable, farmer-type clothes.

'So I can greet this guy looking like I know how to cut a deal. If he thinks I'm a sook he'll lower his price,' Ross told them, while his wife looked worried.

'Heaven help anyone who thinks you're a sook,' Mary retorted. 'Take the painkillers and the ambulance will be here in three hours. If you're not in X-Ray by lunchtime I'll be out here to get you, even if it means both of us walking.'

'You're a hard woman,' Ross said, but he was smiling. He glanced at Ben. 'So you're her bloke?'

'Um…'

'Ben's the guy I pulled out of the water during the cyclone,' Mary said. 'He's the father of my baby.'

And there it was again, his business, out in the open for everyone to inspect.

She had no right…

Except she did have the right, he thought. She was pregnant. He was the father. Why not say it so the district wouldn't spend the next few months playing guessing games?

'Oh, my dear,' Ethel breathed. She fixed Ben with a look that pierced. 'So you'll marry her?'

'It doesn't work like that these days,' Mary said, packing her bag with brisk efficiency. 'They've banned shotguns.'

'I asked her,' Ben said, thinking if she was going to be honest, he could be, too. 'She's refused.'

'He looks okay to me,' Ethel said. 'What's wrong with him?'

'Ethel, why did you marry Ross?' Mary demanded, closing her bag with a loud snap.

'I can't remember.' And then Ethel gave a faint smile and turned her attention to a framed photo on the mantel of a young

Ethel and Ross on their wedding day. 'Okay, I thought he was lovely,' she conceded. 'I wanted to spend the rest of my life with him. No one told me how pig-headed he'd be. We went into our wedding in a cloud of soap bubbles.'

'Do you ever regret it?' Mary asked bluntly, and Ethel coloured. She looked down at Ross and coloured some more.

'I guess not,' she conceded at last. 'He's stubborn and he drives me nuts and dints are everywhere in the fairy-tale image, but enough of the soap bubbles remain.'

'Well, that's why I'm not marrying,' Mary told her. 'I know about the dints, I know about stubborn and I know about independent. My father turned his back on me and it broke my heart. Loving's a huge risk and I'm not being offered one single soap bubble to make up for it.'

'What did that mean?' Back in the car they were headed into town so she could get her car and start her day's work properly.

'What?'

'Soap bubbles.'

'Fantasy,' she said crisply. 'Little girl's dreams. Two hearts become one. Romantic fluff.'

'Is that what you want from me?'

'I don't want anything from you. I told you that. You've made me an offer and I've refused. I'm taking my dreams elsewhere.'

'So you'd like romantic fantasy from someone else?'

'If a hero appears on my horizon maybe I'm available, but he'd have to be something to be worth the risk.' She said it lightly but he sensed a faint note of longing behind the words. Had he imagined it? Did this fiercely independent woman long for romance with all the trappings?

If he had been Jake, he could have supplied it, he thought.

He wasn't play-acting. Life was real. Life was for holding yourself together so you didn't hurt anyone else.

He couldn't supply anything.

* * *

'Is it okay if I stay tonight?' he asked as he dropped her off at work.

'Fine by me,' she managed, although it wasn't. The sooner this man got out of her life, the sooner she might find some sort of equilibrium. Maybe.

'Jake's on location today. He won't be back until tomorrow so I've set the flight back a day.'

That caught her. 'You're seeing Jake only once before you leave? You've come halfway round the world to see him for less than a day?'

'That's like someone I know coming from half a world away to tell me something she might have told me on the phone.'

He was teasing, but she wasn't to be deflected. 'I thought you and Jake were close.'

'Not close.' His voice grew crisp. 'We were dependent on each other when we were kids. We were stupid together. Hopefully we're past that now.'

'Right.' Work was waiting. She knew there'd be a full list of patients. They'd had no one to replace her while she was away and the work would have banked up. She had to go.

But Ben was sitting right next to her.

It didn't matter, she told herself. He was a loner. He didn't need her company and she didn't need his.

But she didn't want to leave.

'I'll bring home fish and chips for dinner,' she told him.

'I'll do dinner.'

'There's no catering in Taikohe.'

'What an insult,' he said, and grinned. 'Go to work and leave the domestic stuff to me. I can manage.'

I bet you can, she thought as she headed inside. It nearly killed her not to turn and watch his car disappear. But managing—alone—that was what Ben Logan was all about.

Work engulfed her. It was after six before she finally finished. Doreen, Taikohe's medical administrator, dropped her off at the cottage with a cheery offer to pick her up the next day and give her a loan to cover the cost of a new car battery.

She accepted the first offer and refused the second. She had enough funds to cover a battery.

Weariness engulfed her as she climbed from the car and headed for the house, a wash of grey fatigue. She'd been feeling nauseous all day. Now, suddenly, she wanted to sit on the front step, put her head in her hands and sleep.

Because Ben was leaving tomorrow?

Because she was facing having Ben's baby alone?

The thought of a long pregnancy with no one beside her was suddenly overwhelming.

She wanted her mother.

She wanted…Ben?

'Because you're pregnant and your hormones are all over the place,' she told herself crossly. 'Get over it. Women have managed on their own for generations. You don't need a male, especially a money-oriented, risk-taking loner like Ben Logan.'

Heinz had come tearing around from the back of the house to greet her. The sound of wood-chopping was echoing over the yard. Ben.

For some reason she didn't want to face him.

Wimp. He'd be gone tomorrow. She could do this.

She rounded the corner of the house to find a mountain of chopped wood stacked against the shed. Ben had his back to her, and the sight made her forget about weariness, forget about nausea. He was wearing boots and jeans and nothing else.

A sheen of sweat covered his skin. The sun was low in the sky, glinting on his broad, muscled back. His hair was ruffled and his boots were grubby.

He had a tattoo. She hadn't noticed it before but a Chinese symbol was etched beneath his armpit.

She had an almost irresistible urge to walk forward and touch it. Somehow she didn't, but it was close.

He looked a world away from the self-contained financier

she knew he was. For just a moment she let herself imagine how it could be if he was here, always. A man to come home to.

Like 'the little wife.' A man, ready with his slippers and pipe. She smiled but the smile was self-mocking.

But still she looked, soaking in the sound and sight of him. This would have to last her forever.

Finally, Heinz, obviously impatient that she wasn't joining him with his new best friend, rushed back to her and barked, and Ben turned and saw her.

He smiled, and with that smile she knew she was in real trouble. This man did things to her heart that she didn't know how to handle.

He was the father of her baby and she loved it that she'd have a part of him forever. But she wanted more.

So go back to New York with him. Accept his offer.

But that was the way of isolation, and she was sensible enough to know it. Romantic fantasy had to be weighed against reality.

Reality was here, now, where Ben was smiling at her.

'This'll keep me going for the millennium,' she managed, motioning to the wood. 'Thank you.'

'It's the least I could do. I've also bought you a new battery.'

'I… Thank you. How much—?'

'Don't be daft. Oh, and I got you a refund on your return fare. I had my secretary cancel your return booking before we left so you'll get a refund.'

Whoa…

'And I'll transfer a set amount to your bank account each month,' he said. He hadn't moved; he was standing amid chopped wood, naked from the waist up, holding his axe, discussing money like it was nothing. 'As the mother of my baby, outside work should be optional.'

'No!'

He didn't answer. One eyebrow hiked, as he stood and waited for her to explain.

As the mother of my baby, outside work should be optional…

What was there in that to make her cringe? What was there to make her back away?

'Work isn't optional,' she told him, and she knew as she said it that she was speaking the truth. Money or not. 'I need…to be needed.'

'Our baby will need you.'

'It's not enough.'

'Mary…'

'You don't get it,' she said. 'You can't. I know that. But thank you for your offer; it's wonderful and generous and I should say yes. But I can't. If you'll set up a trust fund so I can use it for our baby's expenses, education, that sort of thing, I'd appreciate it enormously.'

She summoned a grin, and heaven only knew the strength it took. 'I might even use it to buy a fancy pram. But you'll be paying for your child, Ben, not for me. You and I came together in a storm but that's all it was. A storm. A flash of blood to the head and that was it.'

'You know there's more to it than that.'

'I might know it,' she said. 'But that doesn't mean I intend being Ben Logan's kept woman, wife or not. Your money's between you and our child.' She paused and looked at his wood pile. It was…astonishing. 'But thank you for the wood.' She hesitated, searching for distraction. 'Um…what's the tattoo?'

'It's the symbol for twins,' he told her. 'Jake has one, too. Joined at the breastbone.'

'Are you, though?' She found the idea strangely troubling. This man was so alone. He was standing in the setting sun, facing her, solitary, tough and isolated. For some reason his isolation was doing something to her heart.

There was nothing she could do about it, though. But maybe Jake… 'How often do you see him?' she asked.

'Often enough,' he said, and there was that in his face that told her not to go there.

But she did. Of course she did.

'Ben, this tension between you? Can I help fix it?'

'It's nothing I can't handle.' He slammed his axe into the log he'd been chopping and she knew there was no way he'd share.

This man never shared. Not emotionally. She'd figured that about him now.

Ben Logan, solitary man.

Beautiful man.

'There's lasagne in the oven,' he told her, and she forced herself to stop looking at his body, stop worrying about the unknown Jake, stop feeling sorry for Ben who stood alone because he'd made that choice.

'Kath brought it over?'

'I made it myself!'

'You're kidding me.'

'You don't go straight from rookie to commando in the army,' he said, and somehow his smile reappeared. 'I was appalled to learn there were halfway steps. I was assigned six months' mess duty when I first enlisted. I can now feed battalions.'

'So how much lasagne are we talking?' she asked cautiously, and he grinned.

'Maybe not enough to feed a battalion but I have filled the freezer. I do a mean chicken pie, too. I've made you six.'

'Wow.' She was trying desperately to sound flippant. Inside she was choking. 'Thank…thank you. You want to come and eat? I seem to have enough wood for a battalion as well.'

'I'll pay for someone to chop more when you run out.'

'There's no need—'

'Keeping my baby warm is my need.'

She swallowed. He'd be part of her life from now on, she thought. Part and yet not part. There'd be money arriving when she most needed it, money and help.

But not Ben.

She turned back to the house, unable to look at him. He was doing her head in with the way he looked. He was one gorgeous guy. He was vulnerable and isolated and he wasn't letting anyone in.

'Is there anything wrong?' he asked, as she headed indoors?

'Nope,' she flung over her shoulder. 'What could possibly be wrong?'

They ate dinner in near silence.

'How was your day?' he asked, and she managed a smile.

'The line is, *How was your day, dear?*'

He smiled back, but he didn't feel like smiling. He was all at sea, he admitted. He'd worked himself into the ground all day, trying to do as much as possible for her before he left. Now, with nothing left to do but sit across the dinner table from her, he felt lost.

In the morning he'd walk away. She needed nothing else from him.

If only she'd eat a bit more...

'If I eat more I'll throw up,' she told him. 'Little, often, that's how I'm handling it. I'll snack at midnight.'

He wanted to be around to make sure she did.

She had Kath next door.

One neighbour wasn't enough.

'I'll phone you often to make sure...'

'I don't need phone calls,' she said gently. 'Ben, your relationship will be with our baby, not with me.'

'I'd hope we can be friends.'

'Can you be friends with a guy you've slept with? I'm not sure.'

'We can try.'

'Okay,' she said, but sounded doubtful.

'So phone calls?'

'If you must.'

'Mary...'

'That's it, then,' she said, rising and clearing dishes with noisy efficiency. 'Great lasagne. Thanks, Ben.'

And then the phone rang and she grabbed it as if it was a lifeline. She listened for a moment and then nodded.

'Okay. See you in fifteen.' She disconnected and smiled apologetically. 'Sorry, Ben, I need to go out.'

'Roller derby?'

'How did you guess? They're a man short and it's a final. They were hoping I'd be back.'

'Should you—?'

'First trimester should be okay. Baby's tiny and nicely buffered and the Taimarana Terrors are skilled rather than rough. We play them often. Will you be right here by yourself?'

'Of course I'll be right,' he said, and he couldn't hide an edge of anger behind his words. 'But I'd like to come with you.'

'How are you at counting?'

'What?'

'We're always short on referees. Timer, or maybe a jammer referee if you think you're up to it. How do you feel about wearing a helmet? It's to identify which team you're watching.'

'I know that.'

'You do?'

'I read up on it. How could I not research the interests of the mother of my child?'

'I see.' She sounded disconcerted but she was in a rush. The dishes were forgotten—she was flying around, collecting gear.

'Mary?'

'Mmm?'

'You're pregnant.'

'So I am.'

'It's a contact sport. I don't think you should be playing.'

She paused and looked at him. She glanced down at her tummy and suddenly he saw a wash of something that looked like grief cross her face.

'I… Soon.'

'What do you mean, soon?'

'I'll give it up when I need to.'

'Mary—'

'Not yet,' she said, almost fiercely. 'For the first trimester there's so much amniotic fluid compared to baby size that I'd need to be hit by a truck to make a difference.'

'From what I see, isn't that what roller derby is? Trucks all over the place.'

'The team we're playing tonight is more tactical.'

'But not all teams?'

'Not all,' she admitted. 'So I do need to give it up.' She glanced down at her tummy and once again there was a wash of grief. 'But not yet,' she whispered almost fiercely. 'Not unless I have to. I'll hold to what I have for as long as I'm able.'

She was amazing! Smash 'em Mary was stunning.

The team greeted her with joy; 'We've missed you and, wow, we need you!' She stuck on a helmet bearing two stripes.

The stars meant she was designated jammer.

He could see why. This woman was good.

He'd figured out the rules by now. Mary's job was to pass the entire pack of the opposite team; all the women designated as blockers. Once she got past everyone, the team's score depended on her. She won points for every additional blocker she passed after she'd lapped the entire team.

She was little and quick and agile. She darted in and out of the pack, past women twice her size. The blockers skated to cut her off, using their bodies to keep her behind them, but Mary wouldn't be kept. She weaved with a skill that kept him breathless. She was flying, and she was loving it. From the sidelines the Tigers' supporters whooped her on. Ben was supposed to be keeping time—he was!—but he was whooping, too.

But, hell, some of these women were big. Mary fell once and it was all he could do not to dive out onto the track and grab her. But she was on her feet again, laughing, and flying past the girl who'd just tripped her up.

The more he saw, the more astounded he became. He'd read about this game. He'd watched it on YouTube, but what he hadn't appreciated on the screen was the need for teamwork. You could sit on the sidelines and see a mass of women flying round the track, but when you watched just the one woman you saw how protected she was, and how protective. Each woman was looking out for her teammates. The team was a unit, cohesive and powerful in a way that took his breath away.

The Taikohe Tigers won by a lot and it didn't take the way the women crowded around Mary at the end to know much of that win was down to her. Her team was brilliant but Mary— *his Mary*—was one out of the box.

He felt like shouting it. *My Mary rocks.*

But… But…

She's not my Mary, he told himself savagely. He was leaving tomorrow. He was heading back to Manhattan. Alone.

Leaving Mary with her tribe?

She'd pulled off her skates and helmet, tugged on her coat and was heading towards him. It felt…good, he thought, that this amazing woman was walking towards him.

There was a dumb thought. He'd driven her here. Of course she had to come with him.

'What did you think?' She was lit up like a Christmas tree, exhaustion and happiness radiating in equal measure. 'Wasn't that awesome?'

'Awesome.' There were some things a man just had to agree with.

'I won't be able to do it much longer,' she said, and once again he saw that trace of grief. 'I'll miss it so much. These women are my pack.'

And he'd seen it. The way they'd greeted her, the skill of the blockers as they'd protected her, the yelling of the pivot—the head blocker—aimed at keeping her safe, giving her passage, but more, the underlying respect each woman had for each of the others.

He'd seen this type of respect in the army, in a tight-knit battle situation where every soldier depended on the others for their life.

He'd struggled with it in his personal life, the closeness of interconnecting need. He'd decided he could do without it.

But Mary was loving it. He could see it as she looked back at her team and he could see the regret.

'I'll miss them so much…'

'Hey!'

She turned and there was a woman coming through the door towards them. A woman with vitriol written all over her face.

She was middle-aged, wearing too much make-up, clothes that were frankly tarty. Peroxide blonde. Buxom. Looking rigid with anger. She walked straight up to Mary, and before he could react, before anyone could react, she slapped her hard across the cheek.

Mary's face snapped back and then Ben was between them, grabbing the woman's arm as she raised her hand again, forcing it down.

'What the hell do you think you're doing?'

'And who are you?' The woman's voice was shrill with hate. 'The guy stuck on that island? The stud that got her pregnant? They say you're rich.' She turned back to Mary. 'Is that why you did it, you slut, or did you do it just to hurt Sunrise?'

'I didn't!' Mary sounded appalled, justifiably. She was wearing a handprint inflamed across her cheek. 'I didn't mean—'

'You killed your sister's baby. You think you might have one yourself now, just to rub it in?'

'Leave it, Barbie.' The woman who'd played pivot, still on her skates, headed across to intervene. 'You know everyone says it wasn't Mary's fault. That lawyer who was here—'

'I know what I know,' Barbie hissed. 'And I know that this woman is a slut. I told you before, keep her out of your team. I can't stop her working, but I can tell anyone who socialises with her, forget about coming to our pub. Forget about anyone connected to you getting anywhere in this town. You know my husband's money controls this place. We might have to put up with her but we don't have to like her.'

'Barbie—'

'And you, Hayley Durant,' the woman snarled, poking a painted fingernail into the pivot's chest. 'Your husband works

for Small's Hardware. My husband owns the freehold on that
store. You keep playing nice with *her* and he'll be shown the
door.'

'If that happens,' Ben said, starting to figure who this woman
must be and what power she had, 'then I'll move in. You've already had a hint of what my lawyers can do. Believe me, that's
just a taste. I have money and I have power, and I'll use whatever it takes to keep Mary safe.'

'You can keep her safe,' Barbie snarled. 'But you can't keep
her accepted. She's an outsider here. She doesn't belong.'

'But I don't need to belong,' Mary whispered. 'No, it's all
right, Hayley. Barbie's right, I'm pregnant so I need to give up
roller derby anyway. As long as I can keep working…and she
can't stop me doing that…'

'Where's your father in all this?' Ben demanded. 'Why isn't
he standing up to this woman?'

'Because he's not strong enough,' Mary whispered. 'Because
he loves Barbie and his stepdaughters. He stopped loving me
a long time ago.'

'And you?'

'I don't need him,' she told him. 'You have it right. We don't
really need anyone. You can do it, so I can do it. No, it's okay,
Hayley, no one needs risk anything on my behalf. It's okay, Ben,
I don't need you to defend me. I'm fine on my own.'

'I'll take you home.'

She glanced at her watch. Nine o'clock. 'There's still time,'
she said.

'Time for what?'

'You're going back to your isolation,' she said. 'The Adirondacks are your refuge? Let me show you mine.'

She was tired to death. She should just let him take her home
but she couldn't bear it.

She wanted him so much…so seduce him with her country? It was a crazy thought, but she was past thinking whether

things were crazy or not. All she could think of was that she had this one last night.

This one last chance.

She directed him to the coast, ten minutes' drive away. They pulled up at a collection of motley fishing sheds and a rickety jetty, all dark and deserted They overlooked an inlet, surrounded by mountains on three sides, deep and mysterious, almost a landlocked bay where he couldn't see the outlet to the sea.

'This used to be the base of a fishing community,' she told him. 'But the entrance has silted up. The inlet's still tidal but the water's so shallow at the entrance boats can't get in and out. So it's pretty much a private place.'

The night was completely still. The moon hung low over the water, a shimmery haze. Magic.

'You want to row?' she asked.

'You're kidding.'

'I can row but I'm tired.'

'There's a boat?'

'One of my old patients keeps a rowboat in the far shed and lets me use it. I have a key.'

'Why—?'

'Because I want to show you that I have everything you have and more,' she told him. 'You have a fancy apartment and a housekeeper. I have a cottage and a dog. You have enough money to keep you satisfied and so do I. I have a community as well. This is my final trump card. Adirondacks, eat your heart out.'

It didn't make sense but he was past trying to make sense of what was happening. He was out of his depth and he knew it.

She led him to the last boat shed, inserted a rusty key and found the boat.

The rowing boat was surprisingly neat. The doors of the shed were still oiled. They swung open to the inlet and they were away.

And the moment the boat shed was behind them, he knew why she'd brought him here. He'd visited New Zealand for forty-eight hours but he'd seen nothing. It no longer mattered. For the rest of his life, whenever he thought of this country he'd think of this place.

The mountains loomed majestically around them. The night was whisper quiet. The moon was a vast ball, hung so low and near it was as if they could reach out and touch it.

Flocks of wild swans drifted lazily on the water's surface. As they neared each group, the birds rose, the sweep of their wings on the darkened water a sound he'd remember forever.

Why had she brought him here? It didn't matter. He was awed, as she'd obviously expected him to be awed. She sat quietly in the bow of the boat and he thought…he'd never known such a woman.

And he thought, *She had to marry him.*

'This place is magic,' he said at last into the stillness. 'You're right, it has everything. But for you… You can't tell me you row here at night alone?'

'I do.'

'It's not safe.'

'No,' she said sadly. 'I won't do it again. Not now I have my baby to think of.'

'Our baby.'

'Yes,' she said, and fell silent.

'Everything's changing,' he said softly. 'There's so much, and you're so alone everywhere.'

'I have my job and my workmates. I have Kath next door. The girls in my team will be here for me in emergencies.'

'It'd take a real emergency for them to defy Barbie.'

'Barbie's fury will blow itself out. Things will settle. And my baby will have a community.'

'Is that what this is all about? Hope for a community?'

'Maybe it is.'

'Is it about your dad?' he guessed. 'Are you still hoping?'

She thought about it, while she gazed out at the silhouettes of the swans drifting against the moonlight.

'Maybe I am.' Then she raised her chin and met his gaze, defiant. 'I still love him.'

'Mary, he's never there for you.'

'Once upon a time he was,' she said sadly. 'There was my mum and my dad and me. And then when Mum died there was just Dad and me. Barbie killed that. Dad was wiped by Mum's death and Barbie picked up the pieces, but he's never been whole again. She controls him, but underneath somewhere Dad's there.'

'You'd stick around to wait for him to find the courage to break free? You'd give up everything for something that might never happen?'

'Tell me, Ben,' she said, and she was suddenly sure of herself again, 'what would I be giving up?'

'I can give you a life.'

The chin stayed tilted. 'You can give me an apartment. A place to write. Money for child-raising. As your wife I'd probably have money for stuff I haven't thought of yet. But you wouldn't be giving me yourself.'

'I don't know what you mean.'

'I think you do, Ben,' she said gently. 'You saw it today, with Ross and Ethel. Soap bubbles. That's what they have and they've lived with them for all their lives. I know they may burst at any minute but my mum and dad had them in spades.' She took a deep breath and seemed to firm.

'I know it may never happen for me,' she said softly. 'Especially now I seem—stupidly—to have given my heart to a man called Ben Logan. Ben, I've used my writing as a fantasy and, yes, as a shield. The thought of loving someone, leaving myself open to the sort of pain I felt when Dad turned away from me, has always left me terrified.

'But with you…I have no idea why, but for some stupid reason I'd risk it all. If I let myself love you I could abandon that fantasy. But living down the hall from you and still needing that escape—it'd break my heart. That's not a guess, it's a certainty, and I can't do it.'

'Mary—'

'No.' He'd reached out for her but she held out her hands to ward him off. The boat wobbled and he couldn't move.

'I shouldn't have said that,' she managed. 'More. I shouldn't have made love to you. I shouldn't have got pregnant. Maybe I shouldn't even have told you I was pregnant, but, then, dishonesty's not my way. Okay, I've fallen in love with you and maybe I did the first time I saw you. I have no idea why, or when, or what to do with it, but somehow it'd happened. I don't know how to stop it, but loving you without reciprocation would kill me. Maybe that's me being dumb. Maybe that's why I stay here, hoping against hope my dad will love me again.

'The closest I've ever had to belonging is with my team, my Tigers. Ben, I loved playing again tonight, the closeness, the mutual dependence, the power of more than one. I love sitting here now while you row me, but I need to let it go. I need to let you go. Yes, I'm on my own—but I'm not heading to Manhattan because that way I'll be alone forever.'

And he didn't know how to reply.

She loved him. He wanted to take her into his arms, but rowboats weren't built for passion. And her body language said he shouldn't even try.

'You'll have your baby,' he managed. 'In Manhattan…you won't be alone.'

'*My* baby? That's just it, isn't it, Ben? Sometimes you say it's yours. Sometimes you say ours, but you still feel like it's mine. That's okay. The baby and I will be a unit, but where will you be?'

'If you're in Manhattan I'll be there when you need me.'

'How will you know when I need you? There won't be a pile of unstacked wood. The nanny will do the hard bits. How can you possibly know when I need you?'

'You'll be safe.'

'I'm safe here, Ben. Barbie's not going to eat me.'

He reached out then and took her hand. He tugged her slightly towards him and for some reason she didn't resist. The boat rocked again but he was careful. Very careful.

He touched her cheek. He could feel the heat from the imprint of Barbie's hand. That he hadn't been fast enough to stop her almost killed him.

'It's okay, Ben,' Mary said softly. 'She's the worst of my dragons and, as far as you can, you've slayed her for me. You've done all you can. You can go back to the States with a clear conscience.'

'I can't let you go.' He hadn't meant to say it. It had just come out. He tugged her closer and he felt her yield.

He held her; he just held her, and she let herself be held. For a long, long moment they stayed close while the boat rocked gently in the moonlight. He could feel her breathing against him. His face was in her hair.

He was holding his woman.

She loved him. Maybe if he said it back…

But he didn't know how to. The words were there but they wouldn't come out.

'I'm sorry,' he said at last into her hair, and he felt things change. She'd been leaning into him, seemingly taking warmth and strength from his body. Now she gathered herself and pulled away.

'I'm sorry, too, Ben,' she whispered. 'But thank you for trying. If you ever figure it out… If you ever figure out what love is… Well, I've waited for my dad for twenty years. A few more years won't hurt.'

'And if someone else comes?'

'I hope he does,' she said with sudden asperity. 'If any hero happens by on his white charger, with his heart nicely on his sleeve where I can catch it and hold it, then I won't look back. But that's none of your business, Ben Logan. How long I wait and how much I break my heart while waiting is entirely up to me.'

* * *

They drove home in silence. She ate dry toast and went to bed with hardly a word.

He woke in the night to hear her being ill, and he felt…well, bad was too small a word to describe it.

Why not walk in there, take her into his arms and tell her he loved her? For he did love her, he knew it. The thought of walking away was almost killing him.

But other thoughts kept superimposing themselves, almost as if mocking. The sight of his brother, bloodied and unconscious on a dirty road in Afghanistan. His mother coming home late at night from the theatre, high on adrenalin and who knew what else, hugging him, saying, 'Keep me happy, Ben, make me stay happy.'

Looking in his mother's bedroom doorway the morning she'd died and seeing how he'd failed.

Half a dozen steps would take him to Mary's door and he couldn't take them. If he was to let her down…

Surely leaving her here was letting her down, but taking her back…on her terms…

Her manuscript was lying on the kitchen table. He flicked through it, half smiling but close to tears. In fiction anything could happen. In fiction he could even be a hero.

In her imaginary world, Mary could be safe. What sort of world could he give her where she'd be safer?

This was doing his head in. He rose, half hoping to see Mary coming out of the bathroom, but she was back in the bedroom with her door closed tight. She and Heinz and baby, a team. She'd let him in if he asked, he thought, but it was all or nothing. And all was more than he could give.

Instead, he walked outside and gazed up at the stars, at the Southern Cross hanging low in the night sky. He didn't belong here, he told himself. He had to leave.

He had to walk away from Mary.

'There's nothing else I can do,' he told himself. 'Happy ever after…she can have that in her writing. There's no way I can give it to her. I'd risk breaking all of us.'

Dawn. Time to leave. Jake had post-production meetings all day and wouldn't be able to see him until evening, but staying was doing his head in. He needed to get back to Manhattan, to an unemotional world, where things made sense.

He knocked on Mary's bedroom door, feeling ill himself.

'Come in.'

She was still in bed, looking wan and pale and incredibly small, huddled under her bedclothes.

'How sick—?'

'I'm fine,' she said, managing a rueful smile. 'Okay, I'm not fine, but women have done this before. I'll cope.'

'You don't want me to stay?' He would if she needed him. Practically.

'You've filled my freezer. You've chopped my wood. Why else would I need?'

There was no answer.

'You're leaving now?'

'I… Yes.'

'You want me to kiss you goodbye?' Her words sounded angry and he didn't blame her.

'I can do without it.'

'I'm sure you can. Thank you for the wood and for the food. And for my baby. Goodbye, Ben.'

He couldn't bear it. He crossed to the bed, stooped and kissed her.

Her arms didn't come out from the covers. She simply let herself be kissed.

'I'll be in touch,' he said helplessly.

'Lovely.' She didn't sound like it was lovely. It was the most perfunctory 'lovely' he'd ever heard.

'I'll transfer funds…'

'Thank you.'

'Take care of yourself.'

'And you.'

There was nothing else to say. There was nothing else to do. He turned and walked out the door.

She lay and stared at the door for a very long time. She'd sent him away.

If she'd clung…

If she'd clung he would have picked her up and carried her back to Manhattan and installed her in his sterile apartment.

'At least I'd see him.' She was very close to tears.

'You'd break your heart. You know it. Sit and write, he says, but how can I write fantasy when my hero's real and wants… I don't know what he wants. All I know is what he doesn't want.'

She let herself sob, just the once. If she granted herself more than once she'd be a mess for her entire pregnancy.

Speaking of pregnancy, oh, she felt sick.

'At least it gives you something to think about rather than Ben,' she told herself, but it was small comfort.

'This is going to be a great pregnancy,' she told herself. 'Come on, woman, pull yourself together. It's only two hours until you need to be at work.'

How many minutes thinking of Ben?

How many trips to the bathroom?

'It's hormones,' she said, clutching her stomach. 'I'll get over this.'

'Morning sickness or Ben?' She was talking out loud, a two-sided conversation. Heinz was at the foot of her bed, looking worried.

'Don't you look worried,' Mary told him. 'I'm worried enough for both of us.'

Why? She had herself under control—sort of.

Yeah, she was fine—except her stomach was heaving and the man she loved with all her heart was heading to the other side of the world.

CHAPTER THIRTEEN

HE DROVE TO AUCKLAND. He found a hotel, made a few international calls, did some desultory paperwork—and tried not to think about Mary.

Finally he met Jake. Hell, it was good to see him, but even though the warmth was there, he was instantly aware of tension. There'd been things unsaid since the cyclone, and they were still unsaid.

Maybe they'd been unsaid all their lives.

'Hey, Jake.' A man hug.

'Hey, yourself.'

They headed for a bar Jake knew, drank beer and pretended things were normal. But small talk could only take them so far.

After the cyclone there'd been the relief at seeing each other alive, but their mother's suicide now stood stark and dreadful between them.

But, then, maybe it had always stood between them, Ben thought. Maybe it had always stood between him and the world.

But now Jake knew the facts of his mother's death. Admitting it to Jake meant admitting its reality. Maybe Jake wasn't the only one who'd retreated to make-believe.

'I gather you're not just here to see me,' Jake said, as the small talk died.

'That's why I'm in Auckland.'

'That's not what I meant. Why come to New Zealand?'

'I brought Mary home.'

'Mary?'

'The girl who saved my life. She came to New York but was

ill so I brought her home.' There was a lot more he could say about that, there was a lot more he should say—*Jake was going to be an uncle?*—but right now he wasn't going further. He didn't know where to start.

But Jake knew him well. He was watching his face and Ben knew he guessed a little of what he wasn't saying. That something was wrong. That Mary wasn't just…the girl who'd saved his life.

'So now you're heading back?' His brother seemed almost wary.

'Yes. Tomorrow.'

'How ill is she?'

'She's okay now. Sort of.'

'And you're not getting involved any further?'

'I brought her home. In the company jet.'

Jake snorted. 'That's involvement.'

'Cut it with being snide, Jake.'

'I'm not snide,' Jake said, and suddenly he wasn't. 'I'm worried.'

'She'll be fine.'

'I'm worried about you.'

'Why on earth?' His twin's words brought him up with a jolt. Since when had Jake ever worried about him? It was *he* who did the worrying. It was Jake who got into trouble and it was Ben who picked up the pieces.

'I've met a woman, too, Ben,' Jake said, almost gently. 'Same as you, it's the woman who plucked me out of the sea. Only unlike you, I'm in it up to my neck. But…it's not going so well right now.'

Of course. He might have known. This was all about Jake. Of course it was.

He looked across at his brother's worried, open face, once more bearing tales of woe to his big brother, and something snapped. Here we go again, making him responsible…

'You don't need to tell me. Of course it's not going well. But there's no need to talk about it—I'll be reading about it in the glossies soon enough.' He sighed, raked his hair, feeling infinitely weary. Jake, alias Peter Pan, eternally young, good-look-ing, eternally flying from one disaster to another.

He'd had enough. He didn't have room for more emotion.

Jake was looking taken aback. Fine by him. It was time to tell it like it was.

'Maybe it's time you grew up, Jake,' he snapped. 'Marriages and happy endings belong in one of your movies. They're not the real world. Not for us, that's for sure. You've already tried and failed. You play-acted the perfect husband last time. Wasn't that enough?'

Jake was staring at him, dumbfounded. 'You think I was acting?'

But he wasn't shutting up now. He couldn't. 'You've acted all your life—just like our mother. You don't know what's real and not.'

'I wasn't acting the first time round,' Jake threw back. 'Be-lieve it or not, I thought it was real. But now…I'm sure not act-ing this time. Ellie's different. She's one in a million. This is a million miles from one failed marriage.'

Enough. He'd had it, up to his neck. He was on his feet, his anger surging. 'Then you're even more of a fool than I thought. One in a million—just like the last one. And the next one and the one after that?'

'Will you cut it out?' Jake was also on his feet. The bar was empty save for a lone barman polishing glasses at the other end of the room. He was staring at them, making a tentative move toward them. Pre-empting trouble.

If they'd been ten years old, Ben would have been punched by now. Maybe he still would be. But as he watched, he saw his brother visibly force himself to relax. Jake waved to the barman, a gesture of reassurance, and when he spoke again his anger seemed to have faded. 'Ellie is different, Ben,' he said at last. He hesitated, as if searching for words, and what he finally said was confusing. 'And we're not…we're not our parents.'

What the…? 'What's that supposed to mean?'

'Just that.' Jake sounded as if he was figuring it out as he went, but increasingly he was sounding sure. 'We're our own people. You finally let it out, didn't you? In the life raft, when you said I wouldn't know reality if it bit me. That I was just like Mom. You told me she'd killed herself and you think I'm on the same path. Heading for self-destruction because I can't pick what's real or deal with it.'

'I don't—'

'Yeah, you do. It's gutted me, knowing now that Mom's death was suicide, but it's gutted me even more that you've kept it to yourself all these years. You've been protecting me, but you didn't have to. You've been protecting yourself and that's worse.'

'This isn't making sense.'

'Maybe it's not,' Jake growled. 'But this girl you brought all the way back to New Zealand. Mary. She went all the way to the States to see you?'

'So…what?' He couldn't explain. He couldn't tell Jake she was pregnant. One day soon he'd have to, but not now. It'd escalate this into the stratosphere.

'I'm not even beginning to guess what that was about,' Jake continued. 'But I don't have to guess because it doesn't make any difference. No matter who she is, no matter what she's done, no matter what she means to you, you'll never open yourself up. Because if you do then you open yourself up to that whole mess that was our mom. Our family. And Mom killed herself. Finally I'm seeing why you're so damned afraid.'

'I'm not afraid.' He was having trouble getting his head around this. Jake sounded sure of himself. He sounded almost… sorry for him?

'If you're not afraid of relationships, then why assume that whatever I have going on with Ellie will inevitably be another disaster for the glossies to gloat over?' Jake demanded.

There was a long silence. Jake turned away and stared out into the darkening night, and when he turned back to Ben his voice had changed again. 'Well, maybe it is a disaster,' he muttered, 'but at least I'm involved. I know I'm capable of loving. I'm not running away, like you.'

'Oh, for…' What was his brother on about? He'd never talked like this before. 'I'm not running away from anything.'

'It looks that way to me,' Jake said flatly. 'You run, you hide. Just like you've been hiding from me all these years by not telling me the truth. Shall we go there now, Ben? Talk about it properly? Or do you want to run away from that, too?'

How had this happened? He'd come to talk to his twin. His younger brother. What was Jake offering to talk about? A grief from twenty years ago? Any minute now he'd stick a counselling hat on.

In his dreams. 'I need to go.'

'Of course you do,' Jake said, almost sadly. 'People talk of emotions, you run. You've spent our lives accusing me of being like Mom every time I showed emotion. Play-acting. Yeah, okay, maybe some of it was, but not all of it. I'm trying to figure it out at last. Maybe the real is worth fighting for. The real is even worth hurting for.'

'Yeah, well, good luck with that. What did you say—that things aren't going well between you and this new woman? Amazing. I stand amazed.'

'Get out of here before I slug you,' Jake snapped, and as if on cue Ben's phone rang.

They both ignored it but it broke the tension. No one was going to get slugged.

No one was going to get counselled.

'Maybe you should get that,' Jake said at last. 'Maybe it's Mary.'

Maybe it was. He checked.

'It's work.'

'There you go, then. I don't know why you're not taking it. Work's always been your place to hide, hasn't it, big brother? Why should anything I say make it any different?'

Which explained why he was back in his hotel room, staring at the ceiling at midnight.

There was a cold, hard knot in his gut that didn't let him sleep.

He could have flown out tonight. The plane was at his disposal. Work was waiting.

The conversation with Jake was reverberating in his head.

Mary was four hours' drive away. If he got on that plane…

'It'll make no difference if you go tonight or tomorrow,' he told himself. Work was waiting, piling up. He should go tonight.

He'd be walking away from Jake and his accusations.

He'd be walking away from Mary.

Mary.

She was in his head, brave, funny, alone.

She wasn't alone. She'd told him that. She had her community.

And a family who hated her.

Maybe he could head up to see her father tomorrow. Tell him what he thought of a dad who turned his back on his daughter.

Wasn't that what he was doing—turning his back on his child?

Mary's child?

'You've made the offer…'

Yeah, but it was an empty offer. He knew it. He thought of what Mary had here, Heinz, her nursing, her roller derby, her neighbours. She was coping with hate from her family but she was looking to the future. Her child could have… community.

That was what he didn't get. He'd never needed it.

Even in the army, Jake had embraced the life, enjoyed the communal living, found himself good mates who were still there for him.

He himself had been chosen for missions that had meant working alone. That was what he was best at. He depended on himself. Anyone else depending on him made him feel heavy. Some time, inevitably, he'd let them down.

As he'd let his mother down.

As he'd let Mary down.

He hadn't let her down, he told himself savagely. He'd done what he could for her. He'd always be there in the background.

Why couldn't he get her out of his head?

Jake's words kept replaying. He tried to stop them every way he knew how, but they were burned into his brain, on permanent rewind.

'No matter who she is, no matter what she's done, no matter what she means to you, you'll never open yourself up. Because if you do then you open yourself up to that whole mess that was our mom. Our family. And Mom killed herself. Finally I'm seeing why you're so damned afraid.'

Was he afraid?

'I asked her to marry me.'

'And that was opening myself up?' He was talking out loud. He had the penthouse suite in the best hotel in town. It echoed. There was no one to listen.

That was the way he liked it—wasn't it?

The night was doing his head in. His phone was sending a pale green light from its recharge station. He kept thinking of how Mary had been last night, wan and sick. He could just phone and check…

And do what? Say sorry you're morning sick or night sick or whatever they call it. Say call Kath if you get any worse. Say take care of yourself.

Take care of yourself… What hollow words were they?

'Maybe the real is worth fighting for. The real is even worth hurting for.'

Since when had Jake become a shrink? Hell, if he walked in Jake's footsteps he'd lurch from one emotional mess to another. He needed to get back to the States, immerse himself in his business world, forget this mess.

Was Mary…this mess?

Where was sleep when you needed it? Why had he scheduled the plane for ten the next morning? He needed to be on the plane now, heading back to his life.

His life without emotion. His life without mess.

His life without Mary.

He gave up on sleep, flicked open his laptop and started work. The figures danced before his eyes. If he made any decisions now he risked disaster.

Why could he not stop thinking about Mary?

It'd be different when he got home, he told himself. Life would get back to normal. He could forget Jake's extraordinary outburst. He'd done everything he could for Mary. She'd rejected most of what he'd offered but that was her call.

Her life was no longer his business.

Except she was carrying his child.

Except she was ill.

Except she might need...

Dammit, he was going nuts.

If he got up now he could drive there and back by the time he'd scheduled the plane to leave. He didn't even need to wake her. He could just check...and say goodbye...

He tossed back the bedclothes—and the phone rang.

Did death feel like this?

'Bring it on,' she muttered. Anything would feel better than what was happening to her body. Anything, anything, anything.

'I've called the ambulance.' Kath was there, looking frightened. She'd popped over just before dark, dying to talk about Ben, but she'd found Mary in a mess. Morning sickness had turned into afternoon sickness and afternoon sickness had turned into real trouble. Mary couldn't talk about Ben. She couldn't even think about him. All she wanted to do was die.

But an ambulance? For morning sickness?

'I'll be all right,' she managed, but they were a pretty thready four words.

'You'll be all right in hospital,' Kath said grimly. 'I'm thinking you haven't kept fluids down for twenty-four hours. Is there anyone you want told?'

But Mary couldn't answer. She was in extremis again.

She wanted to die.

* * *

Mary's phone. Mary? At two in the morning?

'Mary!' He almost barked her name, but the voice that came back wasn't Mary's.

'Ben? Ben Logan?'

'Yeah.'

'I've got the right Ben Logan? I'm guessing here. It only says Ben on the phone.'

'Yeah, it's Ben Logan.' He was almost shouting. Why was someone ringing on Mary's phone?

'It's Kath from next door.'

'Kath.' His heart hit his boots. 'The roller derby. The fall. She shouldn't have played.' There was a sick emptiness in the pit of his stomach. 'Has she lost the baby?'

And then came a worse thought, a thought that sucked the bottom from his world. Haemorrhage. Death. The words intertwined with such savagery that his breathing seemed to stop. 'Is she okay?' he managed, and he could hardly get his voice to work.

'She's not okay,' Kath said brusquely. 'But it's nothing to do with roller derby. The doctor's saying she has something called hyperemesis gravidarum. That's a fancy way of saying really bad morning sickness. Apparently she started being sick last night and she can't stop. She's had twenty-four hours' throwing up and she's got nothing left.

'I came by last night to see how she was doing without you and ended up calling the ambulance. She's in hospital now. I tried ringing her dad but her stepmum told me where to get off. I'm sorry but I work milking cows. I need to be at work in four hours. She's by herself. Not that she cares, she's too sick, but I thought someone ought to know.'

He sank on the bed as if dragged there by gravity. He felt sick himself.

She's by herself...

'How...how sick?'

'They've got a drip up but she's still vomiting. Sorry, Ben, that's all I know. Where are you?'

'In Auckland.'

'Is there anyone else I can call for her? I can't think of anyone.'

Of course she couldn't. There was no one.

'No,' he said in a voice that didn't seem to belong to him. 'I'll come.'

You couldn't hire a chopper at two in the morning, not unless you called out the army, and even Logan's influence didn't stretch that far.

He drove. He may have broken the speed limit. Luckily the roads were quiet. The big car ate up the miles while Ben silently went mad.

Mary was in hospital, ill. Mary was ill because she was carrying his baby.

Mary had…what had Kath called it? Hyperemesis gravidarum. He needed to look it up on the internet but he didn't have time.

Hell, why wouldn't the car go faster? It nearly killed him to slow through the towns. Only the thought of spending the night in jail with the car confiscated stopped him hitting racing-car speeds.

Mary.

Mary, Mary, Mary.

She could lose the baby. He'd accept that. He was making bargains, and the baby was his biggest offering.

'I don't mind,' he said out loud. 'As long as Mary lives.'

But he did mind about the baby.

His child. When had it become real?

Just now. The moment he'd heard Kath's voice. The moment he'd thought she'd lost it.

'Yeah, but I'm not giving my Mary up for you,' he told his unborn child, and he wasn't making sense, even to him. But he added a rider and knew it was true. 'I want you both.'

The road seemed endless.

He should have called Jake. Jake would have come with him. This sort of life-and-death situation, this race through the night, would appeal to his twin.

But it wasn't that. It wasn't Jake's energy he wanted now. He just wanted...someone.

He needed Jake.

He needed Mary.

And right there, right then, things cleared. It was like a fog was lifting.

He got it.

The offer he'd made Mary had been crazy. Nothing. It had been a dumb way to closet her neatly into the life that was already his. No wonder she'd refused, because he'd offered nothing.

He hadn't realised then what he was realising now. How much he wanted Mary. How much he needed Mary.

And if he wanted Mary he was going to have to offer a lot more than he had.

What had Jake said? *'I'm capable of loving.'*

'I am, too,' he told the night. 'Please, just give me a chance to show it.'

It was six in the morning when he finally reached Taikohe's community hospital. The nurse in charge took him into Mary's room but told him—sternly—not to disturb her.

'She's been retching for more than twenty-four hours. We've only just got her body to relax. I don't care who you are but if you even think of nudging her awake I'll send you into the middle of next week.'

Mary might not have family here, he thought as he followed the nurse, but she was right, she did have community. Kath had sounded frightened on her behalf. This nurse, who must know Mary personally, sounded fierce.

And then he was ushered into Mary's room and everything else was forgotten.

There was a low-voltage nightlight under the bed, casting a bluish tinge across the room so medical staff could see at a glance what was happening. It made the room seem weird, dark and yet not dark, surreal.

It made the figure in the bed seem…not alive.

He crossed to the bed in three strides, and then just…stood.

She was huddled under the bedclothes, tiny, insignificant, almost as if she was disappearing. Her skin looked almost translucent. That was the light, he told himself fiercely. She was…

'She's okay,' the nurse whispered beside her. 'This light makes everyone look like corpses. It scares the daylights out of our juniors when they first do their rounds. Not that Mary looks exactly pink and healthy but she'll be okay. Now we've stopped her being sick.'

He wanted to touch her. He wanted to feel her warmth.

Smash 'em Mary…what a joke. There was no strength in her. There were tubes attached to her arm, monitors, equipment he didn't know.

He wanted to gather her into his arms and take her home.

Home… Where was home?

Right here, he thought savagely. Home is where the heart is. Home was Mary.

'You want to stay?' the nurse asked, and he nodded. Where did she think he was going?

Nowhere forever, he thought. This was where he belonged.

Where was self-containment now? Jake would mock.

Let Jake mock. He drew up a chair and sat down. Let the whole world mock. Let his dumb armour fall away.

This was his woman, ill with his child.

This was where he belonged.

CHAPTER FOURTEEN

MARY WOKE TO SUNBEAMS, warmth—and someone holding her hand.

For a moment she didn't open her eyes. Why should she? The sun was warm on her face, she was cocooned in comfort—and the appalling sickness had receded.

Right now she felt…okay.

Right now someone was holding her hand.

'Hey,' a voice said gently. 'Hey, Mary, Smash 'em Mary, Mary my love. Could you possibly wake up? I hate to disturb you but apparently we have a date with an ultrasound in fifteen minutes.'

Ben was here.

She was dreaming.

She was so warm. If she opened her eyes the sickness could wash back. If she opened her eyes Ben would disappear into the dream this surely was.

'Mary,' he said again, and his voice was so warm, so tender, and the pressure on her hand was so gently insistent, that she had no choice.

She opened her eyes, and Ben was sitting by her bed, smiling down at her. He was smiling but his eyes were full of worry.

He needed a shave, she thought inconsequentially. He looked…haggard.

And then there was another thought, overriding even the amazement of Ben's presence. An appalling thought.

'My baby?'

Memory was flooding back. By the time she'd reached hospital she'd been in extremis. The retching hadn't abated. Her whole body had seemed to be rejecting her pregnancy.

Why had she stopped being ill?

'Is there something wrong?' she whispered, even though Ben was here. His presence was the most miraculous thing in the world and he was smiling at her and holding her but still… It nearly killed her to say it. 'Have I lost my baby?'

But… *'Our* baby seems to be doing fine,' Ben told her, smiling in such a way it made her heart seem to turn over. 'Except he's making his mother ill. The doctor says this doesn't mean a risk to the pregnancy. On the contrary, this illness means you're producing so many hormones that it's probably ultrasafe. There's nothing to worry about, Mary. Our baby's fine.'

There was a lot to think about in that statement. She was too tired to think much but there was enough to make her sink back onto her pillows and relax a little.

Her baby was safe, but it was *our baby…*

Ben was here.

'You…you're here. Why?'

'You scared the daylights out of Kath,' Ben told her. 'She told me she thought you were dying.'

Good old Kath. She remembered the fear on her neighbour's face last night and understood. 'Maybe I thought I was dying,' she admitted.

Why wasn't she ill now? She was scared to move in case it came back.

She wanted to close her eyes again but Ben was here and she didn't want to chance it.

'Dr Bolton says you were dangerously dehydrated,' Ben said. He sounded matter-of-fact but she knew this man well, and she could hear the tremor behind the words that said there was no matter-of-factness about this. 'Apparently there's a tipping point when you're ill. You get to the stage you're so dehydrated your body is ill because of it and the whole thing compounds into a vicious cycle. You went past that.'

'Yay for me.'

'I should have been here.'

'You're going back to the States.'

'Maybe we need to talk about that,' he said grimly. 'But meanwhile you have IV fluids topping you up and some ultrastrong antinauseant the doctor said he could give you, as long as I understood it's expensive. I've never been more glad I have money.'

She thought about that—and liked it. 'Me, too,' she conceded. 'You think you could put your fancy drug on the child-support expense list?'

'We need to talk about that, too,' he said. 'Mary, I drove for four hours through last night, thinking you might be dying.'

'That's bad,' she whispered. She couldn't get her head around why he was here. All she knew was that he was still holding her hand. He was right beside her, holding her, and he wasn't letting go.

'Mary, I don't intend walking out again,' he said. 'Not ever. Not if you'll have me.'

Whoa… These monitors should be bringing medical staff running with their crash carts, she decided. She was sure her heart had stopped, right there. She was struggling to breathe. She was struggling to take anything in.

If you'll have me…

'W-why?' It was a dumb question but it had to be asked. She felt out of time, out of body. This was happening to someone else, not Mary Hammond. Someone else was lying in a hospital bed, watching the man she loved with all her heart…

'Because I love you with all my heart.' His words were such an echo of what she was thinking that her dream seemed to intensify. The feeling that this wonder couldn't be real. But the pressure on her hand was real. The smile behind Ben's eyes was real.

And the look of fear that still lingered on his face was more real than she ever wanted to see again.

'I'm fine.' She put her hand up and touched his face. 'Ben, I'm okay. You don't have to do this.'

'Fall in love with you?' He shook his head and the fear faded a little. 'How can I not? I think I fell in love with you two months ago, right about the time you dragged me up a cliff in a storm. But it's taken me this long to acknowledge it.'

'So…' She was having trouble getting her voice to work, but she was really trying. Of all things, this was worth the most effort. 'So why acknowledge it now?'

'Lots of reasons. Because it took the thought that I might lose you to make me see. Because Jake called me a coward. Because you called me on being a twin, wearing this tattoo and yet not knowing what it meant. Because you've shown me what community means and how important it is.

'I've finally figured that community's great, I'll buy it, but family's more. I don't think Jake and I ever had a family. The way we were raised, with charades and bullying, we never knew what it was, but suddenly I'm seeing it and I want it. I want it with you, Mary. If you'll have me.'

There was something wrong with her eyes. Drat, they seemed to be watering all over the place. It must be the drips or the drugs or something because she never cried.

She'd never cried until she'd met Ben. Now tears were slipping down her cheeks unchecked and there wasn't a thing she could do about it.

'I can't…I can't live in that mausoleum of an apartment with a nanny between us.' She had to say it. She had to get it out there, even if it almost killed her to say it.

'I'm not asking you to. Mary, it took me four hours to drive down here. In four hours I've reorganised our lives.'

'Wow.' She was still so weak she could hardly take this in but she was trying. Oh, how she was trying.

'Mary, we can't talk about this now,' he said. 'You should be asleep. The doctors are wanting to do an ultrasound, though, just to make sure there's nothing wrong with our baby. Can you do that?'

'As long as I don't have to stand up.' Shock and weakness

were leaving her more than wobbly. If a faint breeze wafted through the window right now she might fly away.

'There's just one thing…'

'Mmm…?' He was still holding her hand. He was smiling at her as if she was the most precious thing in the world. The most precious woman… If this was a dream, she never wanted to wake up, she decided. She was staying in this place forever.

'I need to know…whether you can love me back.' And the fear was back in his voice. 'I know you said you loved me. I need to know…did you mean it? Because if you do, and if I love you, then the way I see it, everything else will follow. It's a huge step for both of us but, combined, our courage can face anything. You and me, Heinz and our baby, the four of us, forever. Do you love me, Mary?'

And there was only one thing a girl could say to that. This was important enough to wake up for. This might, just might, mean the dream could stay with her forever.

She put a hand up and traced the strong contours of his face. She touched his lips and it was as if she'd kissed him.

She loved this man with all her heart, and it was time to tell him.

'I do,' she said, and then she was being kissed and she couldn't speak for quite a while, not until the orderlies came to wheel her away for an ultrasound, not until the world broke in, not until dreams turned to reality. 'I do.'

He sat with her as the radiologist smeared gel over her tummy—a tummy that showed just the slightest suggestion of swelling.

For some reason his heart was in his mouth. When Mary had told him he was to be a father his first reaction had been of dismay. And fear. He wasn't meant to be a father. Ben Logan didn't do family.

Now Ben Logan was sitting by the woman he loved more than life itself—how did that feeling just keep growing stronger?—and he was praying their baby was safe.

He shouldn't have left her. For her to get so dangerously dehydrated this early in pregnancy… If her baby had died…

If his baby had died…

Their baby. His hold on her hand tightened. The radiologist noticed the grip and smiled.

'Scary, huh? You're about to meet your baby for the first time. I'll take photos—you can start boring the world from now on with pictures of your child.'

He thought, suddenly, of his parents. Two people totally caught up in their worlds. The thought of his parents ever showing friends pictures of their children was unimaginable.

They were selfish and self-contained. They'd done their best to destroy their children's childhood.

His mother's suicide had ended his childhood forever.

This baby would have a happy childhood, he vowed, and he'd be a proud dad. He would keep photographs in his wallet.

If things were okay…

'Here we go.' The radiologist was passing her wand back and forth over Mary's slippery belly and fuzzy images were appearing on the screen. A bean-shaped image. An image with tiny buds, hands and feet?

A face…definite symmetry. The beginning of features…

He was going blind staring at the fuzzy image. Mary's fingers were digging into his and her eyes were locked to the screen as well.

'Heartbeat's great,' the radiologist said, but her voice was strange.

Ben's gaze flew to hers. He was good at picking up nuances. There was something…

Back to the image… Her wand was moving back and forward. The image was shifting.

The baby had changed position?

Or not.

The image moved out. The bean-shaped image turned into… two beans.

Two heartbeats. Four tiny buds of arms. Four tiny legs.

Two heads, two hearts, two bodies.

Twins!

'Two,' Mary breathed, and it was half a sob. 'Are we…? Is that…?'

'Definitely twins.' The radiologist was smiling, the tension gone. 'Two lovely healthy babies with two healthy normal heartbeats. No wonder you've been so sick. Multiple pregnancies can be the pits for morning sickness. Is there a history of twins in your family?'

'No,' Mary said.

'Yes,' Ben said, overriding her. 'There's a very strong history of twins in our family.'

Our family.

Twins.

Mary.

If he got any more proud he might burst.

He had done some amazing things in his lifetime. He'd taken extraordinary risks. He'd had a fraught childhood full of stupidity. He'd fought in Afghanistan. He'd controlled the Logan financial empire with an iron fist and he'd made it grow exponentially since his father's death.

But he'd never been more proud of anything than he was right now, holding Mary's hand, looking at the images of his babies on the screen before him.

'Can we get two pictures?' he asked, and if his voice sounded choked he didn't care. 'One of each baby? I want one in each side of my wallet.'

One in each side of his heart, with Mary in the middle.

'You don't mind?' Mary said, but she was smiling and smiling.

'Mind? Why should I mind? We're having two babies. We need to get married right away,' he told her. 'Damn, I should have brought diamonds. How long before she's well enough to shop for diamonds?' he demanded of the radiologist, and she was smiling almost as much as he was.

'Now you're being treated things will be better,' she told Mary. 'And right now is peak for illness. By sixteen weeks the nausea should fade.'

'And looking like an elephant will set in,' Mary retorted, but her smile didn't fade.

'There is that,' the radiologist agreed. 'But if I were you I wouldn't let a bump, no matter how big, get in the way of a man buying you diamonds. That's just unasked-for advice from your elder, dear, so you can take it or leave it.'

'I think I'll take it,' Mary said, and suddenly Ben was gathering her into his arms, gel or not, wand or not, radiologist or not. 'I think I'll take it, if you don't mind. I don't seem to have a choice.'

Hideaway Island. A perfect Sunday afternoon.

They were sitting in front of their cave, looking out over the storm-ravaged island to the turquoise bay beyond.

'I'll buy it,' Ben said, and Mary blinked.

'Pardon?' It had been two weeks since the ultrasound. Ben had stayed on, working from Mary's tiny cottage, sitting on the back porch late at night, with Heinz at his feet, controlling the Logan empire online.

He'd have to return. They both knew it but neither of them talked of it. This had been time out for both of them, time for Mary to recover, time for Ben to take stock of his future, time for them to fall more deeply in love.

Mary had cut back on work but she still worked. Ben still worked online, but at night they lay in each other's arms and the world disappeared.

It couldn't disappear forever. This morning Ben had suggested they hire a boat and come out to the island, and she knew he wanted to talk. About the future.

About his sterile apartment with the nanny in between?

'I need to go back to Manhattan,' he said now, and her heart sank. Here it came...

'But I want to buy Hideaway first. If Barbara and Henry will agree.'

'I think they might,' she said cautiously. 'But...there's lots of upkeep. Are you thinking of visiting it, what, for a couple of weeks a year?'

'That depends on you,' he said, and her heart missed another beat.

'Ben…'

'Mary, listen.' He turned and took her hands in his. The sun was warm on their faces. Heinz was down on the beach, chasing gulls, turning crazy circles on the sand, as happy as a dog could possibly be. 'I've been thinking.'

'Dangerous,' she murmured, and he grinned.

'I know. It's scaring me, too. But I have a corporation to run and I can't ignore it.'

'I wouldn't want you to.' But was that the truth? Yes, she conceded. Ben was who he was. She wouldn't want to change a single part of him.

'The way I figure it, you have a community here but you don't have family,' he told her. 'In New York, I don't have either, but I do have my job. So I started thinking…could we build a community in New York? If we had family…we'd have everything.'

'A nanny's not a community, Ben,' she said bleakly, but it had to be said.

'Forget the nanny,' he told her. 'Dumb idea. There's two of us. If we can't cope with two of them, we're not the powerhouses I know we both are.'

'I'm not exactly feeling like a powerhouse,' she admitted, and he grinned.'

'Okay, nanny if necessary, just for when we need her. But you…you love your nursing?'

'I… Yes.'

'And your writing?'

'It's fun.' She didn't need the fantasy any more, she conceded, but she still loved it.

'And your roller derby?'

'It's awesome.'

'All those things are in Manhattan,' he said. 'We can find them. In fact, I already have.' He hauled a sheaf of paper from his jacket pocket and handed it over. 'The Manhattan Manglers practise four blocks from my…from our apartment and they're always open to new members. They seem to be mostly composed of young mums so team members come and go at need. You could, too.'

'Ben—'

'And district nursing,' he told her. 'There's such a need. New Zealand qualifications are recognised worldwide. You can do as much or little as you want. Manhattan will love you.'

'Ben—'

'And writing,' he said, trying to get it all out before she could object. 'I could take the kids out at weekends, giving you breaks while we bond. You could write all you want. And we can fix our apartment to turn it into a family home, or sell it and buy another if you want. And Heinz is okay to come—I've checked.

'And if we buy Hideaway we could come here for three months a year, maybe even more. I can work online. I can set things up so I train a decent second in command. I'll learn to delegate. I'll do whatever it takes, my love, for us to be a family.'

'You'd really want that?' she said wonderingly, and he tugged her close and kissed her, and then held her for a very long time.

'I want you more than anything I've ever wanted in my life,' he told her. 'I want my family. My last family was a disaster. I don't know if I can resurrect anything of my relationship with Jake—I surely hope so but for now it can't matter. All I know is that the woman I love with all my heart is in my arms. Mary, will you be my family? Will you be my community, my life, my heart? Mary, will you marry me and live happily with me for ever after, for as long as we both shall live?'

And what was a girl to say to that?

There was only one thing she could say.

'Yes,' she said, lovingly and firmly. Her answer rang out over the island where she'd rescued this man and he'd rescued her right back. 'Yes, my love, I will.'

* * * * *

FROM NEIGHBOURS… TO NEWLYWEDS?

BY
BRENDA HARLEN

Brenda Harlen grew up in a small town, surrounded by books and imaginary friends. Although she always dreamed of being a writer, she chose to follow a more traditional career path first. After two years of practicing as an attorney (including an appearance in front of the Supreme Court of Canada), she gave up her "real" job to be a mum and to try her hand at writing books. Three years, five manuscripts and another baby later, she sold her first book—an RWA Golden Heart winner.

Brenda lives in southern Ontario with her real-life husband/hero, two heroes-in-training and two neurotic dogs. She is still surrounded by books (too many books, according to her children) and imaginary friends, but she also enjoys communicating with real people. Readers can contact Brenda by email at brendaharlen@yahoo.com.

Because this series is about brothers, this book
is dedicated to Brett (AKA "BIL").

You became my brother when you married my sister,
and through all the years that you've been part of our
family you've proven yourself to be a terrific husband
and a wonderful father—a true romantic hero.

(PS You're a pretty good brother-in-law, too.)

Chapter One

The house was finally, blissfully quiet.

Georgia Reed mentally crossed her fingers as she sat down at the antique dining room table, hoping for one hour. If she could have a full sixty minutes to focus on the manuscript pages spread out in front of her, she might actually catch up on her work. Unfortunately, the thought of catching a nap was much more tempting than the book she was currently reading.

Though she was officially on maternity leave from her job as an associate editor at Tandem Publishing, she had agreed to accept work on a contract basis to help out the senior editor and keep some money coming in. It had seemed like a good idea at the time, but Georgia hadn't been nearly as productive as she'd hoped to be, especially since she'd uprooted her kids and moved to Pinehurst only six weeks earlier.

She sipped from the cup of herbal tea she'd reheated for a third time and skimmed through the previous chapter to refresh her memory. But just as her mind began to focus on the story, it occurred to her that it was *too* quiet.

The realization kicked her protective instincts into over-drive. She pushed her chair away from the table and raced across the hall to the living room, where she'd left four-year-old Quinn and Shane with a pile of building blocks. The car-pet was littered with the chunky pieces but her boys were both gone—no doubt through the wide-open patio door.

The door had been closed when she settled the boys down to play—closed *and* locked. But the lock was tricky, and sometimes just tugging on the handle would allow the latch to slip and the lock to slide free. She'd talked to her mother about getting it fixed, but apparently that detail had slipped Charlotte's mind.

And now her children were gone.

She hurried back to the dining room to grab the baby moni-tor before racing out the back door.

"Quinn! Shane!" She ran across the deck, cursing when she stepped on a red block. They couldn't have gone far. She'd only left them in the room a few minutes earlier. If anything had happened—

No, she couldn't even complete the thought.

"Quinn! Shane!"

A flash of movement caught the corner of her eye, and she spun around, her heart sinking when she didn't see the boys' familiar faces but the shadowed jaw of a grown man standing on the grass.

"Are you looking for two little guys about yay—" he held a hand about three and a half feet off the ground "—high?"

"Did you see where they went?" she asked hopefully, des-perately.

"They wandered into my backyard." He gestured toward the adjoining property.

Georgia closed her eyes so he wouldn't see that they'd filled with tears. "Oh, thank you, God."

"Actually, my name's Matt—Matt Garrett."

She opened her eyes again and saw that he was smiling at her.

"And your kids are fine," he promised her.

"Only until I get my hands on them," she muttered.

His smile widened.

Now that the panic had subsided and her heart was beating more normally again, she took a moment to look at her new neighbor—and felt a little tug low in her belly.

Matt Garrett had thick dark hair that was sexily tousled, as if he'd been running his fingers through it, a slightly crooked nose and a strong unshaven jaw. His shoulders were broad, his long, lean body well-muscled. And as his deep blue gaze connected with her own, she felt a subtle buzz in her veins that made her feel hot and tingly in a way that she hadn't experienced in a very long time.

"One of the puppies escaped into your yard and caught their attention," he explained.

"Puppies?"

"Come and check them out," he invited.

She hooked the monitor on her belt and followed him, surreptitiously checking out his spectacular backside as she did so.

He'd moved in a few days earlier. She'd noticed the moving truck when she'd gone out to the porch to check the mail Wednesday afternoon—and then she'd noticed the tall, broadshouldered man supervising the unloading of it.

He was in faded denim with an even more faded Orioles T-shirt stretched across his broad chest. Definitely a man's man, she decided, and felt a flutter of something low in her belly. He lifted an arm in casual greeting and flashed a quick smile that actually made Georgia's heart skip a beat before it began hammering against her ribs.

She raised her hand in response, waving her mail at him, then felt the flood of heat in her cheeks as she realized what she'd done. She wasn't sure if it was sexual deprivation or sleep deprivation that was responsible for her distraction, but thankfully, he was too far away to note either her instinctive physical response or her embarrassment. But wow—the man obviously had some potent sex appeal if he could affect her from such a distance.

An appeal that, she knew now, was further magnified up close.

"This is Luke—and Jack," Matt told her, gesturing to the two other men on his porch in turn. "My brothers."

The former was even taller than her six-foot-tall neighbor, with the same brown hair but blue-green eyes; the latter was of similar height but with broader shoulders and slightly darker hair. All three were sinfully handsome.

"I'm Georgia," she finally said, her heart rate mostly back to normal now that the twins were in her line of sight again. "And these pint-sized Houdinis are Quinn and Shane."

"What's a Houdini?" Quinn tore his attention away from the blanket-lined laundry basket for the first time since she'd stepped onto her neighbor's porch.

"A little boy who is in very serious trouble for leaving the house without his mommy," she admonished.

Her son's gaze dropped to his feet, a telltale sign of guilt. "We just wanted to see the puppies."

"Puppies," Shane echoed, and looked up at her with the heartbreakingly sweet smile that never failed to remind her of his father.

She took a few steps closer, as inexorably drawn to the basket as her children had been. But still, she had to make sure they understood that leaving the house for any reason wasn't acceptable.

"If you wanted to see the puppies, you should have told Mommy that you wanted to see the puppies," she said.

"But you told us not to bug you 'cuz you had work to do," Quinn reminded her.

And it was exactly what she'd said when she set them up with their blocks.

"I also told you to never go anywhere—even outside into the backyard—without telling me first."

But how could she blame them for being drawn away when even her heart had sighed at the first glimpse of those white, brown and black bodies wriggling around in the basket?

She looked at her neighbor again. "You have *four* puppies?"

"No." Matt shook his head emphatically. "*I* don't have *any* puppies—they're all Luke's."

"Only until I can find good homes for them," his brother said.

"How did you end up with them?" she wondered.

"I'm a vet," he told her. "And when someone finds an abandoned animal on the side of the road, it usually ends up at my clinic. In this case, the abandoned animal was a very pregnant beagle that, two days later, gave birth to eight puppies."

"Eight?" She cringed at the thought. As if carrying and birthing twins hadn't been difficult enough.

"My receptionist is taking care of the other four."

"They look kind of young to be away from their mother," she noted.

"They are," he agreed.

It was all he said, but it was enough for her to understand that the mother hadn't survived the delivery—and to be grateful that his response in front of the twins wasn't any more explicit than that.

"Nice puppy," Shane said, gently patting the top of a tiny head.

"Can we keep one?" Quinn, always the more talkative and articulate twin, asked her.

She shook her head. As much as she hated to refuse her kids anything, she'd learned that there were times she had to say no. This was definitely one of those times. "I'm sorry, boys. A puppy is too much responsibility for us to take on right now."

But she didn't object when Matt lifted one of them out of the box and handed it to her. And she couldn't resist bringing it closer to nuzzle the soft, warm body. And when the little pink tongue swiped her chin, her heart absolutely melted.

"He likes you, Mom," Quinn told her.

"She," Matt corrected. "That one's a girl."

Her son wrinkled his nose. "We don't want a girl puppy."

"We don't want *any* puppy," Georgia said again, trying to sound firm.

"We *do* want a puppy," Shane insisted.

"'Cept Dr. Luke says they can't go anywhere for two more weeks," Quinn informed her. "'Cuz they're too little to eat and hafta be fed by a bottle."

Shane pouted for another minute, but the mention of eating prompted him to announce, "I'm hungry."

"So why don't we go home and I'll make some little pizzas for lunch?" she suggested.

"With pepperonis?"

"With lots of pepperoni," she promised.

But Quinn shook his head. "We don't wanna go home. We wanna stay with the daddies."

Georgia felt her cheeks burning as her gaze shifted from one man to the next.

Matt's smile slipped, just a little; Luke kept his attention firmly focused on the animals; and Jack actually took a step backward.

"They're at that age," she felt compelled to explain, "where they think every adult male is a daddy. Especially since they lost their own father."

"He's not lost, he's dead," Quinn said matter-of-factly.

The announcement made Shane's eyes fill with tears and his lower lip quiver. "I miss Daddy."

Georgia slipped her arm around his shoulders.

Matt's brows lifted. "You're a widow?"

She nodded, because her throat had tightened and she wanted to ensure she was in control of her emotions before she spoke. "My husband passed away eleven months ago." And although she'd accepted that Phillip was gone, she still missed him, and there were times—too many times—when she felt completely overwhelmed by the responsibilities of being a single parent. "That's one of the reasons I moved in here with my mom."

"Charlotte's your mother?"

"You know her?"

"I met her the first time I came to look at the house," he said. "But I haven't seen her since I moved in."

"She's on her annual trip to Vegas with some friends," Georgia told him.

"Leaving you on your own with two young boys," he remarked sympathetically.

"And a baby," she said, just as a soft coo sounded through the baby monitor she'd clipped on her belt.

"Pippa's waking up." Quinn jumped up, his desire to stay with the "daddies" not nearly as strong as his affection for his baby sister.

"Pippa," Shane echoed.

Matt looked at Georgia, seeking clarification. "You have three kids?"

She nodded. "Four-year-old twins and a four-month-old daughter."

Well, that explained the shadows under her gorgeous eyes, Matt decided. A pair of active preschoolers and a baby would wear any young mother out—especially one without a husband to help ease the burden. But even exhausted, she was one of the most beautiful women he'd ever met.

She had a heart-shaped face with creamy skin, elegantly shaped lips, a delicate nose dusted with freckles, and the bluest eyes he'd ever seen. He'd caught his first glimpse of her on moving day. She'd been casually dressed in a sleeveless yellow blouse and a pair of faded denim jeans with her honey-blond hair in a ponytail, but even from a distance, he'd felt the tug of attraction.

Standing within two feet of her now, that tug was even stronger—much stronger than any self-preservation instincts that warned him against getting involved with a woman with three children who could take hold of his heart.

"You do have your hands full," he said.

"Every day is a challenge," she agreed. And then, to the boys, "Come on—we've got to go get your sister."

"Can we bring Pippa back to see the puppies?" Quinn asked hopefully.

His mother shook her head. "In fact, you're going to apologize to Mr. Garrett for intruding—"

"Matt," he interjected, because it was friendlier than "Mister" and less daunting than "Doctor," and because he definitely wanted to be on a first-name basis with his lovely neighbor. "And it wasn't at all an intrusion. In fact, it was a pleasure to meet all of you."

"Does that mean we can come back again?" Quinn asked.

"Anytime," he said.

"And within two weeks, you'll be calling someone to put up a fence between our properties," Georgia warned.

He shook his head. "If I did that, they wouldn't be able to come over to play in the tree house."

"Mommy says we can't go in the tree house," Quinn admitted. "'Cuz it's not ours."

"But a tree house is made for little boys, and since I don't have a little boy of my own—" Matt ignored the pang of loss and longing in his heart, deliberately keeping his tone light "—it's going to need someone to visit it every once in a while, so it doesn't get lonely."

"We could visit," Quinn immediately piped up, as Shane nodded his head with enthusiasm and Georgia rolled her eyes.

"That's a great idea—so long as you check to make sure it's okay with your mom first," Matt told them.

"Can we, Mommy?"

"Pleeeease?"

He held his breath, almost as anxious for her response as the twins were. It shouldn't matter. He didn't even know this woman—but he knew that he wanted to know her, and he knew that it wouldn't be a hardship to hang out with her kids, either.

"We'll talk about it another time," she said.

Quinn let out an exaggerated sigh. "That's what she says when she means no."

"It means 'we'll talk about it another time,'" Georgia reiterated firmly.

"I'm hungry," Shane said again.

She tousled his hair. "Then we should go home to make those pizzas."

"I'm *not* hungry," Quinn said. "I wanna stay here."

"If you're not hungry, then Shane will get all the little pizzas."

Georgia's casual response earned a scowl from her son.

"And you can help us paint the deck," Matt told Quinn.

The furrow in his brow deepened. "I guess I could eat some pizza."

"I'd take the pizza over painting, too," Luke told him.

"Unfortunately, we weren't given that choice," Jack said in a conspiratorial whisper.

"And since you weren't," Matt noted, "you can go get the painting supplies."

Jack headed into the house while Luke picked up the basket full of puppies and moved it under the shade of a nearby tree so the curious canines couldn't get in the way of their work.

Shane and Quinn stayed by Georgia's side, but their eyes—

filled with an almost desperate yearning—tracked the path of the puppies. And as he looked at the twins' mother, Matt thought he understood just a little bit of what they were feeling.

In the more than three years that had passed since his divorce, Matt had wondered if he would ever feel anything more than a basic stirring of attraction for another woman. Ten minutes after meeting Georgia Reed, he could answer that question with a definitive yes.

"Thank you," she said to him now.

"For what?"

"Being so patient and tolerant with the boys."

"I like kids," he said easily.

"Then you'll like this neighborhood," she told him.

He held her gaze as his lips curved. "I already do."

Matt watched as Georgia walked away, with one of the boys' hands clasped firmly in each of hers. Obviously she wasn't willing to take any chances that they might disappear again—even on the short trek next door.

The first time he'd seen her, it hadn't occurred to him that his gorgeous young neighbor might be a mother. Finding out that she had kids—and not just the adorable twin boys but a baby girl, too—had scrambled his mind further.

Now that he knew about those children, it seemed wrong to admire the sweet curve of her buttocks in snug-fitting denim. And it was definitely depraved to let his gaze linger on the sway of those feminine hips—or to think about the fullness of breasts hugged by the soft blue knit cardigan she wore.

She might have been a mother, but that reality did nothing to alter the fact that she was also an incredibly attractive woman. Something about the sexy single mother next door stirred feelings inside of him that hadn't been stirred in a very long time. And while he was intrigued enough to want to explore those feelings, the kids were a definite complication.

Matt had dated a lot of women without letting them into his heart, but he had no defenses against the genuine friendliness and easy acceptance of children. Especially not when the loss of his son had left a gaping hole in his heart that ached to be filled.

"I know what you're thinking," Luke said, climbing back up onto the porch.

"You think so?"

His youngest brother nodded. "Yeah, she's a pleasure to look at. But she's got *complication* written all over her."

"I was only thinking that it was nice to finally meet my neighbor."

"You were thinking about asking her out," Luke accused.

"Maybe I was," he acknowledged.

Jack dropped an armload of painting tools at his feet. "Don't do it."

"Why not?" he asked, unwilling to be dissuaded.

"Slippery slope."

"You mean like an invitation to dinner might lead to a second date?" Matt didn't bother to disguise his sarcasm.

"And the next thing you know, you're walking down the aisle," Luke agreed.

"You went out with Becky McKenzie last week." He felt compelled to point this out. "But I don't see a ring on your finger."

"That's because when our little brother invites a woman to dinner, it's just an invitation to dinner," Jack explained.

"And maybe breakfast," Luke interjected with a grin.

"But when you ask a woman out on a first date…" Jack paused, his brow furrowing. "Well, we don't actually know what it means, because you haven't been out on a real date with anyone since Lindsay walked out on you."

"I've been out with plenty of women."

Luke shook his head. "You've hooked up with plenty of

women—but you haven't actually been in a relationship with any of them."

Now it was Matt's turn to frown, because he realized that what his brother had said was true.

"And this one comes with quite a bit of baggage," Jack noted.

"A three-piece set," Luke elaborated.

"You're reading way too much into this," Matt told them.

"I'm glad you're thinking about jumping back into the dating pool," Jack said. "But I don't get why you'd want to leap directly into the deep end when there are plenty of unencumbered beautiful women hanging out by the water."

Matt didn't know how to respond. He wasn't sure he could explain—even to himself—what it was about Georgia Reed that appealed to him. Or maybe he was afraid to admit that he'd fallen for the two little boys who had snuck over to look at the puppies even before he'd realized that his pretty blonde neighbor was their mother.

Since the breakup of his marriage, he'd been cautious about getting involved again. Having his heart trampled by his ex-wife was bad enough, he wasn't going to risk having it trampled by anyone else's children.

Not again.

Or so he'd thought—until Quinn and Shane raced into his backyard.

"I'm not looking for anything more than a chance to get to know my neighbor a little better," Matt insisted.

"So get to know her," Luke agreed. "But don't get involved with her. A relationship with someone who lives next door might seem convenient at first, but it can be a nightmare if things don't work out."

"Almost as bad as falling into bed with a woman who was supposed to be a friend," Jack said.

The statement was made with such conviction Matt was sure there must be a story behind it. But since he didn't want to discuss his personal life—or current lack thereof—he certainly wasn't going to grill his brothers about their respective situations.

"If you're lonely, you should think about getting a pet," Luke suggested.

"Like a puppy?" Matt asked dryly.

His brother grinned. "Man's best friend."

"A dog is too much of a commitment."

"Less than a woman and her three kids," Jack pointed out.

Which was a valid consideration, so Matt only said, "Are we going to spend all day sitting around and talking like a bunch of old women or are we going to paint this damn deck?"

"Since you put it that way," Luke said. "I guess we're going to paint the damn deck."

Chapter Two

After Pippa was changed and fed and the boys had helped make little pizzas for their lunch—using up all of the cheese and pepperoni and emptying the last jug of milk—Georgia knew a trip to the grocery store was in order. Since it was a nice day and Quinn and Shane seemed to have energy to burn, she decided they would walk rather than take the minivan.

The twins refused to ride in the double stroller anymore, insisting that they were too big to be pushed around like babies. Unfortunately, Georgia knew their determination and energy would last only so long as it took to reach their destination and not bring them home again, so she strapped Pippa into her carrier and dragged the wagon along beside her.

As she started down the driveway, she caught another glimpse of her hunky neighbor and his equally hunky brothers, and her pulse tripped again. The automatic physiological response surprised her. Since Phillip had died, all she'd felt was grief and exhaustion, so the tingles that skated through her veins whenever she set eyes on Matt Garrett weren't just unexpected but unwelcome.

She did *not* want to be attracted to any man, much less one she might cross paths with any time she stepped outside. But while her brain was firm in its conviction, her body wasn't nearly as certain.

Matt caught her eye and lifted a hand in greeting. She waved back, then quickly averted her gaze and continued on her way. It was bad enough that she'd caught herself staring—she didn't need her neighbor to be aware of it, too.

Of course, he was probably accustomed to women gawking in his direction. A man like that would be.

Not that she had a lot of experience with men like the Garrett brothers, but she knew their type. In high school, they would have been the most popular boys: the star athletes who had dated only the prettiest girls, the boys that other boys wanted to be and that all of the girls wanted to be with.

But not Georgia. She'd been too smart to fall into the trap of thinking that those boys would even look twice in her direction. And they never had. Not until Aiden Grainger sat down beside her in senior English and asked if she'd help out with the yearbook. Even then, she'd been certain he was only interested in her ability to correctly place a comma, and no one was more surprised than she when he walked her home after school one day and kissed her.

And with the first touch of his lips, she'd fallen for him, wholly and completely. They'd dated through the rest of senior year and talked about backpacking around Europe after graduation. Aiden wanted to see the world and Georgia wanted to do whatever he wanted to do so long as she got to be with him.

This willingness to sacrifice her own hopes and dreams in favor of his terrified her. It reminded her of all the times her life had been upended because her mother decided that she had to follow her heart to another city or another state—usually in pursuit of another man.

When Georgia was thirteen and starting her third new school in three years, she'd promised herself that she would never do the same thing. And now, barely five years later, she was preparing to throw away a scholarship to Wellesley College in order to follow some guy around Europe? No, she couldn't do it.

Aiden claimed that he was disappointed in her decision, but it turned out he wasn't disappointed enough to change his plans. He'd said he wanted to travel with her, but in the end, he wanted Europe more than he wanted her. And maybe Georgia wanted Wellesley more than she wanted him, because she went off to college and didn't look back.

But it had taken her a long time to get over Aiden, and a lot longer than that before she'd been willing to open up her heart again. And when she finally did, she'd lucked out with Phillip Reed.

Maybe theirs hadn't been a grand passion, but for almost ten years, he'd made her feel loved and comfortable and secure. It was all she'd ever wanted or needed.

So how was it that, after less than ten minutes, Matt Garrett had made her wonder if there might be something more? How was it that he'd stirred a passion inside of her that she'd never even known existed? And what was she supposed to do with these feelings?

Unable to answer any of these unnerving questions, she pushed them aside and led the kids into the grocery store.

When Matt decided to move, his real estate agent had repeated the same mantra: location, location, location. And Tina Stilwell had promised that this neighborhood scored top marks in that regard. There were parks, recreation facilities, a grocery store and schools in the immediate vicinity, with more shopping, restaurants and the hospital—where he worked as an orthopedic surgeon—just a short drive away. She hadn't mentioned the beautiful blonde next door, and

Matt wasn't sure how that information might have factored into his equation.

He hadn't necessarily been looking for a house—and he certainly wasn't looking for a new relationship. But he believed that real estate was a good investment and this house, in particular, had everything he wanted, not just with respect to location but amenities.

Jack had, logically, questioned why a single man needed four bedrooms and three bathrooms, forcing Matt to acknowledge that it was more space than he needed. He didn't admit—even to himself—that he had any residual hope of utilizing those extra bedrooms someday. Because he had a new life now—a new home and a new beginning, and he wasn't going to waste another minute on regrets or recriminations about the past. From this point on, he was going to look to the future.

But first, he had to cut the grass.

As he pushed the lawn mower across his yard, he kept casting surreptitious glances toward his neighbor's house, eager for any sign of Georgia Reed. He hadn't seen much of her in the past few days, and he knew she wasn't home now because the minivan was missing from her driveway, but that didn't stop him from checking every few minutes.

Thinking about what his brothers had said, he had to admit, albeit reluctantly, that it might not be a good idea to make a move on the woman next door. At least, not until he'd finished unpacking. If he moved too fast, she might think he was desperate. And he wasn't—but he was lonely.

Since his divorce, he'd had a few brief affairs but nothing more meaningful than that. He missed being in a relationship. He missed the camaraderie, the companionship and the intimacy. Not just sex—but intimacy. After a few unsatisfactory one-night stands, he'd recognized that there was a distinct difference.

He missed falling asleep beside someone he genuinely wanted to wake up with the next morning. He missed long conversations across the dinner table, quiet nights on the couch with a bowl of popcorn and a movie, and rainy Sunday mornings snuggled up in bed. He missed being with someone, being part of a couple, having a partner by his side to celebrate not just all of the national holidays but all of the ordinary days in between.

But even more than he missed being a husband, he missed being a father. For almost three years, his little boy had been the center of his life. But Liam had been gone for more than three years now, and it was past time that Matt accepted that and moved on.

With a sigh, he considered that maybe he should let Luke talk him into taking one of those puppies. At least then he wouldn't come home to an empty house at the end of a long day.

Glancing toward Georgia's house again, he was willing to bet that his neighbor didn't know what it meant to be lonely. With three kids making constant demands on her time, she probably didn't have five minutes to herself in a day.

No doubt the twins alone could keep her hopping, and she had the needs of an infant to contend with as well. Although he had yet to meet the baby girl, he found himself wondering what she looked like, if she had the same dark hair and dark eyes as her brothers (which he assumed they'd inherited from their father) or blond hair and blue eyes like her mother.

It had to be difficult for Georgia, being widowed at such a young age. Not that he actually knew how old she was, but if she'd passed her thirtieth birthday, he didn't think she'd done so very long ago. Which meant that she'd likely married when she was young and idealistic and head over heels in love—and that she was probably still grieving the loss of her husband. But even if she wasn't, Matt didn't imagine that she had any interest in—or energy for—a romance with her new neighbor.

A relationship with someone who lives next door might

seem convenient...but it can be a nightmare if things don't work out.

Luke was probably right. So Matt was going to take his brother's advice and step back. Which didn't mean he and Georgia couldn't be friends. Surely his brothers wouldn't have any objection to Matt being friends with the woman next door.

And it seemed obvious that the first step toward becoming friends was to be a good neighbor. He finished the last strip of his grass and pushed the mower over to Georgia's lawn.

Having never owned anything with a yard before, he wasn't sure how he would feel about the required maintenance and upkeep, but so far, he was enjoying the physical work. And mowing the lawn, being unable to hear anything but the rumble of the motor, was almost relaxing. Or it would have been if the hum and the vibration of the machine in his hands hadn't started him thinking about different hums and vibrations that he hadn't experienced in a very long time.

Yeah, it had definitely been too long since he'd been with a woman. Which brought him back to thinking about Georgia again. The neighbor who was, he reminded himself, strictly off-limits with respect to any kind of romance.

But while his mind might be willing to heed the warnings of his brothers, his hormones weren't entirely convinced. Especially when Georgia's van pulled into the driveway and his pulse actually skipped a beat.

As Georgia turned onto Larkspur Drive, she mentally reviewed her plans for the rest of the day. First and foremost was the long-neglected manuscript still on the dining room table. And when she finally got that manuscript finished, she would set Pippa up in her playpen on the deck while Georgia cut the grass. She still had mixed feelings about letting the boys play in the neighbor's yard, but she thought she might indulge them today, trusting they would keep safely out of the way in the tree house.

She hadn't seen much of Matt Garrett over the past few days, which made her realize how little she knew about him aside from his name. She didn't know where he worked or what he did, whether he was married or engaged or otherwise involved. Not that she was interested, just…curious.

And when she turned into her driveway and saw him pushing a lawn mower over the last uncut strip of grass in front of her house, her curiosity was piqued even further.

She parked her minivan, then opened the back door to let the twins scamper out before she unlatched Pippa's car seat. By the time she'd taken the baby into the house, he'd finished the lawn and was making his way toward her.

"Need a hand?" He gestured to the grocery bags in the back.

Georgia turned to respond, but the words dried up inside her mouth. His hair was tousled, his bronzed skin bore a light sheen of perspiration, and the gray T-shirt that molded to his broad shoulders and strong arms was damp with sweat. She'd always appreciated men who were more *GQ* than *Outdoorsman,* but she couldn't deny that there was something very appealing about *this* man.

She swallowed. "No, I've—"

Ignoring her protest, he reached into the vehicle for the remaining two bags.

She blew out a breath. "Okay. Thanks."

He grinned at her, and her knees actually went weak.

Something *very* appealing, indeed.

The first time she'd seen him up close, she'd been struck by his stunning good looks—and unnerved by her body's instinctive response to his blatant masculinity. But she'd managed to convince herself that she'd overestimated his appeal, that he couldn't possibly be as handsome or as sexy as she'd thought. Face-to-face with him now, she was forced to admit that, if anything, she'd *under*estimated his impact.

Those deep blue eyes were both warm and seductive, and

his exquisitely shaped mouth seemed to promise all sorts of wicked pleasure. Not that she was interested in seduction or pleasure; she didn't even have the energy for an innocent flirtation. But the pulsing of the blood in her veins proved that her body was only exhausted, not dead.

Matt followed her into the house and set the grocery bags on the counter.

"Can we come over to see the puppies?" Quinn asked.

Shane looked up at their neighbor, too, the plea in his gaze as earnest as his brother's question.

"The puppies aren't at my house today," Matt told them.

Their hopeful smiles dimmed.

"Where are they?"

"With my brother, Luke, at his clinic."

"He's the doggy doctor," Quinn reminded Shane.

"He's a doctor for all kinds of animals," Matt clarified.

"Maybe we could visit the puppies at the clinic," Quinn suggested.

"Not today," Georgia told him.

Shane pouted. "I want a puppy."

"Well, you got a baby sister instead."

"I'd rather have a puppy," Quinn grumbled.

Matt turned to hide his smile as he washed his hands at the sink. "Those puppies were kind of cute," he agreed. "But your sister is even cuter."

"Do you think so?" Quinn's tone was skeptical.

"Absolutely." He smiled at the baby still securely strapped into her car seat but directed his next words to Georgia. "Can I take her out of there?"

She hesitated. "If you want, but she doesn't have a lot of experience with strangers so she might…"

Her explanation trailed off when she saw that he already had Pippa out of her carrier.

Matt looked up. "She might what?"

"I was going to say 'fuss,'" she admitted. "But obviously she is doing anything but."

Instead, the little girl's big blue eyes were intently focused on Matt's face and her mouth was stretched into a wide, gummy grin that filled his heart so completely, his chest ached.

"She's a charmer," he said, tucking her carefully into the crook of his arm so that her head and neck were supported.

"She has her moments," her mother agreed.

"Mostly she cries," Quinn said.

"'Specially at night," Shane added.

Georgia's sigh confirmed it was true. "Colic."

He'd had his own experience with a colicky baby, and he winced sympathetically. "Are you getting any sleep?" he asked.

"A lot less since my mom went away," she admitted. "But I'm managing—if you disregard the fact that I'm falling behind on my work, housework and yard work."

Shane tugged on the hem of her shirt. "I'm hungry."

"I know, honey. I'll get your lunch as soon as I get the groceries put away."

"Gill cheez?"

She smiled. "You bet."

"I want twisty pasta," Quinn announced.

"You had pasta yesterday," she reminded him. "We're having grilled cheese today. But you can go put cartoons on TV while you're waiting for your lunch, if you want."

Apparently that was an acceptable compromise, as the boys both scampered off to the living room.

"But you're not falling behind with your kids," he said. "And that's what really matters."

The smile that curved her lips was both genuine and weary. "And thanks to you, I'm no longer as far behind with the yard work as I used to be."

He shrugged. "I was cutting my grass anyway."

She took a jug of 2% and a tub of yogurt out of the bag, found room for them in the fridge.

"You should try soy milk," he told her.

She lifted a brow. "Because you have futures in soybeans?"

He grinned. "Because colic can be caused—or aggravated—by an intolerance to the proteins in the cows' milk consumed by a nursing mother."

She crossed her arms over her chest. "How did you know I'm nursing?"

To his credit, he managed to keep his gaze on her face without his eyes even flickering in the direction of her very lush breasts. "No baby bottles in the drying rack or the fridge."

"Very observant," she noted. "And how do you know about the soy milk?"

"I read a lot."

She'd finished putting away her groceries and reached into the drawer under the oven for a frying pan. "I used to read," she told him. "Sometimes even for pleasure."

He smiled. "You will again—someday."

"I'll take your word for it." She retrieved the butter from the fridge. "But for now, we're getting through one day at a time."

"I'd say you're doing better than that. You've got three great kids, Georgia."

She started buttering slices of bread. "I wish you could be here to tell me that at 3:00 a.m." Then she realized how her words might be misconstrued, and her cheeks filled with color.

He knew she wasn't issuing an invitation, but he found himself wishing that he could find some way to help her out, to be the man she turned to when she needed someone, to be the one who could ease some of the fatigue from around her eyes and put a smile on her face. But those were very dangerous wishes. She wasn't his wife, her kids weren't his kids, and he had to stop wanting things that couldn't be.

"I only meant that it would be nice to have *someone* around to reassure me in the early hours of morning when I feel like crying right along with Pippa," she hastened to clarify.

"Sharing a burden makes it lighter," he agreed easily, and scribbled his phone number down on the notepad on the counter. "And if you ever do need a hand—with anything and at any time—give me a call."

"You've already done me a huge favor by cutting the grass." Butter sizzled as she dropped the first sandwich into the hot pan.

"I didn't know there was a limit on good deeds."

She smiled again, and though he could see the fatigue in her eyes, the curving of her lips seemed to brighten the whole room. "I don't mean to seem ungrateful—"

"I wouldn't say ungrateful so much as resistant."

"I lived in New York City for the past dozen years," she told him. "I wasn't even on a first-name basis with most of my neighbors, and the biggest favor any of them ever did for me was to hold the elevator."

"Obviously moving to Pinehurst has been a big adjustment."

"My mother told me it was a different world. She encouraged me to make conversation with people I don't know, and she chided me for locking the doors of my van when it's parked in the driveway."

"You lock the doors of your vehicle in your own driveway?" he asked incredulously.

"When I first moved to New York , I lived in a third-floor apartment in Chelsea. Two weeks later, I wandered down to the little coffee shop on the corner without securing the dead bolt and by the time I got back with my latte, the place had been completely cleaned out."

"I can see how an experience like that would make anyone wary," he admitted. "But around here, neighbors look out for one another."

"Says the man who just moved into the neighborhood," she remarked dryly, turning the sandwich in the pan.

He grinned. "But I grew up in Pinehurst and I've lived here most of my life."

"And probably quarterbacked the high school football team to a state championship in your senior year," she guessed.

"Actually, I was a running back," he told her.

"Yeah, 'cause that makes a difference."

She removed one sandwich from the pan and dropped in another. Then she cut the first into four triangles, divided them between two plates and set them on the breakfast bar. She reached into the cupboard above the sink for two plastic cups, then maneuvered past him to the fridge for a jug of milk.

Though she moved easily in completing tasks she had no doubt performed countless times before, he was suddenly cognizant of the fact that he was just standing around.

"I'm in your way," he noted, moving aside so that he was leaning against the far stool at the counter, the baby still tucked securely in the crook of his arm.

She shook her head as she half filled the cups with milk. "If you weren't holding Pippa, she'd be screaming her head off, wanting her lunch, and I'd be juggling her and burning the sandwiches."

As she called the twins to the kitchen, he glanced down at the baby who had, in fact, shoved her fist into her mouth and was gnawing intently on her knuckles.

"Well, as long as I'm being useful," he said, his wry tone earning him a small smile from Georgia, and a wide drooly one from the baby in his arms.

The quick patter of footsteps confirmed that the boys had heard their mother's call, and they eagerly climbed up onto the stools at the counter.

Georgia moved back to the stove and flipped the next sandwich out onto a plate. She sliced it in half, then surprised Matt by setting the plate on the counter in front of him.

"Milk?" she asked. "Or did you want something else? I've got iced tea or juice or soda."

"Milk is fine," he said. "But I didn't expect you to feed me."

"It's just a grilled cheese."

"Which is much more appetizing than the cold pizza in my fridge at home."

She shrugged. "I figured a sandwich is a small price to pay for lawn maintenance."

"You might get the hang of small-town living yet," he told her.

"I'm trying."

The fact that she was making an effort gave him confidence that their fledgling friendship could lead to something more.

And though Jack's and Luke's warnings still echoed in the back of his mind, they were easily drowned out by the pounding of his heart when Georgia smiled at him.

Chapter Three

Georgia waited until Matt's car was gone from his driveway before she okayed the boys' request to visit the neighbor's tree house. Over the past couple of weeks, they'd enjoyed several adventures in the treetop, but only when their new neighbor wasn't home.

It wasn't that she was avoiding Matt. Not exactly. There was just something about the man that set off warning bells in her head. Or maybe it was tingles in her veins.

He was friendly and great with the kids, and if not for the way her body hummed whenever he was near, she might have thought that they could be friends. But the sizzle of awareness was too powerful for her to be comfortable in his presence, so Georgia decided that it would be best to maintain a safe distance from him at all times—or at least until her post-pregnancy hormone levels were back to normal.

She carted Pippa over to the neighbor's backyard so that she could keep an eye on the boys while they played in the branches.

With the baby cooing happily in her playpen, Georgia settled in a folding lawn chair beside her. She smiled as she listened to the boys' conversation—or rather Quinn's animated chatter and Shane's brief responses. A few minutes later, she saw Shane's sneaker on the top step of the ladder.

"Be careful," she said, instinctively rising from her chair in the exact moment that his foot slipped off the next step. She was halfway to the tree, her heart lodged in her throat, when his body plummeted toward the ground.

Emergencies were par for the course for any doctor, and especially for one who worked in a hospital E.R. But when an emergency surgery was squeezed into a very narrow window between two scheduled procedures, it made an already long day seem that much longer.

After a quick shower, Matt decided to head to the cafeteria for a much-needed hit of caffeine. But then he saw Brittney—a much more effective mood booster than any jolt of java. He slung an arm across her shoulders and pressed his lips to the top of her head.

She, predictably, rolled her eyes. "A little professionalism, Dr. Garrett."

"My apologies, Miss Hampton," he said, not sounding the least bit apologetic.

Brittney Hampton was his former sister-in-law's only child and a student helping out in the E.R.—a co-op placement for which she'd applied without his knowledge, determined to secure the position on the basis of her interview and not because her uncle was a doctor on staff at the hospital. She was loving the experience, and he was pleased to see that she was so intently focused on the pursuit of her goals.

"Are you on a break?" he asked her.

She nodded. "Dr. Layton said I should take one now, while there's a lull in the E.R."

"A lull never lasts long," Matt agreed. "If you're heading to the cafeteria, can I buy you a cup of coffee?"

She made a face. "I hate coffee."

He smiled. "Hot chocolate? Coke?"

"Vitamin water?"

"Sold."

They settled at one of the tables by the window with their beverages.

"How was your morning?" Brittney asked him.

"In addition to the usual hip replacements, I put a plate and five screws in the ankle of a kid who took an awkward tumble on the soccer field."

She winced. "Sounds painful."

"Nah, we put him under so he didn't feel a thing."

She rolled her eyes. "I meant the tumble."

"I imagine it was," he agreed. "How was your morning?"

"I had a test on molecular genetics," she said.

"And?" he prompted.

She shrugged. "I think I did okay."

"So no worries that Northeastern is going to rescind their offer?" he teased.

"Not yet."

"Is Brayden going to Northeastern, too?"

"Brayden is old news," she told him.

"Oh. I'm…sorry?" Truthfully, he was relieved. On the few occasions that he'd met her boyfriend, he'd seemed like a nice enough kid but Matt had worried that the relationship with Brayden would distract Brittney from her studies and her ultimate goal of becoming a doctor like her uncle.

She smiled, at least a little. "It was a mutual decision."

"Then your heart isn't broken?"

"Not even bruised."

"Glad to hear it," he said.

"How's *your* heart?" she countered.

His brows lifted. "Do they have you working in cardiology now?"

She smiled again, but her eyes—when they met his—showed her concern. "Mom told me that Aunt Lindsay is having another baby."

"Yes, she is," he acknowledged, pleased that his voice remained level, betraying none of the emotions that churned inside of him whenever he thought about the family that his ex-wife now had with her new husband. He didn't resent the fact that Lindsay had everything he'd ever wanted, but he was painfully aware of how empty his own life was in contrast.

"You should get married again, too," Brittney said.

"Don't worry about me—I'm doing okay," he said. And it was true. Because he suddenly realized that, since moving in next door to Georgia Reed and her family, his life didn't seem quite so empty anymore.

"You need a family."

"I haven't given up on that possibility just yet."

"Mom was telling Grandma that you need a woman who can appreciate you for all of your good qualities," Brittney continued, "so I've been keeping my eyes open for—"

"I appreciate the thought, but the last thing I need is my sixteen-year-old ni—"

"*Seven*teen," she interjected. "Remember? You came by for cake and ice cream for my birthday last month."

"I remember," he assured her. In fact, he hadn't missed a single one of her birthdays in the past three years, and he was grateful that Brittney's mother had continued to include him in family events after the divorce. Of course, it probably helped that he and Kelsey had been friends long before he married her sister. "But the last thing I need is my *seven*teen-year-old niece trying to set me up."

"Well, I haven't found any candidates yet," she admitted. "Aside from my friend, Nina, who thinks you're really hot. But even I know how inappropriate that would be."

"And on that note," Matt said, pushing back his chair, "I think I should check in on my patient."

Brittney rose with him. "And I need to get back to the E.R."

But before she turned away, she gave him a quick hug.

He was as pleased as he was surprised by the impulsive gesture of affection. But it was the words she spoke— "You'll find someone, Uncle Matt"—that somehow shifted his thoughts to the beautiful widow living next door with her three children and made him wonder if maybe he already had.

Georgia didn't have a lot of experience with her kids and emergency rooms—thank God for small favors—but she knew that "the squeaky wheel gets the grease" was an adage that applied in hospitals as much as anywhere else. And when she finally managed to maneuver her family through the sliding doors, with Pippa fussing, Shane crying (and trying to hold a bag of now partially thawed frozen peas against his wrist), and Quinn shouting "Don't let him die!", she didn't even try to shush them. Or maybe she knew her efforts would be futile anyway.

After she gave the basic details of the incident and handed over her insurance information to the bored-looking clerk behind the desk, she was told—with a vague gesture toward the mostly empty seating area—to wait. But she didn't even have a chance to direct Quinn to an empty chair when a dark-haired girl in teddy-bear scrubs appeared with a wheelchair for Shane. Though the tag on the lanyard around her neck identified her as "Brittney" and confirmed that she was a member of the hospital staff, she didn't look to Georgia like she was old enough to be out of high school.

"I'm just going to take you for a walk down the hall to X-ray so that we can get some pictures of your arm," Brittney explained to Shane.

His panicked gaze flew to his mother. Georgia brushed a

lock of hair away from his forehead and tried not to let her own worry show.

"It's okay if your mom and your brother and sister want to come along, too," Brittney assured him. "Would that be better?"

Shane nodded.

Quinn shook his head vehemently. "I don't want Shane to get a X-ray. I wanna go home."

"We can't go home until a doctor looks at your brother's arm," Georgia reminded her son, holding on to her fraying patience by a mere thread. "And the doctor can't see what's inside his arm without an X-ray."

"*You* can make it better," Quinn insisted. "Kiss it and make it better, Mommy."

Georgia felt her throat tighten because her son trusted that it could be that simple, that she had the power to make it better because she'd always tried to do so. But they weren't babies anymore and Shane's injury wasn't going to be healed by a brush of her lips and a Band-Aid.

Just like when their father had died, there was nothing she could do to ease their pain. Nothing she could do to give them back what they'd lost or fill the enormous void that had been left in all of their lives.

"Unfortunately, that's not going to fix what's wrong this time," she told him.

"Does a X-ray…hurt?" Shane asked.

Brittney squatted down so that she was at eye level with the boy in the chair. "It might hurt a little when the tech positions your arm to take the picture," she admitted. "But it's the best way to figure out what to do next to make your arm stop hurting."

After a brief hesitation, Shane nodded. "Okay."

She smiled at him, then turned to Quinn and sized him up. "How old are you?"

"Four." He held up the requisite number of fingers proudly.

"Hmm." She paused, as if considering a matter of great importance. "I'm not sure if this will work."

"If what will work?" he immediately demanded.

"Well, hospital policy states that no one under the age of five is allowed to drive a wheelchair without a special license," she confided. "Do you have a license?"

Quinn shook his head.

Brittney rummaged in the pockets of her shirt and finally pulled out a small square of blue paper. "I have a temporary one here," she told him, and Georgia saw that the words TEMPORARY WHEELCHAIR LICENSE were printed in bold letters across the top of the paper. "And I can give it to you *if* you think you can steer the chair *slowly and carefully* all the way down the corridor to X-ray."

"I can do it," he assured her.

She looked to Georgia, who nodded her permission.

"Okay, then. But first I have to put your name on here—"

"Quinn Reed."

She uncapped a pen and carefully printed his name. "And the date?"

He looked to his mother for guidance on that one.

"May twenty-second," she supplied.

Brittney filled in the date, then recapped the pen and handed the "license" to Quinn. He studied the paper reverently for a moment before tucking it carefully into the pocket of his jeans and reaching up to take the handles of the chair.

"Just one warning," Brittney told him. "If you bump into anything or anybody, I'll have to revoke that license."

He nodded his understanding, and they set off toward the X-ray department.

Twenty minutes later, Brittney directed them into a vacant exam room with a promise that "Dr. Layton will be in shortly."

But one minute turned into two, and then five turned into

ten. And Pippa, already overdue for a feeding, made it clear—at the top of her lungs—that she would not be put off any longer.

Thankfully, Quinn seemed to have finally accepted that his brother wasn't in any immediate danger of dying, and he crawled up onto the hospital cot and closed his eyes. Shane was still crying, though there was only an occasional sob to remind her of the tears that ran down his cheeks. So Georgia eased Pippa out of the carrier and settled in a hard plastic chair to nurse the baby.

She tried to drape a receiving blanket over her shoulder, to maintain some degree of modesty, but Pippa was having none of it. Every time she tried to cover herself, her daughter curled her little fingers around the edge of the fabric and tugged it away, until Georgia gave up. Besides, she didn't imagine a nursing mother was either an unusual or scandalous sight in a hospital.

Of course, that was before Matt Garrett walked in.

In the few moments that Matt had taken to review the digital images before he tracked down the patient, he didn't manage to figure out why the name Shane Reed seemed familiar. Then he walked into exam room four and saw one little boy on the bed and an almost mirror image in the wheelchair parked beside it, and he realized Shane Reed was one half of the adorable twin sons belonging to his gorgeous neighbor. And sure enough, Georgia was seated beside the bed, nursing her baby girl.

The baby's tiny hand was curled into a fist and pressed against the creamy slope of her mother's breast, and her big blue eyes were wide and intent while she suckled hungrily. It was one of the most beautiful sights Matt had ever witnessed. And incredibly arousing.

"Mommy." It was Shane who saw him first, and he tapped his mother with his uninjured hand. "Mr. Matt's here."

Georgia's gaze shifted, locked with his and her pale cheeks filled with color.

"You're not Dr. Layton," she said inanely.

"Things are a little chaotic in the E.R. right now, so Dr. Layton asked me to take a look at Shane's X-ray."

Quinn sat up. "Are you a doctor, too?"

Matt nodded.

"You don't look like a doctor," he said accusingly.

"Quinn," his mother admonished.

But Matt was intrigued. "How does a doctor look?"

The little boy studied him for a minute. "Older," he decided. "With gray hair and glasses."

"I'm older than you," Matt pointed out.

"You still don't look like a doctor."

"Actually, I'm an orthopedist," he explained.

"See?" Quinn said triumphantly to his mother.

"An orthopedist *is* a doctor," she told him.

The boy looked to Matt for confirmation.

He nodded. "An orthopedist is a doctor who specializes in fixing broken bones."

"Is Shane—" Quinn swallowed "—broken?"

He managed to hold back a smile. "No, your brother isn't broken, but a bone in his arm is."

"I falled out of your tree house," Shane said quietly.

Matt winced. "All the way from the top?"

The little boy shook his head. "I missed a step on the ladder."

"And reached out with his arms to break his fall," Georgia finished.

He noted that she'd shifted Pippa to nurse from her other breast, and he quickly refocused his gaze on his patient. "And broke your arm, too," Matt told Shane. "Do you want to see the picture of your arm that shows the break?"

Shane sniffled, nodded.

Matt sat down in front of a laptop on the counter and tapped a few keys.

"This here is your radius—" he pointed with the tip of a pencil to the picture on the screen "—and this is your ulna."

Though the occasional tear slid down the boy's cheeks, his gaze tracked the movement of the pencil and he nodded his understanding.

"Do you see anything different about the two bones?"

"I do," Quinn immediately replied, as Shane nodded again.

"Well, since it's Shane's arm, I think we should let Shane tell us what's different," Matt said.

Quinn pouted but remained silent.

"What do you see, Shane?"

"The ra-di—" he faltered.

"Radius?" Matt prompted.

"It has a line in it."

"That line is the break, called a distal radius fracture."

"It hurts," Shane said, in a soft voice that was somehow both wounded and brave.

"I know it does," Matt agreed.

"Can you fix it?" Quinn asked. "You said you can fix broken bones."

He nodded. "Yes, I can, and I will."

Georgia tried to concentrate on what Matt was saying, but her mind was still reeling from the realization that her new neighbor wasn't just gorgeous and charming but a doctor, too. She couldn't have said why the information surprised her so much or what she'd expected.

While he was occupied with Shane, she took a closer look at him, her gaze skimming from his neatly combed hair to the polished loafers on his feet. This man certainly didn't bear any resemblance to the sexy gardener who had tended to her overgrown yard. If she'd taken a guess as to his occupation that day, she probably would have said that he was employed in some kind of physically demanding field, like construction work or firefighting. She certainly wouldn't have guessed that he was an M.D.

Maybe the Mercedes in his driveway should have been her first clue, though she'd never met a doctor who hadn't managed to reveal his profession within the first five minutes of an introduction. And she'd been living next door to the man for more than three weeks without him giving even a hint of his occupation. But as she watched *Dr.* Garrett now, she could see that he was completely in his element here.

As he explained the process of casting a broken bone, he used simple words that the boys could understand. Despite his careful explanation, though, Quinn remained wary.

"Is Shane going to die?" he asked, obviously terrified about his brother's potential fate.

Though Georgia instinctively flinched at the question, the doctor didn't even bat an eye.

"Not from a broken arm," he assured him.

Shane looked up, his dark eyes somber. "Do you promise?"

She felt her own eyes fill with tears when she realized that the question wasn't directed to her but to Matt. Which made perfect sense, since he was the doctor. But it was the first time since Phillip had died that either of the twins had sought reassurance from anyone but their mother, and emotionally, it cut her to the quick.

"I absolutely promise," he said.

And Shane's hesitant nod confirmed that he'd accepted the man's word.

"Can I ask you a question now?" Matt asked.

Shane nodded again.

"What's your favorite color?"

"Blue."

"Then we'll put a blue cast on your arm," the doctor announced, and earned a small smile from his patient.

He left the room for a few minutes, then came back with

Brittney and an older woman. The gray-haired nurse helped lift and maneuver Shane's arm while the doctor applied the cast and Brittney looked on, observing and providing a running commentary of the process to entertain the twins. When it was done, Matt tied a sling over Shane's shoulder and explained that it would help keep the arm comfortable and in place.

"Do you use your right hand or your left hand when you eat?" Brittney asked Shane.

"This one," he said, lifting his uninjured hand.

"Do you think you could handle an ice cream sundae?"

Shane nodded shyly, then looked to his mother for permission.

"They would love ice cream," she admitted to Brittney, reaching for her purse.

The girl waved a hand. "It's on Dr. Garrett—part of the service."

Matt passed her a twenty-dollar bill without protest.

"Does my wheelchair driver still have his license?"

Quinn pulled the paper out of his pocket.

"Then let's go get ice cream."

"Thanks, Britt," said Matt with a smile.

Georgia had mixed feelings as she watched her boys head out with the young nurse. They were growing up so fast, but they would always be her babies as much as the little one still in her arms.

"She's been wonderful," she said to Matt now. "I don't know that I would have survived this ordeal without screaming if she hadn't been able to engage the boys."

"It can't be easy, juggling three kids on your own on even a normal day."

"What is a normal day?"

He smiled at that. "I'm not sure I would know, but I'm sure it's not strapping three kids into car seats for a trip to the hospital."

"Mrs. Dunford did offer to look after Pippa and Quinn so I didn't have to bring them along but—" She knew there was no reason to feel embarrassed talking to a doctor about a perfectly natural biological function that women had been performing since the beginning of time, but that knowledge didn't prevent a warm flush of color from rising in her cheeks again. "But the baby was almost due for a feeding and Quinn was absolutely terrified at the thought of his brother going to the hospital."

"He has a phobia about hospitals?" he asked.

"They both do," she admitted.

"Any particular reason?"

She nodded. "Because their father—my husband—was in the hospital when he died."

"That would do it," he agreed.

"It was a heart attack," she explained. "He recognized the symptoms and called 9-1-1, but the damage was too severe. All the boys know is that he was alive when they put him in the ambulance and dead at the hospital."

"Now they think anyone who goes to the hospital is going to die," he guessed.

She nodded again. "I've tried to explain that it wasn't the doctor's fault—that it wasn't anybody's fault—but they don't seem to believe me."

"Which one is Mrs. Dunford?"

She smiled. "Across the street. Always outside at 7:00 a.m. in her housecoat, watering her flowers. She has a magic touch with geraniums."

"And gingersnap cookies," he said.

"She baked you cookies?"

"She wanted to welcome me to the neighborhood."

"More likely she wanted to set you up with her grand-daughter."

"Then she should have gone for chocolate chip—they're my absolute favorite."

"I'll be sure to let her know."

He shook his head. "I'd prefer to get my own dates—although even Brittney thinks I need some help in that regard."

"Brittney—the nurse who looks like she's fifteen?"

"She's seventeen."

"Then she's not a nurse?"

He laughed. "More like pre-pre-med. Actually, Brittney's a high school co-op student who also happens to be my niece."

"She's been fabulous with the boys."

"She plans to specialize in pediatric medicine."

"That's quite an ambition."

"She's very determined. And she's one of the most sought-after babysitters in town."

"I'll keep that in mind if I ever find myself in need of one," she promised, certain Brittney would have graduated from medical school before that would ever happen.

So she was more than a little surprised when Matt said, "How about Friday night so I can take you out to dinner?"

Chapter Four

For a minute, she just stared at Matt as if he'd spoken in a foreign language. And with every second that ticked away during that interminable minute, he wondered if he should rescind his impulsive invitation.

He wasn't usually the impulsive type, a truth that was proven by the fact that he'd kept the condo he'd lived in with his wife and child for three years after they'd gone rather than take a hit on the downturned real estate market. Or maybe he just hadn't been ready to move on until now.

But he was ready now. And if Georgia agreed to go out with him—even just once for dinner—it would hopefully convince his niece to put her matchmaking efforts on hold.

"Are you asking me out...on a date?"

Except that her question, along with the skepticism in her voice, made him question whether he truly was capable of getting his own dates.

It can be a nightmare if things don't turn out.

He ignored the echo of Luke's words in the back of his

mind. While he trusted that his brother had his best interests at heart and believed that there was some legitimacy to
his warning, Matt couldn't deny the instinct that was urging
him to get to know Georgia a whole lot better.

"Let's not put a label on it," he said instead.

"So it's not a date?"

"It isn't anything until you say yes."

She considered for another few seconds, then shook her
head. "I can't."

"You can't have dinner with a friend? A neighbor?"

"I can't leave my kids with a stranger—even if she is one
of the most sought-after babysitters in town."

But he thought that, for just a minute, she'd been tempted.

"Quinn and Shane seem to like her just fine," he pointed
out.

"She's been great with the twins," she said again. "But
Pippa is another story. There are certain things that no one
but Mommy can do for her."

Okay, he didn't need to be hit over the head. At least, not
more than once. And if his gaze automatically dropped to her
breasts, well, he made a valiant effort to yank it away again.

Not so quickly that she didn't notice—as was attested by
the color flooding her cheeks.

"Okay, then, how about dinner at my place so you're not
too far away if you're needed?"

"Look, I appreciate the invitation, but I'm doing okay.
You don't have to feel sorry for me because I'm on my own
with three kids."

"Is that what you think—that I feel sorry for you?"

"I don't know what to think," she admitted. "But it's the
only explanation I can imagine that makes any sense."

"Maybe it did occur to me that a few hours away from
your responsibilities might be appreciated," Matt allowed.
"But I don't feel sorry for you. In fact, I think you're lucky to
have three beautiful children, and that they're lucky to have

a mother so obviously devoted to them." Because he knew from firsthand experience that there was nothing quite like the bond between a parent and child—and that nothing else could fill the void when that bond was broken.

"I am lucky," she said softly. "Although I don't always focus on how very lucky—and I don't always know how to respond to unexpected kindness."

"You could respond by saying you'll come to my place for dinner on Friday."

She shook her head, but she was smiling. "You're persistent, aren't you?"

"That's not the response I was looking for," he reminded her.

"I'll come for dinner on Friday," she finally agreed. "*If* Brittney is available—and willing—to watch the kids."

"Is seven o'clock good?"

"Shouldn't you check with the babysitter first?"

"Brittney will make herself available," he assured her.

"Then seven o'clock should be fine," Georgia said.

"Any food allergies or aversions?"

She shook her head.

"Favorite food?"

She smiled. "Anything I don't have to cook."

It was a long night for Georgia.

She gave Shane some children's acetaminophen to take the edge off of the pain, but she could do nothing to combat his frustration. He was usually a tummy sleeper, and he didn't like having to stay on his back with his injured arm elevated on a pillow, even if it was what "Dr. Matt" had recommended.

And she didn't have any better luck settling Quinn. While he'd been happy enough to wheel his brother around the hospital and indulge in ice cream, neither activity had succeeded in completely alleviating his worry about his twin.

But aside from checking on Shane and reassuring Quinn

and nursing and pacing with Pippa, what really kept Georgia awake through the night was second-guessing her agreement to have dinner with her sexy new neighbor.

He was a genuinely nice man who was wonderful with her kids, and if those were the only factors to consider, Georgia wouldn't have hesitated to accept his invitation. But Matt Garrett made her feel things she hadn't felt in a very long time—if ever before—and the stirring of those unexpected feelings made her wary.

Her mother had always said that falling in love was kind of like jumping into a pool without testing the water. And there was no doubt that Charlotte had always enjoyed that crazy sense of plunging into the unknown. Georgia had never been the type to leap without looking—she liked to gauge the temperature first and ease in slowly.

And that was the perfect analogy for her relationship with Phillip. She'd loved her husband, but their affection had grown over time along with their relationship. They'd started out as friends who'd shared common interests and values—and a mutual distrust of romance. Phillip had been engaged previously, but that relationship had ended when he found his fiancée in bed with his cousin. Georgia had, as a result of her mother's numerous relationships more so than her own experience, mostly steered clear of any romantic entanglements.

But Phillip had been as persistent as he was charming, and one date had led to another until, before Georgia knew what was happening, they were exchanging vows. They'd had a good relationship, a solid marriage. They'd been compatible enough, even if the earth hadn't trembled when they made love, and she had sincerely loved him.

When they'd decided to get married, she'd had no reservations. It wasn't that she couldn't live without him so much as she didn't want to—he was her best friend, the one person she knew she could always rely on, and the one person she always felt comfortable with.

She didn't feel the least bit comfortable around Matt Garrett.

She was thirty-one years old and a mother of three children, and she didn't have the first clue about what to do with these feelings that he stirred inside of her. She wished, for just a minute, that Charlotte was here so that she could talk to her about this inexplicable attraction. Four marriages— and four divorces—had given her mother a lot of experience with love—and heartbreak.

Except that Georgia didn't need to talk to Charlotte to know what her advice would be. "Go for it. Have fun—and make sure you have orgasms. Life's too short to fake it."

She smiled, almost hearing the echo of her mother's voice in her mind even as she chided herself for jumping the gun. After all, just because the man had invited her over for dinner didn't mean he was looking for anything more than that. Just because her heart pounded wildly inside her chest whenever he was near didn't guarantee that he felt the same attraction.

"I'll be glad when your Gramma's home tomorrow," she said to her daughter. Not that she expected her mother would be able to put the situation in perspective for her, but she would help out with the kids so Georgia could get some sleep. Because after more than a week of serious sleep deprivation capped off by an unexpected trip to the emergency room, she was starting to feel more than a little frazzled. But she was confident she could handle things on her own for twenty-four more hours.

The first few weeks after Pippa's birth had been pure bliss. The baby had slept and nursed and cried very rarely, and Georgia had been completely enthralled with her. And then, around four weeks, Pippa had started to get fussy. She still slept and nursed frequently, but the sleeping was for shorter periods of time, the nursing more frequent, and the crying much louder and longer.

After a thorough checkup, Dr. Turcotte had announced

that there was absolutely nothing wrong with her aside from "a touch of colic." He'd been sympathetic but unable to help. And though Charlotte had offered to cancel her annual trip with "the girls," Georgia couldn't imagine letting her do it. Because if she'd accepted that offer, it would be like admitting that she couldn't handle her own baby. Besides, Charlotte had already done so much for her daughter and her grandchildren.

When everything had started to fall apart in Georgia's life, her mother hadn't hesitated to invite her to come home. Not that Pinehurst, New York, had ever actually been *her* home. In fact, Charlotte had only settled in the picturesque upstate town about half a dozen years earlier, long after Georgia was living and working in New York City. But Georgia hadn't needed a familiar environment so much as she'd needed her mother. As she needed her now.

She was passing the kitchen when the phone rang, and she grabbed for the receiver automatically, forgetting for a moment that she didn't need to worry about the noise waking the baby because Pippa was already awake and snuggled happily—at least for the moment—in her carrier.

Georgia recognized her mother's voice immediately. "Hey, Mom, I was just talking to Pippa about you."

"How is my beautiful grandbaby girl?" Charlotte asked.

She always sounded upbeat, but Georgia thought she sounded even more so today. Not that it took much to make her mother happy—something as simple as winning a couple of hands at the blackjack table or scoring front-row seats to see Wayne Newton could be responsible for her joyful mood.

"She seems content enough right now," Georgia said, not wanting to let her mother know how difficult the last few days had been.

"Oh, I miss my grandbabies so much," Charlotte said. "Have you been givin' them all big hugs and kisses from me every day?"

"I have," she assured her mother. "But they're looking

forward to getting them directly from you when you come home tomorrow."

"Well, that's actually why I was callin'," Charlotte began, and Georgia felt a sinking sensation in the pit of her belly. "There's been a little bit of a change in my plans."

"What kind of change?" She tried to keep her voice light and borrow the brave face her mother always wore.

"I met someone." The excitement fairly bubbled over in Charlotte's voice again. "Oh, honey, I didn't think I would ever fall in love again. I certainly didn't expect it. I mean, I've already been so lucky in love—"

Lucky? Only Charlotte Warring-Eckland-Tuff-Masterton-Kendrick would think that four failed marriages somehow added up to lucky. On the other hand, her effervescent personality and unfailing optimism were no doubt two of the qualities that continued to draw men to her, in addition to the fact that she looked at least a decade younger than her fifty-four years.

Okay, Georgia thought, trying to be rational about this. Her mother had met someone. She certainly didn't have any philosophical objection to Charlotte having a romantic relationship—not really. But she did object to her mother, or anyone for that matter, believing that she'd fallen in love with a man she couldn't have known for more than a handful of days.

"—but the minute our eyes met across the baccarat table," Charlotte continued, "I felt a jolt as if I'd just stuck my finger in a socket."

Georgia had to smile at that. "I'm glad you're having a good time—"

"The *best* time," Charlotte interjected. "And after the ceremony last night, Trigger got us upgraded to the honeymoon suite, and I swear, I drank so much champagne my head is still spinnin'."

Right now, Georgia's head was spinning, too. Ceremony? Honeymoon suite? *Trigger?*

"Mom," she said, attempting to maintain a rational tone in the hope that it would calm the panic rising inside her. "Are you telling me that you married this guy?"

"Honey, when love comes knockin' on the door, you don't just open up, you grab hold with both hands and drag it inside."

Georgia banged her forehead softly against the wall.

"So yes," Charlotte finally answered her question. "I am now, officially, Mrs. Trigger Branston."

"His name is really Trigger?"

"Oh, his real name's Henry," she told her daughter. "But they call him Trigger 'cause he's so quick on the draw."

"Quick on the draw?" she echoed, fingers crossed that this whole conversation was some kind of bizarre waking dream induced by her own mental and physical exhaustion.

"With his gun," Charlotte clarified. "He's a *bona fide* member of the Cowboy Fast Draw Association and World Fast Draw Association and he's won all kinds of contests."

"That's...um...impressive?"

"You bet your cowboy boots it is," Charlotte said.

Georgia didn't remind her mother that the only boots she owned were of the snow-shoveling kind. What would be the point?

"So...this is what he does for a living?" she pressed.

Her mother laughed. "Of course not—the gun-slingin' thing is just a hobby. Trigger's ranch keeps him too busy for it to be anything else."

"Where is this ranch?"

"In southwestern Montana."

"You're moving to *Montana*?"

"Well, he can hardly bring the sheep and goats all the way to upstate New York," Charlotte pointed out.

Sheep and goats?

Georgia didn't want to imagine. Besides, she had a more pressing concern. "What are your plans for the house here?"

"Oh, I haven't even thought about that. But naturally you and my grandbabies can stay there as long as you want."

The statement was typical of her mother—equal parts impulsive and generous. And while Georgia appreciated the offer, her main reason for packing up her family and moving them to Pinehurst was that Charlotte was there.

But she bit her tongue. How could she do anything else when her mother sounded so happy and proud? What right did she have to begrudge her mother a new life just because her own had completely imploded?

So even while her eyes burned with tears, she said, "Congratulations, Mrs. Branston."

Her mother's laughter bubbled over the line. "I knew you'd be happy for me, baby girl."

And she was—at least, she really wanted to be. Because Charlotte Warring-Eckland-Tuff-Masterton-Kendrick-Branston had the biggest heart in the world and she deserved to be happy. But when Trigger Branston trampled all over that big heart with his Montana cowboy boots, Georgia thought ominously, he was going to answer to her.

Or maybe she was being too cynical. The fact that none of her mother's four previous marriages had worked out didn't mean that this one wouldn't. And really, who was she to judge? Just because Georgia didn't want to follow in Charlotte's footsteps didn't give her the right to condemn her mother's choices.

Maybe she had no interest in a steamy romance or a hunky man because she only wanted a few hours of sleep—preferably dreamless sleep. Because over the past couple of weeks, it seemed as if every time she closed her eyes, she couldn't help but dream about the sexy doctor next door.

Matt was wrapping potatoes in foil when the doorbell rang. Since it was just past six o'clock and, therefore, too early to be Georgia, he decided to ignore it. When he heard the door open and heavy footsteps in the foyer, he knew it had to be one of his brothers. An assumption that was proven accurate when Jack strolled into the kitchen.

His brother automatically reached for the handle of the fridge. "Do you want a beer?"

"No, thanks. But help yourself," Matt said dryly.

Jack did so and deftly twisted the cap off of a long-neck green bottle, his gaze zeroing in on the package of steaks. "Either you're really hungry or I picked the right night to stop by for dinner."

"You're *not* staying," Matt told him.

Undeterred, his brother dropped into a chair. "Why—you got a hot date or something?"

"As a matter of fact, I do."

Jack's bottle thunked down on the table. "You really have a date?"

"Is that so hard to believe?"

"Actually, yes."

Matt scowled as he tossed the foil-wrapped potatoes into the preheated oven. "I date."

His brother shook his head. "You've never invited anyone back to your place."

"It felt strange when I was still at the condo," Matt admitted. "Being with someone else there."

"Then you should have moved out of that place three years ago."

"Maybe I should have," he acknowledged. He'd known, long before the divorce was final, that his marriage was over. But he'd still been reluctant to leave the home that held so many memories of the little boy who had been his son for far too brief a time.

"So who is she?"

Jack's question drew him back to the present. "No one you know. Now finish your beer and get out."

"Maybe I should hang around to get to know her," his brother teased. "Maybe she'll like me better than you."

"You have enough women falling at your feet without homing in on mine."

Jack's brows lifted. "Is she? Your woman, I mean."

"It's a first date, Jack." And then, in a not-so-subtle effort to change the topic of conversation, he asked, "So what's going on with you?"

His brother shook his head. "It's the mom, isn't it? That's why you're trying to change the topic."

"I'm just curious as to why you're dateless on a Friday night," Matt hedged.

"Things were getting a little intense with Angela, so I decided to take a break from the dating scene for a while."

"I thought you really liked Angela."

"I did," he agreed. "And then I noticed that she was starting to stockpile bridal magazines."

"Someday you'll find the right woman and take the plunge again," Matt assured him.

Jack shook his head and reached for his beer. "I like to think I learned from my mistakes. One failed marriage is enough for me."

"Did you hear that Kelly Cooper's moving back home?"

"Yeah, I heard."

"I just wondered if that might be the real reason you decided to end things with Angela."

"Our youngest brother was the one who was always tight with the girl next door."

Matt couldn't help but laugh at that. "Because they were best friends—not because there was any kind of romantic connection."

Jack shrugged, but Matt knew that his brother's efforts to appear unconcerned only proved that he cared more than he wanted anyone to know.

"I always wondered why she never came home," Matt

mused now. "We all knew she was excited about going to school in Chicago, but no one expected that she would go from Chicago to Dallas to Seattle, or that she would stay away for so long."

"I'm sure she had her reasons."

"Would you be one of those reasons?"

Before Jack could respond, a knock sounded at the back door.

"I guess that's my cue," he said, picking up his almost-empty bottle to finish it off.

Matt didn't protest. The last thing he wanted was his brother hanging around all night. But he refused to let Jack off the hook so easily. "We'll get back to this," he promised.

But apparently Jack wasn't letting him off the hook, either, because instead of heading out the front—the same way he'd come in—he went to the back door as Matt was opening it to his guest.

"Hello, Georgia," Jack said.

"Oh, hi." She seemed taken aback by the other man's presence. "Jack, right?"

He smiled, pleased that she'd remembered his name. "It's nice to see you again."

"Jack was just on his way out," Matt said pointedly.

His brother shook his head. "I'm not in any huge rush," he denied.

Georgia's gaze shifted from Matt to Jack and back again. "Am I interrupting?"

"No, *you* were invited," Matt reminded her. "*He's* interrupting."

"He's right," Jack acknowledged. "And I promise I won't stay for long. I just wanted to meet my brother's mystery date."

"I didn't know that I was a mystery—or that this was a date," Georgia admitted.

"It's just a friendly dinner," Matt affirmed, shooting a

warning glance at his brother. "Did you want something to drink? I've got sparkling water or juice or—"

"Water would be great," Georgia said. "Thanks."

But before he even had a chance to pour her drink, Matt's pager went off.

He swore silently, but he couldn't ignore it. Not wanting the night to be a complete write-off for Georgia, he reluctantly left Jack in charge.

Then Matt headed toward the hospital, already devising a plan to secure a second date—and hopefully a first kiss.

Chapter Five

Georgia was disappointed that Matt had to cancel their plans to go to the hospital, but she understood. She didn't understand why he'd insisted that she stay to enjoy the dinner he'd promised her, and she didn't know how to decline Jack's offer to barbecue without sounding rude. Her only hope was that Pippa would wake up and pitch such a fit next door that Brittney would call and demand that Georgia return home.

Of course, her cell phone remained stubbornly silent.

"Looks like Matt's taken care of everything," Jack told her, returning with the plate of steaks from the grill. "There's a green salad, baked potatoes and dinner rolls."

"He didn't have to go to so much trouble," Georgia said, feeling more than a little guilty that he wouldn't get to enjoy the meal himself. "I would have been thrilled with a burger."

"Obviously my brother thinks you're worth the trouble," he said.

Despite the compliment implicit in the words, something in Jack's voice warned Georgia that he wasn't so sure.

He set a steak on her plate. "Well done."

"I like my steak medium."

"Matt told me to cook it all the way through to ensure there's no risk of any bacteria."

Her smile was wry. "Does he try to take care of everyone?"

Jack dropped a spoonful of sour cream onto his baked potato. "He and Luke both—it's the nurturing-doctor thing."

"What's your thing?" Georgia wondered.

He grinned. "I'm the heartless lawyer."

She shook her head. "I don't believe that."

"I have a law degree to prove it."

"It's not the educational qualifications that I doubt—it's the claim of heartlessness."

"There are more than a few women in town, including my ex-wife, who would assure you it's true."

"You're close to, and protective of, your brothers," she noted.

He didn't deny it.

"And for some reason, you disapprove of Matt and I being friends."

"I don't disapprove of your friendship," he assured her.

"But?" she prompted.

"But—and I know Matt would kill me for saying this—he's vulnerable."

"And you think I'm going to take advantage of him in some way?"

"I don't know what to think," Jack admitted. "Because I don't know you."

"That's fair," she acknowledged. "Would it reassure you if I said that I'm not in the market for a husband or a father for my children?"

"Not really."

"Why not?"

"Because I know my brother and he doesn't give up on anything he wants."

"And you think he wants me?"

"I know he does," Jack told her. "Because he called dibs."

She set down her water glass. "Excuse me?"

"The day he moved in—the first time he saw you on the porch—he warned the rest of us to back off."

She wasn't sure whether to be amused or insulted. "I would think the three kids would be warning enough."

He shrugged. "It's all about balancing pros and cons. We're guys and you're hot—for most of our species, those factors outweigh everything else."

"I'm not sure how to respond to that," she admitted, blushing. "Thank you?"

"It was a compliment," he said, and grinned again. "And you're welcome."

"But I do think you're misreading the situation between your brother and me."

"I doubt it."

"Even if he might have been interested when we first met, I'm sure the brief interactions he's had with my kids since then have cured him of any romantic notions."

"If you really believe that, you don't know Matt at all."

"I'd be the first person to admit that I don't," she told him.

"Which is probably why he invited you for dinner tonight," Jack noted.

"He's been incredibly helpful and generous."

"Don't kid yourself into thinking that he doesn't want to see you naked."

"You are blunt, aren't you?"

He shrugged easily. "I believe in telling it the way it is. But as much as he does want to get you naked, I know he could easily grow to care for you, too, and that makes the situation even more complicated."

"I'm not looking for a relationship," Georgia said.

"Sometimes we don't know what we want until it's right in front of us."

"That's quite the philosophical statement from a man who claims to value a woman on the basis of her 'hotness.'"

He flashed that quick grin again. "I can't be philosophical and shallow?"

She sliced off a piece of steak. "I think you're not nearly as shallow as you want people to believe."

Jack just shrugged, but Georgia suspected there were a lot more layers to each of the Garrett brothers than they let anyone see. Which was just one more reason for her to steer clear of all of them.

Her life was complicated enough right now without adding a man to the mix, especially one who had the potential to send her life—and her heart—into a tailspin, as she suspected Matt Garrett had already started to do.

Matt had just finished pouring his first cup of coffee Saturday morning when his youngest brother walked in.

"What are you doing here?" he asked Luke.

"Jack told me about your date last night."

"It wasn't much of a date," Matt admitted, pouring a second cup of coffee for his brother and adding a generous splash of cream.

"Yes, he said that you were saved by the bell—or at least your pager." Luke accepted the proffered cup.

"What is it, exactly, that I was supposedly saved from?" Matt asked. "A few hours in the company of a beautiful woman?"

"Let's put aside the fact that she's a beautiful woman—and your neighbor—for just a minute," Luke suggested, "and focus on the fact that she has three kids."

"I like kids."

"I know—and I saw the look on your face when those two little boys scampered across your backyard."

"What look was that?" Matt lifted his cup to his lips again.

"Pain. Regret. Longing."

He snorted. "Really? You got all that from one look?"

Luke shrugged. "I know you, and I know what you've been through."

"Ancient history," he said dismissively. Because while the scars from his failed marriage and the loss of his son had not completely healed, they had started to fade—and even more quickly since he'd met Georgia and her kids.

"Your marriage is history and Liam is gone," his brother agreed. "But I doubt you've given up on wanting a family."

"If we're going to start talking about our feelings, I'm going to need something a little stronger than coffee," Matt told him.

"I get that you're lonely," Luke continued as if his brother hadn't spoken. "But zeroing in on the first woman who crosses your path—"

"Georgia's hardly the first woman to cross my path in the past three years," Matt chided.

"But she's the first one you've invited over for a home-cooked dinner."

"It was a couple of steaks on the grill, not a six-course meal."

Luke just stared at him over the rim of his mug.

"Okay," he finally acknowledged. "So I like her. What's the big deal?"

"The big deal is that you're setting yourself up for heart-break all over again. She was married to another man—presumably because she was in love with that other man—and her kids are that other man's kids."

"The situation is not the same," Matt denied, though he could understand why his brother might worry about the similarities. "Georgia is a widow."

"Which doesn't mean she's not still in love with her husband."

He knew it was true, but he also knew that there was a

definite crackle in the air whenever he was near Georgia, and he didn't believe he was the only one who felt it.

"I'm only suggesting that you expand your horizons," Luke said now.

Matt eyed him warily. "Expand my horizons—how?"

"Come out to Maxie's with us tonight."

"Maxie's? Are you kidding?" While he and his brothers had frequented the popular dance club when they were younger, the loud music and louder women didn't appeal to him anymore.

"It might be just what you need," Luke said.

"I doubt it."

"Come anyway," his brother cajoled. "If you don't have a good time, I'll back off and not say another word about your infatuation with your neighbor."

Matt snorted his disbelief.

"And I'll buy the beer."

"Well, in that case…"

Matt spent the afternoon framing the unfinished basement to divide the space into individual rooms. Although the house already had a lot of space, he thought it would be convenient to have a home gym so that he didn't have to head out whenever he wanted some exercise. And until the room was ready, he figured the construction itself was a pretty good workout.

The physical labor occupied his hands but not his mind, and he found himself wondering what Georgia was doing, if the twins were behaving, if Pippa was napping. He remembered those first few months with Liam, how he and Lindsay had struggled to meet the baby's needs and establish some routines. His life had never been quite as chaotic as it had been back then, and he was surprised to realize that he missed it. Of course, spending time with his neighbors had given him brief glimpses of that pandemonium again, and spending time in close proximity to Georgia had stirred his hormones into a frenzy. He hammered the final nail into a board and tried to push those thoughts from his mind.

He was covered in sweat and sawdust and heading for the shower—prompted by the text message Luke had sent to remind him of their plans (because his brother knew Matt would forget, or at least claim he'd forgotten, without such a reminder)—when the bell rang.

Since his brothers had already proven that they had no qualms about walking right in, he let himself hope that it might be Georgia at the door. And while a quick glance through the sidelight revealed a pair of shapely, tanned legs, the hem of a short skirt and a pair of slender arms wrapped around an enormous ceramic pot from which towered a plant with lots of glossy, green leaves, his hopes were dashed.

He opened the door, made a show of looking around the greenery. "I really need to find a landscaper who can deal with these weeds. They're out of control."

"It's not a weed, it's a schefflera."

"Kelsey?" He parted some branches, peeked between them. Maybe she wasn't the woman who had preoccupied so many of his thoughts over the past few weeks, but she was one of his best friends, and he was genuinely happy to see her. "Are you in there?"

His former sister-in-law shoved the pot at his midsection, causing the air to whoosh out of his lungs. "Happy house-warming."

He maneuvered back through the door and carefully set the pot on the floor. "It's a killer plant," he said, after he'd managed to catch his breath again. "Although chances are, I'll kill it first."

"It's low maintenance," she assured him. "But don't leave it by the door in the winter. And it needs lots of light, but not direct sunlight."

"Low maintenance like most women are low maintenance," he grumbled.

She just smiled as she kissed his cheek, then moved past him and into the foyer. "This is a great house."

"Why do you sound so surprised?"

"Because it's a house—and nothing at all like your condo. Even the furniture's different."

"I was ready for a fresh start."

She nodded, understanding, and continued toward the kitchen. "I'm sorry I didn't get a chance to stop by sooner," she said. "One of the cruise lines is having a summer sale and things have been crazy at the office."

"You know, a ticket for a cruise would have been a better housewarming gift than a plant."

"Except that you don't take vacations," she reminded him. "In fact, I don't think you've gone on a holiday since..."

"Since my honeymoon?" he guessed, when her words trailed off.

She winced. "I'm sorry."

"The divorce has been final for three years," he pointed out.

"I know," she admitted.

The sympathy and worry in her deep brown eyes made him realize that he'd given her cause for concern in those three years because he hadn't taken any concrete steps to prove that he was moving on with his life. Hopefully seeing him in his new home would prove to her that he was doing so now.

He opened the refrigerator, peered inside. "Beer, wine, soda, juice?"

"Juice sounds good."

He pulled out the jug of orange juice, filled a tall glass, grateful that she'd dropped the topic of his ex-wife—her sister.

"Am I going to get the grand tour?" she asked.

"Actually, you caught me just as I was about to hit the shower," he told her. "So you can wait fifteen minutes or poke around on your own."

"I'll wait," she said. "Unless this is a bad time, in which case I can just go. I should have called first, anyway."

He waved off her apology. "You're always welcome. But I really need to clean up."

"Another hot date tonight?" she teased.

"Yeah," he said dryly. "With my brothers at Maxie's."

"Maxie's?" She wrinkled her nose. "Aren't you guys getting a little old for that scene?"

"We're guys," he reminded her, though he didn't disagree with her statement. "Our maturity level always lags behind our physical age."

"Tell me something I don't know."

He didn't have to think long to fulfill her request. "Luke has eight puppies he's trying to place in good homes."

Kelsey groaned. "Remind your brother that, in the past five years, he's already conned me into taking two cats, a parrot and an iguana."

"And you love the whole menagerie."

"That doesn't mean I'm taking any more," she said firmly.

"Brittney's always wanted a puppy," he pointed out.

"Unfortunately, the residences at Northeastern have a strictly enforced 'no pets' policy, so she'll have to be satisfied with visiting yours when she comes home."

He shook his head. "I'm not taking one of Luke's puppies." He tried to sound firm—to ignore the voice in the back of his head that promised the twins would be absolutely overjoyed if he did. And when the twins were happy, Georgia was happy, and her smile did all kinds of crazy things to his insides.

"You were going to shower," Kelsey reminded him.

He nodded and turned away. He did need to wash away all of the sawdust and sweat—and he was hopeful that the chilly spray might finally help banish wayward thoughts of Georgia that continued to pop into his mind.

Georgia didn't let herself think twice. If she did, she would think of all kinds of reasons that walking across the yard and knocking on Matt's door was a bad idea. Then she'd convince herself not to do it and she'd end up eating two dozen freshly baked chocolate chip cookies all by herself. Besides, it was just a plate of cookies—it wasn't as if she was propositioning her neighbor. Even if there was something about the man that intrigued her, despite the fact that she didn't want to be intrigued.

He was more attractive than any man had a right to be, but it wasn't just his physical appearance that appealed to her. There was a warmth in his eyes that hinted at a kindness in his soul, and a twinkle in his smile that attested to a sense of humor. And when he looked at her, she felt some of the weariness in her bones fade away and an unexpected warmth spread through her belly. Which was just one more reason she should not be making the man cookies.

She'd meant what she'd said to Jack the night before—she wasn't interested in any kind of romantic relationship and she didn't want to send mixed signals. On the other hand, it was possible that Jack had misinterpreted his brother's intentions and that Matt wasn't even reading any of her signals. Just because the man gave *her* tingles didn't mean that *he* felt the same sizzle of attraction. After all, it was extremely unlikely the sexy doctor would ever be interested in a weary widow with a lot of kid-sized baggage.

The mental lecture didn't do much to reassure her, but she accepted that the truth needed to be faced. Her children were her priority right now, and it would be a very long time before she even considered adding a man into the equation. So resolved, she lifted a hand to press the buzzer.

A moment later, she heard light footsteps—much lighter than she would have expected from a man of her neighbor's size and build—then the door was opened.

"Oh. Um." Georgia wasn't expecting anyone but Matt to answer the door, and finding herself face-to-face with a stunningly beautiful brunette left her momentarily speechless.

"You're looking for Matt," the woman guessed.

"I was," Georgia admitted. "But I don't want to interrupt—"

"Please." The other woman laughed as she held up a hand to halt her apology. "You're not interrupting anything."

"Are you sure?"

"Matt is a very old and close friend and nothing more than a friend. I just stopped by to drop off a housewarming gift and to make sure he was getting settled," she explained, stepping away from the door so Georgia could enter.

She held out the plate of cookies. "Actually, if I could just leave these with—"

"Georgia."

Before she could make her escape, he was there—fresh out of the shower, if his damp hair and the subtle scent of soap were any indication. And when he smiled at her, a smile filled with both warmth and pleasure, her heart actually skipped a beat.

"I'm sorry for just stopping by. I didn't know you had company."

"Kelsey's not company," Matt said, winking at the brunette.

The other woman rolled her eyes. "Didn't I tell you?"

Georgia smiled, then turned to offer the plate to Matt. "When you fixed up Shane's arm, you mentioned that you were partial to chocolate chip."

"I am," he agreed. "But I'm not sure I follow the connection between the hospital and the baked goods."

"I wanted to thank you for last night," she said, then felt her cheeks heat. She glanced at Kelsey and hastened to explain. "For dinner, I mean." And then, to clarify further, "When I lived in Manhattan, I didn't socialize with the people in my building—to be honest, I didn't even know most of them—so this whole neighbor-helping-neighbor thing is all new to me. But you've been really great, and I thought baking some cookies might be a nice way to say thanks."

"It wasn't necessary, but I appreciate it." He breathed in deeply. "They smell fantastic."

"Well, I should get back," she said.

"How is Shane managing with the cast?" Kelsey asked.

Georgia must have looked startled by the question, because the other woman smiled.

"Brittney, your hospital assistant and babysitter, is my daughter," she explained.

"Your daughter?" Georgia was genuinely baffled by this revelation. "You don't look old enough to be the mother of a seventeen-year-old."

Kelsey laughed. "Oh, I *do* like you."

"Shane's doing okay," she said, in response to the original question. "Mostly because his brother is catering to his every whim. Although I suspect that will wear thin in another day or two."

"How's Pippa?" Matt asked. "Has she been sleeping any better?"

She shook her head again.

"Colic doesn't last forever," he told her.

"It only seems like forever," Kelsey warned.

"It already does," Georgia admitted.

"And yet," Kelsey mused thoughtfully, "somehow a woman who has her hands full with three small children, including a fussy newborn and a preschooler with a broken arm, still found the time to make cookies for her new neighbor."

"It took a lot less time to make the cookies than it would have to cut my grass, which Matt did for me the other day," Georgia explained, wanting to ensure that Kelsey didn't get any wrong ideas.

"So this is...tit for tat?"

Georgia wasn't sure if the emphasis on "tit" and "tat" was

deliberate, but the implication had her cheeks flooding with color again. "Something like that," she agreed lightly.

"Did you want some of these cookies and a cup of coffee? I could make decaf," Matt said, coming to her rescue again.

"Thanks, but I just had a cup of tea with Mrs. Dunford—and I've left her alone with the kids for too long already." She turned back to Kelsey. "It was nice meeting you."

"You, too," Kelsey said. "Next time, I hope you'll have time for that cup of coffee."

"That would be nice," Georgia said.

Matt followed her to the door. "Sorry about Kelsey."

Her lips curved. "Why are you sorry?"

"Because she's the sister I never wanted."

Despite the disclaimer, the tolerant affection she'd seen when Matt looked at Kelsey had been obvious. But when she glanced up now to find him looking at her, what she saw in his eyes wasn't tolerant affection but something hotter and more intense. And this time, the tingles that started low in her belly spread through her whole body.

She had to swallow before she could speak. "I really have to get back."

"Thanks again for the cookies."

"Thank you," she said. "For everything."

He smiled. "See? You're getting the hang of small-town living."

"I'm trying," she agreed.

"And from the neighbor-helping-neighbor thing, it's just a short hop, skip and a jump to friendship."

"I haven't had a chance to meet many new people since I moved here," she admitted. "I'd like it if we could be friends."

"I'd like that, too," he said.

Matt stayed where he was, watching until Georgia had disappeared through the back door and into her house.

In the few weeks since he'd moved in, he'd made more

progress with the beautiful blonde next door than he'd anticipated. She'd gone from being distant and wary to baking cookies for him, which gave him confidence that they were well on their way to becoming friends.

And from there, he was optimistic that it was just another hop, skip and a jump to something more.

Chapter Six

Matt stayed out with Luke and Jack later than he'd intended. Not because he was having a good time, but he figured if he at least pretended he was, it might get his brothers off his back for a while. He had a couple of beers early in the evening, because Luke was buying, but then he switched to soda. It was rare for Matt to overindulge, he never had more than a couple of drinks when he was driving, and he didn't drink at all if he was on call.

By the time he left the bar, his head was pounding from the throbbing beat of the music, his muscles ached from the sawing and hammering he'd done in the afternoon, and he was exhausted. And when he pulled into his driveway at nearly 2:00 a.m., he was stunned to see Georgia carrying Pippa's car seat toward her own vehicle, with the twins—in their pajamas—shuffling along beside her.

He shifted into Park and turned off his vehicle. Even through the closed window of his car, he could hear the baby's cries. In fact, he wouldn't be surprised if she was screaming loud enough to wake Mrs. Dunford across the street—and she was almost 80 percent deaf.

As he exited the vehicle, he had to admire the baby's lung capacity. He lifted a hand in greeting, but Georgia didn't see him. And as she passed beneath the streetlight, he saw that Pippa wasn't the only who was crying. The wet streaks on Georgia's cheeks were his undoing. He forgot his own fatigue and crossed the patch of grass that separated their two driveways.

"What are you doing?"

She finished locking the car seat into its base, then made sure the boys were securely belted in their booster seats. Straightening, she wiped the telltale traces of tears from her cheeks. "I'm going for a drive."

"At 2:00 a.m.?"

"Is that a violation of street curfew?"

"No, just common sense," he told her.

She reached for the driver's-side door, but he scooped the keys out of her hand.

"What are *you* doing?" she demanded.

"You're too exhausted and emotional to get behind the wheel of a car," he said. "Especially with your infant daughter and two little boys in the backseat."

"I'm tired because Pippa won't sleep. Hopefully, a quick trip around the block will change that, then I can come back home and we'll all get some shut-eye."

He opened the passenger-side door and gestured for her to get inside. She just stared at him, uncomprehending.

"I'll drive," he told her.

She opened her mouth as if to protest, then closed it again without saying a word and climbed into the vehicle.

He knew she wasn't accustomed to having anyone look out for her, and that she was probably more suspicious than appreciative of his efforts, but tonight she was too tired to put up a fight.

He'd just turned onto Queen Street when he realized that she was right—the motion of the car had quickly succeeded in putting Pippa to sleep. A glance in the rearview mirror confirmed that both Quinn's and Shane's eyes were closed, too. He started to comment to Georgia on the obvious success of her plan, then saw that she was as deeply asleep as her children.

Matt continued to drive, with only the radio for company, because he was concerned that Georgia would wake up as soon as he pulled back into her driveway, and he knew that she needed the rest as much as—or maybe even more than—her daughter. But half an hour later, his eyes were starting to feel heavy, too, so he turned the vehicle back toward Larkspur Drive.

Luckily, Georgia's house key was on the same ring as the van key, so he was able to let her sleep while he opened up the door and transferred the kids, one at a time, from the vehicle to their beds. He couldn't figure out how to unlatch Pippa's car seat, so he finally just unbuckled the belt and lifted the sleeping baby into his arms. She didn't stir. Obviously her sleepless nights were taking as much of a toll on the baby as they were on her mother.

When Pippa was settled in her crib, he went out to the van again to rouse Georgia. He touched her shoulder gently; she jolted.

"What— Where?"

"You're home," he told her.

She turned automatically to the backseat. "Where are the kids?"

"They're all inside, tucked into their beds."

Her eyes widened. "Really?"

He nodded. "Now it's your turn."

"Okay." She let him help her out of the car and toward the back door. "I didn't mean to fall asleep, too."

"Obviously you needed it."

"I guess so," she said, and lifted a hand to cover her yawn.

He steered her in the direction of the staircase. She automatically turned toward Pippa's room, but he guided her across the hall to what he assumed was her own. "Just go to sleep," he said softly.

"Pippa—"

"Is already in her crib."

"I should change her diaper."

"I checked it before I put her down."

She blinked. "You did?"

He smiled. "She's clean and dry and sleeping—you should do the same."

"Okay," she finally relented. Then she lay down on top of the covers, fully dressed, and closed her eyes.

"Sweet dreams, Georgia."

But she didn't respond, because she was dead to the world again.

Georgia awoke in a panic.

The sun was streaming through the partially open blinds and a quick glance at the clock on her bedside table revealed that it was 8:02 a.m.

She didn't believe it. The last time she'd nursed Pippa was around two, just before she'd gone out to the car to take her for a drive. But Pippa had never slept for six straight hours. She wondered if she might have awakened in the night and nursed the baby without realizing it, but her painfully engorged breasts immediately refuted the possibility.

Aside from the uncomfortable fullness, she felt good. Relaxed and rejuvenated. She crossed the hall to Pippa's room, a genuinely contented smile on her face.

The contentment and the smile disappeared fast when she discovered that her little girl's crib was empty.

She bolted across the hall to the twins' room and found it

was empty, too. She raced for the stairs, her heart hammering against her ribs. "Pippa?"

She couldn't have said why she was calling for her—she knew the baby wouldn't answer. But she wasn't thinking rationally. She wasn't thinking about anything except that her children weren't where they were supposed to be.

"She's here." Matt must have heard the panic in her voice, because he met her at the bottom of the stairs with Pippa in his arms and Quinn and Shane at his side.

Her breath rushed out of her lungs and her knees went weak. Matt reached out, catching her arm to hold her steady. "You okay?"

She nodded as she took Pippa, cuddling the little girl close to her chest. The baby cooed happily. "I am now."

"Why is Mommy crying?" Shane wanted to know.

She hadn't known that she was, and wiped hastily at her cheeks with her free hand, then touched his head. "I just got scared when I woke up and didn't know where you guys were."

"Pippa's a Who-dee-na, too," Quinn announced.

"Houdini," Matt corrected the boy automatically. Then, to Georgia, "I'm sorry. I thought I was doing you a favor by letting you get some sleep."

"You were. You did. I just didn't expect that you'd still be here, and when I saw that her crib was empty and I didn't hear the boys..." They wandered off now, back into the living room where she could hear their favorite cartoons on the television.

"You panicked. Understandably," he said. "And I'm sorry."

She wanted to be mad, but he was so genuinely contrite that she couldn't hold on to her anger. Especially not when he spoke again and asked, "Are you hungry? I hope you don't mind but I pilfered through your cupboards and was just about to make some French toast."

"No, I don't mind," she said. "Especially not if you're offering to make French toast for me, too."

"Absolutely," he assured her. "If for no other reason than to be able to tell my brothers that I had breakfast with my beautiful new neighbor."

She knew he was teasing, and she wasn't sure how she was supposed to respond to that. From their first meeting, he'd been friendly and flirtatious, but maybe he was just the type of guy who flirted with every woman who crossed his path. Because the idea that he could be interested continued to baffle her—and never more so than right now, as she suddenly remembered her wrinkled clothing, disheveled hair and unbrushed teeth.

"Do I have time for a quick shower?" she asked.

"Twenty minutes enough?"

She nodded and turned back toward the stairs.

"Are you planning to take Pippa into the shower with you?"

"No, but I figured she was overdue for a feeding," she said. Despite the fact that the baby certainly wasn't acting like it had been more than six hours since her last feeding, Georgia's aching breasts confirmed the fact.

"She had a bottle an hour ago," he said.

That stopped her abruptly in her tracks. "She had a bottle?"

"I found your stash of breast milk in the freezer."

Georgia was impressed, and more than a little surprised. Because on the few occasions that she'd tried to coax her daughter to take one, Pippa had refused to latch on to the artificial nipple. "She was okay with the bottle?"

"She was hungry," he said simply.

She couldn't help but smile as she secured Pippa into her bouncy chair. "You really do go above and beyond, don't you?"

"It wasn't a big deal," he assured her.

But to Georgia it was. Six hours of uninterrupted sleep was a very big deal—and she was very grateful. But now she wondered, "Where did *you* sleep?"

"Your couch, in the living room."

Having caught some quick naps there herself, she didn't recommend it. "I hope you don't have to work today," she said, wondering how he could get through a day at the hospital on only a few hours of sleep on a sofa.

"I work twelve-hour shifts for four days, then I'm off for four days, barring emergencies. This is one of my days off."

"Then you should be taking advantage of the opportunity to laze around in bed."

His lips curved. "Is that an invitation?"

"No!" She was shocked by the idea—and just a little bit tempted by the wickedly explicit thoughts that sprang to mind in response to his suggestion. "I only meant that you didn't have to hang around here taking care of my kids."

"I like your kids," he told her.

And they absolutely adored Matt, but that was hardly the point. She couldn't help but remember what Jack had said about his brother and worry that she was taking advantage of his generous nature. She hadn't asked him to help her out last night, but she hadn't objected to his offer, either. And she certainly hadn't asked him to spend the night so that she could get some sleep, but she was immensely grateful that he'd done so.

Matt took a step closer, lifted a hand to tuck an errant strand of hair behind her ear. "And I like you."

The contact was brief, casual. But the touch made her shiver; her heart started to pound; her throat went dry.

All he'd done was touch her, and her hormones had gone haywire. Was she so lonely, so desperate for human contact, that such a simple gesture could affect her so deeply? Apparently so, because not only was her pulse racing, her body was aching, yearning.

"Well, I'm going to go take that shower now," she said, and turned to make her escape.

What was he doing?

It was a question Matt had asked himself countless times

through the night and one that continued to plague his mind as he got breakfast under way.

He found a package of bacon in the fridge, started the meat frying on the stove while he gathered the rest of the tools and ingredients for French toast. The twins had been playing in the living room but, drawn by the sounds emanating from the kitchen, ventured into the room to investigate.

Quinn looked quizzical as he watched Matt turn the strips of bacon that were sizzling and popping. "Are you really gonna make breakfast?"

"Sure." He set a lid over the bacon to cut down on the grease spatters.

"Can I watch?"

"Sure," he said again. "You can even help, if you want."

The little boy's eyes went wide. "Really?"

"Why not?"

Shane, silent until now, frowned. "Daddies don't cook."

"Says who?" Matt challenged.

"My daddy."

The assertion, so firmly stated, gave Matt pause. He didn't want to contradict any memories the boys had of their father, but he couldn't imagine that Georgia wanted her sons growing up with the outdated assumption that the kitchen was strictly a woman's domain. "Your dad never scrambled eggs for you on a Sunday morning so your mom could sleep in?"

Shane shook his head. "Mommy doesn't sleep in."

Which was apparently a situation that had existed long before Pippa came along.

"She slept in today," Quinn pointed out.

"And we're going to make her breakfast today," Matt said.

"We could order pizza."

Matt had to smile. "For breakfast?"

"Daddy knew the best places to get pizza," Quinn said loyally.

"Well, I'm going to make French toast. And if you don't want to help, I'll crack all the eggs myself."

Shane shifted closer, looked up at him with solemn dark eyes. "I wanna crack eggs."

"Then let's get you washed up," Matt said.

He supervised the boys' washing their hands, or—in Shane's case—washing the only hand he would be using. Then he sat them at the table with a big bowl and gave them each three eggs while he took the bacon out of the frying pan and set it on paper towels to absorb the grease.

"Hey! You're not 'sposed to put the shell in the bowl."

Matt glanced over in time to see that Quinn's criticism had Shane's eyes filling with tears.

"It's hard with one hand," Shane said, his voice wavering.

"You're doing a great job," he assured the child. "And it's easy enough to fish the pieces of shell out again," he told Quinn. Then he gave Shane a spoon and showed him how to do it.

But Quinn was still scowling over his brother's clumsiness. "What if he doesn't get them all?"

"Then we'll have an extra dose of calcium with our breakfast."

"What's calsum?" Shane asked.

"It helps build strong bones and teeth."

"Like milk," Quinn said.

"That's right," Matt agreed. "Because milk is a source of calcium."

He poured a generous splash of it into the bowl with the eggs and let them take turns whisking the mixture. After reminding them that they should never go near the stove without an adult close by to supervise, he let them each dip a piece of bread in the liquid and then place it in the frying pan.

It was as much fun for Matt as it obviously was for the twins, and all the while, that same question echoed in the back of his mind: What was he doing?

But this time, the answer was obvious: He was getting too close.

Aside from the fact that she was a widow, he knew very few details about Georgia's life before she came to Pinehurst. Had her marriage been a happy one? Was she still in love with and mourning her husband? What did she want for her future?

Of course, he didn't know the answers to any of those questions. He only knew that he was extremely attracted to her—and totally captivated by her children. They were a family without a daddy, and he very much wanted to be a daddy again.

That, he knew, was his problem. He wasn't sure that he could separate his desire for Georgia from his affection for her children. And the closer he got to all of them, the more difficult it would be. He needed to take a step back, distance himself from the situation.

So that was what he was going to do—right after breakfast.

Chapter Seven

Georgia did feel better after her shower. Fresh and well-rested, and completely in control of her wayward hormones. She could smell bacon and coffee as she made her way down the stairs and inhaled deeply, confirming that Matt had found the tin of French roast her mother kept in the freezer. Georgia had given up caffeine when she found out she was pregnant with Pippa and, more than a year later, it was the one thing she still craved. Unfortunately, Pippa's fussiness and sleeplessness ensured that it was something she continued to avoid.

"Mommy's coming!" She heard Quinn's excited whisper summoning his brother.

Shane appeared at the bottom of the stairs. He was still in his pajamas, but he bent at the waist in an awkward bow. "I'm your eksort."

"And a very handsome escort you are," she told him, and was rewarded with one of his shy smiles.

She took his hand and let him lead her to the dining room where the table had been set with mismatched plates on Mickey Mouse place mats with a centerpiece of wilting dandelions in a drinking glass. Georgia took in the scene in about two seconds, and that quickly, the firm grip she held on her emotions slipped.

During their eight-year marriage, Phillip had taken her to plenty of fancy restaurants with exclusive menus and exemplary service. But no Crepes Suzette or Eggs Benedict had ever looked as appealing to Georgia as the platter of overcooked bacon and slightly mangled French toast on her mother's dining room table.

She swallowed around the lump in her throat. "Somebody's been busy."

"We were!" Quinn said proudly. "We made it together—all of us."

She didn't—couldn't—look at Matt, because she didn't want him to see the tears that swam in her eyes. Instead, she focused on her boys. "Did you really?"

"'Cept for Pippa," Shane told her.

Georgia noticed that Matt had moved the baby's bouncy chair into the dining room so that her mother would be able to keep an eye on her while she had breakfast. Pippa kicked her legs and smiled now, as if she knew that she was the subject of their conversation.

"You did a wonderful job," Georgia said, and because Matt had spearheaded the effort, she lifted her gaze to meet his now. "Thank you."

"You're welcome." He pulled out a chair for her. "Now sit and eat before it gets cold."

The brusque command was exactly what she needed to keep the tears at bay. Following his direction, she sat and loaded up her plate. But before she could sample her own breakfast, she had to cut Shane's French toast. Then she turned to do the same for Quinn, only to find that Matt had already completed the task.

"Eat," he said again, though more gently this time.

So she sliced off a corner of the fried bread and popped it into her mouth.

"Do you like it, Mommy?" She heard the anxiousness in Shane's voice and wondered why it was that her youngest son worried so much about doing everything just right while his sibling always forged ahead without concern. Sometimes it was hard to believe they were brothers, never mind twins.

"It is the best French toast I have ever tasted," she assured him.

"That's 'cuz it's got extra calsum," Quinn told her. "From the shells Shane dropped in the bowl."

She sent a quizzical glance in Matt's direction. He just smiled and lifted one shoulder.

"That must be it," she agreed.

Georgia ate two slices of French toast and three strips of bacon and savored every bite. When the twins had finished their breakfast, they carried their plates and cups to the kitchen and went to wash up.

As she heard them clamoring up the stairs, she turned to Matt. "Thank you," she said again. "Not just for cooking breakfast, but for including the boys in the process."

"It was fun." He said it so simply and matter-of-factly, she knew he meant it.

"Can I ask you something?"

"Sure."

"Why aren't you married?"

The blunt question seemed to take him aback, and he lifted his mug for a sip of coffee before answering. "I was," he finally admitted. "Now I'm divorced."

She winced. "Excuse me while I take my foot out of my mouth."

"No need. The divorce was final more than three years ago. I'm over it. Mostly."

"Mostly?"

He shrugged. "It's always hard to accept the loss of something you really wanted."

A truth that she knew far too well. And though she knew it was a question she had no right to ask and none of her business anyway, she heard herself say, "Do you still love her?"

"No." This time he replied without hesitation and emphasized the response with a shake of his head. "Whatever feelings we'd once had for one another were gone long before the divorce papers were signed."

"Then why aren't you dating anyone?"

"How do you know I'm not?" he challenged.

"Because you spent Saturday night sleeping on my couch."

He smiled at that. "Okay, I'm not."

"Why not?" she asked again.

"I've been out with a few people—I just haven't met anyone who made me want to take the step from a few casual dates to a relationship."

"You're so great with my kids," she told him, "I'd have thought you had half a dozen of your own."

He looked away as he shook his head. "I don't."

And then, in an obvious effort to put an end to that topic of conversation, he reached across the table to tickle Pippa's bare toes. The baby kicked her legs and cooed joyfully in response to his attention.

"When she's happy, she's really happy, isn't she?"

Georgia smiled at her daughter. "Yeah. So much that I sometimes almost forget the hell she's been putting me through over the past few weeks."

He went to the kitchen to refill his mug of coffee, then returned to his seat across from her. "When did you say your mother would be back from Vegas?"

"The original plan was for her to come home yesterday."

"What happened?"

"She decided to go from Nevada to Montana."

He sipped his coffee. "Why Montana?"

"Because that's where her new husband lives."

His brows lifted. "When did she get married?"

"A few days ago."

"You don't approve of the man she married?" he guessed.

"I don't know him," she admitted. "In fact, *she* didn't know him before their eyes met across the baccarat table."

His lips curved. "She's a romantic."

"That's a more favorable word than the one I would have chosen," she admitted.

"I take it you're not a romantic?"

"I like to think I'm a little more…practical." It was so easy to open up to him, to tell him things she hadn't spoken aloud to anyone else—not even either of her sisters. In fact, if not for the way her body hummed whenever he was near, she might have thought that they could be friends.

But the awareness between them was too powerful for her to be completely comfortable in his presence. And when she glanced up to see him studying her, she was suddenly conscious that the awareness was sizzling even now.

"You've never been swept off your feet?" he challenged.

She shook her head. "I don't want a man to sweep me off my feet, although I wouldn't object to a man who was willing to sweep the floors every once in a while."

"I can sweep floors," he told her. "But I don't do windows."

She smiled. "I'll keep that in mind."

"No, you won't."

His blunt contradiction took her aback. "Excuse me?"

"You're so busy trying to do everything yourself that it doesn't occur to you to ask for help every once in a while."

"Maybe," she acknowledged. "But I'm learning to accept it when it's offered."

"That's a start," he said, and rose from the table to begin clearing the rest of the dishes.

Georgia gathered the napkins and cutlery and followed him into the kitchen.

"I don't like to feel inadequate," she finally admitted.

He turned and stared at her. "Are you kidding? You're juggling the responsibilities of a home, a job and raising three kids."

"Which is no more than a lot of women do."

"A lot of women have a partner to share the burden," he pointed out.

She dropped the napkins into the garbage and put the cutlery into the basket in the dishwasher. "Truthfully, even before Phillip died, he wasn't at home enough to share much of the burden." Then, because she didn't want to sound critical of the man she'd married, she felt compelled to add, "He was a good husband and father, but he had an incredibly demanding job. He worked a lot of long hours and weekends."

Too late, she recognized that she was making excuses about her husband to a man whose job as an orthopedic surgeon was undoubtedly more demanding and stressful than that of a trader. And yet, Matt didn't seem to have too much trouble making time for the things he enjoyed. Which was one of the concerns that had plagued her throughout her marriage: If Phillip really wanted to be with her, why had he chosen to spend so much time away from her?

She knew the situation wasn't that black-and-white, that her husband's drive originated from the hard lessons he'd learned in his life. And no matter what she said or did, she couldn't convince him that they should take time to enjoy what they had. It was never enough for Phillip—he wanted to work harder, earn more, buy more. In the end, he worked himself into an early grave, leaving his wife alone and his children without a father.

Her eyes filled again. Obviously she wasn't as in control of her emotions as she'd hoped, but this time she managed to hold the tears in check. "I'm sorry. I'm not usually such an emotional basket case."

"You don't have to apologize to me," he told her.

"Yes, I do. You've been nothing but helpful and kind, and I shouldn't repay you by crying on your shoulder."

"I'm not afraid of a few tears," he promised.

She managed a smile. "You're a good man, Matt Garrett."

"Don't say that too loud," he warned. "I have a reputation to protect."

"Believe me, every time I go into town I hear all about the string of broken hearts you left behind you in high school," she admitted. "Although rumor has it, you've matured into a responsible citizen since then."

"Just a nasty rumor," he assured her. "Don't believe it for a second."

This time, her smile came more easily.

However, before Georgia could respond, Shane ventured into the kitchen. "I built a hosp'al with my bricks," he told her.

Since his trip to the E.R. the previous week, he'd been understandably curious about hospitals and doctors and everything related to the medical profession, so his chosen project was hardly a surprise to Georgia.

"Did you want me to come take a look at it?" she asked.

He nodded, then glanced shyly at Matt and quickly away again. "Dr. Matt, too."

"I'd love to take a look at it," Matt said.

And when he held out his hand to the little boy, Shane hesitated less than half a second before he lifted his own and tucked it inside the doctor's much larger one.

Georgia stood rooted to the spot as fresh tears pricked her eyes. Shane was her introverted son—the little boy who hovered in the background while his brother basked in the spotlight. It was rare for Shane to make any kind of overture, especially to a stranger.

Okay, so Matt wasn't exactly a stranger, but being neighbors for a few weeks didn't make him a close acquaintance, either. Of course, the fact that he'd fixed up the little boy's broken arm might have helped the doctor breach Shane's usual guard, but Georgia suspected her son's ready acceptance of the man had more to do with the man himself. And that was something she was going to have to think about.

When she entered the living room, she saw that Matt was already hunkered down beside the twins to examine their construction projects. He admired the "fine craftsmanship" of Shane's hospital and the "creative design" of Quinn's fire station and commented that there were enough bricks left over to build a whole city.

"Do you want to help us?" Quinn asked.

But Shane was shaking his head before Matt even had a chance to respond.

"Daddies don't play," he reminded his brother, and the matter-of-fact tone of his voice made Georgia's heart ache.

Phillip had loved his children—she had never ever doubted that fact. But she'd never understood, until she'd seen how easily Matt interacted with the boys, how much the twins had missed out on by not having a hands-on dad. She knew they'd felt rebuffed when Phillip had been too tired to show much interest in whatever they were doing, and she'd tried to make it up to them. But no matter what she did, she couldn't be the father they needed.

"Some adults don't have time to play," Matt acknowledged. "But sometimes adults need to play—" he glanced up at Georgia and grinned "—just to prove they're still kids at heart."

"Are you a kid at heart?" Quinn wanted to know.

"Definitely," Matt said, and dug into the bin of bricks to prove it.

Georgia left the boys to their toys and set about cleaning up the kitchen. Matt and the twins had made a pretty good attempt at destroying her mother's stove, but the wielding of a scrubber with some serious muscle eventually succeeding in removing the last traces of egg from the ceramic cooktop.

Still, the cleanup was a small price to pay for everything Matt had done for her. Not only had he let her sleep through the night—and oh, what a glorious indulgence that had been!—he'd helped her boys make breakfast for her. And now, when she thought he would have been more than anxious to get back to his own house and his own life, he was playing with her children, giving them the male attention they needed more desperately than she'd guessed.

But as grateful as she was to Matt, she was also wary. It was obvious to Georgia that the boys already adored their new neighbor and she was worried that they would start to rely on him for too much. Because as great as Matt had been, he wouldn't stick around. Because no man in her life had ever stuck around.

If that was cynical, well, she had reason to be cynical. Her biological father had walked out before she was three years old, and not one of the three stepfathers who had passed through her life had stayed for much longer than that. The few casual and short-lived relationships she'd had as a teenager had done nothing to alter her opinion. It wasn't until she met Phillip that she let herself look to the future and trust that he would be there. But it turned out that she'd been wrong about that.

She knew that her husband hadn't chosen to leave her, and yet, the end result was the same. He was gone and she was alone. Well, not entirely alone. And she would forever be grateful to Phillip for their three beautiful children.

But as happy as they seemed most of the time—discounting Pippa's colic for the moment—she couldn't help worrying about them, about the void in their lives that only a father could fill.

Since Phillip's death, she'd sometimes found herself wondering if Charlotte's string of impetuous unions had been— even in part—an attempt to provide her daughters with a sense of family. Except that her daughters were all grown up now and Charlotte was still following her heart—wherever it might lead.

Georgia had no intention of following that same path, not for any reason and certainly not on the hunt for a substitute father for her children. She wasn't willing to risk her heart again, and she certainly wasn't going to risk theirs.

But as she heard the boys giggling in response to something Matt had said or done in the other room, she had to wonder if it wasn't already too late.

Matt made a conscious effort to keep his distance from his neighbor and her kids over the next week. Work at the hospital kept him busy enough for the first few days—it was his days off that caused him trouble.

In the space of a few weeks, he'd become accustomed to seeing Georgia and her kids almost every day, even if it was only for a few minutes of conversation on the sidewalk. He missed Quinn's endless barrage of questions, Shane's intense focus as he listened to his responses, and the joyful light in Pippa's eyes whenever she saw him. But mostly he missed spending time with Georgia.

Every time he pulled into his driveway, his gaze automatically swung toward the house next door. More than once, he considered stopping by just to see how she was doing and to check if the shadows under her eyes had faded. Too many times, he'd started to head in that direction before his self-preservation instincts kicked in and turned him around again.

Instead, he did some more work in the basement. He hung drywall, taped seams, plastered nail holes. The physical labor kept his hands busy, but it didn't stop him from thinking about Georgia. He spent some time hanging out with his brothers and took a fair bit of ribbing for having struck out with the beautiful blonde next door. It was easier to accept their jabs than admit that he'd walked away from the plate before the first pitch had ever been thrown. He'd been nicknamed Mr.

Clutch in high school, because he'd always played his best in the biggest games. But if this was a game, it was the big leagues, and there was more at stake here than a score.

Georgia wasn't just a beautiful woman, she was the mother of three beautiful children, and they were a package deal. He couldn't take one without the other, and he was afraid to admit how much he wanted the whole package. And so, instead of stepping up to the plate, he'd walked away. Mr. Clutch had been face-to-face with what was potentially the biggest opportunity in his life, and he'd choked. And if his brothers knew the truth, he'd never hear the end of it.

So he let them think that he'd struck out and he tried not to think about Georgia while he listened to Jack boast about the clerk who had propositioned him in the judge's chambers. But when Luke started rambling on about the exploits of the puppies, he couldn't help but remember how totally enthralled the twins had been by them—and that those puppies had played a pivotal role in his first meeting with his neighbors.

It was readily apparent that Luke was trying to convince one or both of his brothers that their lives would not be complete without a canine companion. He'd found good homes for five of them, he admitted, and had decided to keep one for himself, which meant that there were only two left.

Jack, who was hardly ever at the penthouse apartment he paid an astronomical rent for, refused to be swayed. He didn't have the time or the energy that a puppy would demand, not to mention the havoc that an untrained animal would wreak on his designer furniture and hardwood floors.

So Luke gave up on Jack and focused his efforts on his other brother. Matt was able to tune out most of his arguments, but he couldn't forget the awe and excitement on both Quinn's and Shane's faces when they'd seen the puppies in his backyard. And he couldn't forget the stubbornness and longing in Shane's voice when he told his mother, "We *do* want a puppy."

And Matt knew he was fighting a losing battle, because he couldn't refuse anything that would put a smile on the boys' faces—and maybe Georgia's, too.

Chapter Eight

Matt was avoiding her.

Georgia didn't know why, but she knew it was true.

There was a part of her that insisted the "why" didn't matter. All that mattered was that Matt had done what she expected him to do—he'd walked away. But another part insisted that there had to be a reason for his withdrawal. And whether or not he wanted to be friends, they were neighbors, and she didn't want there to be any awkwardness between them when their paths crossed.

More than a week after he'd made her breakfast, on a rare night in which Pippa had actually settled down at a reasonable hour, she waited outside on her back porch to catch him when he came home from work.

She recognized the quiet hum of the engine as he pulled into his driveway, and her heart started to beat just a little bit faster.

She was unaccountably nervous, and already second-guessing her decision to confront him. Maybe he hadn't been avoiding her. Maybe he'd just been busy. Or—and this was a possibility that left her slightly unsettled—maybe he'd done some thinking after their breakfast conversation and had started dating someone. And wouldn't she feel like a complete idiot if she went over there now and he wasn't alone?

She decided that knocking on his door after ten o'clock at night, in the absence of an emergency, might make it look like she'd been waiting for him. And although she had been, she didn't want him to know it. A realization that only made her feel more ridiculous.

She had just turned to go back into the house when the light over Matt's deck came on and he stepped outside. Alone.

He dropped down onto the top step, his forearms on his knees, a beer bottle dangling from his fingertips.

Georgia hesitated. She was pretty good at reading body language, and the weariness in Matt's broad shoulders was visible even in the shadows from fifty feet away. He lifted the bottle to his lips, took a long swallow.

Her decision made, she ducked back into the house to make sure all of the kids were settled and sleeping, then she clipped the baby monitor onto her belt and made her way across the yard.

Despite his preoccupation, he must have heard her footsteps rustling in the grass, because his head came up and he peered into the darkness. She stepped into the circle of light.

"Georgia." She saw surprise flit across his face and heard the pleasure in his voice before he seemed to shut down all of his emotions.

It confirmed her suspicion—he had been avoiding her. For some reason, he was deliberately trying to put distance between them. But right now, she didn't care about any of that. All that concerned her was the look of abject misery on his face.

"Rough day?"

He just nodded.

Though he hadn't invited her to sit down, she did so anyway, settling onto the step beside him. "Can I do anything?"

He shook his head and lifted the bottle to his lips again.

The silence stretched between them, broken only by the chirp of crickets and the occasional hoot of an owl in the distance.

"Want to talk about it?"

He shook his head again. "Not really."

She waited another minute, hoping he would change his mind. He remained silent, and she pushed herself back to her feet.

"But I wouldn't mind if you stayed awhile," he said. "I thought I wanted to be alone, but that's not really a great place right now."

She glanced back at her own house. It wasn't really so far, but she didn't like to be away from her children, even when they were sleeping. "Can you bring your beer over to my step?"

"You want to be able to hear the kids," he guessed.

"I know it seems silly when I have this—" she tapped the monitor clipped on her belt "—but I feel more comfortable being close."

"It doesn't seem silly at all," he told her, rising to his feet. "In fact, I wish more parents were as concerned about their children as you are."

She sensed that his comment was somehow connected to his dark mood, and wondered what had happened at the hospital. He'd already said he didn't want to talk about it, and she didn't want to pry, but she wanted him to know that she was there for him—as he'd been for her when she needed him.

When they were settled on her deck, she decided to open up the channels of communication. Even if they didn't talk about what was bothering him, she thought it might help him just to talk.

"After living in Manhattan for so long, it took me a while

to get used to the sights and sounds outside of the city. It seems so quiet here—" she smiled wryly "—at least it is when Pippa's not screaming. At first, it seemed *too* quiet. But now, I sit out on the porch sometimes just to listen to the crickets, and I feel a sense of peace that I've never known anywhere else."

"I used to take it for granted," he admitted. "Growing up around here, I didn't really know anything else. But the years I spent away at college gave me a new appreciation for this town."

"I never thought I wanted anything like this. But now that I'm here, I can't imagine a more perfect place to raise my kids. I want to watch them run around the backyard, chasing butterflies and playing tag. I want to hear them giggle when they jump into piles of leaves we've raked up together."

"You'll have lots of leaves," he assured her, looking around at the towering maples that lined the back of her property. "Probably more than you want to rake."

"Luckily, I have this wonderful neighbor who's been a very big help with a lot of my outdoor chores."

"It's not as if I enjoy cutting the grass—actually, I do enjoy cutting the grass," he decided, sounding almost surprised by the realization. "The mindless physical work is a welcome diversion after a twelve-hour shift at the hospital."

"Then I'm sure raking leaves in the fall will provide similar benefits."

"And shoveling snow?"

She smiled. "If it works for you, I wouldn't want to deprive you of the pleasure."

"Believe me, there are other—and much more pleasurable—stress releases."

She felt her cheeks color, but refused to follow where his train of thought was trying to lead her. "Talking about the cause of stress also helps," she agreed.

"I wasn't talking about talking," he informed her.

"I know," she admitted. "But it can help. And if you ever decide you do want to talk, I'm happy to listen."

He was silent for a moment, considering her offer. She didn't expect he would actually open up to her. It had been apparent that whatever was bothering him wasn't something he wanted to discuss, but he finally said, "I performed surgery on a four-year-old girl with a spiral fracture tonight."

"What's a spiral fracture?"

"It's a break caused by twisting the bone—a common type of injury suffered by skiers. Their feet are tied into boots locked into skis, and when a ski twists around, the leg automatically twists with it."

"It seems unlikely that she was skiing anywhere around here in May."

"She wasn't. And it wasn't her leg, it was her arm."

It didn't take her long to make the logical jump. "She was abused?"

"The mother is denying it, but X-rays revealed that the child's arm had been broken before and healed improperly because it wasn't treated. So when I fixed the new break, I also had to rebreak and repair the previous injury."

Georgia's eyes filled with tears. "And she's only four?"

He nodded.

"I'd say that was a pretty rough day," she agreed.

"I'm doing okay now."

She touched her lips to his. Softly. Briefly.

He stilled. "What was that for?"

"A kiss to make it better," she said lightly. "Because you're hurting."

Georgia started to draw back, but Matt snaked his arm around her waist and held her close.

"I'm feeling a lot of things right now," he told her. "And hurt isn't anywhere near the top of the list."

Her eyes grew wide, her breath hitched, and he could see the pulse point at the base of her jaw fluttering.

"I think we're getting a little sidetracked," she hedged.

"Are we? Or are we finally back on the track that we've been heading toward all along?"

"How is it possible that we were heading anywhere in the same direction when you've been avoiding me all week?"

His lips curved, just a little. "Did you miss me?"

"Yes," she admitted, sounding piqued. "For almost three weeks, it seemed as if I couldn't step outside my door without tripping over you, and then, just when I got used to you being around—when I started looking forward to you being around—you disappeared."

"If it counts for anything, I missed you, too. All of you."

Her gaze softened. "The boys kept asking me why you didn't want to play with them anymore."

"I'm sorry," he said, and meant it.

"I don't want you to be sorry, I just want to know if it was something I said or did."

"No," he assured her. "It's all on me."

"Why?"

"Because I knew that if I didn't put some space between us I wouldn't be able to stop myself from doing this."

She knew he was going to kiss her. He could see the conflict in her eyes—the war between wariness and wanting. Not wanting to give her another second to worry or wonder, he dipped his head.

She held herself immobile and kept her eyes open, as if she was willing to tolerate his efforts but was determined not to participate. He kept his gaze locked on hers, his hand splayed against her lower back, as he brushed his mouth against hers. A soft sigh sounded in her throat and her eyelids flickered, just a little, proving she wasn't as immune to him as she wanted to believe.

Since the end of his marriage, he'd been with other women,

but sex without intimacy had left him feeling oddly unful-filled. The problem with meaningless flings, he'd quickly dis-covered, was that they were meaningless. Truthfully, Georgia was the first woman he'd been sincerely attracted to in a long time, the first woman with whom he could imagine himself having a relationship rather than a one-night stand.

He also realized that he was probably thinking further ahead than she was. She was a young widow with three kids, and he knew he would have to take things slow until he was sure she wanted the same thing he did. Right now, she didn't seem to know what she wanted—but at least he knew he had her full attention.

His mouth cruised over hers again, savoring her texture and flavor. Her lips were soft, lush and deliciously seductive. He traced the shape with the tip of his tongue, and swallowed her soft sigh as her eyelids finally drifted shut.

He took his time, teasing her lips further apart, testing her response. She lifted her hands to his chest, and he half expected her to push him away. He would have been disap-pointed, but not really surprised. But then her hands slid over his shoulders to link behind his head, and she pressed herself closer, so that her breasts were crushed against his chest, her hips pressed against his.

She had to know he was aroused—there was no way she could think the erection throbbing inside the front of his pants was anything else—but she didn't pull away. His hand slid under the hem of her T-shirt, skimmed up her back. She shiv-ered in response to his touch on her bare skin and moaned in pleasure. It was that low, sexy sound deep in her throat—proof that she wanted this every bit as much as he did—that nearly undid him.

He'd wanted to kiss her—and now that he had, he wanted so much more. But he'd promised himself that he would take things slow, which was a lot harder to do than he'd expected with his heart pounding so fiercely inside his chest and his blood pulsing hotly in his veins.

He eased his lips from hers but kept his arms around her to ensure she couldn't flee. Because he could see, even in eyes still clouded with desire, the first hint of panic beginning to set in. And her words, when she spoke, confirmed her worry.

"That was a really bad idea," she told him.

"I have to disagree."

"We're neighbors and, hopefully, friends."

"I'd say that's a good start to any relationship."

She shook her head. "I'm not looking for a relationship."

"Because you're still grieving for your husband," he guessed.

"Because I need to focus on my kids," she clarified. "And they don't leave me enough time or energy for any kind of romantic involvement."

"Okay—we'll put a hold on the romance portion of things."

"That includes the kissing portion."

"You kissed me first," he pointed out.

"Not like that," she protested.

"You didn't like the way I kissed you?"

She rolled her eyes. "Is your ego so fragile that you need to fish for compliments?"

"So you *did* enjoy kissing me," he surmised.

"It seems you're a man of many talents, Dr. Garrett."

"That kiss barely scratched the surface."

"That's what I'm afraid of," she admitted.

"There's something between us," he told her.

"It's a basic physical attraction."

"It's more than that."

She shook her head again. "I won't let it be anything more than that."

He smiled. "You think it's your decision to make?"

"Yes." Her tone was firm and unequivocal. "I make my

own choices, and I'm *not* getting romantically involved with you."

But he caught the slightest hint of desperation in her tone now and was torn between wanting to offer reassurance and challenge her conviction. Instead, he opted for a casual shrug. "Okay."

Her gaze narrowed suspiciously. "Okay?"

"You've obviously made up your mind," he acknowledged.

"I have," she confirmed. "And I appreciate that you're respecting my decision."

"I do," he agreed. "But that doesn't mean I'm not going to do everything in my power to change your mind."

"You'll be wasting your time," she warned.

He shrugged again. "I figure it's my time to waste."

Her sigh was filled with exasperation. "But why would you want to waste your time with me when there are any number of women in this town who would be thrilled to be with you?"

He grinned. "Any number, huh?"

"As if you didn't know that everywhere you and your brothers go, female heads swivel in your direction."

"It's been like that since high school," he admitted. "It's a curse."

"And how long ago was high school?" she asked, in what seemed to him an abrupt shift in the conversation.

"Almost twenty years," he admitted. "Why?"

"Because in the past few weeks, every time I go into town someone refers to me as the young mother from New York City who moved in next to Dr. Garrett—conveniently overlooking the fact that I was here before you. And on top of that, I've had at least half a dozen people tell me about the grand slam home run you knocked out of the park in the bottom of the thirteenth inning to bring home the district championship."

"Only half a dozen?" He frowned. "I guess my legend is truly fading."

She just shook her head.

"Did you ever play baseball?" he asked.

"Just in gym class at school or the occasional pick-up game at the park when I was a kid."

"Are you any good?"

"I was never the first one picked for a team, but I wasn't the last, either."

"Because we play a co-ed charity softball tournament on the Fourth of July and I'm putting together a team, if you're interested."

She shook her head. "I'm not playing any games with you—you're completely out of my league."

"I got to first base with you tonight," he teased. "And you didn't seem to have any trouble keeping up."

Her cheeks flushed. "It won't happen again."

He just grinned. "I guess time will tell."

"Matt," she said warningly.

"I'll see you soon," he promised.

His step was much lighter as he made his way across the grass to his own house, and he knew the sizzling kiss he'd shared with Georgia was only part of the reason. Another—maybe even bigger part—was just being with her.

He hadn't appreciated how much he'd missed having someone to open up to at the end of a difficult day until she'd sat down beside him and invited him to talk. And she not only listened to him ramble about the stress of his day, she empathized with him. And then she'd kissed him.

True, it had been little more than a casual brush of her lips against his, but he figured it had to mean something that she'd made the first move.

He figured it meant even more that she hadn't balked—at least not too much—when he made the second.

A few days later, Matt had just walked into the house after a visit to his brother when his phone rang. Picking up the receiver, he was pleased to hear Georgia's voice on the other end of the line, and even more pleased when she said, "Have you had dinner yet?"

"No," he admitted.

"Because we just ordered a party tray of pizza and thought you might want to come over to share it with us."

"Why did you order a party tray?"

"Because it was the special of the day," she told him. "And because you've cooked for me—twice now—so it only seems fair for me to return the favor. I didn't actually make the pizza, but I thought I would earn some points by providing the meal."

"You're the only one keeping score," he said.

"Maybe, but the boys would like to share their pizza with you, if you don't have other plans."

Adding the kids to the equation obliterated any resistance. "I don't have other plans," he admitted. "And pizza sounds great, but would it be too much trouble if I asked you to bring it over here?"

"Not too much trouble," she told him, "but likely a lot of fingerprints you'll have to clean up around the house after."

"I'm not worried about fingerprints," he assured her.

"Then we'll be over in five."

As much as Georgia tried to convince herself that taking pizza over to Matt's house was just being neighborly, she knew that wasn't entirely true. One kiss had changed everything.

One unbelievably hot, mind-numbing, toe-curling kiss.

Since Matt had planted his lips on hers, all kinds of lustful thoughts had taken root in her mind. Thankfully, she wasn't just taking pizza but three kids, too, and she was grateful for the buffer that their presence would provide.

Maybe her hormones had been stirred up by that kiss, but she was confident that she still had enough self-control not to jump Matt's bones in front of her children. Because she'd meant what she'd said to him—she had neither the energy nor the inclination for a romantic relationship, even if she was suddenly, achingly aware that it had been more than a year since she'd had sex.

When Matt stepped out onto the back deck, the twins raced toward him, Shane, predictably, lagging a few feet behind his brother.

"We've got pizza!" Quinn announced.

"I hope it has pepperoni," Matt said, smiling as he took the long, flat box from him.

"Lots and lots of pepperonis," Shane chimed in. "'Cuz they're my favorite."

Matt winked at him. "Mine, too."

He glanced at Georgia, who had Pippa strapped against her chest, a diaper bag in one hand and a plastic bag in the other, then gave the pizza box back to Quinn with instructions to put it on the table in the dining room.

"Let me give you a hand," he said.

"Thanks."

"What have you got in here?" He took the grocery bag.

"Paper plates and napkins, veggies and dip, juice boxes for the boys."

"I do have plates and napkins."

"It didn't seem right to bring dinner then leave you with dirty dishes."

"I would have let you wash them," he assured her.

She smiled at his teasing, relieved that there didn't seem to be any evidence of the awkwardness she'd feared. "This way I don't have to."

When Georgia got Pippa settled on a blanket with her favorite toys, she saw that the boys were already seated at the table, eager to dig into dinner. She put a slice on each of their plates and added a few veggies—broccoli and carrots for Quinn and cucumber and red pepper for Shane.

Quinn wrinkled his nose. "Don't like veggies."

"Yes, you do," she reminded him.

He ignored the vegetables and picked up his pizza.

Matt reached into the box to take a couple of pizza slices. Then he looked at the boys' plates and, with more resignation than enthusiasm, he added some carrot sticks and cucumber slices. Georgia was grateful, because she knew that neither of the boys would protest any further about eating their vegetables if Dr. Matt was eating them, too.

She had just bit into her second slice of pizza when she heard a noise emanating from behind a closed pocket door that led to Matt's kitchen. She'd noticed the closed door earlier but had assumed he had a sink full of dirty dishes he didn't want guests to see. When the noise—a whimper?—came again, she suspected that he was hiding something much more significant than unwashed plates.

The boys were already finished eating—including their vegetables—when Matt confirmed her suspicions.

"Do you guys want to see what I've got in the kitchen?" he asked them.

"Is it ice cream?" Quinn asked hopefully.

"Sorry," Matt said. "It's not ice cream."

"I like ice cream," Shane told him.

He ruffled the little boy's hair, and Shane smiled shyly in response to the casually affectionate gesture. "Then I'll make sure I have ice cream for next time."

"Whatcha got this time?" Quinn wanted to know.

In response, Matt started to open the door. He'd barely slid the barrier a few inches when a tiny bundle of fur wriggled through the narrow opening. He held his breath, not entirely sure that this surprise would go over as well as he'd anticipated. Not that he doubted the twins' response, but their mother's reaction wasn't quite so easy to gauge.

"A puppy!" Quinn announced.

The boys were already on the floor, fussing over it. Georgia pushed away from the table to join her sons.

"Are you pet-sitting for your brother?" she asked Matt.

"No," he admitted.

Her eyes widened. "He's yours?"

"Actually—" he opened the door farther and picked up a second puppy "—they're both mine."

"Two?"

He shrugged. "Well, they were the only two left, and they're brothers."

She looked up at him, her blue eyes reflecting equal parts amusement and approval, and he felt as if his heart had actually swelled inside of his chest.

"You really are a softie, aren't you?" she said.

"I'm thinking 'sucker' is more accurate," he admitted, and bent to put the second puppy down on the floor with the first.

"What are their names?" Quinn wanted to know.

"I only just brought them home," Matt said. "I haven't had time to give them names yet."

"You hafta pick good names," Quinn told him. "Not like Fluffy or Buttercup." He wrinkled his nose in obvious disapproval of such choices.

"No Fluffy or Buttercup," Matt promised solemnly.

Shane giggled as a tiny pink tongue swiped his chin. "Finnigan," he said.

Matt's brows lifted, as surprised by the unusual suggestion as the fact that Shane had offered it.

"Finnigan?" he queried.

"And Frederick," Quinn declared.

"They're characters on a television show," she explained.

Shane looked up at him. "They're brothers."

"In that case," Matt said, "I guess the only question now is, which one is Finnigan and which one is Frederick?"

The boys were in complete agreement about the assignment of the names, and it warmed Matt's heart to see their enthusiasm about the puppies. Then he looked up and saw Georgia looking at him, and the small smile on her lips warmed every other part of him.

Chapter Nine

Since bringing the puppies home, Matt had more than a few moments when he wondered, *What the hell was I thinking?* When he saw Quinn and Shane fussing over Finnigan and Frederick, he understood that he had been thinking of this exact moment. Not that he'd brought the puppies home just to score points with the little boys, but he couldn't deny that their apparent affection for the animals had been a factor in his decision.

"A tree house and puppies," Georgia mused. "My kids are going to be spending more time in your backyard than their own."

"That's okay with me," he said, dropping his voice so that the boys couldn't hear him. "Especially if their mom comes with them."

She picked up Pippa, who had begun to fuss. "Are you flirting with me?"

"Obviously I'm not doing a very good job of it if you have to ask."

"I just don't know why you'd bother when you know I have no intention of getting involved with you."

"I know that's what you said," he acknowledged.

She lifted a brow. "You don't think I meant it?"

"I think I can change your mind."

"I think you should take the puppies and the boys outside while I clear up in here," she countered, in an obvious attempt to change the topic of conversation.

"Don't worry about clearing up, I'll take care of it later."

"Okay, then, why don't you take the puppies and boys outside so I can feed Pippa?"

And he finally grasped that she hadn't been trying to change the topic so much as she'd been trying to get him out of the house so she could have some privacy. Not that he had any objections to the sight of a woman nursing her child, but he understood that Georgia might be a little self-conscious about baring her breast in front of him, especially now that she knew he wanted her in his bed.

"Matt?" she prompted.

"Take the boys and puppies outside," he agreed. "I can do that."

So he did, and he sat on the deck watching as the boys and their canine companions ran and jumped and wrestled in the grass. He tried to remember what Liam had been like at the same age, then felt a pang deep in his heart when he recalled that his son had been gone from his life before he'd celebrated his third birthday.

Matt shoved the painful memories to the back of his mind. He'd spent far too much time wishing for what he'd lost and wondering what might have been. When he'd finally sold his condo and bought this house on Larkspur Drive, he'd promised himself that he was finished living in the past and vowed to focus on the future. Now he found himself hoping that his future might include his beautiful neighbor and her three kids.

But convincing Georgia that she wanted the same thing was going to take some work.

Much to Quinn's and Shane's disappointment, the puppies tired out long before they did.

"How come he doesn't wanna play with me no more?" Quinn asked, stroking the soft fur of the puppy that had fallen asleep in his lap.

"He's just tired out right now," Matt told him. "He's still just a baby, even younger than your sister."

"Are the puppies gonna wake you up at night?"

"I hope not," he said fervently.

"What if they do?" Quinn pressed, followed by Shane's question, "Are they gonna sleep in your bed?"

"No." His response to the latter question was firm.

"I'd let him sleep with me," Shane said. "If I had a puppy."

"I think your mom might have something to say about that," Matt told him.

"She lets me sleep in her bed when I have a bad dream," Quinn said.

Matt didn't think that excuse was going to get *him* access to Georgia's bed, but he hadn't given up hope that he would be there. Preferably sooner rather than later, because he was getting tired of cold showers.

"I wish I had a puppy," Shane said wistfully.

"A puppy's a lot of work," Matt told him. "And your mom already has a lot to do, taking care of you and your brother and your sister."

"I'd take care of the puppy. She wouldn't hafta do nothin'," Quinn vowed.

Matt couldn't help but smile in response to the fervent promise that countless boys had used on their mothers over the years—mostly ineffectively.

"I think you'd have a better chance of convincing your

mother if she saw you were willing to help out with Finnigan and Frederick every once in a while."

"I'll help every day," Quinn promised.

"Me, too," Shane chimed in.

"Well, you'll have to check with your mom on that," Matt told them. "But if you can, I'd appreciate it."

"Does that mean we're friends again?" Quinn asked.

Not too much surprised Matt, but this question did. "I didn't know we stopped being friends."

"You stopped coming over."

The little boy's matter-of-fact statement made him appreciate that you could fool some people some of the time, but you couldn't fool a four-year-old. Obviously Georgia wasn't the only member of the Reed family who had recognized his avoidance.

"There was a lot of stuff going on at the hospital," he hedged.

"Did you fix more broken arms?"

He nodded. "A couple of those. A broken femur—" he tapped the little boy's thigh "—that's the bone in there, a hip replacement, some knee arthroscopies."

"What's arrow-scope-peas?"

Matt smiled. "Arthroscopy," he said again, enunciating the word more carefully. "It's an operation that uses a tiny camera to see what's inside the joint so that the doctor can fix whatever's wrong through little cuts in the skin."

Quinn drew back in horror. "You cut people?"

"Only when necessary," Matt assured him.

"You didn't cut me," Shane said.

"Because the X-ray let me see that the bone was only broken, not out of position, so we just had to put a cast on your arm to make sure the bone wouldn't move before it was healed."

The little boy considered this explanation for a minute,

then he said, "Mommy says we can't go back in the tree house till my cast is gone."

"She's probably worried that you might fall again."

"Maybe you could talk to her," Quinn suggested hopefully. "She'd listen to you, 'cuz you're a doctor."

"Nice try, but doctor's orders do not override Mommy's rules," Georgia said, stepping out onto the deck.

Matt noticed that she'd strapped on the infant carrier again and Pippa, obviously sated and happy, was snuggled inside.

Quinn let out a long-suffering sigh. "It was worth a try."

"And you get an A for effort," she told him. "But you don't go back to the tree house until *I* say so."

Shane pouted silently.

"Now take the puppies inside," she said. "It's time for us to go home so that you guys can have a bath before bed."

"Don't wanna bath," Shane said.

"I know, because you're a four-year-old boy and dirt is your best friend, but you're going to have a bath anyway."

Shane shook his head. "Quinn's my best friend, and then Finnigan and Frederick."

"Then you shouldn't mind getting rid of the dirt," Georgia said dryly, while Matt tried not to laugh at the little boy's solemn statement.

Quinn stood up, careful not to disturb the sleeping puppy in his arms. "It's okay," he told his brother. "We can come back and see the puppies tomorrow. Dr. Matt said so."

"I said *if* it was okay with your mom," he interjected quickly, before Georgia had to remind her sons again about doctor's orders and Mommy's rules.

Shane looked up at her pleadingly. "Can we, Mommy?"

"We'll figure that out tomorrow."

Quinn's lower lip jutted out.

"But if that's not acceptable, I can say 'no' now," she suggested.

Matt had to admire the quickness with which the boy

sucked his lip back so that it was in a normal position again before she'd even finished speaking.

"I guess that's acceptable then?" she prompted.

Both boys nodded as they carried the puppies back into the house.

Georgia waited until they were out of earshot before she said, "It looks like we'll be seeing you tomorrow."

"I'm already looking forward to it."

He stayed out on the deck, watching as they made their way back to their own house and wishing that they could have stayed. Not just for a little bit longer, but maybe even forever. Because somehow, over the past few weeks, he'd fallen head over heels for Georgia and her three adorable children.

He winced as tiny claws pressed down on his bare foot. He glanced down to see Finnigan—or was it Frederick?—trying to climb up his leg, wanting some attention. He scooped the puppy up and tucked him into the crook of his arm. Almost as soon as he had done so, his canine sibling appeared.

As Matt retreated back into the house with the puppies in his arms, he was consoled by the fact that he wouldn't be completely alone tonight.

Georgia didn't get much sleep that night, and she couldn't even blame Pippa because her baby girl had actually slept for almost five hours straight. Unfortunately, even while Pippa was sleeping, Georgia was tossing and turning—thinking about Matt Garrett. *Wanting* Matt Garrett.

She wasn't used to having her hormones all stirred up, especially not by someone who wasn't her husband. She wasn't sure what to do about it, or even if she wanted to do anything at all.

Matt was stirring her up on purpose—of that she had no doubt. To an outside observer, his treatment of her had been nothing but circumspect throughout the evening. He certainly hadn't done anything obvious or inappropriate. But when he led her to the table, he placed a guiding hand at the small of her back. When he sat in his own chair, he let his knee brush against her legs. When he wanted to get her attention, he'd touch a hand to hers. And every single touch, no matter how brief or casual, made her pulse jolt and her body yearn.

She didn't know if her response was specific to her neighbor or just a symptom of the fact that she'd been celibate for so long. She suspected it was specific to Matt, because no one—before or since her marriage—had ever affected her the way he did, and she didn't have the first clue what to do about it.

She could sleep with him. That seemed the most obvious and simple answer. *If you have an itch, scratch it,* Charlotte was fond of saying. But Georgia and her mother often had differing philosophies.

And there were a lot of reasons for Georgia not to get involved with her neighbor—one of them being that he was her neighbor. If they hooked up and things didn't work out, she still had to live next door to him.

But the primary consideration was her three children. Not only did their presence complicate the situation and decrease the likelihood of finding any alone time, she had to consider how any kind of romantic involvement would affect them. She didn't doubt that Quinn and Shane would be in favor of a relationship between their mother and "Dr. Matt" because they loved hanging out with him. But if things didn't work out, how difficult would it be for them to lose that connection? They'd been devastated by Phillip's death. For weeks after the funeral, they'd been plagued by nightmares; and for several more months, they'd frequently awakened Georgia in the night just to make sure she wasn't dead, too. They'd already grown so close to Matt, and she couldn't imagine what another loss would do to them. And because she didn't know, she wouldn't let herself risk the possibility of starting something that might only end with heartbreak—for her children and herself.

But what if things *did* work out?

Georgia wasn't sure she was willing to consider that possibility; she didn't want to look too far ahead. She didn't want a relationship—even if she was increasingly tempted to explore the chemistry between them.

As for what Matt wanted...she wasn't entirely sure. He'd admitted that he was attracted to her, so she was pretty sure he would go along with the sex thing. She just didn't know what—if anything—he wanted beyond that.

But the more time that passed, the more she thought about him, the more she wanted him. For a lot more reasons than the fact that his proximity made her all hot and bothered.

He was a good man. She knew that not all doctors had chosen the profession for benevolent reasons. But she didn't doubt that Matt had. It was his nature to help people, whether that meant fixing a broken bone or performing lawn maintenance or late-night taxi service. She knew he wasn't perfect—if he was, he wouldn't still be single. And while she couldn't deny a fair amount of curiosity about his marriage and divorce, she didn't feel it was her place to ask when they weren't really anything more than neighbors—even if the air fairly crackled whenever they were together.

But the physical attraction aside, he was innately kind and considerate, and he was great with kids.

He paid attention to her children. He looked at them when they were talking to him, he listened and responded to what they said, and he seemed to genuinely enjoy being with them. That alone was almost enough for Georgia to fall in love with him.

And the knowledge that she could fall in love with him was what terrified her.

If she thought she could scratch the proverbial itch and be done with it, she might have been more willing to take that next step. But she worried that scratching would only make the itch more intense—because the more time she spent with Matt Garrett, the more she wanted to be with him.

It turned out that the answer to Quinn's question was a resounding yes—the puppies did wake Matt up in the night. Three times, in fact. And each time that he was up, he noticed that there was a light shining in Pippa's room, so he knew Georgia was up, too.

A couple of times, he saw her shadow through the curtains as she passed in front of the window. He could barely keep his eyes open on night one with the puppies, so he could only imagine how exhausted she must be after more than four months of sleepless nights.

When he'd asked, Georgia told him that Pippa was sleeping better and her bouts of fussiness were less frequent and intense. Since Matt couldn't hear the baby crying, he figured that was probably true, but he still didn't think Georgia was getting much sleep.

A suspicion that was proven by the shadows under her eyes when he knocked on her door late the following morning.

"I was just going to take Finn and Fred for a walk and thought the boys might want to come with me," he said.

"We want to," Quinn responded before his mother could.

"Pippa's just gone down for a nap," Georgia told him.

"Why don't you do the same?" Matt suggested.

"You're going to take two boys and two puppies by yourself?"

"Don't I look capable?"

"It's not your ability I doubt, it's your desire."

Even before his lips curved, her cheeks filled with color as she realized how her statement could be interpreted.

"I thought we answered that question definitively the other night," he teased.

"I meant your willingness to take a walk with two boys and two puppies."

"I'm willing—and capable," he assured her. "And we won't be gone too long."

She looked down at the hopeful faces of her sons. "Go get your shoes."

The twins raced down the hall to the closet, and Matt took advantage of their temporary absence to dip his head and kiss their mother. It was a brief touch, barely more than a brush of his lips against hers. Certainly not enough to satisfy him, but enough to thoroughly fluster Georgia.

Before she could say anything, the boys were back.

"We're ready," Quinn said.

Matt took each boy by the hand. "Then let's go get the puppies."

Georgia intended to take advantage of the boys' absence to get some work done. But after checking her email and replying to the messages that needed replies, she found herself struggling to concentrate. And it was Matt Garrett's fault—even when he wasn't around, she couldn't seem to get him out of her mind.

She'd always been extremely focused and never, in her entire life, had she let herself be so easily and completely distracted by a man. Not that she was "letting" herself be distracted now—she just couldn't stop thinking about him.

And it wasn't just because she had let the twins go off with him. In fact, she wasn't the least bit worried about her children with Matt, because he'd proven that he was more than capable of looking after the boys and she absolutely trusted that he would do so.

But while she wasn't worried about her children, she was worried about herself. Because somehow, Matt Garrett had taken hold of her heart and she didn't have the first clue what to do about it.

The slap of the screen door against its frame jolted her back to the present.

"Mommy?"

"In the dining room," she said.

Quinn raced into the room, his brother on his heels and Matt right behind them, looking completely at ease with her children—and far too handsome and sexy for her peace of mind.

"We tired the puppies out," her son told her proudly. "Dr. Matt had to carry them home 'cuz they were too tired to walk."

"Then you guys must be pretty tired, too," she said, ruffling her son's hair.

"Nuh-uh," Shane said. "We're goin' for ice cream."

She lifted a brow. "Ice cream?"

"You haven't heard of it?" Matt teased. "It's a frozen dairy dessert."

She rolled her eyes. "I've heard of it. In fact, I've actually tasted it once or twice before."

"But have you experienced the bliss of Walton's ice cream?"

Georgia shook her head, thinking that there were a lot of blisses she would willingly experience with this man.

"You haven't really had ice cream until you've had Walton's," he told her.

She forced herself to ignore the clamoring of her suddenly hyperactive hormones. "It's almost time for lunch." She felt compelled to point this out to all of them.

"Walk on the wild side," he suggested, "and eat your dessert first for a change."

The low, sexy tone of his voice raised goose bumps on her flesh, but she ignored the physiological response of her body and focused on more practical matters.

"If the boys have ice cream now, they won't eat their lunch."

"A kiddie cone," Matt cajoled.

"Pleeeease," Quinn and Shane chorused.

She believed it was important for the boys to understand that there were rules to follow, but she wasn't so rigid that she would never bend those rules. And though she was tempted to bend this time, she shook her head. "Pippa isn't up from her nap yet, and when she wakes up she's going to need to be changed and fed."

As if on cue, the sound of Pippa babbling and cooing came through the baby monitor.

"Pippa's up," Quinn told her.

"It sounds like she is," Georgia agreed.

"Ice cream?" Shane said hopefully.

"Let me take care of Pippa, and then we'll go for ice cream."

Because that was one blissful experience she could justify, but personal fantasies about the doctor next door she could not.

Chapter Ten

When Matt had agreed to take the remaining two puppies from his brother, he'd worried about how much time and attention they would need. Luke had somehow convinced him that having two puppies would be less work than one because they would be company for one another and content to play together. After a few days, Matt had found that was generally true. He'd also discovered that Finnigan and Frederick were never happier than when they were playing with Quinn and Shane—and the twins seemed equally enamored of their furry friends.

It was, to Matt's mind, a win-win situation. Or maybe it was a win-win-win situation, because when the boys were hanging out with the puppies, it gave him an excuse to hang out with Georgia. Since keeping a distance hadn't stopped him from thinking about her, he'd abandoned his campaign of avoidance for a new tack—spend as much time with her as possible in the hope that she would want him as much as he wanted her.

He knew she wasn't there yet, but he knew she was thinking about him. He saw it in the awareness in her eyes when he touched her, heard it in the huskiness of her voice when he stood close, and he'd definitely tasted it in the sweet softness of her lips when he kissed her.

Yeah, she was thinking about him, and hopefully—with just a little bit of a nudge in the right direction—she would be thinking about a lot more.

As they made their way toward Walton's, Georgia carrying Pippa in her baby carrier and Matt pulling the twins in their wagon, he considered that today just might be the day to give her that nudge.

"How did I not know this place was here?" she wondered, taking in the long row of freezers, the candy toppings displayed in glass containers and the list of menu items that stretched across the long wall behind the counter.

"You're new in town," he noted.

And because it was her first visit, she took her time surveying the offerings while the boys raced back and forth, pointing out one flavor then another.

Matt gave her a few minutes before he asked, "What looks good to you?"

"Everything," she said, and then she sighed. "But I'm going to have to pass."

He shook his head. "You can't come into Walton's and walk away from the counter empty-handed."

"Is that written into the local bylaws?"

"If it's not, it should be," he told her.

"I followed your advice and cut out dairy and it seems to have helped alleviate some of Pippa's colic. So as tempted as I am, I'm not going to sacrifice my sleep for a brief taste of sinful decadence."

But he heard the regret in her voice, and couldn't resist teasing, "Sinful decadence is the best reason I can think of to sacrifice sleep—but I'm not talking about ice cream."

The flush in her cheeks confirmed that she knew what he was talking about. "These days, I'm not sacrificing my sleep for *anything*."

He just grinned and turned her toward the freezer on the other side of the counter. "Nondairy sorbets."

She nibbled on her bottom lip, obviously tempted, as was he—but not for ice cream.

He might have been teasing when he'd responded to her comment about sinful decadence, but his desire for her was very real. There were all kinds of deliciously sinful things he wanted to do to her body, all kinds of decadent pleasures he wanted to share with her.

"The orange mango looks really good," Georgia finally said. "But so does the piña colada…and the raspberry…and the lemon lime."

"Raspberry gets my vote," Matt told her. "Or you could go for the sampler bowl and try three different flavors."

She shook her head. "I'll stick with the orange mango for today. I have a feeling the boys are going to want to come back here on a regular basis."

Matt ordered an orange mango cone for her and a raspberry for himself, while Georgia tried to help the boys narrow down their choices. Through the bits and pieces of conversation that he overheard, it sounded as if Quinn was vacillating between chocolate chip cookie dough, chocolate fudge brownie and chocolate peanut butter cup. Apparently the kid really liked chocolate. Surprisingly, Shane seemed to have already made up his mind.

"Two kiddie cones," Georgia finally told the teen behind the counter. "One chocolate peanut butter cup and one vanilla."

Vanilla? To Matt's way of thinking, that was almost as bad as not having any ice cream at all.

"Wait." He held up a hand to the server and turned his attention to Shane. "Vanilla? Really?"

Shane looked down at his feet, but he nodded.

"That's your absolute favorite flavor?"

"I like 'nilla," he said. But the quiet statement was hardly a rousing endorsement.

"Better than cotton candy or bubble gum or—" Matt looked at the Kids' Favorites labels "—superhero or alien invasion?"

That got the kid's attention.

Shane lifted his head. "What's alien 'vasion?"

Matt boosted him up so that he could see into the freezer case.

"It's lime sherbet with blueberry swirl and fruit juice gummies," the server said, then winked at Shane. "And one of my favorites."

The little boy nibbled on his bottom lip, considering.

"You want to give it a try or do you want to stick with vanilla?" Matt challenged.

The server scooped a tiny spoon into the bin and offered Shane a taste.

He looked to his mother for permission before accepting the spoon and cautiously sliding it between his lips. He hesitated for another minute, then pointed to the green ice cream. "That one. Please."

They decided to eat inside in the hope that Quinn and Shane might be able to finish their cones before they melted. Georgia seemed worried that, despite the sample, Shane would change his mind about alien invasion. But after a few more tentative licks, he pronounced it "the best ice cream ever" and she finally turned her attention to her sorbet—and had Matt's attention completely riveted on her.

Quinn gobbled his ice cream, as if he was afraid someone might try to take it from him. Shane—happy to have broadened his flavor horizons—worked at his cone methodically and steadily. Georgia savored every lick, closing her eyes and humming in appreciation as the sorbet melted on her tongue.

She somehow turned the consumption of a single scoop of sorbet into a blissful, sensual experience, making Matt wonder: If she was this passionate about dessert, how much passion would she exhibit in the bedroom?

"Doncha like it?"

Shane's question snapped Matt out of his reverie and back to the present.

"'Cuz you can share mine if you don't like yours," the little boy offered.

Matt shook his head. "Thanks, but I think I'll leave it up to you to gobble up all the alien invaders."

Shane smiled at that and took a bite of his cone.

The boys finished quickly—probably because they had as much ice cream on their hands and faces as in their bellies, the result of Quinn deciding to dig a peanut butter cup out of his cone in exchange for one of the gummy aliens from his brother's—and Georgia sent them to the washroom to clean up.

Though he knew it would only increase his own torture, he convinced Georgia to sample his raspberry, and nearly groaned aloud as he watched the tip of her tongue lap delicately at the sorbet. But when he tried to finagle a taste of her orange mango, she refused.

"You said the raspberry's the best," she explained. "Which implies that you've already tried every flavor."

It was true, but her obvious enjoyment of the orange mango made him suspect that it might taste better than he'd remembered. But since she wasn't sharing, he leaned over and touched his mouth to hers.

"Mmm." He swiped his tongue over her bottom lip. "Maybe that is better than the raspberry."

She drew back and when he shifted, as if to kiss her again, she stuck the cone between them to keep him at a distance.

He nibbled at her sorbet; she narrowed her gaze.

"You think you're clever, don't you? Tricking me into letting you taste my sorbet."

"The sorbet was my consolation prize—what I really wanted was a taste of you."

"You got that, too, didn't you?"

His gaze dropped to her mouth. "Not nearly enough."

Georgia and Matt finished their cones and they headed back outside. Pippa was still comfortably snuggled in her baby carrier, so as soon as the boys had climbed back into their wagon, they were ready to head out. She automatically reached for the handle of the wagon, only to find that Matt had beat her to it.

He kept telling her that she didn't have to do everything on her own, and Georgia was starting to believe it. But as nice as it was to have someone around who was willing to lend a helping hand, Matt had done so much for her already and Georgia didn't want to let herself rely on him too much.

She'd always prided herself on her independence. If she didn't count on anyone else, then she wouldn't ever be disappointed. But she found that she was starting to depend on Matt, not just because he helped her out in so many ways, but for his company and conversation. She liked having him around, just knowing he was there.

And the more time she spent with Matt, the more that growing attachment concerned her. And it wasn't only her own feelings that she was worried about.

"You're awfully quiet," Matt noted. "Something on your mind?"

She shook her head, unwilling to admit that *he* was the reason for her preoccupation. But after a moment, she realized there was something else bothering her, too.

"Shane always has vanilla," she said.

"Did I overstep by suggesting that he try something different?"

She shook her head again. "No. I'm just surprised that he was willing. His dad was strictly a vanilla guy," she admitted. "And I think one of the reasons Shane always had vanilla was a subconscious attempt to be more like his dad."

That maybe having something in common would cause Phillip to pay more attention to him. But of course she didn't say that part out loud. "He's always been so painfully shy, so much quieter than Quinn. Part of it, I suspect, is being Quinn's brother. My sister likes to joke that Shane doesn't talk much because he never has a chance to get a word in edgewise."

Matt glanced back at the wagon, where Quinn was entertaining his brother with a running commentary of one thing or another. "There might be something to that theory," he mused.

"Maybe," she acknowledged with a smile. "But he's talked more to you in the past three weeks than he's talked to anyone else in the past three months."

"Is that good or bad?" he asked cautiously.

"It's good." Now she looked over her shoulder at the boys in the wagon. "Spending time with you has been good for both of them."

"And yet you say that as if it's a bad thing," he noted.

She sighed. "I just don't want them to start expecting too much, depending on you."

"Because I'm not dependable?"

"Because they're not your responsibility."

"Why does it have to be about responsibility?" he demanded. "Why can't I just hang out with you and your kids because I enjoy hanging out with you and your kids?"

"You're twisting everything around," she protested.

He paused in the middle of the sidewalk. "*I'm* twisting things around?"

"Yes. I'm just trying to establish some boundaries—"

"And every time you throw up boundaries, you only tempt me to breach them," he warned, deliberately dropping his gaze to her mouth so she knew that he was thinking about kissing her again.

Georgia had spent more than enough time remembering every minute detail of their first kiss and, with her lips still tingling from the much briefer but more recent kiss in the ice cream parlor, she decided it would be smart to heed his warning.

"I'll keep that in mind," she promised.

Satisfied by her response, he started walking again.

Georgia fell into step beside him, as baffled as she was intrigued by this man. But it was a nice day for a walk, so she tried to concentrate on the scenery rather than her frustrating neighbor.

She'd always scoffed at the idea that people moved faster in the city. Life in New York hadn't seemed so fast when she was moving at the same frenetic pace as everyone else. Whenever she and Phillip had gone out anywhere, they'd rushed to the subway so the underground train could whisk them to their destination. They'd always been in a hurry to get where they were going. As odd as it seemed, she couldn't even remember just taking a leisurely stroll with her husband.

For a lot of reasons, she'd been reluctant to leave Manhattan. She hadn't wanted to take the boys away from everything familiar, but she'd felt so isolated and alone in the city. Maybe Phillip hadn't been a very hands-on dad, but he'd at least been there so she wasn't completely on her own. When he'd died, she'd become painfully aware of how truly alone she was. And with three-and-a-half-year-old twins and another baby on the way, she'd also felt completely overwhelmed.

When Charlotte left for Vegas, Georgia had been alone again, although not for long. Matt had moved in next door and suddenly she had a neighbor, a friend, a confidante... and maybe even more.

And she wanted more, even if she wasn't ready to admit it.

For the past year, she'd focused on being a mother to the exclusion of almost everything else. Being with Matt made her remember that she was a woman, with a woman's wants and needs.

She just hadn't yet figured out what, if anything, she was going to do about those wants and needs.

Five days later, Georgia still didn't have any answers. Since four of those days had been Matt's days at the hospital, she didn't see much of him. It was just like the man to get her all stirred up and then disappear, and she didn't doubt for a single minute that he'd done it on purpose. He was giving her time to think, to wonder, to want. She could no longer deny that she wanted.

But while she'd spent the better part of four days thinking about Matt, he'd apparently been busy planning a party, because when she took the boys outside late Saturday afternoon, there was quite a crowd gathered on his back deck. Even from a distance, she recognized both of his brothers and a woman that she thought might have been Kelsey, but most of the other guests were unfamiliar.

"Finnigan and Frederick are out," Quinn said, already heading in that direction.

Georgia caught his arm just before he raced past her. "I know you want to see the puppies but you can't just go over to someone else's house uninvited."

"Dr. Matt said we could go anytime," Quinn reminded her.

"I know that's what he said, but he has other company today and it isn't polite to intrude."

"I don't wanna be polite," her son protested. "I wanna see Finn."

She had to fight against a smile. No matter his faults, at least he was honest.

"I'm sure you'll see Finn tomorrow, and the day after that, and the day—"

"I wanna see him today!"

And apparently the puppy wanted to see him, too, because before Georgia could admonish her son, the puppy came tearing across the grass, racing as fast as his little legs could carry him. As usual, Fred was right behind him, neck-in-neck with a third puppy.

"Look, Mommy." Shane's eyes were wide. "Finn and Fred have a friend."

"I'm thinking he might actually be another brother," Georgia said.

Finnigan and Frederick were ecstatic to be reunited with their pint-sized playmates, and they jumped and danced around the twins while their companion went exploring. He put his nose deep in the grass and followed a trail—directly to Pippa's blanket.

Georgia watched as the baby and puppy eyed one another. Pippa lifted a hand, as if to touch him, and the puppy pulled back, out of reach. She dropped her hand, he moved closer, sniffed her face, then swiped his tongue across her chin. Pippa giggled.

The puppy licked her again; the baby giggled some more.

And then a strong arm reached down and scooped the puppy up and away. Pippa tipped her head up, wondering where her furry friend had disappeared to, and smiled when she saw him wriggling in Luke Garrett's hold.

"I'm so sorry," Matt's brother apologized. "I didn't think he would venture too far—or so quickly."

"No worries," Georgia assured him. "And he might not have ventured this way on his own, but he followed Finn and Fred."

"I should have been keeping a closer eye on him, so he didn't slobber all over your child."

She shrugged. "A little doggy spit never hurt anyone."

"I wish you could tell that to my date from last night."

Georgia's brows lifted. "She had a different opinion?"

"Oh, yeah," he told her. "When I took her back to my place after dinner—"

She held up a hand. "I'm not sure I want to follow wherever you're going with this."

Luke grinned. "Strictly *G*-rated. All that happened was Einstein licked her hand—not even her face, just her hand. And just once. And she jumped up screaming 'I've got dog germs' like Lucy in the old cartoons."

She couldn't help but smile at the image his words evoked. "First question—how did you end up dating a woman who doesn't like animals?"

"It was a blind date," he said. "I didn't know she didn't like animals."

She didn't even ask about the fact that he'd taken a woman, on a first date, back to his place. Obviously a lot of things had changed since the last time she'd been on a first date. Instead, she said, "Second question—Einstein?"

He sighed. "Because he's not."

"Having a little trouble training him?"

"More than a little," he admitted. "I have never met an animal so determined not to do what he's told."

"Wait until you have kids."

He shook his head. Emphatically.

"Not that I dislike kids," he hastened to explain. "And yours are great. I just don't see myself as a father—not anytime in the near future, anyway."

"That's because he's still a kid himself," Matt said.

Georgia hadn't seen her neighbor approach, and her heart gave a little jolt when he winked at her now. And she wasn't the only female affected—Pippa's eyes lit up and she gave him a gummy smile.

Matt picked up the little girl, who settled comfortably in his embrace, and Georgia realized that her boys weren't the only ones getting attached to "Dr. Matt." And she wondered again how it was that a man who so obviously doted upon children didn't have half a dozen kids of his own.

"Undeniably," his brother admitted with a grin.

"Then I would guess that's a family trait," Georgia noted. "As common as the broad shoulders and brown hair."

"We're not as similar as people think," Luke denied. "Matt's the smart one, Jack's the charming one, *I'm* the good-looking one."

She chuckled at that. "I think you all got more than your fair share of brains, charisma and looks."

"And they're all heartbreakers," Kelsey warned, joining their conversation.

Matt tugged on the end of her ponytail. "Don't you be telling tales out of school," he warned.

"I wouldn't dream of it," she said sweetly. Then she spotted the puppy in the crook of Luke's arm. "Ohmygoodness—he is such a sweetie."

"You had your chance to take one," the vet told her.

"I've already taken enough animals off of your hands," she retorted, stealing the puppy from him—at least for the minute. "Is this one Finnigan or Frederick?"

"That one's Einstein," Luke said.

"He's sooo adorable." She tore her gaze away from the puppy for a minute to explain to Georgia, "Brittney was dying to see Uncle Matt's puppies, so I brought her over and crashed the party."

"It isn't a party," Matt protested.

"Tell that to the dozen other people hanging out on your back deck."

"I didn't invite any of those people," he denied.

"I did," Luke admitted. "Think of it as an impromptu housewarming."

Georgia glanced over at Matt's deck. "None of those people look like Brittney."

"She's in the house, on the phone with her ex-boyfriend, attempting to remind him of the 'ex' part," Kelsey told her.

Georgia winced. "That's awkward."

"Yeah. Almost as awkward as not inviting your neighbor

to a backyard barbecue," she said with a pointed glance in Matt's direction.

"I would have invited my neighbor if I'd been planning a barbecue," he retorted, before turning to Georgia to say, "Apparently I'm hosting an unplanned barbecue."

"Apparently," she agreed, trying to hold back a smile.

"So—" he nudged her playfully, caused tingles to dance down her spine and toward all of her erogenous zones "—do you want to come over for a burger?"

When he looked at her the way he was looking at her now, she was almost ready to admit that she wanted a lot more than a burger. But she wasn't going to get into that kind of conversation in front of his family and friends.

Instead, she forced herself to match his casual tone and said, "Yes, I think I do."

He held her gaze for another minute, then turned to call out to Shane and Quinn. "Come on, boys. Let's go get lunch."

Chapter Eleven

The twins were racing across the yard before Matt finished speaking.

"I remember when Brittney was that young—and that active—and wishing I could figure out a way to bottle that energy," Kelsey said to Georgia.

"I wish the same thing," she agreed. "Every single day."

Matt wanted to be part of her every single day—to share the joys and responsibilities of raising a family with her. But as much as he wanted it, the prospect also scared the hell out of him.

After the failure of his marriage, he'd thought he might never heal, and he'd vowed that he would never give his heart to anyone again. Somehow, over the past few weeks, Georgia and her kids had stolen it away from him. And he didn't know whether to be frustrated or grateful that she didn't seem to have a clue.

Luke's elbow jamming into his ribs severed his wayward

thoughts. "Since you've got your arms full of adoring female, I'll take Finn and Fred back to the house."

Matt nodded and glanced down at the little girl in his arms. He didn't know if she was adoring, but she was absolutely adorable, and gazing up at him with big blue eyes just like her mother's. And just like her mother, she had firmly taken hold of his heart.

Luke and Kelsey headed back across the yard with the puppies, while Georgia gathered up Pippa's supplies. By the time she and Matt made their way across the yard, Jack had the food line moving. Hot dogs and hamburgers were available at the barbecue and an assortment of potluck dishes were set out on the picnic table. Brittney—having finally ended her conversation with Brayden—held Shane's plate so that he could load it up. Like his brother, he opted for the hot dog with a side of macaroni salad and homemade baked beans.

"Beans are awesome!" Quinn declared. "They make you fart real loud!"

Though everyone chuckled—even Adam, the baker of the beans—Matt saw the color rise in Georgia's cheeks, the natural blush making her eyes look even bluer than usual and somehow more beautiful.

By the time she settled Pippa in her bouncy chair and they joined the food line, the boys were half finished with their meals. Matt introduced Georgia to various guests who passed by: Adam Webber and Melanie Quinlan; Tyler Sullivan; Tyler's brother, Mason, and Mason's wife, Zoe, and their kids; Gage and Megan Richmond and their three-year-old son, Marcus.

"And there's Megan's sister—"

"I'm never going to remember everyone," Georgia warned him.

"—Ashley Turcotte and her husband, Cameron."

But she smiled as the couple drew nearer. "I'll remember those names, because Dr. Turcotte is our new family doctor."

"I'm only a doctor when I'm wearing the white coat," Cameron said, protesting her use of his formal title.

"Or when there's a scraped knee in the vicinity," his wife added, offering her hand.

"I'm Georgia Reed."

"The city girl with the three kids who moved in next to Dr. Garrett," Ashley noted.

"He moved in next to me," Georgia pointed out, with just a hint of exasperation in her tone.

The other woman chuckled. "I know, but the rumor mill always orbits around the locals."

"Which is just one more reason to be glad you're an import," Matt told her. Then, to Ashley, "Where are Maddie and Alyssa?"

"Our daughters discovered your tree house."

"Have they eaten?" Cameron asked.

"Maddie said that they needed to go exploring to work up an appetite first," his wife explained.

"Those are my boys," Georgia told Ashley, pointing out the twins who were seated on a blanket with Brittney. "They always seem to have an appetite."

"But their mom needs to eat, too," Matt said, nudging Georgia toward the barbecue where Jack had a long-handled spatula in one hand and his own burger in the other.

"Make sure you try Zoe's broccoli salad," Ashley advised.

Matt and Georgia loaded up their plates and found a couple of empty chairs near Brittney and the twins. A few minutes later, Kelsey and her husband, Ian, joined them. And when everyone had a plate, Jack finally abandoned the grill and came over.

"Hey, Britt, I heard Matt talked you into playing on our softball team for the Fourth of July tournament," he said.

"Despite my protests and against my better judgment," she said. "Which I'll remind you again when I strike out for the umpteenth time."

"We've got three weeks to practice—we'll get you hitting the ball," he said confidently.

The teen shook her head. "I really suck, Uncle Jack."

"I'm sure you're not that bad." Kelsey tried to assure her daughter.

"Actually she is," Luke said, dropping onto the blanket beside the twins.

Brittney wadded up her napkin to throw it at him—and missed her target by a mile.

He winked at her. "Thanks for proving my point."

"You can show her how it's done at practice tomorrow," Matt told his brother.

"Three o'clock at the park," Jack confirmed.

"There's swings at the park," Shane said.

"And monkey bars!" Quinn added.

"Do you guys want to go to the park?" Brittney asked.

They both nodded enthusiastically.

She looked at their mother. "Do you mind if I take them over there for a while?"

"They would be thrilled and I would be grateful," Georgia told her.

"Why don't we round up all the kids and I'll go with you?" Luke offered. He looked at Jack, as if he expected to rope him into babysitting duty, too.

Jack shook his head. "I'm going to check the food supply, make sure no one goes hungry."

Ian stood up. "Actually, I could go for another burger."

"Me, too," Matt said, then he turned to Georgia. "Do you want anything?"

"Brittney to live with me so she can keep the boys entertained 24/7?" she asked hopefully.

"You'll have to talk to her mother about that," he said, heading back toward the barbecue.

Georgia turned to see Kelsey was already shaking her head. "Sorry, but Northeastern has dibs."

"But not until September, right?"

"Not until September," she agreed, then sighed. "Damn, I'm going to miss her."

"I can imagine," Georgia admitted. "The boys are only starting kindergarten in the fall, but already I'm thinking about how quiet the house will seem when they're at school."

"Don't blink," Kelsey warned. "Because before you know it, they'll be packing their bags for college."

Georgia watched the boys, each one holding on to one of Brittney's hands, with a trail of other kids behind them. They were in their glory, not just because they had Brittney's attention but because there were other kids to play with, too.

"I'm not accustomed to anything like this," she told Kelsey.

"Like what?"

"Big, noisy get-togethers. Growing up, it was just my mom and my sisters and I. Obviously, I didn't know what I was missing."

"You mean the chaos and confusion?" Kelsey teased.

Georgia smiled. "No, that came along with the twins. What I meant was the camaraderie, and the sense of comfort that comes from knowing that there's always someone there. Matt and his brothers might argue and tease one another mercilessly, but there's no doubt that each one would go to the wall for the others."

"And they have," Kelsey confirmed. "You don't have that kind of relationship with your sisters?"

Georgia shook her head. "Maybe it's geography—I'm here, Virginia's in Texas and Indy's in Alaska."

"That's a lot of distance," the other woman noted.

"I sometimes wonder if we went our separate ways because we never had a sense of belonging anywhere."

"It makes a difference," Kelsey agreed. "Matt and Jack and Luke all went away to school, but they all came back to Pinehurst in the end."

"How about you?" Georgia asked.

The other woman shook her head. "My sister was the one with wanderlust. I never wanted to be anywhere else."

"I had mixed feelings about moving to Pinehurst after my husband died. But now, I'm so glad that I did. This is what I want for my children—a home in a community where everyone looks out for their neighbors."

"Is that a diplomatic way of saying 'where everyone butts into everyone else's business'?"

"That thought never once crossed my mind."

Kelsey laughed, because she saw right through the lie. "So tell me, now that you've accepted we're all busybodies, what has Matt said or done that has you worried?"

Georgia wasn't usually the type to confide in a woman she barely knew, but she didn't know many people in Pinehurst and she desperately needed someone to talk to. And Kelsey seemed a more logical choice than the elderly Mrs. Dunford.

"He kissed me," she admitted.

"And that surprised you?"

"Maybe not the kiss itself," she admitted. "But the intensity of it."

"Matt's never been the type to do anything by half measures," Kelsey said. Then, after a beat, she asked, "How was it?"

Just the memory of that kiss had Georgia's blood humming. "Beyond spectacular."

The other woman grinned. "Go Matt."

"That's the problem," Georgia said. "I don't know if I'm ready for this…attraction…to go anywhere."

"You're deluding yourself if you think you can stop it."

Georgia frowned at that.

"You're thinking about the kids," Kelsey guessed. "'What if I get involved with this guy and things don't work out?'"

She nodded, surprised that a woman she barely knew could be so attuned to her thoughts and concerns. Except that Kelsey was a mother, too, so maybe it wasn't surprising at all.

"Pippa's probably young enough that you don't have to worry about her too much, but the boys are already looking at Matt as if the sun rises and sets in him, and what will happen if things don't work out and he's not part of their lives anymore?"

She blew out a breath. "You're good at this."

Kelsey shrugged. "I'm a student of human nature—and I can see the situation a little more clearly because I'm not personally involved.

"I can also tell you," she continued, "that Matt isn't the type of guy to play fast and loose with anyone's heart. Despite my teasing, he wouldn't have invited you here tonight, with his family and his friends, if this wasn't where he wanted you to be."

"Or maybe he just figured I'd be less likely to complain about the music if I was invited to the party."

"You really don't see it, do you?"

"See what?" she asked warily.

"How completely smitten he is."

"He's been a good friend—"

Kelsey snorted.

"—and he's absolutely terrific with the kids."

"I've never known a man better suited to being a father or more deserving of a family," the other woman said. "Which is why I know Matt would never risk everything we just talked about if he wasn't sure he wanted a future with you."

"I think you might be reading too much into the situation."

Kelsey just smiled. "He already loves your kids, Georgia. When are you going to figure out that he's more than half-way in love with you, too?"

"No." She shook her head. "Now you're definitely reading too much into things."

"And that instinctive panicked reaction is probably why he hasn't told you how he feels," Kelsey said.

Then she gathered up the empty plates and headed up to the house, leaving Georgia alone to think about what she'd said.

She decided that just because Kelsey and Matt were good friends didn't mean that the other woman knew what was in his heart. Certainly he'd never given any indication that he was "halfway in love" with her, or even "completely smitten." Sure, he flirted with her, and he'd kissed her once—okay, a few times, but the more recent kisses had been too quick to really count, even if she'd felt tingles all the way down to her toes—but he hadn't given any indication he wanted to take things any further than that.

She wanted to put Kelsey's words out of her mind, but her gaze kept zeroing in on Matt as she watched him mingle with his friends, and she couldn't help but admire his easy manner. She also couldn't help but admire the way his shorts hugged his spectacular backside, and felt that now-familiar throbbing in her veins. There was no doubt about it, Matt Garrett was a fine specimen of masculinity.

It was only Pippa's fussing that succeeded in tearing her attention away from the doctor next door, and she ducked into the house to find a private corner to nurse her. When the baby was finally sated, Georgia rejoined the group that had gathered on Matt's back deck. With all the other kids at the park with Brittney and Luke, Pippa was the star attraction, and she was happy to let herself be passed from one set of arms to another, charming all with her big blue eyes and even bigger smile.

Georgia was chatting to Adam Webber—a fifth-grade teacher at the school the boys would be attending in the fall—when Matt made his way back to her. Adam, catching a look from the host, excused himself to grab another drink. When he did, Matt stepped into the space his friend had vacated and slipped an arm around Georgia's waist.

She eyed him warily. "You're going to give your friends the wrong idea about us."

He nuzzled her ear, and she couldn't quite suppress the delicious shiver that skated down her spine. "I'm trying to give you the *right* idea about us."

"You haven't listened to anything I've said, have you?"

"I've listened to a lot of things you've said," he countered. "But all your protests about not wanting to get involved can't override how right you feel in my arms. Or the fact that your body's instinctive reactions contradict your verbal responses."

She just sighed. "I don't know what to do about you."

"I have a few ideas," he teased. "But I'm not sure you're ready to hear them just yet."

"We're *friends,*" she said firmly.

"Believe me, I'm feeling very friendly right now."

She shook her head, but she couldn't help smiling. "You are far too charming for your own good."

"The Garrett curse," he lamented.

"I'll bet it is."

Somehow, Georgia was still there when the rest of Matt's guests had cleared out. The twins had played for hours outside—first with the puppies, then at the park with Brittney and the other kids, then with the puppies again—until they were as tired out as their four-legged friends. Georgia had wanted to take them home to get them ready for bed, but they'd balked at that idea. When Matt suggested they could go inside to watch TV, they'd jumped all over that offer with both feet.

Pippa was awake again, but happily playing with the soft toys attached to her bouncy chair. Her fussy nights finally seemed to be a thing of the past, for which Georgia was immensely grateful. But while Georgia was getting more sleep, she wasn't feeling any more rested because her sleep continued to be disturbed by erotic dreams starring one very handsome doctor.

"I didn't think they would ever leave," Matt said, as the last car pulled out of the driveway.

"You have an interesting group of friends," she noted. "Have you known them all very long?"

"Most of us go back to grade school," he admitted.

"Really?"

"Why do you sound so incredulous? You must keep in touch with friends you went to school with."

She shook her head. "There were too many schools to keep track from one year to the next. In fact, it was rare for me to walk out of class in June at the same school I'd started in September."

"Was your father in the military?"

"No, my mother was following her bliss."

"Really?"

"She's settled down in recent years—or so I thought until I got the phone call informing me that she'd found husband number five."

"Where's your dad?" Matt wondered.

"Somewhere in Atlanta."

"Is that why you're named Georgia?"

She nodded. "And I have a half sister named Virginia and another half sister named Indy."

"Short for Indiana?" he guessed.

"No, she was actually named for the Indy race circuit. Her father was a member of one of the pit crews and we traveled so much from track to track that summer, Charlotte couldn't be sure whether the baby had been conceived in Wisconsin or Iowa, so she decided to go with Indy."

He smiled. "A good choice, considering the other options."

She nodded her agreement. "Charlotte always said the only

crime in life is in not following your heart wherever it wants to lead."

"And you disapprove of that philosophy?" he guessed.

"I didn't see that following her heart ever led to anything more than heartache."

"Did you never follow yours?"

She glanced away. "I believe the desires of the heart need to be balanced against the reason of the mind."

"How long did it take you to balance the desires of your heart with the reason of your mind when your husband proposed?" he teased.

"He never actually proposed."

"He never proposed?" Now Matt was the one who sounded incredulous.

"The topic of marriage came up in conversation and we decided it was what we both wanted, so we got married. The formalities weren't as important as being together to either of us."

He shook his head. "Next you're going to tell me that you got married at city hall."

"What's wrong with that?"

"Not a thing—if that's what you wanted," he said.

She'd told herself that it was, that she didn't need a white dress or a bouquet of flowers. She wasn't the type to be influenced by romantic trappings or swayed by amorous words. She wasn't like her mother.

But there had been a few occasions—usually other people's weddings—when she found herself wishing they'd done things a little differently. Not that she'd ever admitted it to anyone, and she wasn't going to do so now. Instead, she stood up. "I should check on the kids."

She'd set the twins up in the living room to watch a program on the Discovery Channel, but now they were both fast asleep.

"I hope this isn't a premonition," she murmured to Matt, who had followed her into the house.

"Of what?"

"Their attention span for educational instruction. I don't want them falling asleep in class when they start kindergarten in September."

"I don't think you need to worry. They just crashed because they had an incredibly busy day."

She nodded, acknowledging the point. "But regardless of how exhausted they were, if I'd put cartoons on TV, they'd still be awake."

"Which is obviously why you didn't put cartoons on."

But now that they were asleep, she was second-guessing her choice. Because Quinn and Shane were supposed to be her chaperones, and she was suddenly conscious of being *un*-chaperoned with her sexy neighbor. "I should get them home."

"You're going to wake them up to take them home so they can go to sleep?"

"They should be in their beds," she insisted.

"They seem comfortable enough," he noted.

Looking at her boys cuddled up with the puppies, Georgia couldn't disagree. But that didn't make her any less uneasy.

They moved into the kitchen, where their conversation wouldn't disturb the kids, and Matt said, "I should have considered that you might be tired. How are you holding up?"

"I didn't do anything all day. Your brother cooked the burgers, your friends supplied the rest of the food, Brittney occupied the boys, and everyone else took turns with the baby." She looked up at him and smiled. "In fact, I was thinking we should do it again tomorrow."

The implication of her words registered too late, and she immediately tried to backtrack.

"I didn't mean to imply... I mean, I don't expect you to spend all of your free time hanging out with me and my kids."

Matt just shook his head. "When are you going to figure out that I like hanging out with you and your kids?"

"It's starting to sink in," she told him.

"Maybe this will help," he said, and lowered his mouth to hers.

Chapter Twelve

Matt prided himself on being a patient man. When he'd decided that he wanted Georgia—about three minutes after their first meeting—he'd accepted that it would probably take her some time to come to the same realization. He also figured there was no harm in nudging her in that direction.

He braced his hands on the counter, bracketing her between them, and brushed his lips over hers softly, slowly. Her eyes fluttered, closed. He traced the shape of her mouth with just the tip of his tongue. She breathed out a sigh.

Apparently she didn't need as much nudging as he'd anticipated, because when he swept along the seam of her lips, they parted willingly. His hands moved from the counter to her hips; her palms slid over his chest, her hands linking behind his neck.

He deepened the kiss, stroking the inside of her mouth with his tongue. He didn't demand a response but coaxed it from her. Their tongues danced together in a sensual rhythm of advance and retreat that had all the blood rushing from his head. Part of him felt as if he could go on kissing her for hours, but another part refused to be satisfied with kissing.

His hands moved up her rib cage, over her breasts. She moaned and pressed closer. This was exactly how he wanted her—warm and willing in his arms. His hands curved around her bottom, pulling her tight against him. He was rock hard and aching with wanting her, and she was rubbing against him, her movements so natural and sensual she nearly pushed him to the brink.

Determined to regain control of the situation, he eased his lips from hers to trail kisses across her jaw, down her throat. He nipped at the nape of her neck, and she shuddered against him. His tongue traced over her collarbone, then along the edge of the lacy cup of her bra. Her skin was so soft, her breasts so perfect and round, and when he nuzzled the hollow between them, he could feel her heart racing.

He brushed his thumbs over her nipples, and she shuddered again. But when he reached for the clasp at the front of her bra, she pushed his hand away, shaking her head.

Reminding himself that he'd promised to be patient, he didn't push back. Instead, he cupped her face in his hands.

"What are you afraid of, Georgia?"

"I'm not sure," she admitted.

"I'm not going to push for more than you're ready to give," he promised.

Her smile was wry. "Maybe that's what I'm afraid of. Because there's a pretty big disparity between what my body wants and what my brain is thinking."

He brushed his lips against hers. "Would it be wrong for me to encourage you to listen to your body?"

"Believe me, my hormones are clamoring loudly enough without any encouragement."

"At least you're no longer trying to deny the chemistry between us."

"That would be hypocritical, considering the way I was pressed up against you less than a minute ago."

"I liked the way you were pressed up against me," he assured her. "In fact, feel free to press up against me anytime."

She shook her head. "That was a temporary state of mindlessness induced by an overload of hormones after more than a year of celibacy."

"Is that what you think it was?" He had to fight to keep his voice level, his tone casual. "Just a combination of factors that really had nothing to do with you and me?"

Her gaze shifted away. "It seems like the most reasonable explanation."

"Then let's be unreasonable," he suggested, and lowered his head again to nibble on her bottom lip.

His efforts were rewarded by a soft moan low in her throat.

"I can be unreasonable," she agreed.

Which sounded like a green light to Matt.

He allowed his hands to stroke over her shoulders, down her arms, while he continued to kiss her. Deeply. Hungrily. And she responded with equal passion.

His hand slipped down the front of her shorts, dipped inside her panties. She gasped as his fingers sifted through the soft curls in search of her womanly core. He had to bite back his own moan when he found her hot and wet and oh-so-ready.

He slid a finger deep inside of her, and let his thumb zero in on the tiny nub of her most sensitive erogenous zone. She moaned again but made no protest as he slowly and inexorably coaxed her closer and closer to the pinnacle of her pleasure.

She was mindless now, writhing and panting. He didn't disagree that hormones played a role in what was happening here, but he knew that it was more than that. And he wanted more than hot, meaningless sex—he wanted intimacy. From the first, he'd sensed that deeper level of connection with Georgia, and he'd be damned if he'd let her dismiss what was between them as nothing more than a transitory urge.

He slid his finger in again, then two fingers. In and out, deeper and faster now, while his thumb continued to stroke her nub. He felt the clamp of her inner muscles around his fingers in the exact moment that her teeth sank into his bottom lip, the unexpected shock of erotic pleasure nearly bringing him to climax. He clamped his other arm around her waist, holding on to her, while the shudders racked her body.

She eased her lips from his and dropped her head against his chest. But several minutes passed before she said anything, and then it was only, "Oh. My. Wow."

He managed to smile, though his own body was screaming for its own release. And when she reached for the button of his shorts, her fingertips brushing the top of his aching erection, it took more willpower than he knew he possessed to stop her.

But he caught her hands in his, held them at her sides. "It's late. You should be getting home."

She just stared at him, stunned. "But don't you want to... finish?"

"What I want," he told her, "is to take you upstairs, slowly strip every piece of clothing away, and spend hours touching and kissing you all over until you're begging for me."

She swallowed. "So why...are you sending me away?"

"Aside from the fact that your screams of pleasure might wake your kids?"

Her cheeks flushed. "I guess that's a good reason."

"But the main reason," he continued, "is that I'm not going to make love with you until I know it's what you want, too. Not because you need a release, but because you want *me*."

She glanced away, but not before he saw that her eyes had filled with tears. Cursing himself, he put a hand on her arm.

Not surprisingly, she shrugged away from his touch.

"Should I thank you for taking the edge off?"

Except that there was still an edge—he could hear it in her voice.

"It wasn't all for you," he said, because it was true. "Touching you was definitely my pleasure."

But she turned away, proving that his words hadn't swayed her. "I need to get the kids home."

He held back a sigh. After all, he was the one who had reminded her it was getting late.

"You take Pippa, I'll bring the boys."

She opened her mouth as if to protest, because even now, she didn't like to accept help from anyone.

"Unless you really want to make three trips," he said.

"Thank you—I would appreciate your help." Except that her sharp tone and narrowed gaze contradicted her words.

She slung Pippa's diaper bag over her shoulder and lifted the bouncy chair with the baby securely fastened and contentedly slumbering in it. It was a little more awkward for Matt to juggle the twins without waking them up, but he managed.

He kicked off his shoes inside the front door and carried the boys upstairs to their bedroom while Georgia changed Pippa. He ignored the pajamas that were neatly folded at the foot of each bed and laid Quinn gently on top of his mattress.

He'd done this before—tucked a sleeping child into his bed. And while the memories of his son usually tore at his heart, tonight—with Georgia's little boy cuddled up against his chest—he was able to smile at the remembrance.

Then he eased Shane down onto his pillow and carefully tucked the covers around him. He brushed away a lock of hair and impulsively touched his lips to the child's forehead.

"Night-night, Daddy."

Matt froze.

He'd always wanted to be a father, and even after he'd lost Liam, he'd been confident that he would have other children someday. But he hadn't realized how much he wanted to be a father to Georgia's kids until he heard the word *Daddy* slip from Shane's lips. He knew the little boy was asleep, and that the words had been murmured subconsciously, but that knowledge didn't prevent them from arrowing straight to his heart.

He took a moment to compose himself before he moved back to Quinn's bed, tucked his covers around him and kissed his forehead. He wasn't sure if he was relieved or disappointed when this twin didn't stir.

Georgia was just leaving Pippa's room when he stepped into the hall. She followed him down the stairs.

"Thank you," she said formally. "For helping with the boys and for inviting us to dinner."

"You're welcome," he said.

And because he couldn't resist, he touched his mouth to hers, softly, fleetingly.

She kept her lips tightly compressed, but her lack of response didn't faze him. Because he knew now, without a doubt, that she wanted him as much as he wanted her.

Now he just had to wait for her to come to the same realization.

He was driving Georgia insane.

Six days after Matt had given her an up-close-and-personal glimpse of the stars and the heavens, he was acting as if absolutely nothing out of the ordinary had happened. Then again, maybe arousing women to the point of climax in his kitchen wasn't out of the ordinary for him. But it had been an extraordinary experience for her—and an incredibly frustrating one.

She hadn't meant to insult him when she'd tried to explain away the sizzle between them as a basic physiological response to their proximity. It made sense to her that more than twelve months of celibacy in combination with post-pregnancy hormones would fuel an attraction to the sexy doctor. But Matt had taken exception to her reasoning and endeavored to prove that what she wanted wasn't just sex but sex with him.

And he was right, damn it. Because when she went to

sleep that night, she didn't dream about hot, sweaty sex with nameless, faceless partners, she dreamed about hot, sweaty sex with Matt Garrett. And she woke up craving his kiss, aching for his touch, yearning for the fulfillment she knew only he could give her.

Since Phillip had passed away, she'd been a mom first and foremost. She'd been dealing with the twins' grief and her own pregnancy. She hadn't missed sex—in fact, she hadn't even thought about it. For more than a year, it was as if every womanly urge in her body had simply shut down. And then Matt Garrett had moved in next door.

Being around him stirred all kinds of wants and needs inside of her. He made her feel like a whole woman again. Except that, in the past six days, nada. Not one kiss, not the brush of a single fingertip on her skin, nothing.

Not that he was avoiding her. In fact, she was practically tripping over him every time she turned around. He was solicitous and helpful and he continued to spend a lot of his free time with the boys. He'd even taken it upon himself to make a trip to the local garden center and arranged for a delivery of sand to fill the empty box at the back of her mother's yard. And he was out there with the boys now, driving dump trucks, bulldozers and cement mixers through the sand right alongside them.

Yeah, he was having a great time with the boys, and he hadn't made a single move to touch her or kiss her in six days. At first she'd thought he was punishing her, then she started to wonder if he'd lost interest, maybe he'd decided that she wasn't worth the effort. Except then she'd catch him looking at her, and the intense heat of his stare certainly didn't telegraph disinterest.

Stepping outside, she called to the boys. "Quinn, Shane— lunch is ready."

The boys jumped up, wiping their sand-covered hands on their shorts before they raced toward the house. Matt followed behind them, at a more leisurely pace. While the boys went inside to wash up, she waited for her neighbor.

"I made a pot of chili, if you wanted to join us."

"Thanks, but I've got some things I have to do."

She stepped in front of him, blocking his path. "Are you going to stay mad at me forever?"

"I'm not mad at you," he told her.

"Then why haven't you kissed me in six days?"

The corner of his mouth tilted up in a half smile. "You've been counting the days?"

She lifted her chin, met his gaze evenly. "Have you changed your mind about wanting me?"

The answer was evident in his eyes before he spoke. The glint of amusement in his gaze immediately replaced by desire—hot and hungry and unrestrained. "No," he said slowly. "I haven't changed my mind."

"So why haven't you kissed me?"

"Because I was afraid that if I started, I wouldn't be able to stop."

She swallowed. "Maybe I wouldn't want you to stop."

He took a step back. "Let me know when you can make that statement without the 'maybe.'"

"I'm sorry," she said with a sigh. "I'm not playing hard-to-get. At least, not on purpose."

His smile was wry. "I know."

And then he pressed a quick kiss to her lips.

It was almost too quick, and he was walking away before the fact even registered in her brain. But it had certainly registered in her body, zinging through every nerve ending from the tip of her head to the soles of her feet and everywhere in between.

If she thought about it, she might have worried that her response to the casual touch was too much. But in the moment, all she could think was that she wanted much more. That she wanted him to kiss her and touch her and never stop.

But she wasn't ready to say the words out loud. And even if she was, it was too late.

He was already gone.

A few days later, Georgia decided to reward herself for finishing her reports on three slush pile submissions with a trip to the park. Since the boys had mostly behaved and let her focus on her work, she decided to take them with her. It wasn't until they got to the park and she saw Matt in the outfield that she knew his team—the Garrett Gators—was practicing today.

While the boys played—Shane no longer encumbered by the cast that had been removed the day before—she put Pippa on her blanket on the grass. Her daughter had recently learned to roll from her stomach to her back and vice versa, and she happily spent a lot of time practicing her new skill. While Georgia was proud of her daughter, she was also a little wary. Pippa's increased mobility required even greater diligence because Georgia knew that if she turned her back for a moment, the baby might roll out of sight. For the moment, however, she seemed content just to go back and forth.

"Heads up!"

Georgia spun around to see the ball pop high into the air and over the backstop of the baseball diamond. Instinctively, she cupped her hands and snagged the ball before it dropped near the baby. There was a smattering of applause from the field as she tossed the ball back to the catcher.

"Sign her up!" somebody yelled from the field.

Georgia ignored the commentary and turned back to Pippa who had, in her mother's brief moment of inattention, rolled all the way to the edge of the blanket. With a mock admonishment, she scooped up the baby and set her in the middle of the quilt again.

"Mrs. Reed?"

She glanced up to see Brittney jogging toward her. Georgia smiled at the girl. "Another practice for the Fourth of July tournament?"

"Yeah," the teen responded with a complete lack of enthusiasm. "And I still completely suck. Unfortunately, there are strict rules about the number of men and women you can have on each team, and uncle Matt's team needed another female body on the field."

"I'm sure you'll do just fine," Georgia told her.

Brittney shook her head. "After half a dozen practices, it's still my instinct to get out of the way when the ball's coming toward me. I haven't fielded a single hit and I haven't hit a single pitch past the pitcher's mound."

"Why are you telling me this?"

"Because when that ball came at you, you didn't even think about it—you just reached out and grabbed it."

"A mother's instinct," she explained. "I was protecting the baby."

"Still, it proved that you'd be a much better asset to the team than I am," Brittney told her.

"Matt asked me if I wanted to play, but—" she gestured to the boys on the climber and Pippa on the blanket under the tree "—I can't sit them in the bleachers and expect them to stay put."

"I'd be happy to hang out with the kids if you took my spot at second base. No, I'd be *thrilled*," the girl amended.

Still, Georgia hesitated. "I haven't played baseball in more years than I care to admit."

"Give it a try now," Brittney urged, offering her glove.

And that was how Georgia found herself playing second base for the Garrett Gators on the Fourth of July.

The local sports complex had been turned into a carnival for the holiday, including a family fun zone with an enormous ball pit, a twenty-foot inflatable slide, a puppet theatre, and face painting and balloon animals for the little kids. For the bigger kids, there was a midway area with thrill rides and games of chance and skill. And since everyone in attendance had an appetite, food vendors offered everything from hot dogs, popcorn and snow cones to perogies, schnitzel and sushi. But one of the biggest draws of the day was the Sixth Annual Co-ed Softball for Sick Kids Hospital Tournament.

Brittney's best friend, Nina, had offered to help out with the kids, but Georgia still couldn't help worrying that the twins and Pippa would be too much for the girls over the course of the day. And she was feeling more than a little guilty that she wasn't able to spend the day with her family. But the twins were happy to wander off with the teens, who pushed Pippa along in her stroller, leaving Georgia with nothing to do but play ball.

There were two divisions of three teams in the tournament, so every team played a five-inning game against each of the others in its division to determine standings. Then the two first-place teams played for the championship trophy.

Georgia nursed Pippa between games and made sure that the girls had enough money to keep the twins occupied and supplied with snacks. At the end of the first round, it was announced that the Garrett Gators would be facing off against the Sullivan Swingers for the hardware.

"A rematch of last year's final," Ashley Turcotte said, in a tone that warned Georgia that game had not ended well for the Gators.

"What happened?" she asked.

"Tyler Sullivan cranked a solo home run over the right field fence to win it for the Swingers in the bottom of the ninth."

"Ty got lucky on that one," Luke grumbled.

"And for months afterward by retelling the story to any female who would listen," Jack chimed in.

"We've got a better team this year," Matt said confidently.

"So do they," Karen, Luke's receptionist and their right

fielder, noted. "They finished with a better run differential, so they're the home team again."

"Then let's get ready to bat," Matt suggested.

Matt had always loved baseball. Hardball or softball, wind-mill or slo-pitch, it was a fun game. And while the annual charity tournament didn't have quite the same intensity as the high school state championship, there was definitely a rivalry between the Gators and the Swingers, and Matt really wanted payback.

This year's game, just like the previous one, was a close contest. The Gators would go up by a couple of runs in the top of the inning, then the Swingers would catch up when they batted in the bottom. And just like the previous year, the game was on the line in the bottom of the ninth when Tyler Sullivan stepped up to the plate with two outs. But this time, he didn't need a big hit. With his sister-in-law at third base, he only needed a single to score her and tie the game.

In center field, Matt pulled his ball cap lower and focused his attention on the plate. Tyler took a big swing at the first pitch, fouling it back and out of play. When the second pitch came off of his bat, Matt immediately knew by the crack of the bat that it had made contact right at the sweet spot.

Cursing under his breath, he watched the ball fly...straight at Georgia. As if in slow motion, she lifted her glove and the ball disappeared inside its pocket.

The umpire held up his closed fist to signal the final out; Tyler dropped his bat in disgust; the spectators went crazy. Matt stood still, stunned.

Georgia barely had time to toss the ball back toward the pitcher's mound before she was lifted off her feet and swung around. Jack, from his position at shortstop, had reached her first, and when he finally put her feet back on the ground, he planted a kiss right on her mouth. Luke, who had been on first, was next in line. Following his brother's example, he gave her a smack on the lips, too.

Adam Webber showed a little more restraint. After high-fiving her, he said, "I'm just glad the ball wasn't hit to third. I mean, I like all these guys, and I don't mind them patting my butt, but I draw the line at kissing."

"I draw the line at kissing you, too," Jack told him.

There were more high fives all around, and then the Gators lined up for the post-game handshakes with the Swingers.

After the trophy had been presented and the crowd began to disperse, Matt saw Tyler Sullivan approach Georgia to ask, "So what are you doing next Fourth of July?"

She just chuckled. "I don't make any plans that far ahead."

"So you're not on the Gators' permanent roster?" he pressed.

"Back off, Sullivan," Matt growled.

Tyler just grinned. "Can't blame a guy for trying."

"Are you trying to steal my second baseman or snag my woman?"

Georgia seemed as startled by the question as Tyler.

"Your woman?" she echoed.

Tyler, sensing that the fireworks might start hours ahead of schedule, held up his hands in a gesture of surrender and backed off.

Matt slipped his arm around Georgia's waist. "Any woman who can snag a line drive for the final out in the bottom of the ninth and go three-for-four at the plate is the woman for me."

"The ball was hit right into my glove and it's pretty hard to strike out when your own team is pitching to you."

"Cam managed to do it," Luke said. "Twice today."

"They were foul tips," Cam pointed out in his defense. "They don't count as a third strike in real baseball."

Ten-year-old Maddie, who had been their bat girl, patted his shoulder. "You're still a hero to me, Daddy."

He kissed the top of his daughter's head. "That's all that

matters to me." Then he draped an arm over his wife's shoulders. "That, and scoring when I get home."

Ashley shook her head, but she was smiling as they walked away.

"Speaking of scoring," Karen said, winking at Georgia. "I have to admit that I'm curious. Now that you've been kissed by all three of the Garrett brothers, which one would you score the highest?"

Georgia's cheeks filled with color, but she responded lightly, "I'm not the kind of girl who kisses and tells."

"At least tell me this—is their reputation warranted?"

She smiled. "Absolutely."

Chapter Thirteen

Thankfully, before Georgia could be pressed for more details, Quinn and Shane came running onto the field. She bent down to receive their hugs and kisses. As sweaty and dirty and exhausted as she was, just holding her boys was enough to make her forget everything else.

"You were awesome, Mommy!" Shane's voice was filled with admiration, and her heart swelled with pride.

"Better than the Yankees!" Quinn declared, because that was undoubtedly the highest praise he could think of.

"A performance that definitely warrants ice cream," Matt noted.

"Ice cream?" Quinn said hopefully.

"Well, don't you think your mommy deserves a reward after that terrific game?"

Shane nodded. "Me, too."

Matt grinned. "You bet. Ice cream for everyone. Go tell Brittney and Nina that they're invited, too."

Georgia held back a groan as the twins raced away again.

"You, too," Matt told his brothers. "If you want to join us."

But Jack shook his head regretfully. "I've got a huge file to review before a trial on Monday."

"And I just got a call from Peggy Morgan asking me to take a look at Southpaw."

"She still has that old cat?"

"Probably not for much longer," Luke said. Then, to Georgia, "Make him spring for a double scoop—you more than earned it today."

"I guess it's just you and me," Matt said to Georgia when his brothers had gone.

"And two teens, two preschoolers and an infant," she added. And then, more hopefully, "Or you could let me beg off, too."

"You don't want ice cream?"

"Right now, I just want to go home, wash all the sweat and dust from my body and crawl into bed."

"That sounds even better than ice cream," he said.

"Alone," she said pointedly.

His smile never wavered. "A doctor knows all the muscles in the human body. I'd be happy to help you work out some of the kinks."

"A tempting thought, but I think I'll pass." She tossed him the baseball glove she'd borrowed.

He caught it against his chest, then took a step closer. "Is it?" he wanted to know. "A tempting thought?"

"If you're asking if I've thought about your hands on my body, the answer is yes."

His eyes darkened. "I should have known you'd make that admission at a time and place where I can't do anything about it," he grumbled.

She smiled sweetly. "It seemed safest."

He stepped closer. "Do you want to see the fireworks tonight?"

She lifted a brow; he grinned.

"That wasn't some kind of secret code," he assured her. "The town puts on a fabulous fireworks display back here after dark. I'm sure the boys would love it."

"They probably would," she agreed. "But I don't know about Pippa."

"Brittney could keep an eye on Pippa and the puppies at my place."

"She's been watching my kids all day."

"She owes me, for bailing on the team."

"I thought you said you owed her a 'thank you' for that," she reminded him.

"I'll thank her tomorrow," he promised. "After she babysits tonight."

Of course, Georgia wouldn't really disappoint her boys by bailing on a trip for ice cream, so they all piled into her van and made the short drive to Walton's. Unfortunately, the lineup at Walton's was not short, and she suspected that everyone who'd been at the game had the same idea as Matt. But they finally made their way to the cashier and placed their orders: s'mores sundae for Brittney, hot fudge with nuts for Nina, a chocolate chip cookie dough kiddie cone for Quinn, alien invasion again for Shane—apparently he had a new favorite—lemon-lime sorbet for Georgia, and the colossal banana split for Matt.

By the time they polished off their treats and headed back home, the boys could barely keep their eyes open and Georgia knew there was no way they would stay awake for the fireworks show. In fact, she still had doubts about whether *she* could stay awake, but she owed it to Matt to make the effort.

While he went home to shower and change, she steered the boys into the bathroom and filled the tub. When they were clean and dry, she instructed them to put their pajamas on and brush their teeth while she took her turn in the shower. By the time she finished, Pippa was hungry again, so Georgia sent the boys downstairs with Brittney and Nina while she fed the baby, promising them a story when she was done.

Matt returned to find the twins hanging out with the teens, waiting for their mom to read them a bedtime story. When he suggested that he could read the story, the boys exchanged wary glances.

"Mommy tells the bestest stories," Shane told him.

"But you can read to us now," Quinn said, handing him the book he'd picked out. "'Cuz Mommy's busy with Pippa."

"All right, then," Matt agreed, and opened the book.

"Upstairs," Shane told him.

"It's not a bedtime story if we're not in bed," Quinn explained.

"I don't know what I was thinking," Matt said, and followed them up to their room.

When the boys were settled with Matt sandwiched between them—in Shane's bed tonight, because apparently they alternated and it was his turn—he opened the book again. It was a story about a funny, furry monster that had the boys giggling out loud at various parts, sometimes even before Matt read the words on the page, so he knew it was a story they'd heard several times before. By the time he got to the last page, both boys were snuggled in close and struggling to stay awake.

When he closed the cover, Shane tilted his head back to look up at him. "Maybe you could be our new daddy."

It was the hopeful tone even more than the words that squeezed Matt's heart. And he wanted, more than anything, to agree with the little boy's suggestion. But it wouldn't be smart to get Shane's hopes up—or his own—until he knew that Georgia was on board with the idea, too.

"If you were our daddy, then me and Shane could take care of Finnigan and Frederick for you all the time," Quinn said.

Matt had to clear his throat before he could speak. "Well, that's definitely something to consider."

"But you'd hafta marry Mommy to be our daddy," Quinn continued.

He was mildly amused and incredibly humbled by their reasoning. "Is that how it works?"

Both boys nodded.

"You do like her, doncha?" Shane asked.

"Yes, I like her," he admitted, fighting against the smile that wanted to curve his lips. "And I like you guys, too."

"That's good, 'cuz we like you, too."

Georgia paused just outside the door of the twins' bedroom. She hadn't intended to eavesdrop—she hadn't even known that Matt was back until she heard his voice down the hall. And she hadn't overheard much of their conversation, just enough to get the impression that they were having a meeting of the mutual admiration society.

But when Quinn said, "That's good, 'cuz we like you, too," she saw Shane shake his head. And her heart broke, just a little, when her shy son looked up at him and said, "I love you, Dr. Matt."

She'd worried that she was making a huge mistake in allowing herself to get close to Matt; she'd been even more worried about the twins. And just as she'd suspected, her boys had already given him their fragile, trusting hearts. Now she stood frozen in the doorway, waiting for him to respond to her son's heartfelt confession.

Matt lifted a hand and gently tousled Shane's hair. "I love you guys, too," he said, his voice husky with emotion.

And Georgia's heart tumbled right out of her chest to land at his feet.

Over the past couple of months, she felt as if she'd gotten to know Matt Garrett fairly well. She knew he was a dedicated surgeon who cared about his patients, a brother with close ties to his siblings, a neighbor always willing to lend a hand, and the man who made her heart beat faster whenever

he was near. He was good with kids and kind to animals—
and he kissed like there was no tomorrow. He was smart and
sexy and far too charming. But he was also steadfast, reli-
able and trustworthy.

She pressed a hand to her rapidly beating heart and prayed
that she wasn't wrong about that part. Because she'd decided
that she was finally ready to prove that she trusted him, with
her body *and* her heart.

But first she had to get her kids to sleep.

Obviously Matt was thinking along the same lines, because
he said, "Now let's get you both tucked into your own beds
before your mom comes in to check on you."

Quinn climbed out of his brother's bed and into his own,
pulling his sheets up under his chin and closing his eyes tight.

"Well, look at this," she said, stepping into the room. "My
two handsome boys with their jammies on and teeth brushed,
all snuggled down and ready to go to sleep."

Quinn's eyes popped open and he exchanged a guilty
glance with Shane.

"You did brush your teeth, didn't you?"

Of course she knew that they hadn't, because she'd checked
their brushes on her way past the bathroom and found they
were still dry.

"We forgot," Shane admitted.

"Then you better go do it now," she advised.

"But I'm already in bed and I'm really tired," Quinn protested.

"Then the hot dogs and cotton candy and ice cream on
your teeth will be a delicious feast for the cavity monsters
who come out when you're asleep."

She held back a smile as the boys scrambled out of bed
and raced to the bathroom.

While they were brushing, she crossed the room to where
Matt was standing and kissed his cheek. "Thank you."

"For what?"

"Being so great with the boys."

"They're great boys," he said, with an ease that assured her he meant it.

"I think so," she agreed, then smiled. "Most of the time, anyway."

The boys raced back into the room, stopping in front of Georgia and opening their mouths for the ritual inspection to ensure there wasn't anything left for the cavity monsters to snack on in the night.

"Looks good," she said approvingly.

Then there was a round of hugs and kisses and she tucked them into bed again. Matt glanced at his watch as he followed her into the hall, and she knew he was eager to head back over to the park. But when they made their way down the stairs and into the empty living room, he frowned.

"Where did Brittney and Nina go?"

"I sent them home." She hoped she sounded more confident than she felt, because now that they were really alone, her stomach was in such a mess of knots she didn't think they'd ever untangle.

"I thought we were going back to the park to see the fireworks."

"I changed my mind."

"Don't I get a vote?"

She shook her head. "No, but you have a choice."

"What choice is that?" Matt asked her.

She lifted her arms to link them around his neck. "You can go back to the park for the fireworks—" her fingers cupped the back of his head, drew it down towards hers "—or we can make some of our own right here."

And then she kissed him.

To his credit, it didn't take him long to catch on to the change in their plans. In the space of a heartbeat, surprise had given way to seduction. He didn't respond to her kiss so much as he took it over—and she let him, because she'd never known anyone who kissed like Matt Garrett, with singular purpose and intense focus.

His lips were firm and masterful, confident and seductive. His tongue slid between her lips, stroked the roof of her mouth. Tingles of anticipation danced over her skin, desire shot through her veins. She wanted this—wanted him—more than she'd realized. And as glorious as it was to be kissed by Matt Garrett, she wanted more. She slid her hands over his chest, where she could feel the beat of his heart beneath her palms—strong and steady. Just like Matt.

She wanted to touch him, to feel the warm texture of his skin beneath her hands. Intent on her goal, she started to tug his shirt out of his pants, and nearly whimpered in protest when he caught her wrists in his hands and held them at her sides.

She eased her mouth from his and looked up at him, her gaze steady and sure. "I want you, Matt. Now. Tonight."

His eyes darkened, as much she suspected with satisfaction as with desire, but she didn't care. He could be as smug and self-righteous as he wanted, so long as he was with her.

"No doubts?"

She shook her head. "No doubts."

His lips hovered over hers again, tantalizingly close and oh so far away. "Are you going to let me strip every piece of clothing off your body, then touch you and kiss you all over until you're begging for me?"

Georgia wondered how she'd so quickly lost control of the situation. She'd set out to seduce him, and with just a few well-chosen words spoken in that low, sexy voice, he practically had her on the brink of climax. It made her wonder what would happen when he finally touched her—and made her desperate for his touch. But before that could happen, she had to make one thing clear. "I don't beg."

He grinned. "We'll see."

He captured her mouth again, kissing her so deeply and thoroughly she wanted to beg him to never stop. He finally released his hold on her wrists, skimming his fingers up the length of her arms to her shoulders, over her collarbone. Her skin burned everywhere he touched, and her body yearned everywhere he didn't. He traced the V-neckline of her blouse, raising goose bumps on her flesh. Then his thumbs brushed over her nipples, and she moaned as sharp arrows of pleasure shot to her core.

His hands immediately dropped away. "Did I hurt you?"

"No." She shook her head and grasped his wrists, drawing his hands back to her breasts. "I love the feel of your hands on me."

"Good. Because I want to touch all of you. I want to explore every inch of your satiny skin, every dip and curve of your exquisite body." As he spoke, his hands moved over her, from her shoulders to her breasts to her hips and her thighs, making her shudder.

"Are you planning to do all of that in the middle of my living room?" she asked.

"I guess a room with a door would be a better option."

"Upstairs," she said.

"I know," he said, and scooped her into his arms.

He knew because he'd taken her to her bed once before. At the time, she'd been practically comatose and unable to appreciate having a strong, handsome man at her disposal. She was definitely going to appreciate him tonight.

And despite having told him that she never wanted a man to sweep her off her feet, she couldn't deny that there was something incredibly romantic about being held against a solid, masculine chest with a pair of strong arms around her.

He set her on her feet just inside the room, then turned and closed the door with a soft click. Then he waited, as if giving her one last chance to change her mind. She took his hand and led him over to the bed.

Her heart was racing and her knees were shaking, not because she was afraid but because she'd never wanted anyone as much as she wanted this man now. He laid her down gently on the mattress and lowered himself over her. Then he kissed her again, and she sighed in blissful pleasure.

She wasn't aware that he'd unfastened the buttons of her shirt until he pushed the fabric over her shoulders and down her arms. Then he dipped his head to kiss the hollow between her breasts before he unclipped the front of her bra and parted the lacy cups. She tensed, because her breasts were ultra-sensitive as a result of nursing Pippa, and nearly lost it when he touched his tongue to her nipple.

He continued to focus his attention on her breasts, alternately licking, kissing and suckling until she was very close to begging. And then his mouth moved lower, raining kisses over her rib cage, the curve of her belly, and lower still. She tensed, her hands fisted in the covers, as he removed her jeans.

His fingers trailed along the soft skin inside her thighs, coaxing them to part. Then his tongue followed the same path to the apex of her thighs, and with the first touch of his tongue to her center, she simply and completely shattered.

"Matt." His name was both a whimper and a plea, but not even Georgia knew if she was begging him to stop—or not.

He didn't alter course. With his lips and his tongue and his teeth, he continued to tease and torment her, driving her higher and higher, ever closer to another pinnacle of pleasure. She bit down hard on her lip to keep from crying out. She wouldn't have thought it was possible, but somehow the second climax was even more explosive than the first.

"Now. Please now."

He paused only long enough to take care of protection, and her body was still pulsing with the aftershocks when he finally levered himself over and into her. She cried out as another wave of pleasure crashed over her. She didn't think it was possible, that she'd had anything left to give, but Matt proved her wrong once again. As her body found its rhythm in concert with his, she was flooded with new sensations, unimaginable pleasures.

She arched beneath him, lifting her legs to hook them over his hips, drawing him even deeper inside her. His groan mingled with hers, and he began to thrust faster, harder, deeper. Her fingers dug into his shoulders, the short nails scoring his flesh, as her body tensed again.

This time he rode the wave with her, crest after crest, until he finally shuddered his release into her.

Matt had dreamed of Georgia, hot and naked and screaming his name. But as vivid as those dreams had been, they paled in comparison to the reality of the woman in his arms. Making love with her had transcended all of his expectations. She was passionate and playful, and the result was an experience both gloriously intense and unexpectedly fun.

But the best part about making love with Georgia was that even after his body was sated, he still wanted to be with her. He wasn't proud to admit it, but he'd had a few interludes after which he couldn't wait to put his clothes back on and go home. And that, he'd finally understood, was the difference between meaningless sex and true intimacy. Both served a purpose, at least with respect to satisfying basic physiological needs, but he'd quickly grown bored of attraction without affection. Thankfully, with Georgia, there was plenty of both.

When he finally managed to catch his breath, he propped himself up on an elbow and couldn't resist teasing, "You begged."

One bare shoulder peeked out from the sheet as Georgia shrugged. "It seemed to matter to you."

"Oh, yeah?" He touched a fingertip to that bare shoulder, traced a path down below the sheet, over the curve of her breast to circle a taut nipple. "That was the only reason?"

"That and the fact that—" her breath caught when he gently tweaked her nipple "—you made my knees weak and my head spin."

He frowned, feigning concern as he shifted his attention to her other breast. "Sounds like a serious medical condition. Maybe you should see a doctor."

She smiled at that. "You don't really expect me to let you play doctor with me, do you?"

"I don't care what you call it—" he replaced his hand with his mouth, gently licking and nibbling until she was writhing and panting "—so long as you let me play."

"I can't think…of any…immediate…objections."

His hand slid over the gentle curve of her belly to the center of her femininity. And smiled with satisfaction when Georgia's breath whooshed out of her lungs and her eyes drifted shut.

"In fact…I can't think…at all."

"I like when you don't think," he told her.

She bit down on her lower lip. "Part of me wonders if I should be insulted by that remark."

"And the other part?" he prompted.

"All the other parts are too aroused to care."

"Are you going to beg again?"

"Make me," she challenged.

And because he'd never been able to resist a challenge, he did.

Chapter Fourteen

Georgia had known that Matt would be a good lover. He was too attentive and thoughtful in every aspect of his life to be otherwise in the bedroom. Not that she had much experience for comparison. She'd never been with anyone but Phillip, and she didn't know if that was the kind of admission she should have made to a potential lover.

She didn't know what Matt's expectations were when he took a woman to his bed. All kidding aside, the man did have a reputation. He'd dated a lot of women, probably slept with a lot of women—women who were likely more sophisticated and experienced than she. And women whose bodies didn't bear the evidence of having carried three babies.

She wouldn't trade any one of her children for anything in the world, but that didn't stop her from wishing—at least in the moment—that her hips were a little less round and the skin on her belly a little more taut. But Matt didn't seem to have any issues with her body during their two intense rounds of lovemaking. Which might explain why she was so thoroughly exhausted—three games of baseball followed by energetic bedroom activities would wear out anyone.

Georgia stretched her arms up over her head, trying to ease some of the kinks out of her body. Rolling over to face the other side of the bed, she was surprised to find it empty.

Obviously Matt had decided to go home, and while she was undeniably disappointed, she figured it was for the best. They really hadn't talked too much before they'd fallen into her bed, so it was probably wise for them both to take some time to think things through and reestablish boundaries. Because there had been absolutely no boundaries when she'd been naked in his arms.

After a quick trip to the bathroom, she noticed that soft light was spilling out of Pippa's partially closed doorway. Tiptoeing closer to peek into the room, she saw Matt in the rocking chair, feeding Pippa a bottle.

He'd pulled on his pants but not bothered with a shirt, and the sight of her baby girl cradled against his solid, masculine chest took her breath away. He should have looked ridiculous—a half-naked man in the midst of all the ultra-feminine décor; instead, he looked perfect—as if he belonged there.

"I raided your freezer stash again," he explained, whispering so as not to startle the baby.

"I can't believe I didn't hear her fussing."

"She didn't make too much noise," he assured her.

"You should have woken me up."

"I figured it was at least partly my fault that you were so exhausted, and I wanted to let you sleep."

Even before tonight, even before she'd watched him with her boys, she'd been more than halfway in love with him. But she'd refused to admit it, so sure that she could control her emotions. Then she'd made love with him, and she'd tumbled the rest of the way.

Now, seeing him here with Pippa, looking every bit as if he belonged there, made her wish that Matt Garrett could be a part of her life—and her children's lives—forever. Except that there had been too many stepfathers in and out of her life for Georgia to let herself even hope. Nothing was forever, and the sooner she put an end to such foolish fantasies, the better.

As he rose to put the sleeping baby back in her crib, Georgia turned away so he wouldn't see the shimmer of her tears. But he was somehow attuned to the change in her mood, because he followed her into the hall and tipped her chin up, forcing her to meet his gaze.

"What's going on, Georgia?"

She shook her head. "Nothing. You're right—I'm just really tired and…I think you should go now."

He seemed more amused than offended by her impulsive suggestion. "Where do I have to go?"

"Home."

"Why?"

The gentle patience in his tone made her want to scream. How could he be so calm when she was on the verge of a full-scale panic?

"Because it's late," she snapped.

He smiled at that. "I don't have anyone waiting up for me."

"The puppies," she suddenly remembered, seizing upon the excuse. "Don't you have to let them out?"

"I already did," he told her.

"Won't they be scared, alone in the house without you?"

"They'll be fine," he insisted, and drew her into his arms. "What I want to know is why you're suddenly scared to have me in your house with you."

"I'm not scared," she lied. "I just think we should take a step back."

His amusement faded. "You want to take a step back?"

She nodded. "Sex is sex, but sleeping together implies a certain level of intimacy."

"Yes, it does," he agreed. "And I intend to spend the night

with you, Georgia—to sleep with you in my arms and wake up with you in the morning."

She wanted that, too, far more than she should. Because if she let him stay tonight, she would want him to stay the night after that and the night after that, and eventually she would start to count on him being there.

"Do you want me to beg?" His tone was deliberately light, but she could tell by the intensity of his gaze that he understood this was a big deal to her.

"Would you?" she wondered.

His gaze never wavered. "I would do anything for you, Georgia. Don't you know that by now?"

"I guess I do," she finally said. "And maybe that's what scares me."

"Have there been so many people in your life who have let you down?"

"Each of my mother's four husbands, including my own father. Every single one of them claimed to want her and her kids, and every single one of them dropped out of our lives."

"And then your husband did the same," Matt noted with surprising insight. "Not that it was his choice, but the result was the same. He promised to be with you forever, and then he was gone, leaving you alone and your children without a father."

She nodded.

"And if even he didn't stick around, why should you trust that I will?"

She nodded again. "And before you point it out, yes, I know that I was the one trying to push you out the door."

"Because then it would be *your* choice," he noted.

Even she hadn't consciously understood the rationale behind her actions, but now she realized he was right. Every time her mother had walked out on one of her husbands, it had been Charlotte's choice, and her daughters had no option but to follow her out the door.

"Okay, you get to decide," he said. "Do you want me to stay—or do you want me to go?"

She should have been relieved that he was letting her choose, because her choice was already made. Except that somehow, during the course of their conversation, she'd started to question the wisdom of her decision to push him away. He'd proven that he understood her as no one else ever had, and he wanted to be with her anyway. And the fact that he had enough faith in her to put the choice in her hands gave her the courage to trust her heart.

She reached for his hand and linked their fingers together. "Stay."

Matt understood how hard it was for Georgia to say that single word. Because while it might have seemed like an easy response to a simple question, he knew that it was much more than that.

For Georgia, admitting that she wanted him to stay was the equivalent of putting her heart directly in his hands. And he was both grateful and relieved that she'd found the courage to do so, because whether she knew it or not, his heart was completely in hers.

This time when he took her back to bed, he showed her with his hands and his lips and his body the words he knew she wasn't ready to hear. And in the morning, when he woke with her in his arms, he had absolutely no doubt that this was how he wanted to wake up every day for the rest of his life.

Over the next several days, they resumed their normal routines with only a few minor adjustments—the puppies' bed was moved into Georgia's kitchen in the evening, he spent the nights in Georgia's bed, and she'd stopped pretending that she didn't want him there.

But as much as he enjoyed the new physical aspect of their relationship, he also enjoyed just being with her. There was so much he didn't know about her, so much he wanted to learn, and they often stayed awake late into the night just talking.

One night, after filling her in on the exploits of Finnigan and Frederick during a recent trip to Luke's office for their nine-week checkup, Georgia commented, "You've got a great relationship with your brothers, but I've never heard you mention any other family."

"That's because both of my parents died a few years back."

She winced. "I'm sorry—I shouldn't have pried."

"It's hardly a big secret," he said, and certainly not in comparison to the other, bigger secret that he'd yet to confide. Not because he didn't want to tell her, but because he knew that the time and place of the telling were crucial to ensuring her understanding, and this was not the time or the place.

Then when? the nagging voice of his conscience demanded.

Followed by Georgia's question: "Can you tell me what happened?"

It took him a second to comprehend that she was referring to the loss of his parents and not the failure of his marriage. "After my dad retired, they decided they wanted to see the world—the Great Wall of China, the Australian outback, the Serengeti—and they were having a great time. Then they decided to sail around Cape Horn, but the captain's years of experience were no match for the storm that capsized their boat. My parents—and all the crew—drowned." She took his hand, a silent gesture of comfort and encouragement.

"That must have been horrible for you and your brothers—losing them both at the same time," she murmured.

He nodded. "It was hard to find solace in anything under those circumstances, but once we'd started to get over our frustration and grief, we were able to take some comfort in the fact that they were together. Because we knew that, after almost forty years of marriage, neither one of them would have wanted to go on without the other.

"Losing them so unexpectedly was tragic," he continued.

"But we were lucky to have been witness to such an example of a strong and stable marriage, to have seen, day in and day out, the evidence of their deep love and enduring affection for one another."

"My mother has never found that kind of forever-after love," she told him. "And not for lack of searching. Yet she still believes it exists."

"It does," he said, and lowered his head to press a soft kiss to her lips.

"Did you think you'd found it with your wife?"

He leaned his forehead against hers. "Are you trying to kill the mood?"

"I guess I'm just curious," she said. "I can't imagine that you would get married without believing it was forever, and—believing it was forever—I can't imagine you ever giving up on your vows. At least not easily."

"It wasn't easy," he admitted, resigned now to spilling the whole sordid story of his ex-wife's deception.

Except that the puppies suddenly broke into a chorus of yelps and howls.

Georgia froze. Matt threw back the covers and swung his legs over the edge of the mattress, but she grabbed his arm, halting his movements.

In the midst of all the frantic puppy sounds, the muttering of a female voice could be heard. Matt couldn't actually make out the words, but he thought they sounded like, "You'd think she could have told me about the dogs."

"You stay here," Georgia said, reaching for her robe. "I'll go."

He shook his head, baffled that she would even suggest such a thing. "There's someone in the house, and there's no way—"

"It's not just someone," she interrupted. "It's my mother."

Georgia had faced more than a few curveballs in her life, and having Charlotte Warring-Eckland-Tuff-Masterton-

Kendrick-Branston show up unannounced and in the middle of the night was only the latest one.

The puppies heard the creak of the stairs before Charlotte did, and they happily abandoned the unfriendly stranger in favor of the human who occasionally fed them dinner and took them for walks. Georgia bent to pat them both on their head, reassuring them that they were excellent watchdogs, before she addressed her mother.

"This is a surprise, Mom."

Charlotte kissed each of her daughter's cheeks in turn before she offered a smile that was wide, and just a little bit forced.

"Well, that was my plan—to surprise you. But I didn't mean to wake you up, baby girl," she said, a note of apology in her voice. "And actually, I don't think I did, it was the dogs. Why didn't you tell me that you were turnin' the house into a kennel?"

"It's only two puppies, and they're not mine."

"Then why are they here?"

"I'm helping out a friend," she hedged. "Why are you here?"

"As far as I know, this is still my house."

"You know it is," Georgia agreed. "But why are you showing up here at two o'clock in the morning?"

"Because it's nearly a three-hour drive from the airport," she said, as if that explained everything.

"Okay," Georgia said, trying not to lose patience. "Why did you choose to make the trip from Montana at this particular point in time?"

"I was just missin' my grandbabies so much I simply couldn't wait another day to put my arms around them, so Trigger bought me a plane ticket and here I am."

There was something about Charlotte's explanation that struck Georgia as a little off, or maybe it was the deliberately casual tone that tripped her radar. Whatever the reason,

Georgia was suddenly convinced that there was more to this impromptu trip than her mother needing a baby fix. And she was pretty sure she knew what it was.

"You left him, didn't you?"

"What are you talkin' about?"

"Trigger—your husband. The one who made you feel a jolt as if you'd stuck your finger in a socket," Georgia reminded her.

Charlotte pressed a perfectly manicured hand to her chest, right over her heart. "It was just like that," she agreed.

"So where is he now?"

"At his ranch, of course. He couldn't just abandon his animals 'cause I had a whim to see my baby girl and her babies."

"You're actually sticking to that story?"

"Really, Georgia May, I don't understand why you're being so confrontational."

Upstairs, she could hear Pippa starting to fuss, wanting to be fed, and Georgia was eager to get to the baby before her mother decided to trek up the stairs.

"I'm sorry. Maybe we should continue this conversation in the morning—or rather, at a more reasonable hour in the morning."

"Sounds good to me," Charlotte agreed. "It's been a long day and I could definitely use some shut-eye."

Georgia nodded, though she didn't expect that she would get to sleep any time soon. First she'd have to feed and change Pippa, then when the baby was settled back down and she was sure that Charlotte was asleep, she'd have to get Matt out of the house. She didn't doubt he would balk at being shoved out the back door but even though she was thirty-one years of age, Georgia still wasn't willing to risk her mother catching a man in her bed.

Another soft coo drifted down the stairs, followed by a chattier babble that was the little girl's version of a conversation. Which meant that Matt had heard the baby and, knowing that Georgia was occupied downstairs, had gone in to Pippa's room to check on her.

"Oh, the baby's awake," Charlotte said, her voice filled with genuine pleasure. "I have to take just a little peek—"

"Why don't you wait until morning?" Georgia suggested. "If she sees you now, she won't settle down again."

Charlotte waved a hand dismissively as she started up the stairs. "Don't be silly. She'll settle down just fine if she's tired."

Short of physically restraining her mother, Georgia knew there was no way to prevent Charlotte from going into Pippa's room. Which meant there was no way that she wasn't going to cross paths with—

"Matthew Garrett," Charlotte said, her voice tinged with both surprise and approval. "I was wonderin' whose size-thirteen shoes I nearly tripped over downstairs."

"Well, that wasn't as awkward as I thought it might be," Matt said, after Georgia had finished nursing the baby and Charlotte had gone back to the main floor master bedroom.

"It felt plenty awkward to me," Georgia told him.

"You're just embarrassed because your mom gave you two thumbs up before she said good-night," he teased.

"The fact that she approves of our involvement does make me wary," she admitted. "My mother has notoriously bad taste in men."

"Are you saying that because her exes were of questionable character or because the relationships were unsuccessful?"

"I'm not sure the distinction really matters."

"Sure it does. If she truly made poor choices, then you should be wary. But if they were good men, then there could be any number of reasons that things didn't work out."

"Like her habit of bailing whenever a relationship hits a snag rather than trying to find a solution?" she suggested.

"That could be an issue," he agreed.

"I don't think she's here for a visit," Georgia finally said. "I think she left Trigger."

"Wouldn't she have told you if that was the case?"

She shook her head. "No. Not until she's figured out a way to spin it so that it isn't her fault."

"That's kind of harsh, don't you think?"

She sighed. "Maybe. And maybe I'm wrong. I honestly I hope that I am, because if she did walk out on her marriage, her heart is completely shattered but she won't let anyone know it."

"I guess that proves you come by your tough demeanor honestly enough."

"You think I'm tough?"

"On the outside," he said. "On the inside, you're all soft and gooey like a marshmallow." He lowered his head to kiss her, softly, deeply. "And very, very sweet."

"Mmm." She hummed her approval as she linked her arms around his neck. "You're trying to distract me, aren't you?"

He slid his hands beneath her shirt and unfastened the front of her bra so that her breasts spilled into his hands. Her breath hitched; her nipples pebbled. He rubbed his thumbs over the taut peaks, making her moan. "Is it working?"

Her breath shuddered out between her lips as he nibbled on the lobe of her ear. "Is what working?"

Smiling, he lowered her onto the bed.

Matt got called in to the hospital early the next morning, leaving Georgia to face her mother's barrage of questions and unsolicited advice alone. And Charlotte didn't disappoint. In fact, Georgia had barely begun cracking eggs into a bowl when her mother said, "You picked a good man, baby girl."

Considering that Matt hadn't moved in until after her mother had left for Vegas, she had to ask, "How do you know?"

"There's no disputing the Garrett boys were all players in

their youth, but everyone in town agrees that they've grown into fine, upstanding citizens. Or at least Matt and Luke," her mother clarified, a slight furrow in her brow. "There seems to be some difference of opinion with respect to Jack."

"That's your source of information—town gossip?"

"News—good and bad—travels fast in Pinehurst. And I've heard nothin' but good things about Matt Garrett." Charlotte dropped her voice, as if revealing confidential information. "Did you know that he's a doctor?"

She focused on whisking the eggs and ignored the fact that her mother actually thought Georgia might sleep with a man without knowing something as basic as his occupation. "Yes, I know he's a doctor. In fact, he put the cast on Shane's arm when he broke it."

Her mother nodded. "Smart, charming and very handsome. It's almost too much to hope that he'd also be good in bed."

"Mom!" Georgia felt her cheeks burn hotter than the skillet on the stove.

Charlotte smiled. "Well, well. My baby girl's discovered that there's passion in her blood."

"A true revelation after having three children delivered by the stork," Georgia said dryly.

"The earth doesn't have to move for a woman to get pregnant," her mother pointed out as she gathered plates and cutlery for the meal. "And while I never doubted that Phillip was a good man, I did wonder if he was a good husband."

Georgia was baffled by the statement. "Why would you ever wonder about that?"

"Because I never saw him look at you the way Matt looks at you—and vice versa."

Georgia hated to admit that it was probably true. In so many ways, she and Phillip had been well suited, but while they'd shared a certain level of attraction, they'd never generated any real sparks. Certainly nothing that could compare to the kind of sparks that flew whenever Georgia and Matt were together, but acknowledging that fact—even to her mother—seemed disloyal somehow. "I loved my husband."

"I know you did," Charlotte said. "But do you love Matt?"

She pushed the eggs around in the pan. "I've only known him a couple of months."

"I only knew Trigger a couple of days," Charlotte reminded her. "But that was long enough to know that I wanted to spend the rest of my life with him."

Except that, for some inexplicable reason, she was here and her husband was in Montana. But Georgia wasn't going to get into that with her mother today. Instead, she only said, "I'm not ready to make that kind of leap."

"Well, don't wait too long," Charlotte advised. "If you don't snap up that sexy doctor quick, another woman will."

"If he let himself be snapped up that easily by someone else, then maybe I'm better off without him."

Charlotte huffed out a breath, unable to dispute her daughter's logic, and Georgia took advantage of her momentary silence to call the boys to the table.

They were just settling down to eat when the doorbell rang. Not just once but three times in rapid succession, and then, before Georgia could even push her chair back, a fist was pounding on the door.

A quick glance across the table revealed that her mother's face was whiter than the napkin she'd twisted around her fingers. Since she obviously had no intention of going to the door, Georgia did, pulling it open to a tall, broad-shouldered cowboy, complete with hat and boots. "Can I help you?"

The man on the porch swiped the Stetson from his head, revealing neatly trimmed salt-and-pepper hair. "I'm Henry Branston. I'm here to get my wife."

Chapter Fifteen

"Your driveway's starting to look like a rental-car agency," Matt commented to Georgia when he got home from the hospital later that afternoon.

"I know. I walked to the grocery store with all the kids today because it was easier than moving three vehicles around. That and it allowed me a brief opportunity to escape from the drama."

"You can always stay at my place," he offered. "If you want some extra space."

"I might take you up on that if they don't go back to Montana soon, because after all the accusations and tears were done and they'd kissed and made up, they went straight down the hall to her bedroom and locked the door. And then I heard *noises*." She shuddered at the memory.

"Does that mean they've worked things out?" he asked cautiously.

"I think so. But what's even more bizarre, from what I

overheard of their argument, I think I understand why she left. I don't agree with her decision, but I understand."

"Want to explain it to me?"

"My mother felt as if she was the only one who made any kind of sacrifice when they got married. She left her home and her family and moved to an environment completely unfamiliar to her in order to be with the man she loved. And the more time she spent in Montana, the more she recognized that his life hadn't changed at all.

"She didn't necessarily want him to make any changes, she just wanted to know that he loved her enough to be willing to do so. The fact that he dropped everything to follow her halfway across the country to take her back home seemed to prove to her that he did love her enough."

"And now everything's okay?"

"Apparently."

"So when are they heading back to Montana?"

"Probably not soon enough," she said.

He chuckled. "As long as they're not leaving today, then I don't have to change our plans for tonight."

"Our plans?"

"Last night, when you were nursing Pippa, your mom offered to babysit the kids so that I could take you out on a real date."

She lifted a brow. "Have we had fake dates?"

He nudged her with his shoulder. "You know what I mean."

"Actually, I'm not sure that I do," she admitted. "What is a real date?"

"Dinner in a restaurant that doesn't have a kiddie menu, a movie that isn't a cartoon."

"Those things are beyond my realm of experience," she warned.

"Are you willing to give it a try?"

"We could," she allowed. "Or we could order pizza with spicy sausage, hot peppers and black olives, and watch a movie on the TV in your bedroom."

"You're assuming I have a TV in my bedroom," he pointed out.

Her lips curved. "If you don't, I'm sure we could find something else to occupy the time."

He decided to go with her plan, but upgraded it a little by setting the table with candles and champagne flutes filled with sparkling grape juice. And for dessert, he picked up some miniature pastries from the Bean There Café.

After the pizza had been eaten, Matt asked Georgia if she had any update on her mother's plans.

"They want to stay for two weeks," she told him, making the "two weeks" sound like "forever."

"Charlotte misses her grandchildren," he guessed.

"I think she does, but it was actually Trigger's idea to stay for a while, to get to know his new family." But she didn't sound very enthusiastic about the prospect.

"And you're afraid that if you get to know him, you'll like him, and if your mother walks out a second time, you might never see him again."

"That's certainly been the history," she admitted. "But honestly, I think Trigger is different. I think my mother could walk out a dozen times, and he'd track her down and take her back, because he loves her."

"Does that mean you now believe they did fall in love over a baccarat table?"

"It seems that I do."

"Then it wouldn't be completely out of the realm of possibility that a man could fall in love with his next-door neighbor after only a couple of months?"

She picked up her juice, sipped. "I guess not, but I'm hardly an expert on the subject."

"Okay, as a non-expert, do you think there's any chance that she might someday feel the same way?"

She nibbled on her lower lip for what seemed like an eternity while he waited for her response.

"I think it's possible that she already does," she said, and he was finally able to release the breath he'd been holding.

"I know you probably think I'm rushing things—even I thought I was rushing things," he admitted. "But Charlotte convinced me that sometimes the heart just knows what it wants."

"You're taking relationship advice from a woman who's been married five times and divorced four?"

"It takes courage to follow your heart."

"Then she has to be the bravest woman I know."

"She probably is," Matt agreed.

"And you think I'm a coward."

"I think you're wary," he said. "And I understand why you would be."

"My kids are my priority."

"I don't have a problem with that," he assured her. "And I don't think your kids have any problem with us being together."

"They don't, because they want you to be their new daddy. But they've already lost one father—how will they feel if things don't work out?"

"I'm thirty-eight years old and long past the stage of wanting to sow any wild oats. I wouldn't be with you—I wouldn't risk getting close to your kids—if I wasn't serious." He put his hand in his pocket and closed his fingers around the box from Diamond Jubilee. He set it on the table in front of her. "Very serious."

Georgia's breath caught when she recognized the logo. Matt hadn't opened the lid, but that didn't matter. She didn't care if he'd chosen a diamond solitaire or a cluster of cubic zirconias, it was the significance of the box itself that had her mind reeling.

"This isn't how I planned to do it," he told her. "But I couldn't let you continue thinking this is just a fling, because it's not. Not for me."

"I kind of liked the idea of a fling," she said, keeping her tone light and her hands clasped together. "I've never had one before."

"Because you're not the type of woman to share your body without giving your heart. At least, I hope you're not."

That heart was pounding frantically now, though she didn't know if it was with excitement or apprehension. "I'm also not the type of woman who believes that an intimate relationship has to lead to a walk down the aisle."

"And I've never felt compelled to propose to a woman just because I slept with her," he pointed out. "But I've been married before and if the failure of that marriage taught me nothing else, it at least taught me that there are no guarantees in life.

"After the divorce, I learned to appreciate every moment—and I vowed that if I was ever lucky enough to find someone with whom I wanted to share those moments, I would never let her go." He reached across the table and linked their hands together. "I want to share all of my moments with you."

The heartfelt words brought tears to her eyes. And while she could appreciate that he was putting it all on the line, she was too cowardly to do the same.

"I wasn't ready for this," she protested. "I'm *not* ready for this."

He released her hands and tucked the box back into his pocket. But removing it from the table didn't make her feel any less pressured, because now she knew it was there.

"I wasn't pushing you for an answer. Not right now," he said. "I just wanted you to know that I was looking toward a future for us—all of us—together."

"And I was looking forward to tonight—just the two of us."

She could tell that he was disappointed in her response, but she didn't know what else to say. Or maybe she was afraid to admit what was in her heart. She wasn't just wary—she was terrified, because what she felt for Matt was so much bigger than anything she'd ever felt before.

"Then let's start with tonight," he said, and led her upstairs to his bedroom.

Georgia wouldn't have thought it was possible, but she was almost more nervous now than the first time they'd made love. Because then she'd had no hopes or expectations beyond that single night. And when one night had become two, she'd still been content to live in the moment.

I want to share all of my moments with you.

As Matt's words echoed in the back of her mind, Georgia knew without a doubt that she wanted the same thing. From this moment to forever.

He paused in the act of unbuttoning her shirt. "You're trembling," he noted.

She could only nod.

"It can't be nerves," he said, in a gentle, teasing tone. "Because I've seen you naked at least once or twice before."

"But I never knew it wasn't just a fling before."

"But you know it now?"

She nodded again. "You matter to me, Matt. And I don't want to screw this up."

"You won't," he assured her.

"How do you know?"

"Because we're in this together, and I won't let anything screw this up for us." He kissed her then, softly, deeply, thoroughly. "I love you, Georgia."

She wasn't sure if it was the kiss or his words, but suddenly her head was spinning and her knees were weak. Her fingers curled into the fabric of his shirt, holding on. "Show me."

So he did. With each kiss, every touch and every caress,

with his lips and his hands and his body, he showed her the depth and truth of his feelings. She had never felt more treasured or cherished. Her pleasure was his pleasure. He gave and gave until she couldn't take any more, until she didn't want anything—not even her next breath—as much as she wanted him inside of her.

And when their bodies finally joined together, Georgia knew that their hearts and souls were equally entwined.

Afterward, when she was snuggled against his chest waiting for her heart rate to return to normal, she appreciated that this was one of those moments he'd been talking about. A moment that she wanted to share with only Matt. Not just because they'd had earth-shattering sex together, but because, when she was in his arms, she felt as if she truly belonged there. And because there was nowhere else in the world that she would rather be.

And along with that certainty came the courage to finally admit what she wanted. "Was there really a ring in that box you pulled out earlier?"

"You want to see it, don't you?" His lips curved, just a little. "It's always about the bling, isn't it?"

"No, I don't want to see it," she denied. "I want to wear it. But only if I hear a proper proposal." It really hadn't mattered to her that Phillip had never formally proposed. But he was her past and Matt was her future—and she wanted this time to be different. She wanted this time to really be forever.

His brows quirked. "Does that mean I have to get dressed?"

She shook her head. "It only means you have to ask."

He leaned over the edge of the mattress, searching for the pants that had been discarded on the floor to retrieve the box from the pocket. He fumbled a little, trying to open the lid, but she covered his hand.

"The proposal," she reminded him.

"Now *I'm* nervous," he admitted.

She smiled, relieved to know that she wasn't the only one. "Would it help if I told you that I'm probably going to say yes?"

"Probably?" he echoed. "That's not very reassuring."

"Well, I can't say anything until you ask the question."

"I really didn't plan to do it like this. I wanted to have all the right words to tell you how much you mean to me, how just knowing you has changed my life and made every day a little bit better."

"That sounds pretty good so far," she said.

"Being with you makes me happy," he told her, "and the only way I could imagine being any happier would be with you as my wife. But I don't just want to be your husband, I want to be your partner in every aspect of your life. I want to share your hopes and dreams, to help raise your children, to celebrate with you when you're happy and hold you when you're sad. I want to share every moment of the rest of your life, and that's why I'm asking, Georgia Reed, will you marry me?"

She blew out a shaky breath. "I don't have any words that can top that."

"There's only one word I want to hear," he said.

"Yes." She pressed her lips to his. "Yes, Matthew Garrett, I will marry you."

"You haven't even looked at the ring," he chided.

Because it seemed so important to him, she dropped her gaze to the box in his hand. And this time when her breath caught in her throat it was because she was absolutely stunned by the enormous princess-cut diamond set in a platinum band.

"So it's not about the bling?" he teased, slipping the ring onto her finger.

She couldn't deny that she liked the way the diamond sparkled on her finger, but far more precious to her was the love in his heart. A love that matched her own.

"No," she said, and kissed him again. "It's all about the man."

Georgia had hoped to keep the news of their engagement on the QT for a while—at least until she had a chance to get used to it herself. She didn't count on the fact Charlotte could sniff out a diamond at twenty paces. Georgia had barely walked into the kitchen the next morning when her mother let out a squeal of delight and snatched up her daughter's hand for a closer inspection.

"Look at the size of that rock," she said approvingly. "If that doesn't say 'I love you,' nothin' does." But then her gaze narrowed. "So why is it that your cheeks are glowin' but there's worry in your eyes?"

"I guess I'm just feeling a little like I'm venturing into new territory."

"You were married once before," Charlotte reminded her.

"I know, but everything was different with Phillip. I felt safe with Phillip."

"You're feelin' vulnerable," her mother guessed.

She nodded.

"Every time you put your heart out there, you put it at risk," Charlotte acknowledged. "You just have to trust that it's worth the risk."

"I loved Phillip, but it was a comfortable kind of love. What I feel for Matt is so much more intense, so much more all-encompassing. So much more...everything."

"Love can be scary," her mother agreed. "It's both exhilaratin' and terrifyin', much like those roller coasters you enjoyed so much as a kid."

"That was Indy," Georgia reminded her. "I *hated* roller coasters."

Charlotte chuckled. "That's right. You used to scream

bloody murder whenever your sister convinced you to strap yourself into one."

"She didn't convince me—she bribed me." Usually by offering her share of the cotton candy or caramel corn Charlotte had bought for them. Georgia would happily devour the treat—and then promptly throw it up again when she got off the ride.

And she couldn't help wondering if she was making the same mistake now. The idea of a future with Matt was like a trip to the carnival—both thrilling and terrifying. She had never loved anyone as she loved him, which meant that no one had ever had so much power to break her heart.

But when she was in Matt's arms, she had absolute faith that he wouldn't do so. He was like the safety bar that held her tight, that would keep her in the car, protect her through all of the ups and downs and corners and curves. He would be the partner who shared not just her life but her hopes and her dreams, and a father for her children.

When Phillip died, she'd mourned for her children even more than she'd mourned for herself. She'd cried for her sons who had absolutely doted on their father, and who had been devastated to know that he was never coming home again. And she'd cried for her unborn child who would never even know her daddy. But she hadn't cried for herself, because the truth was, she'd been living life on her own for a long time before she buried her husband.

"So when's the weddin'?" Charlotte asked.

"We just got engaged," Georgia reminded her.

"Which means it's time to start thinkin' about a weddin'," her mother insisted. "Better yet, let's go out today to find you a dress."

"I'm not rushing into anything," Georgia protested.

"But it would mean so much to me to see my baby girl happily married before I go back to Montana."

She shook her head. "There's no way I'm planning a wedding in two weeks."

"You don't need to do a lot of plannin'," Charlotte said, her eyes twinkling. "You and your fiancé can just fly down to Vegas—"

"No."

Her mother frowned. "Why not?"

"Because I don't want to get married by a second-rate Elvis impersonator in some tacky chapel..." She felt the flood of color in her cheeks as her brain finally halted the flow of words from her mouth. "I'm sorry. I didn't mean—"

Charlotte waved off her apology. "Most of those chapels are tacky, but some of those Elvises are real good. Not the one who married me and Trigger, mind you, but I didn't care about the settin' so much as the vows." Then she winked. "And the weddin' night."

Georgia cringed. "Too much information."

"Honestly, Georgia May Reed, I don't know how any daughter of mine grew up to be such a prude."

"Did you know that the word 'prude' provides the root of the word 'prudence,' meaning the exercise of sound judgment?" she asked, undaunted by the criticism.

"Nothin' would show more sound judgment than movin' forward with your life with that sexy doctor," Charlotte told her. "And I'd feel so much better about goin' back to Montana if I knew you were settled and taken care of. But if you won't do it for me, do it for your children."

Georgia narrowed her gaze. "Don't you use my children to manipulate me."

"I'm just askin' you to consider how happy they'd be to have a full-time daddy in their lives again. Especially the twins, since they'll be startin' kindergarten soon." Her mother refilled her mug with coffee, added a heaping teaspoon of sugar. "When they're asked to draw those pictures of their family, I'm sure they'd like bein' able to put a daddy in the scene."

It was, as Charlotte had to know, the only argument that could sway Georgia from her conviction not to rush into anything.

Matt was surprised but not opposed when Georgia suggested a date for their wedding that was less than two weeks away. And he was determined that doing it on short notice didn't mean they couldn't do it right. While Georgia went shopping with her mom for a dress and made arrangements for a minister, flowers and cake, he enlisted the aid of his brothers to get the upstairs bedrooms ready for the kids.

He'd let the twins decide what they wanted for their room and was pleased with the sports-themed border and green paint they selected. Since the room had been empty, he ordered new furniture for them, too—a set of bunk beds, and dressers and desks. Georgia picked out the paint for Pippa's room and lace curtains for her window and pitched in with the decorating whenever she could spare a few minutes in between taking care of the kids and dealing with wedding details.

They were both so busy that they rarely had any time alone. And when they did manage to steal a few minutes of private time, they usually only stayed awake long enough to make love and then fall asleep in one another's arms. But as the date of the wedding drew nearer, Matt knew they needed to find time to talk. Except that now, with the wedding only a few days away, he couldn't help but worry that he'd already waited too long.

He was in the midst of hanging the border in the twins' room when he remembered that he needed a utility knife. When Georgia walked in to check on his progress, it seemed logical to ask her to get the knife out of the top drawer of his desk. It wasn't until she'd started down the stairs that he re-membered the photo that was in that same drawer.

Panic clawing at his belly, he dropped the border and raced after her, desperate to get to her before she opened that drawer. But when he reached the doorway, he saw that he was already too late.

Georgia stood behind the desk, the utility knife in one hand and a wallet-sized photograph in the other. He couldn't see the picture from where he was standing, but the image was burned into his mind. A six-year-old boy with dark hair, dark eyes and a broad grin, wearing a mortarboard and gown and holding a rolled-up scroll. Liam's kindergarten gradu-ation photo.

He took a tentative step into the room. "Georgia?"

She looked up at him, and his heart broke to see the doubts and confusion swirling in her eyes. "Who is he?"

He blew out a breath. "His name's Liam.... He was my son."

Chapter Sixteen

Georgia could only stare at him, uncomprehending. She thought he'd said "my son" but that wasn't possible. There was no way he could have a child he'd never mentioned. But the expression on his face—a combination of guilt, regret and remorse—was silent confirmation of his words.

She sank into the chair behind the desk. "You have…a child?"

"I did," he said. "For almost three years."

Three years? But that didn't make any sense either, because the boy in the photo was clearly more than three years old.

"Maybe you could fill in some more details," she suggested, still trying to wrap her head around this sudden and unexpected revelation.

He nodded, but he didn't say anything right away, and she knew that he was struggling to find the right words to explain the situation.

"I married Lindsay because she was pregnant," he finally

said. "And because she told me the baby was mine. It turned out that he wasn't."

Though his words were casual, she heard the tension—and the hurt—in his tone, and her heart ached for him. She could only imagine how he'd responded to the disclosure. And because she knew Matt fairly well now, she knew he wouldn't have just felt hurt and betrayed, he would have been wrecked. "How did you find out?"

"Liam's real father finished his tour of duty in Iraq and decided to track down his ex-girlfriend, only to find that she'd married someone else less than two months after he was deployed."

"Did he know that she was pregnant?"

"No. Apparently Lindsay didn't even know when he left. And even when she knew she was going to have his baby, she didn't want to tell him because she was convinced he would never make it home. Instead, she decided to find another father for her baby."

As a mother, Georgia understood wanting what was best for her children, and she would—without question—do absolutely anything to protect them. But she couldn't imagine any woman being as coldly calculating as Matt was describing this woman to be.

"And I was the perfect patsy. She'd known me for years, because of my friendship with Kelsey. We'd even gone out a couple of times in high school, but it had never gone any further than that. Then suddenly she comes back from California after several years away, spinning this tale about how she never stopped thinking about me. She was beautiful and determined, and I let myself be flattered and seduced."

"She knew you would do the right thing," Georgia guessed. And it made her furious to think that this kind, generous, wonderful man had been ruthlessly targeted for those qualities.

He nodded. "I never even hesitated. I wasn't in love with her but I already loved the baby we were going to have together, and I believed our affection for one another would grow during the course of our marriage."

"I'm so sorry, Matt." And she was, her heart aching for everything he'd gone through.

Having witnessed firsthand how effortlessly he'd connected with her children, it was all too easy to imagine the deep and immediate bond he would have formed with a baby he believed was his own. And when the truth came out, he would have been absolutely devastated.

But he still wouldn't have turned his back on the child. Blood ties or not, in every way that mattered, he had been the little boy's father. His next words confirmed it.

"When Lindsay told me that she wanted a divorce so that she could take Liam back to California to be with his real dad, I was stunned and furious. So much that I thought about suing for custody.

"Although I wasn't Liam's biological parent, Jack assured me that I had a good chance of success, that the courts wouldn't look kindly on Lindsay's blatant deception and might believe that maintaining the status quo was in the child's best interests."

"What changed your mind?" she asked, though she suspected she already knew the answer to that question.

"Seeing the three of them together. It was immediately obvious to me that Lindsay and Jarrod loved one another in a way that she and I never had. And when he first saw Liam, when he realized that he was looking at his son—" Matt cleared his throat. "I just couldn't deny them the chance to be a family."

"Even though it broke your heart," she said softly.

He didn't deny it.

"Do you see him anymore?"

"Not since they moved back to California. Lindsay sends a card and a picture every once in a while, but Liam—" his gaze shifted to focus on the watercolor on the wall behind her "—he doesn't even remember me."

Georgia knew that was likely true. Even the twins' memories of their father were starting to fade. She knew they wouldn't ever forget Phillip—she would make sure of that—but their recollections would dim. For her, that sad truth had been countered, at least in part, by the pleasure of watching her sons bond with Matt.

She looked down at the photo again, her heart aching for the little boy who had been a pawn in his mother's game, thoughtlessly shifted from home to home, from father to father. As a result, Matt had lost his son. And then he'd moved in next door to a woman with three children who had lost their father. But the implications of that were something she wasn't ready to examine too closely just yet.

"This was his kindergarten graduation," she guessed.

He nodded.

She had to moisten her lips before she could ask, "How long ago was that?"

"A few weeks."

So much for thinking that the photo had been in the drawer for so long he'd forgotten about it. He'd only received it a few weeks earlier, and she didn't—couldn't—understand why he'd never mentioned it to her.

"I know I should have told you," Matt began.

And she waited, wondering what explanation he could possibly come up with that might make sense of the whole situation for her. He'd told her about his marriage—no, he'd only told her about his divorce, she realized now. When she'd asked him why he wasn't married, he'd only said that he was divorced. He'd never given her any details and he'd certainly never mentioned that his wife had given birth during the course of their marriage.

Even if it had turned out that the child wasn't his, it was a pretty significant omission. And it made her wonder why he'd been so closemouthed about the situation. In the beginning, okay. She hadn't spilled all the details about her marriage the first time they'd met. But as they'd grown closer, she thought he'd opened up to her. For God's sake, he'd asked her to marry him, their wedding was only three days away, and he'd never given her the tiniest glimpse into this part of his life.

Maybe she should have asked. Certainly his ease with her children, especially with Pippa, should have been a major clue that he had experience with kids. But when she'd questioned why he didn't have half a dozen children of his own, he'd never mentioned that he'd once had a son. He hadn't said anything at all.

Just like he didn't say anything else now, and Georgia finally understood that he wasn't going to. He wasn't going to explain why he hadn't told her about the beautiful little boy who had been his son. She knew it couldn't be easy for him to talk about Liam, to remember the child he'd loved and who had been ripped from his life. She could understand that experience would leave a huge hole in anyone's heart. But this wasn't just anyone, it was Matt—the man who claimed to love her.

And now she couldn't help but wonder if his affection for her was real, or if he just missed being a father.

He'd always been so good with her kids—forging a deep and enduring connection with each of them. At first, it had worried her, how quickly and easily the twins had taken to their neighbor. And Pippa hadn't been far behind. The little girl had never known her father, but she lit up like a neon sign whenever Matt walked into the room.

But Georgia's wariness had slowly faded and she'd been

grateful that she'd fallen in love with a man who so obviously loved her children. *I wasn't in love with her, but I already loved the baby we were going to have together.*

As Matt's words echoed in her mind, she had to wonder what had been the precipitating event in their relationship: his attraction to her or his affection for her children?

"Say something, Georgia, please."

She searched for words—any words—to describe the chaos of emotions churning inside of her. In the end, she only said, "Yes, you should have told me."

And she handed him the utility knife and walked out.

Georgia had introduced Trigger to the twins as Henry, not wanting to explain the origin of his nickname, but as soon as they found out he was married to Gramma, they decided that made him their Grampa. The boys had never had a Grampa before and Trigger had seemed so pleased with the designation that she didn't bother to nix the boys' decision.

And Gramma and Grampa were more than happy to look after the kids while Georgia ran some errands. At least that was the excuse she gave for going out again as soon as she'd returned from next door. And she probably did have errands that she needed to run, but in the moment, she couldn't remember any of them with all the doubts and insecurities churning in her mind.

She needed to talk to someone—she needed to vent and cry and try to figure out what Matt's revelation meant for their future. But she still didn't know very many people in Pinehurst and the one person she might consider talking to—Kelsey—had been Matt's friend for a long time.

She'd known me for years, because of my friendship with Kelsey.

That part of his explanation hadn't really registered at the time. In comparison to all of the other details, it had hardly seemed significant. But now Georgia knew that Kelsey might be the one person who had some of the answers she so desperately needed.

She walked down Main Street, past Emma's Flower Shop and Beckett's Sporting Goods until she found herself in front of Postcards from the World—Travel Agents & Vacation Planners.

Kelsey spotted her as soon as she walked through the door and waved her over. "Matt said you guys weren't going to plan a proper honeymoon until you'd weaned Pippa, but I had some ideas...." Her excited chatter faded away as Georgia got closer. "Obviously you're not here to inquire about vacation destinations."

"No, I'm not," Georgia agreed. "And I probably shouldn't have just dropped in, but I was hoping you might have a few minutes."

Kelsey looked around the mostly empty room. "Right now I have a lot of minutes. Did you want a cup of tea?"

Georgia nodded. "That would be great."

There was a small kitchen in the back, and Kelsey gestured for her to sit while she filled the kettle and put out a plate of cookies. When the tea was ready, she took a seat across from Georgia and said, "What did he do?"

Georgia wasn't surprised that the other woman had so quickly zeroed in on the heart of the problem, and the bluntness of the question encouraged her to respond equally succinctly. "He forgot to mention that he had a son."

"Are you saying that he didn't tell you until today?"

"He didn't tell me at all. I found a graduation photo of a little boy in his desk."

Kelsey winced. "Sometimes I wonder how that man ever got through medical school with only half of a working brain." Then she sighed. "Of course, he's not really an idiot, he just leads with his heart instead of his head sometimes.

That's why it was so easy for Lindsay to manipulate him. She played her cards exactly right to get what she wanted from Matt."

"Sounds like you knew her well," Georgia commented.

Kelsey paused with her cup halfway to her lips. "What did he tell you about my connection to his ex-wife?"

"He just said that he knew her because of his friendship with you. I assumed that meant you were a friend of hers, too."

The other woman shook her head. "Lindsay is my sister."

Now Georgia felt like the idiot. "I should have realized… I know Brittney calls him 'Uncle Matt,' but I thought that was just because you and he were such close friends."

"She refers to Jack and Luke as 'uncle' for that reason," Kelsey acknowledged. "But there's a real family connection to Matt through his marriage to my sister."

Georgia sipped her tea and tried to assimilate all of this new information.

"What are you thinking?" Kelsey asked gently.

"I don't know what to think. My head is spinning with so many questions and doubts that I don't know if I can articulate any of them."

"I can understand the questions, but what are you doubting?"

"Matt's reasons for wanting to marry me."

"The fact that he's head over heels in love with you isn't enough?"

"Is he?" Georgia asked, finally speaking her greatest fear aloud.

Kelsey looked startled by the question. "Do you really doubt it?"

"He married Lindsay to be a father to her baby," she reminded the other woman. "How do I know he isn't marrying me to be a father to my kids?" It was a possibility that tore at Georgia's heart.

"Ask him," Kelsey said. "That's the only way you can be sure."

It was good advice. Georgia certainly agreed that she and Matt needed to do a lot more talking, but first she went home to nurse her baby and hug her boys. Being with her children always helped her put things in perspective, through all of the best and worst times in her life. Since Matt had come into their lives, they'd enjoyed some of the best, and losing him, if that were to happen, would be one of the worst.

A short while later, Charlotte tracked her down in the laundry room where she was folding clothes.

"Did you pick up your wedding dress while you were out?"

Georgia shook her head. "No, I forgot."

"Forgot?" Her mother laughed. "How could you forget when you're gettin' married in three days?"

"I don't know if there's going to be a wedding," she admitted.

"Don't be silly," Charlotte chided. "Of course, there's goin' to be a weddin'. The church is booked, the flowers and cake have been ordered, and I know two very handsome boys who are lookin' forward to walkin' their mama down the aisle."

Georgia's eyes filled with tears. "This is all happening too fast. I knew Phillip three *years* before we got married—I've barely known Matt three *months*." She swallowed around the tightness in her throat. "And as it turns out, I'm not sure I really know him at all."

Charlotte waved a perfectly manicured hand. "You're just havin' some pre-weddin' jitters. Not to worry—every bride does."

"Mom, I'm not a virgin bride fretting about my wedding night," Georgia said, frustration evident in her tone. For once she wished her mother could be her mother, not the cliché-spouting Southern Belle that she played so well.

"Then tell me what it is about."

So, with no small amount of reservation, she did.

Charlotte was silent for several minutes after Georgia had finished talking, and when she finally spoke, it was only to ask, "Do you love him?"

"It's not that simple," she protested.

"Do you love him?" her mother asked again.

"You know I would never have let him put a ring on my finger if I didn't."

Charlotte nodded. "But do you know that marriage is a leap of faith as much as a testament to love?"

"How am I supposed to trust a man who hasn't been honest with me?"

"He should have been more forthcomin'," Charlotte agreed. "But I don't think you can say he was dishonest. I mean, he never actually told you he didn't have a son, did he?"

"That doesn't make it okay."

"I'm not sayin' it's okay." Her mother's tone was placating. "I'm just sayin' that you need to cut him some slack. No one's perfect, baby girl, and if you expect him to be, you're just goin' to be disappointed."

"You're right," Georgia finally said, because it was easier to agree with her mother than to expect that she might ever see things from her daughter's perspective.

"I understand why you might question his motivations," Charlotte said now. "But you might also consider that he's been so focused on his future with you that he wasn't thinkin' about the past. His ex-wife and her little boy are his past, you and your children are his future.

"You can postpone the weddin'—cancel it even, if that's what you feel you have to do," her mother continued. "But before you make that decision, make sure you think about all of the consequences."

"The boys would be so disappointed," Georgia admitted.

Charlotte shook her head. "Though you're right that puttin' off the weddin' would likely break their hearts, this isn't about my grandbabies. It's about you and about why you said yes when he proposed to you in the first place."

"Because I love him," she admitted.

Her mother looked her in the eye. "And are you willin' to spend the rest of your life without the man you love?"

* * *

After her conversation with her mother, Georgia had gone next door to talk to Matt, only to find out—from his brother Jack, who was cursing as he attempted to assemble bunk beds—that he'd been called in to the hospital. So she went back to her mother's house, but she kept peeking out the window to watch for his return.

It was late when she saw his headlights turn in the driveway, but their conversation couldn't wait any longer. Knowing his routine, she slipped on a pair of sandals and went out the back door. Sure enough, Matt was out on the back deck, watching the puppies run around on the grass. The sky was black, but the moon and the stars gave off enough light that she was able to navigate her way across the yard.

The puppies spotted her first and greeted her with a cacophony of ecstatic barks, jumping at her heels as she made her way to where Matt was sitting.

"Hey," he said, trying for casual, but she heard a world of uncertainty in that single syllable.

She sat down beside him. "Hey, yourself."

Finnigan and Frederick were jumping all over one another, vying for her attention, so she took a moment to play with them while she tried to find the right words to say what she wanted to say.

But Matt broke the silence first, cautiously asking, "Are you still mad?"

She considered the spectrum of emotions that had churned through her system over the past twelve hours. "Mad isn't even part of what I was feeling," she told him. "Unless you count being furious with your ex-wife for what she did to you."

"I wish there was something I could say or do to explain," he said, "but I honestly don't know that there's any explanation."

"You're an idiot?" she suggested.

He managed a smile. "You've been talking to Kelsey."

Georgia nodded.

"I am an idiot," he agreed. "Because the absolute last thing I ever wanted to do was to keep anything from you."

"Then can I ask you something?"

"Anything," he promised.

"Why did you ask me to marry you?"

He shifted so that he was facing her. "That's your question?"

She nodded again.

"I screwed up even worse than I thought if you don't know how much I love you."

"I know you said you do," she acknowledged. "But I need to know that you want to be with me and didn't just see the widow next door and her fatherless kids as an opportunity to have a family again."

"Obviously you know how much I care about Quinn and Shane and Pippa, but as completely as your children won my heart, I never would have proposed to you if I didn't want to be with *you*.

"We've both been married before," he reminded her. "And I don't know about your vows, but I'm pretty sure that mine included something like 'so long as we both shall live' and not 'until the kids grow up and go off to college.'"

She had to smile at that. "The difference this time being that the kids aren't an obscure concept but an immediate reality."

"I couldn't love Quinn and Shane and Pippa any more if they were my own, but I wasn't thinking about them when I proposed to you," he assured her. "When I asked you to marry me, I wasn't thinking about teaching Quinn to throw a curveball or watching Shane knock it out of the park or even about the huge princess party we're going to throw for Pippa's first birthday."

"Although you've obviously given all of those ideas some thought."

"Because when I think of the future with you, it encompasses everything that I've ever wanted, but none of it matters without you." He took her hands, linked their fingers together. "I asked you to marry me because when I thought about my future, I couldn't imagine it without you. The kids are a bonus—I won't deny that—but it's you that I want by my side for the rest of my life."

The sincerity in his tone, the depth of emotion she could read in his eyes, brought tears to her own.

"But if you want to reschedule the wedding, that's okay," he told her. "Just don't push me out of your life. Give me a chance to prove how much I love you. Please."

"Do *you* want to reschedule?"

"No," he replied without hesitation. "I want to spend the rest of my life with you, and I want the rest of our life together to start as soon as possible. But if you've got any doubts at all…"

She shook her head, because she didn't. Not anymore. "I don't want to postpone the wedding," she said. "I want to marry you because I love you, and I want the rest of our life together to start as soon as possible."

He hauled her into his arms and kissed her firmly. And then he drew back to say, "In the interest of full disclosure—"

Georgia instinctively tensed. "Is this another secret from your past?"

"No, it's an idea for our future."

She exhaled. "Okay."

"I just wanted you to know that I've thought about some-day adding to our family."

"You'd want more children?" She hadn't considered the possibility. Maybe because Pippa was still just a baby, the idea of having another baby had never crossed her mind. But now that Matt had mentioned it, she knew that she would love to have another child—Matt's child.

"Only if you do," he hastened to assure her. "I just thought, we've already got two boys, it might be nice for Pippa to have a sister."

It was the *we* that had her eyes filling with tears, the ease with which he'd spoken that one word that made her accept the truth of his feelings for her. He hadn't put the ring on her finger to make them a family—they already were a family. The ring really was about his love and commitment to her.

"Why don't we hold off any discussion about another baby until I've finished nursing this one," Georgia suggested.

"That sounds fair," he agreed.

"Besides, we have more important things to do right now if we're going to move into your house after the wedding in three days."

"I finished hanging the border in the twins' room," he told her. "Do you want to see it?"

"You're just trying to get me upstairs, conveniently down the hall from your bedroom," she guessed.

He smiled. "Am I that transparent?"

She framed his face in her hands so that she could look into his eyes and clearly see his love for her shining through.

"Yes, you are," she said, and touched her lips to his.

"I love you, Georgia Reed."

"And I love you, Matt Garrett," she told him. "Now, let's go check out that border."

He took her hand and led her into the house that was no longer his own but the home they would share—just like their future—together.

Epilogue

The day of the wedding wasn't very different from any other day that Matt had experienced since moving in next door to Georgia and her kids—which meant that it was pretty much chaos from beginning to end.

He knew it was his own fault, since he'd convinced his bride-to-be to let the twins spend the night at his house. He'd been confident that he could handle the routines of two little boys and get them ready for church the next day. Besides, he had backup in the form of Jack and Luke.

When the boys were fed and washed and dressed—and looking way too darn cute in their little tuxedos, despite the fact that Quinn kept complaining the shoes were too tight—they wanted to play. But all of their toys were next door, so he put cartoons on the TV. That occupied them for all of about thirty minutes, after which he finally agreed they could go outside with the puppies *so long as they didn't get dirty*.

Both Quinn and Shane nodded their understanding of the rule, and Luke went outside with them to ensure they followed it. Unfortunately, no one could have anticipated that Finnigan would find "something stinky and dead" (as Quinn later described it) in the yard and decide it would make a tasty snack, but not so tasty that he didn't later throw it up on Shane's pants.

Luke—the expert on all kinds of puppy puke—brought them back inside for cleanup. It was shortly after that when Jack discovered Quinn's shoes in the toilet of the downstairs bathroom. Apparently Mommy never let him put wet shoes on his feet for fear he'd catch "new-moan-ya," so he'd stuffed them in the toilet to get them wet and unwearable.

When Matt rounded everyone up for a last inspection before they headed off to the church, he decided that the boys' tuxedos didn't look too bad with running shoes. Then he made the mistake of reminding the twins that they were going to walk down the aisle on either side of their mom to give her away. He said the words without thinking, and both Quinn and Shane burst into tears, protesting that they didn't want to give away their mommy, they wanted to keep her forever and ever.

By the time he dried their tears, clarified their role in the ceremony and confirmed that they were *all* going to be together forever and ever, his head was throbbing.

A grinning Luke handed him a glass of water and a couple of Tylenol. Jack followed that up with a tumbler of scotch.

But all the drama was forgotten as soon as he saw Georgia. Wearing a sheath-style dress of cream-colored lace and carrying a bouquet of red roses, she completely took his breath away.

It seemed to take forever for her to reach the front of the church—which might have been because Quinn and Shane were almost literally dragging their feet—but when the minister instructed them to join hands, Georgia's were steady and warm. And in her eyes, he couldn't see any evidence of lingering doubts, just love and joy shining in the beautiful blue depths.

But as a reminder, in case the vows hadn't been enough, he whispered to her, "I love you, Mrs. Garrett."

"I know," she said. "I love you, too."

And when his lips brushed over hers, he heard Quinn clearly announce, "We gived her away, but she's still our mommy."

As soft chuckles sounded from the gallery, Georgia drew back to look at him, silently questioning.

Matt could only shake his head. "Let's just say that the only thing that got me through the last few hours on my own with those boys was the knowledge that, after today, I would always have you by my side."

"Always," she promised.

As Georgia and Matt made their way back down the aisle, they were flanked by Shane and Quinn with Pippa in her mother's arms.

Now, officially, a family.

* * * * *

THE BONUS MUM

BY
JENNIFER GREENE

Jennifer Greene lives near Lake Michigan with her husband and an assorted menagerie of pets. Michigan State University has honored her as an outstanding woman graduate for her work with women on campus. Jennifer has written more than seventy love stories, for which she has won numerous awards, including four RITA Awards from the Romance Writers of America and their Hall of Fame and Lifetime Achievement Awards.

You're welcome to contact Jennifer through her website at www.jennifergreene.com.

To the real "Lilly,"
who is likely to get a zillion more dedications
from me. You're the light of our lives, sweetheart!

Chapter One

When the oven bell dinged, Rosemary sprinted for the kitchen faster than the sound of a fire alarm. She'd added a ton of amenities to the old MacKinnon lodge in the past six months, but a new stove never made the budget. The temperature gauge in the oven could be downright cantankerous.

This time, thankfully, the old monster behaved. She grabbed a hot pad and pulled out a tray of cream puffs, all swelled up, their surface a golden-brown. Perfect.

While the puffs cooled, she headed outside to cart in an armload of peachwood. Outside, a blustery wind bit her face with needles, but considering it was December 19, Rosemary figured she was lucky. There could be snow or a serious ice storm on top of Whisper Mountain by now. A little wind was nothing.

Back inside, she knelt in front of the massive fieldstone fireplace. The grate already had a huge bed of

snapping, orange coals, just needed a stir and a poke
and fresh logs. Moments later, she had a sassy crackle
of fire back, warming the whole living room.

She stood up and stretched, dusting her hands. The
MacKinnons had spent a lot of Christmases here when
she was a kid. She couldn't remember the last holiday
when the place hadn't been a complete wreck. By now,
there should be a giant Christmas tree in the corner,
already dropping needles. Dusty Santas and holiday
tchotchkes should be cluttering every surface. Instead,
there was no tree, no winking lights, no tinsel or glitter, no wrapping paper and crushed bows anywhere in
sight. The place was fabulously tidy and clean.

Truth to tell…she hated it. She had no problem working alone, being alone. But darn it, at this time of year
she loved the chaos, the clutter, the razzle-dazzle, the
messes, the feasts and for darned sure, the time with
her family.

This year she just couldn't do it. So…she'd decided to
ignore the holiday altogether. She'd work, and when she
got sick of work, she planned a heap of silly distractions.

Like wasting time on *Judge Judy* and old sappy movies.

Like having cream puffs for dinner—with vanilla
bean ice cream and hot, dark chocolate sauce. And cherries.

She foraged for a big spoon, and had just pulled the
steaming-cold container of ice cream from the freezer
when the front door suddenly blasted open. She went
to the kitchen doorway, figuring she must not have ad-
equately latched the front door—but that wasn't the
issue at all. Over the wheeze and whistle of wind came

the unmistakable sound of screams and cries. Human screams and cries. Girls. Children. Dozens of children, judging from the volume of cries.

She dropped the spoon, dropped the ice cream, peeled out of the kitchen.

There were children. Not a herd of them, just two girls, red-faced and shaking and crying.

They spotted her, and as if identifying a woman was all it took to let go, thundered toward her in a nonstop sputter of tears and words.

"You have to help us! There's a bear chasing us! A huge *grizzly* bear! He wants to kill us!"

"He's right *out* there. We ran and ran. I ran so hard my side hurt and I still kept going—"

"We didn't know where we were going. Anywhere. We just had to keep running because it kept coming after us!"

"It's still out there! It could still get us!"

"You think it could break windows? It was huge! I thought we were going to die!"

"And what if there's more than one? What if that bear was *married* and there's a wife, too, and he has baby bears only they're all big like that—?"

Rosemary raised her hands, and finally managed to squeeze in a few words. "Hold it. You're both safe. No bear is getting in here. Let's get your coats off, sit down by the fire. I want to hear the whole story, everything you want to say, but let's calm it down a few octaves, okay?"

They'd closed the front door—slammed it, actually, and she bolted it. The front closet had a shotgun, locked on the top shelf. The girls' jaws dropped when they saw it.

"Are you going to kill the bear?"

"Afraid I'm not much on killing anything. But I'm going to shoot a couple blasts in the air. There's a good chance he'll scare off."

"Oh. Can we watch?"

"You can watch from the window. I'm guessing neither one of you are in a hurry to go back outside this minute, right?"

"Oh. Right."

She looked outside, both north and east windows, before opening the door. If a bear had been close—seriously close—she would have smelled it. Nothing smelled quite like a wild bear. She didn't want to steal the girls' thunder by telling them grizzlies didn't live anywhere near Whisper Mountain, South Carolina. Besides, black bears definitely did. They usually snoozed through the cold months, but never went into total hibernation. She stepped outside, clicked off the safety, and aimed a shot at the sky. Then a second one.

She was only gone for a minute—max—but when she stepped back in and relocked the door, the girls were sitting on the old leather couch, staring at her openmouthed.

"Something tells me you girls weren't raised in the country," she said wryly.

That started them talking again. They came from Charleston. Their dad had taken them out of school a little early and rented this place on the mountain. They were doing the whole holiday here. It was because their mom had died about a year ago. Just before Christmas. She'd been Christmas shopping with them. A big truck hit her. Their mom died and both girls ended up in the hospital. They'd missed a heap of school, and Pepper had two casts, and Lilly really wrecked her left foot and had some scars, but not so much now. Anyway, their dad thought it'd be hard to have Christmas at home this year, because it was like an anniversary from when their mom died, so they were here. Having fun mostly. Until the bear.

Rosemary took in this information between handing out drinks and waiting through bathroom breaks.

At some point, one of them wandered toward the kitchen, and that started them on a different track. One picked up the dropped ice cream container, the other honed straight for the cream puffs. They immediately confessed that they'd never had a cream puff and didn't think they could live another minute before trying one. They were desperately hungry. It was from all that running away from the vicious, angry bear.

One of them abruptly realized that they should have phoned their dad right off—and promptly took out a cell. The line was busy, but that wasn't a problem, because their dad never talked on the phone long, and rather than leave him a message that they'd been in terrible danger because of the bear, they figured they'd just call him in another couple minutes.

Rosemary's ears were ringing by then…but she'd more or less sorted them out. They were twins. Eleven. Lilly and Pepper. They were both blonde, both colt- ish and lanky. They both had straight, fine hair, shoul- der length, but one had a red streak and the other had a green one. They had purple jackets that matched, skinny jeans, blue eyes…but not identical blue eyes. Lilly's were uniquely blue, with a dark ring around the light blue iris—the effect was mesmerizing and striking. Pepper had a tendency to scrunch up her nose and prance around, restless, curious, irrepressible.

They were both cute.

They were both going to be breathtaking.

Rosemary figured once they left, she was going to need a long nap. After they'd finished talking, they started on her with questions. How come she lived here? She *really* studied orchids? What was a university grant? So was she wearing a Duke sweatshirt because that's where she got the grant? She *really* had her own gun? Oh, my God, was that a dark room, and could she develop pictures by herself? Could they see? Was she married? Well, if she wasn't married, what was she doing for Christmas?

"Wait a minute. You can't spend Christmas alone," Lilly said firmly.

Right about then Rosemary suggested they call their father again.

Pepper grabbed the cell phone from Lilly—they only had one cell phone between them, which apparently caused arguments several times a day. This time their dad promptly answered, and Pepper went on a long rendition of the walk, the bear, the bear chase, the house, Rosemary, the cream puffs.

"Can you come and get us, Dad? We really got lost when we started running. And now it's already dark, even though it's so early…. I told you, we're at Rosemary's. Oh. Well, no, I…" Pepper lifted the phone and arched her brows to Rosemary. "Could you tell my dad where we are?"

Rosemary was almost laughing as she pressed the cell to her ear. Pepper had a ditsy side, for sure. She'd sounded as if she assumed her dad had some magical ability to automatically know where she was.

"Hi— I'm Rosemary MacKinnon," she said immediately.

"And I'm Whit Cochran."

She took a quick breath. He just had one of those unique guy voices, a clear tenor, that put a shiver in her pulse. It didn't matter if he was ugly as sin or plain as a sloth—she had no way to know, and didn't care. It was just that his voice made her think of sex and danger. Preferably together.

"Just tell me quick," he started with. "Are the girls hurt in any way? And are they okay now?"

"They're fine—except for conning me out of ice cream probably before they've had dinner."

"There really was a bear?"

"I didn't see it myself, but black bears regularly wander around here. Normally they don't bother humans, but they'll venture close when they're scrounging for food. At this time of year, it's pretty rare to come across one."

"I like your voice, Rosemary MacKinnon."

The comment was so unexpected, she got an inexcusable warm fuzzy feeling in her tummy…but obviously, she'd relieved his mind about his girls and he was just getting his breath back, not thinking clearly. "I'm guessing you'd like my address," she said quickly.

"Yes, of course."

"You're not far. There aren't that many places near the top of Whisper Mountain. I'm on the east side, and most of the land up here is MacKinnon property. I'd guess you're either in the Landers place or the Stewarts…they often rent out at Christmas. The Stewarts' place is brick, double kitchen, double deck—"

"That's the one."

"So. If you're driving a car, you're going to have to go down the mountain road—there's only one, as you probably know. Where it ends in a Y shape, turn left. Give or take a half mile, you'll see a wood sign for MacKinnons—that'll lead to the house here. Take you ten, fifteen minutes. On the other hand, if you have some way to go cross-country—"

"A Gator."

"Okay, so it's your choice…with the Gator, you go up that same mountain road…you'll run into a gravel road, turn right, then zip along that way until you run into a battered old MacKinnon sign, turn in."

"So the girls really weren't far."

"I don't know…they could have circled and back-tracked a zillion times if they were trying to outrun a bear. Speaking of which…until you get here, I'll be talking bear defense with your girls."

"Maybe you'd better have that talk with me, too."

She laughed, so did he…but when she clicked off the phone, she found both girls sitting side by side on the leather couch, staring at her.

"Your dad'll be here in two shakes." When they kept up with the stare, she cocked her head. "What?"

"You laughed. And we thought we heard Dad laughing."

Rosemary didn't understand. "He did laugh. But not because he thought your bear was funny. He had to hear that you two were safe. So he was relieved, and naturally he got in a happier mood."

Lilly said, "Our dad hasn't done a whole lot of laughing since Mom died."

She didn't know what to say. The girls had already spilled a lot of information about their personal circumstances that was none of her business. She didn't want to pry—but actually, she was relieved to understand their circumstances. She could have said something painful or insensitive accidentally, if she'd never known the girls had lost their mom, and that they were trying to have a different kind of Christmas to keep the grieving memories at bay.

"Hey. Should we call you Mrs. MacKinnon? Or Miss MacKinnon? Or Rosemary? Or what?" Lilly was clearly the one who wanted to know the rules.

"You can call me Rosemary. And I'm a Miss, not a Mrs."

"How come?" That was definitely Pepper. No boundaries on Pepper's tongue.

"Because I was happy being single."

"Oh. Okay. Can we look around, while we're waiting for my dad? It's about the most beautiful house I can remember."

"Yes, you can look around…except in the first room down that hall. For a long time it was a utility room, but I turned it into a dark room to develop photographs. When that door's closed, you'll see a red light next to the knob, and that means you shouldn't open the door."

"You really develop pictures? Yourself? Right here?"

It had been a while since she'd "awestruck" anyone...much less had anyone treat her like a goddess. Her family—at least her parents—rarely had a pleasant word to say to her. Since June, whenever they called, it was invariably to make sure she knew her Terrible Mistake hadn't been forgotten, and probably never would be. Her two brothers would have defended her against the world—and always had—but even they skirted around the question of why she'd done such a "damn fool thing."

The girls talked her ears off—and asked more questions than a teacher on a test. But after being raised with two brothers—and working alone all these months since June—Rosemary didn't mind. She inhaled all the girl talk.

She never heard a knock on the door, never heard anything until the girls both squealed, *"Dad!"*

They'd ended up in the kitchen—both girls had chosen to ignore the table, and instead sat on the counter with their legs swinging—some body part *always* seemed to be in motion with them. They'd somehow conned her into wrapping up three more cream puffs to take home with them. Possibly she'd been easily conned. Besides, she'd made the full recipe, and even sugar-greedy as she was, couldn't possibly eat a dozen.

"Dad! We're having so much *fun!* Can we stay a little longer?"

And then, "Dad, this is Rosemary. Rosemary, this is Dad—"

"He's not Dad when you're introducing him, dummy.

He's Whit. Dad, this is Rosemary. Rosemary, this is Whit. *Wait* until you taste these cream puffs! Rosemary's giving us some to take home."

"She has a darkroom, Dad. And she has a *gun*. A big *rifle*. That she *owns*. It's all hers. Everything!"

Over the bouncingly exuberant girls, their eyes met. She was both laughing and rolling her eyes—there was no shutting the girls up, no chance to temper their exuberance. And his eyes were filled with humor, too....

But somehow she'd expected the girls' father to be... well, fatherly looking. A lot older than her twenty-seven. Sure, she'd expected him to be reasonably good-looking, because the girls were adorable, but he'd been married awhile. He should have looked more staid, the way settled down guys tended to get, more safe, less... how would a woman say it?...less hungry.

Whit radiated all the safety of a cougar just freed from a cage. He was tall, rangy and sleek. He had the shoulder and arm muscles of a guy who was physical and exceptionally strong. He wore an old canvas jacket, jeans and country boots.

His hair was sort of a dusty blond shade, rumpled from the wind, a frame for the rugged bones in his face. The haircut was the choice for a guy who didn't waste time on grooming. Straight eyebrows set off his eagle-shrewd eyes—shrewd, except when he looked at his daughters.

Then his gaze turned into a helpless puppy's.

"Did they drive you crazy?" He said it under the relentless stream of eleven-year-old chatter.

Oh, right. Like she'd kick a puppy in the teeth. The

girls were obviously the sun and the moon to him. Besides, even if they had driven her a little crazy, they'd been fun. "They're wonderful," she said.

"Yeah. I think so. But…"

"I never had a chance to give them the 'bear' talk. They should know…you don't run from a bear. You don't leave food in the wild, ever, and if you make loud noises, he'll likely turn tail and take off. A bear doesn't want to hurt a human—unless it's spring and it's a female with cubs. Or it's fall, and he's filling up on every berry he can find. So if they spot one from a distance, just move away. Make noise. Trust me, he doesn't want to eat you. He just wants you out of his space."

Pepper had been listening, but she wasn't buying this advice wholesale. "But what if he's crazy? You know. What if it's a people-hater bear. Like the bear in that movie, where the model's in Alaska—"

"If he's crazy, you're up a creek. But the population of black bears around here doesn't have a bad reputation. If a crazy one showed on the radar, DNR and rangers would be all over it. So if you just use common sense and do the regular safe things, you should be fine."

"Dad, do you see how much she knows? Even about things like bears? And she's a girl."

"I noticed that."

Her head whipped toward him again. There was nothing suggestive in his tone. Just in his eyes. There was just something there that sparked a sizzle in her pulse…and Rosemary was too darned practical to feel sizzles—in her pulse or anywhere else.

"I think it's time we got out of this nice lady's hair."

"But she likes us, Dad. She said so."

"Of course she likes you. You're the angels of the universe. But we're still giving Rosemary her life back and going home. It's already dark."

"You sure didn't call us angels when we put the red and green in our hair. Even though we told you and told you and told you it'd wash out. And everybody does it."

The adults barely exchanged another word—they had no chance. Rosemary was amused—and surprised—by the violent silence when she closed the door after them. She was used to silence. Or she should be. She was happy living alone.

Or that's what she'd been telling herself for six months now.

Maybe she'd been telling herself that her whole life. If you're waiting for someone else to make you happy, you're waiting for a spit in the wind. It has to start on the inside. Being content with who you are.

Rosemary always thought she was. Content within herself. Until last June, and since then she couldn't seem to fit in her own skin.

She turned away from the window, fed the fire and turned her attention back to things that mattered. Another cream puff, for starters.

And what a hunk of a man that Whit was. Maybe she could have a hot, steamy dream about him tonight. He was the kind of guy that looked all sexy and dangerous when he was sweaty.

Not that Rosemary was attracted to sweat and oiled shoulders and bad boys.

But losing a wife and raising two young girls alone—

that was a tough road. Tougher than her own problems, by far.

Which was probably why she couldn't get him off her mind.

Chapter Two

Whit opened the refrigerator and stared at it blankly. He'd bought a truckful of groceries. The fridge was full. He just couldn't seem to find anything to eat.

At least anything that didn't involve cooking and dishes and cleaning up.

"What are you hungry for, you two?" He called out to the living room, and then wondered why he'd asked.

The answer came in joyous unison. "Mac and cheese. From the box."

Followed by, "And don't burn it this time, Dad."

He still had two boxes, thank God. All the green stuff he'd bought was going to waste. But the sugary cereals, the mac and cheese and the ice cream—after two days, he was nearly out of those. He could probably feed the kids on five bucks a day—if they had their way. Instead he'd spent better than $500 on stuff that was good for them.

Why wasn't that in the parenting rule book, huh? That short of putting an eleven-year-old in a coma, there was no way to get anything fresh and green down them without a war that involved pouting, door slamming, dramatic tragic looks, claims of being misunderstood, claims of being adopted, claims of child abuse…and… that torture could go on for hours. Sometimes days.

He scrounged for a pan, and filled it with water. Read the directions on the mac and cheese box for the millionth time. When he turned around, Lilly was leaning on the blue-and-white tile counter.

It was a trick, since he knew she hadn't come in to help. He was in trouble. He just didn't know over what. And the truth—which Lilly possibly knew—was that he'd do anything she asked. Anything.

He was terrified of both daughters, but Lilly more than Pepper. Lilly had stopped talking after her mom died. She'd just lain there, in that hospital bed next to her sister, but where Pepper would cry and shriek, Lilly just carried that silent look in her eyes. Grief too deep to understand, grief that made her go still, as if in any motion, no matter how tiny, could tip her over the edge. She couldn't take more.

Eventually Lilly started talking again, but it went on and on, that grief of hers. She answered questions, and talked about things like school and dinner, but it was months before she volunteered anything. Months before that unbearably sharp grief started to fade. Months before he won a real smile—and he'd done everything but stand on his head and grovel, to bring her beautiful smile back.

"What?" he said, when she kept leaning there, looking at him, kind of rolling her shoulders.

"Nothing. I was just thinking...."

That was the other problem with Lilly. Pepper, thankfully, said anything that was on her mind. It came out like froth; he never had to work to figure out where her head was. But Lilly was the thinker, the one who stored hurts on the inside, the one who never said anything he could anticipate. Nothing in the universe could make him feel as helpless as Lilly.

And he'd have to kill anyone who dared cause her any grief again.

"Didn't you think she was pretty?" She asked him as if his answer was of no consequence, while idly scratching the back of one knee with a slipper.

"The lady?"

"Rosemary, Dad. You heard her name. And yeah. Didn't you think she was pretty?"

"Sure."

Lilly rolled her eyes. It was a default response when Whit did something inadequate on an eleven-year-old's terms. "Something's wrong with her."

"Like what?"

"I don't know. But she's pretty. And she's spending Christmas all by herself. And she's working, she showed us some stuff on orchids. But you'd think it was July or June or something. There's no tree or presents. No stuff. No lights."

"Maybe she's of some other religion."

"You mean like Buddhist or Muslim or something? No. It's not that."

"How do you know?"

"Because I know." Another default answer, usually accompanied by, "I'm a girl and I know. You wouldn't understand."

"Maybe she's Jewish?"

"Dad. We know five Jewish people. And they do Christmas with presents and trees just like we do. Except that they get to do their Hanukkah holiday, too, so they get even *more* presents. In fact, I was thinking about turning Jewish."

"Were you?"

"Hey, people fight wars all the time over religion. I think they should stop fighting wars and concentrate more on giving presents. Especially presents for their kids." Possibly out of boredom, she plucked a raw carrot from the glass of carrots and celery on the counter. It was the first time he'd seen her eat anything nutritious since they'd come up here. "But back to Rosemary. The thing is…she's our neighbor. In fact, as far as I can tell, she's our only neighbor up here. At least the only one we know about. So maybe we should do some Christmas stuff with her, so she's not alone."

"Honey, she may be alone by choice. She may not want company or neighbors around."

"Well, then, why were her eyes sad?"

The water started to swirl and bubble. He dumped in the dry pasta, asked Lilly to get some milk and butter from the fridge and called Pepper to set the table. Then he did what he always did when he needed a diversion. He called dibs on the TV as of eight o'clock.

That immediately raised the decibel level in the great room to rock concert levels…and for sure, diverted Lilly.

But Rosemary's face flashed back in his mind. She *did* have sad eyes. At first...well, at very first, he'd only seen his girls, because he'd nearly had a heart attack about their bear encounter. No matter what they'd claimed on the phone, he had to see them both in flesh and blood to breathe again.

Still, the minute he realized the kids were both fine, he swiftly turned on Rosemary. First, he noticed her vibrancy. With three females in the same room, naturally all three of them were talking at once, with volume, and were all in constant motion besides. But over and above his twins' chatter, he caught...the energy of her. The life-lover zest.

Her build was lithe and lean, a woman comfortable with her body, used to doing physical things and spending time outdoors. Even in December her nose had a hint of sunburn, with a thin spray of freckles.

Her eyes were faded blue, the color of a hot sky in summer. She wore her hair grass-short and styled wash-and-wear, not all that much different than his, but no one would ever mistake her for a guy. Everything about her was soft and female. The long sleeved T-shirt in navy blue, the battered-soft jeans, the sculpted fine bones in her face. None of her clothes were fancy but distinctly feel-good styles, easy to move in, easy to live in. She wore no makeup—of course, since she lived alone, why would she paint her face? But it was more than that. Her skin had that wind-fresh, sun-friendly wholesome look. Her breasts were small and pert; her hips barely held up her jeans. There was no vanity in her. No embellishments. Just...beauty.

The real kind of beauty.

The kind that rang his chimes. Only no one—real or not—had rung his chimes since Zoe died.

Sooner or later, he figured he'd get his libido back. He'd always been overcharged, not under, but Zoe's death seemed to kill something off in him.

He'd never identified it that way. Never thought of it at all.

Yet one look at Rosemary, and his libido showed up and started singing bass. With drums.

And yeah, the sadness in her eyes touched him—maybe should have warned him. But that sadness wasn't *her*. It was about something that had happened to her. And…

"*Dad!* You're burning the mac and cheese again!"

He glanced down at the pot. How had that happened again?

By the time they sat down at the table, Whit realized that something was up. A father of twins learned some things the hard way. Two children were just two children—but twins were a pack. Like wolves. Or badgers.

Especially like badgers.

"Listen, Dad." Pepper shoveled in the mac and cheese, but took time to offer him a beguiling smile. She was always the troublemaker.

"I'm listening."

"We're really happy up here. It's awesome and all. And we know you want us to forget Mom this Christmas."

He frowned. "No. No, you two, not at all. I just thought this Christmas would be extra hard without your mom. By next year, we could do the holiday completely differently. Make a point of remembering your mom, in fact—like making some of her favorite holiday dishes. Remember her strawberry pie? Or putting the tree in the corner where she thought it looked best. I don't ever want you to forget your mom, I just—"

"Dad, wind it up." Pepper again, using her impatient tone. "We're okay with all that. You don't have to go on and on."

"But here's the thing." Lilly, always the pacifier, jumped in when she thought her sis was being abrasive. "We don't know Rosemary very well. But she's alone. And we're alone this Christmas, too. Like you said before, maybe we'd be an intrusion. But maybe not. I mean, what if we just—like when we're cutting down our own tree tomorrow—cut one down for her, too?"

Pepper started her fidgety thing, dropping a napkin, then her fork. "And then we could just bring her the tree—and see if we're in her way or if she really needs to work or something. Because maybe she really wants some company around. Especially us girl company. She *said* she loved girl talk."

"It's not just that," Lilly interrupted again. "You know when I was little—"

"As compared to your being an old lady now?"

"Quit it, Dad. We're having a talk. No joking."

"Okay, okay."

"When I was little, I remember the neighbor who came over for Christmas. Mom said she was alone because she lost her husband. So she asked her over for Christmas dinner. Mom said, and then you said, that Christmas isn't just about presents. It's about people being together. Sharing something good."

"Sometimes you two worry me. You have this tendency to use things I've said against me."

"Come on, Dad. We can take Rosemary a tree tomorrow, right?"

Whit couldn't imagine how they could just show up at Rosemary's back door with a tree out of the complete blue. But at least temporarily, he couldn't figure out a way to say no that would make sense to the girls.

Rosemary bent over the corkboard. Heaven knew how she'd gotten hung up on the sex life of wild orchids in South Carolina. The subject would undoubtedly bore most people to tears. But when she needed her mind off stress, she'd always been able to concentrate on work.

Her stomach growled. She ignored it. She was pretty sure she'd ignored it a couple times before this.

It had taken quite a while to completely fill the corkboard on the coffee table. She'd pinned photos of local orchids—and their names and location—until the entire space was filled. Some of the names were so fun. Little lady's Tresses. Small whorled pogonia. Yellow fringed orchid. Crested coralroot. Downy rattlesnake plantain.

Absently, she picked up her coffee mug. It was cold, and since it was also the last in the pot, it was thicker than mud. She still swallowed a slug.

She'd never planned on turning into an egghead. It was all sort of a mistake. When she'd cancelled the wedding, escaped from George (as she thought of it now) the two-year grant from Duke had struck her as a godsend. She could make a living—or enough of a living—and seclude herself up here.

The goal hadn't been to get a Ph.D. She'd never

wanted a Ph.D. She just wanted to work so hard she could forget about everything else for a while. Until she put her head back together. Until she figured out what to do with her life. Until she could analyze exactly what had gone so bad, so wrong, with George.

Mostly she had to figure out how she could have been so stupid.

She leaned forward, studying the photo of the small whorled pogonia. A white lip hung above the five green leaves. The species was teensy. It was hard to find, hard to notice. And it was probably the rarest orchid near the eastern coastline—which made it one of her treasures.

That was the thing. It wasn't about academics. Or getting a Ph.D. It was about…survival. Why did some species fail and others thrive? How could a fragile, vulnerable orchid like this conceivably survive in such a hostile environment?

Not that she thought of herself as vulnerable. Or that she feared she couldn't survive the mess she was in.

It was just that everybody believed the old adage that only the strong survived. Because it always seemed to be true. Except with these fragile orchids.

There had to be a reason. A logical explanation. Something in delicate orchids that enabled them to survive, when far tougher species died out.

A sudden knock on the door almost made her jump sky-high. A spit of coffee landed on her sweatshirt; she set the mug down, went to the door.

The twins huddled together like bookends, a platter in their hands covered with tin foil. "Hi, Rosemary. We can't stay. We can't bother you."

"But we made some brownies to thank you for saving our lives yesterday."

Clearly their opening lines had been prepared.

"The brownies," Pepper added, "have some mints and some cherries on the inside. We didn't sample any of these, but we've made them this way before. Honest, they're really good. Although we usually put in marshmallows, only this time, we didn't have any marshmallows so we couldn't."

Lilly's turn. "We were trying to make it red and green on the inside. You know. Like to be Christmasy." She took a breath. "Dad said we absolutely can't bother you. So we're leaving right now, this very instant."

She noticed the golf cart behind them. Saw the hope on their faces, no matter what they said. "You can't even come in to sample a brownie? That's an awful lot for just me to eat by myself."

"I don't think we can. No matter how much we want to." Pepper let out a massive sigh.

"Hmm. What if I call your dad and asked him myself if you could stay awhile?"

"Oh." Both girls lit up like sparklers. "Yeah. If *you* call him, it'll be okay."

There ended her bubble of solitude. She called Whit first, so he knew the girls were safely with her, said they wanted to share a brownie with her, and she'd have the girls call when they were headed home. It wouldn't be long.

Just that short conversation invoked symptoms she'd suffered when she met him yesterday. It was as if she'd been exposed to a virus. She felt oddly achy and restless, hot—when there was no excuse in the universe to react like a dimwit toward a perfect stranger.

But the girls distracted her from thinking any more about their father. The first priority was testing the brownies—which were fabulous. Both girls could somehow eat and talk nonstop at the same time.

Pepper went first. "Our dad thought we couldn't handle Christmas at home. But we both know he's the one who can't. He hasn't been out one single time since mom died. You know what that means?"

Rosemary was afraid to answer. "How about if you tell me what you think it means."

"It means that he's trying to be there for us 24/7. Rosemary, he's driving us *nuts*. He wants us to *do* things together all the time."

"And that's bad?" She might not have a chance to think about Whit in connection with herself, but if the conversation was going to be all about him…well there's not much she can do about it. She reached for a second brownie, feeling self-righteous as the devil herself.

"It's not *bad*. Because we love him. But can you picture a pajama party with seven girls and my dad trying to fit in?"

"Um…no."

"Everybody in our class at school likes going to the movies. It's like a couple miles, though, so if the weather's good, we walk. Otherwise one of the moms drive. But Dad, when it was his turn, he wanted to go inside with us. He sat in the back. Like the kids wouldn't know he was there?"

"Um…" Rosemary eyed a third brownie.

"We know he's lonely. He really loved our mom.

He just can't seem to get over it. But it's been a *year*. I mean, we miss her, too."

Lilly said softly, "I think about her every day."

"I do, too!" Pepper said defensively.

"But really, we would have been fine just being home for Christmas. Then we could have had friends over. Or gone to their houses. See the Christmas movies and all that. So…" Lilly looked at her sister.

"So…" Pepper picked up the refrain.

"So…we were wondering if you would do some things with us. I don't mean every second, like when you have to work and stuff. But we're going to do a tree. And make some ornaments. Bake some cookies. It's stuff we're already *doing,* so we're not asking you to *work.* We'd just like you to be, well, another person."

"She *is* another person, stupid." Pepper, naturally.

"I *know* that, numbskull." Lilly turned to her again. "I meant, so Dad could see he didn't have to be hovering over us all the time. That it's okay. We're eleven. Practically adults. We don't need a parent in the same room with us every single minute."

"Besides, we want you there for ourselves. Because I'm sick of this hairstyle. And we've been arguing about how it'd look best. Lilly thinks we should both grow it way long. I think we should go short, and like, with spikes. You could help us with an opinion."

Lilly took her plate to the counter. "We wanted to bring you a tree. We're cutting down our tree tomorrow, so we told Dad, why don't we get one for Rosemary, too? But he said we had no way to know if you even wanted one. Don't you want a Christmas tree?"

Every direction she turned, she seemed to face the

gruesome problem of taking sides. And all their dad conversation was prickly—they kept relaying things that were private and none of her business. Even their enthusiasm at being around her was touchy—they were fun; she really wouldn't mind visits from them now and then. It wasn't as if she'd had a choice to spend the holiday alone. But Whit might not appreciate a stranger in the middle of their private holiday, no matter what the girls thought they wanted.

"Where did you get the golf cart?" she asked, hoping for a diversion.

"It was in the shed with the Gator. It came with the property. It'll go a few miles, like four or something, and then you just plug it back in. Dad won't let us drive the Gator, but he said we could use the cart to carry the brownies to your house and then come back."

"You weren't scared you'd run into your bear again?"

"A little. But we can go pretty fast in the cart. And we brought cookie sheets to make noise. We read a bunch about bears last night. Mostly it's like the stuff you told us. If a person doesn't do something that upsets him, the bear's really not interested in humans anyway." Pepper was about to jump up from the table, when her sister gave her a finger point. She rolled her eyes, but grabbed her dish and took it to the counter. "Anyhow, I know we're supposed to go home, like now, but could you just show us your darkroom really quick? Show us how you make pictures?"

That sounded like a fine idea to Rosemary.

And the kids had a blast. The three were crowded in the small space, and the girls seemed entranced with everything.

"The thing I'm confused about," Pepper said, "is why you're making your own photographs. I mean, couldn't you just get a digital camera? Or a phone where you could take pictures?"

"I could do both those things—and sometimes do," Rosemary explained. "But when I do these myself, then I own those photos. It's a legal thing. I'm responsible for the research and the work, so I wouldn't want anyone using my photos without my permission. It's like a protection."

"I get it." Lilly then had questions about the house—why it was so big and interesting, and was it really old, and how did she make the darkroom?

"The lodge has been in the MacKinnon family for generations—so lots of family members used it for summer getaways and vacations and holidays and just family gatherings. It was always kept pretty rustic, but when I knew I was going to be staying here for quite a while, I put in electricity and ran cable wires and all that." She motioned. "This used to be a utility room. It already had a sink and rough shelves. But when I set it up as a darkroom—well, one problem is that everything has to be put away perfectly—because once you've turned out the lights, you have to find what you need in the dark."

"So we can turn out the lights?" Lilly asked.

"Sure. But first let me show you what certain things are used for." The blackout shades had the obvious purpose. The extractor fan sucked out the chemical odors. She pointed out the safelight. And next to the old sink was a long "wet bench" made of something similar to Formica. "That's where the developing trays go—where you're developing the photos…and at the far end, there's a squeegee to remove excess water from the prints."

"This so beyond awesome," Lilly said.

"What's this stuff?" Pepper said as she pointed.

"All large bottles of solution are stored on the floor. Every single thing that's used in here has a place. And no matter how tired or busy I am, it all has to be put back in that place before I leave—or I'd never find it in the dark the next time."

"Well, that'd probably be too hard for me," Pepper admitted. "Dad says I shed stuff every place I walk, like a dog sheds fur."

"So what's that?" Lilly didn't want to listen to her sister. She wanted to hear Rosemary.

"Okay…on the other side of the room—and I know it's hard for the three of us to operate in this narrow space, but when I'm by myself, it's not so bad. So this is an enlarger. It does just what it sounds like. Makes the prints larger. It might make them blurrier, too—so you can't just ask it to enlarge something and then go take a nap. You have to watch the process."

"Rosemary?" Lilly again. "Could we do this with you sometime? If we didn't move and didn't get in your way and didn't do anything wrong? If we just watched?"

"Sure. If it's okay with your dad. And you guys are only going to be here for a week, aren't you?"

"We're not sure exactly. We think we're going home a day or two after Christmas, but Dad only promised that we'd be home by New Year's Eve, because we're sleeping over with a bunch of girls from school."

"We're going to stay up all night and have popcorn and stuff."

"Sounds like great fun." She heard a vague sound, turned her head, and abruptly realized that someone was knocking on the front door.

She hustled out, glanced out the peephole and felt her stomach jump five feet. She yanked open the door at the same time she looked at her watch.

"My God, Whit. I'm so sorry. I swear I didn't realize how much time had gone by."

"It's not a problem, except that when you gave me your cell number—"

She nodded. "I never heard it ring. I'm sorry. I think I left it on the fireplace mantel. And we were in the back of the house, the darkroom."

"Like I said, it's okay. But I did figure by now you'd need rescuing."

She did. Not from his girls. From him.

The minute he walked in the room, she suffered from a cavorting heartbeat and instant noodle knees, annoying her to no end. So he was a hunk. So he was so brawny he made her feel like a sweet little Southern belle. So he had the sexiest eyes this side of the Mississippi.

It was just attraction.

Last she knew, that problem was embarrassing but not fatal.

The kids leaped on him as if he'd been missing for six months. "Dad! Rosemary took us in the darkroom, and showed us all about the enlarger and the paper safe and the squeegee panels—"

"And where you keep the chemicals and the big extractor fan and solution and stuff—"

Since Whit was getting pulled inside, Rosemary interrupted with the obvious. "Would you like some tea or coffee? I've got both."

"Coffee, definitely, if it's not too much trouble."

By the time she brought two mugs back in, the girls had yelled for permission to play games on her iPad, and they'd taken root on the floor with couch pillows behind them. Whit, hands in his back pockets, was circling the corkboard display on the coffee table.

He smiled when she walked toward him, cocked his head toward the girls. "They've made themselves at home."

"It's the iPad. Not me."

"I don't think so. You keep gaining goddess status."

She laughed. "I'm not doing anything, honest."

"Maybe not, but we'll have to brainstorm some way to take you down a peg in their eyes. Otherwise, they're going to pester you nonstop."

He'd lowered his voice so the girls wouldn't hear. His whisper was just as evocative as his normal tenor.

"Well, if you think up something evil I could do, give a shout, would you?"

He chuckled. They shared a smile that made her feel like a lit sparkler in a dark room. But then he motioned toward her corkboard.

"The girls said you were doing a project with orchids."

She nodded. "The wild orchids in South Carolina— especially rare and endangered ones. Duke gave me a two-year grant, but I think I can finish the project sooner than that. When I came up here in June, that's all I did, traipse around the mountains, taking photographs and collecting specimens. So most of the gut research is done. I just have to put it all together, which is going to take a serious block of time." She knew she was babbling, but he honestly looked interested.

"Landscaping's my work."

"The twins said you owned a business."

He nodded. "I'm the family disgrace. I have three siblings, two lawyers and my sister is a CPA. I'm the only dirt bum. Love working with my hands. Love taking a piece of land—don't care whether it's small or big—and analyzing the soil, the shapes and contours, figuring out which plants and trees will thrive there, what will show it off. I have no idea where I picked up the addiction, but I sure have it hard-core."

"My parents are both surgeons, and they expected the three of us kids to follow in their footsteps…but at least I could share disgrace with one of my brothers. I went for botany, and Tucker has a retreat camp on Whisper Mountain here. Ike was the only brother who turned into a doctor, like we were all supposed to."

"Being a disgrace is tough."

"Well, I was a disgrace for more than one reason," she admitted, and then wanted to shoot herself. That wasn't information she meant to share with Whit—or anyone else, for that matter.

He didn't ask. He looked at her, as if waiting to hear the "other reason" she was a disgrace. But when she didn't say anything more, he turned his attention back to the corkboard of photographs.

"Are you only photographing them when they're in flower?" he asked.

"Good question. No. I marked the spot where I found each orchid—the location, the environment, the plants growing near them, tested the soil for acidity and all that. Then I went back every month to record that information all over again. Different predators showed up in different months. Different plants became dormant in different months. There were different insects, different temperatures, different rainfall."

"Man. I'd love to have done this kind of study. I don't know anything about orchids. But the how, why, when and where certain plants or grasses grow is of enormous interest to me."

"You didn't go for a botany degree…?"

"No, I went after a landscape architecture degree from Michigan State. It was a long way from home to go to college, but they had a great program for what I wanted. Never regretted it. But the study you're doing crosses paths with so much I'm interested in."

But he looked at her as if he were far more fascinated in her than her study. She couldn't remember the last time anyone wanted to hear what she thought, what she felt.

"Hey, Dad!" Pepper leaped up from the tablet and hurtled toward them at her usual speed—a full gallop. "Can we all stay and watch a movie if Rosemary says yes? There's one that starts in just a few minutes. We'll miss the beginning if we have to go home."

"I think our family's imposed on Rosemary enough for today."

"But *Dad*. It's *Princess Bride!* And it's on right now."

"You never have to see that one again. You know all the words. Hell. I know all the words. Please. Anything but that. Anything. We can even go home and talk about…clothes."

He herded them out, over a new round of protests and pleas and outright begging. Grabbed jackets. Found shoes. Listened to chatter.

Over their heads, before he whooshed them out the door, he looked at her. Really looked at her. As if they'd been connecting in a private way since the moment they met...the moment he walked in. Every moment they found themselves together.

She thought: he wanted to kiss her.

It was there. In his gaze. In how privately he looked at her, how silently he looked...worried. Worried but determined.

When she finally closed the door, the sudden silence in the cabin struck her again as unexpectedly lonely—when she'd been content living alone. Or she thought she'd been content.

She ambled through the living room, picking up mugs and glasses, doing little cleanups—and lecturing herself at the same time. She was imagining those "looks" from Whit. The guy was still in love with his wife, from everything the girls had said. He was still loving her, still mourning her, still grieving.

And she had no business volunteering for trouble, besides. She was still in deep emotional shock over George—the man everyone assumed she'd be thrilled to marry, thrilled to spend her life with. She hadn't discovered his turnip side until it was almost too late... which unfortunately said a whole lot about her lack of judgment in men.

She was afraid to trust her judgment again. Not because she was a sissy. Because she was smart.

She had to be smart. Her confidence had been crippled, not by George, but by misjudging a man she thought she loved. It was a mistake she couldn't risk making again.

Chapter Three

They'd been home a half hour. The girls were parked in front of *The Princess Bride,* mesmerized, as if they'd never seen the movie fifty times before. But Whit couldn't settle, couldn't shake an odd case of restlessness.

He prowled the rented house from room to room. The mountain cabin suited him far better than their home in Charleston—but Zoe loved the city side of life, so a city house was what she'd wanted.

He liked it here. The quiet. The clean air. The mists in the morning, the smell of pine, and the house itself had a dream of a layout. The great room had a massive corner fireplace, and the kitchen/dining area was all open. You could feed two or twenty in the same space. Glass doors everywhere led to a wraparound porch. The back door opened onto a practical mudroom and downstairs bath, and beyond that was a good size master bedroom.

The upstairs was a simple open loft—a bedroom and den type of area—the girls had squealed nonstop when they first saw it, thought it was "beyond awesome" to have a whole floor to themselves. He thought it was equally "awesome" that they were always safely within his sight.

When he'd prowled the house enough, he settled with a mug of cider in the great room—as far away from *The Princess Bride* movie as he could get—and accidently found himself staring out the glass doors to the west. More precisely, he wasn't staring out, but staring up.

He couldn't see the MacKinnon lodge through the thick forest, but without those trees, he suspected he'd easily be able to locate Rosemary's place, maybe even see her, if she were outside on her front deck.

Mentally he could still picture her long legs, the careless, easy way she wore clothes. Her hair was short, blond as sunshine, always looking finger-brushed, framing her delicate face so naturally. The way her sun-blushed skin set off added to her looks being striking, interesting.

More than interesting. He hadn't felt his hormones kick like this in a long, long time.

There was a reason—there had to be a reason—why a smart, delectably attractive and downright interesting woman was living alone. It gnawed at him to think of her being alone, especially during the holidays. It wasn't as if there were close neighbors or friends who could easily stop over for a visit. Whit understood that she'd won that academic grant, that she loved the study, that whole business.

But that still didn't explain her holing up alone for the holidays.

And it didn't begin to explain the sadness in her blue blue eyes.

Abruptly he heard the tune on his cell phone, flipped it open and heard the country drawl of Samson, one of his truck drivers. No emergency, Sam just wanted to relay that he was headed to Savannah for his Christmas family gathering, and he hoped Whit and the girls would have a good holiday.

The conversation lifted his spirits. His employees had been together for years now, except for a few extra college kids he'd hired over the summer. They'd turned into a team, the kind who shared good times and bad, who attended each other's christenings and graduations.

Whit didn't know what that really meant until Zoe died, and the crew hung closer to him than sticky glue. Someone called every day; someone else brought food; and all of them offered help with whatever needed doing—either for Whit or for the girls. It taught him forever that "family" could mean a lot of things, and wasn't always defined by blood kin.

When he finished the call, he almost put down the phone...but instead flipped it open again. Rosemary's number was already in his phone's memory, from their first call. It only took one impulsive, brainless moment to dial it.

Her line was busy.

So, he thought, she did have someone to talk to.

He couldn't call again for a couple hours, because the

movie ended and the girls immediately claimed starvation. The vote for dinner was a made-from-scratch pizza—one of the few things he could do well in the kitchen. It just always seemed to require every dish and every counter to put it together.

The girls helped clean up. Some. Predictably, though, they scattered faster than dust in the wind when he turned on the news.

Once they ran upstairs, he tried calling Rosemary again.

For the second time, her line was busy. So she either had another person to talk with, or she'd talked for three solid hours to her first caller. The former seemed more likely, but as the girls came back down to con Whit into an old fashioned game of Clue, he got the niggling idea that possibly she was in trouble. Maybe she hadn't been talking. Maybe her phone wasn't working, because for a hermit to be occupied with two calls seemed odd. A puzzle piece that didn't fit.

If that thinking was flimsy, he figured out the obvious. He wanted to talk with her. Any excuse he could conjure up was good enough.

He checked on the girls, found them in their Christmas pj's, lying on their tummies reading. He stole a good-night kiss from each, then took his cell phone into his room downstairs.

He kicked off his shoes, flipped off the light and sank into the recliner facing the west glass doors. The master bedroom suited him like a good pair of gloves. Nothing fancy, just a giant bed with a serious mattress and a warm, dark pine comforter. The best part was the view. The glass doors looked straight up the mountainside. A few nights before there'd been a full moon. He'd been close enough to touch it.

Okay, so maybe not that close. But he'd moved the recliner to the window that night, and that's where he'd spent the past few evenings since, a short brandy in his hand, the lights off, to just inhale the mountain, the air, the peace.

When he dialed Rosemary's number this time, she answered. "Whit? Trouble at your house?"

She sounded breathless, animated. "No trouble. Did I catch you in the middle of something?"

"Yeah. Stargazing."

She didn't chuckle but he could hear the smile in her voice.

"I was doing that here, too. I just shut off the lights. I can't get over how many stars I can see from this altitude."

"It's the mountain. You know the mountain's full of magic, don't you?"

"Oh, yeah. I'm a real believer in magic," he said drily.

Again, he could hear the smile in her voice. "Whisper Mountain has a legend. The 'whisper' business is supposed to be real. Except that only true lovers can hear the mountain whisper. It's a sign."

"You mean like a stop sign or a construction warning sign?"

"No, you lunkhead. It's a *magic* sign."

"Did you just call me a lunkhead?"

"No, of course not. That was the other woman on the phone. Not me. I don't even know what a lunkhead is. I never heard the word before."

"Well, would you put Rosemary back on the line?"

"Can't. She's in the bathtub shaving her legs. Took a glass of wine and a candle with her, so I doubt she's coming out soon."

"Is it me, or is this conversation coming out of never-never land?"

"What do you expect? You're living with two pre-teen girls and I live alone. After nine o'clock, I don't think it's reasonable to expect rational conversation."

"Well, I swear, there was a rational reason why I called you. But now—"

"You can't remember it? You're feeling a little discombobulated?"

"That wasn't the first word that came to mind. But once you said it, yes."

"Well, I can pretty well guess why you called. I thought a little estrogen-spiced conversation might scare you off, but so far it doesn't seem to be working.... So yeah, I'll go Christmas tree hunting with you three tomorrow."

For a moment he was speechless. "How did you know I was calling for that?"

"Because your girls brought it up about fifty times—that you were going to find your own tree, bring it home, do the really traditional holiday things. And after spending a couple hours with the twins, I figured you'd started to realize that an entire week alone with two girls that age could strain your sanity—no matter how much you love your daughters. And they're adorable. Anyway..."

Sitting on a chair, Whit couldn't figure out why he felt so dizzy. "Anyway?"

"Anyway, the last thing I want to do is intrude on

your family time. I'm not an Aunt Matilda, who you have to invite for holiday stuff because she's alone. I'm fine here. One hundred percent fine. Two hundred percent fine even. Just because the girls were bubbling with invitations, you're talking to me now, and I promise, I didn't take them seriously."

"I'm going to have to hang up pretty soon, because you're starting to make sense and that's scaring me." Then he added quickly, "But tomorrow, we figured on taking the Gator, doing a search-and-cut for Christmas trees. I figure around ten in the morning, if it's not raining? And that's a 'please come' from all three of us, not just Pepper and Lilly."

"All right, all right! I'll come. I can't resist the three of you! But…I'm going back to my stargazing now. If I quit doing this, I'll have run out of excuses for not working. I've got hours of soil samples I have to analyze, so you can't imagine how happy I am that you called. I got to postpone work even longer."

She rang off before he could reply. His first impulse was to shake his head, hard, see if he could get some airflow back to his brain.

But his second impulse was to just laugh. Hell. He could feel a wreath of a smile on his face. The call had been completely off the wall and nonsensical…but he couldn't remember laughing in a long time. Even smiling some days was a job.

Since Zoe died, he'd almost forgotten that he used to be a happy-go-lucky kind of guy. Laughter used to come to him easy as sunshine. As a kid, he'd been prone to a little trouble, couldn't shake the mischief gene, but marriage had shaped him up. The twins came six months after the wedding. Neither he nor Zoe was ready for marriage, but she'd had an early ultrasound, so they knew about the twins.

There was no way they could give up two. Or raise two without each other. He was a little mad at first. So was she. Before the babies, they'd both realized that their love affair was more of a lust affair, and the marriage was on precarious ground. But then the girls came. Whit still remembered the first time he'd held his newborn daughters.

He'd been a goner. That fast. That completely. He never knew he had a daddy streak, much less that he would go head over heels hopeless for the squirts. Neither slept at night. They cried in unison, never a little whine, always screams loud enough to wake the dead. If one didn't have a messy diaper, the other did.

The babies had not only terrorized him; they'd terrified him. In spite of that—in spite of everything—the bond kept growing. He'd have given his life for them. Without a qualm.

Abruptly he heard a noisy attack of giggles coming from the loft. Since they were obviously still awake, he ambled toward the stairs. They were going to love the news that Rosemary was joining them tomorrow.

Still, just from talking on the phone with her, he felt a goofball smile glued on his face. She had that kind of dry humor, the way she talked total nonsense in such a serious tone.

Whit might have killed for his daughters…but it had been a long time since he'd felt anything to live for, beyond the girls. He couldn't remember smiling…just for himself. He couldn't remember the last time he'd felt lighthearted—and he had no idea why or how Rosemary had evoked those forgotten emotions in him.

But he was glad he was seeing her tomorrow.

After that…well, he'd just have to see.

Rosemary was trying to pull on thick wool socks and hold the cell phone at the same time. It was not an easy balance act.

"I swear, Tucker, no one could be more of a pain than a brother—unless both you and Ike were calling me at the same time. Just tell me how the new wife is. And how her pregnancy is going. And how the boys are—"

"Everybody's fine." Tucker would do anything for her and she knew it, but her oldest brother was more stubborn than a mule. "But I still want you to agree to have Christmas with us. You don't have to see Mom and Dad. You could just—"

"Tucker! I told you and Ike both that I can't do that. I don't want to hurt the parents. I just can't handle one more conversation about why I canceled the wedding, what George must have done, what I must have done, how I could fix it all if I just called him, etcetera, etcetera, etcetera. I've heard it too many times. I don't *want* to miss any of you at Christmas. Even though you're both total pains, I love you. And your families. I even love Pansy, that damned bloodhound Ike made me babysit for."

"But—"

She wasn't about to hear him repeat his argument. "But nothing. I told Mom and Dad that I had to work. If anyone in the universe could understand that, it's them.

And it's not like I won't catch up with all of you. I already sent heaps of presents to the kids—"

Tucker, of course, interrupted with different persuasive arguments. Being relentless wasn't totally his fault. Growing up with absentee parents—and their parents were such terrific surgeons that they were always on call—Tucker had taken on the role of Dad. Being the only girl, Rosemary had tried to play the role of Mom, but since she was the youngest, all she could really do was hand out suckers when the boys were sick. The point, though, was that Tucker thought she needed a caretaker.

Which she did. But not a brother or a dad or a lover. Not a man at all.

She needed to be her own caretaker.

Still, she listened to her older brother's rant—or mostly listened—as she walked to the closet to retrieve her serious jacket, then ambled over to the front window. Whit and the girls would be here any moment. It was after ten now.

Outside, there was brilliant—but misleading—sunshine. She'd hiked before dawn, almost froze to death. The sleet had started in the middle of the night and stopped before daybreak. But there were still tears dripping from every pine branch, crystal ice on every puddle. She needed wool mittens, and wasn't sure where she'd seen them last.

"Rosemary...Ike said something about a guy there."

"Oh, for heaven's sake. You two are like mother hens, I swear."

"Well, you're all alone up there. And if it were me

all alone, you'd be checking out how I was doing. No difference."

"Of course it's different. You think because I'm a girl, I'm less capable. Who whipped you at poker last time, huh? Who beat you in the kayak race last fall? Who—?"

"Those were technicalities. I'm the big brother, so I had to let you win."

She made a rude sound into the phone, making him sputter with laughter. Her eyes were still peeled on the gravel road, though. It didn't matter if Whit was late or early. They were on vacation during the holiday week, so it's not as if they were compelled to stick to a schedule.

Tucker eventually circled back to his nosy grilling. "About this guy."

"I only mentioned my temporary neighbor to Ike because he was bugging me about being alone—he wasn't as awful as you, but close. Anyway, that's why I mentioned that a very, very nice guy rented a house for the holidays. He has twin daughters, around eleven—"

"Very nice, huh?"

"If you won't interrupt, I'll fill in the blanks. He's a widower. Major car accident a year ago, and his wife was killed. So he came up here with his girls to have a private Christmas away from the memories."

"Okay."

"Get that tone out of your voice, Tucker, or I swear, I'll sock you when I see you next, in front of the boys."

"I was just asking…." Tucker had that innocent tone down by rote.

"He's grieving. Hard. For his wife. It's pretty obvious he's still in love with her and can't get over the loss. The girls accidently came across to the lodge. That's the only reason we met."

"Okay, that sounds…" Her brother searched for a word. "Nice."

"It is nice. He's nice. The girls are nice. But the only thing on their minds is the loss they suffered last year. It's a sad time of year for them. That's all."

"Okay, okay, I got it. Sheesh." Tucker hesitated. "All the same, if you wanted, I could run a background check on him—"

She hung up. Sometimes that's all you could do with brothers. It was something in the male sibling gene. When they got a bone between their teeth, they all turned into Neanderthals.

And just then, she saw a sturdy SUV winding up the driveway. The girls were here.

And so was their dad.

Whit couldn't take his eyes off her. She bounced out of the house like a kid, a stocking hat yanked over her head, wearing old hiking boots and skinny jeans and a Christmas red parka.

"Hey, Rosemary!" the girls called out.

"Hey right back! Does everybody have mittens?" She opened the passenger door, but didn't climb in yet. The girls had automatically taken the backseat, assuming anyone of adult age would want to sit up front. Which pretty much meant they intended to lean over Rosemary's seat the whole time.

"Who'd have guessed it would be this cold?" Rosemary said, and kept talking. "I figured you'd change your mind about the Gator and bring a bigger car. Don't know how we'd carry trees and the four of us together, otherwise. Anyway, I have spare mittens and hats and gloves in the lodge, if anyone needs stuff like that. Nothing pretty. Just warm."

Lilly said, "I brought gloves, but Pepper didn't. She always says she doesn't need them, but two seconds later, she's freezing to death."

"You *lie,*" Pepper shot back.

"I'm not lying, I'm—"

Rosemary shot Whit a wink, then just hustled back in the house and came out moments later with a bag full of cold-weather gear. She jumped back in, belted up, handed the bag to the girls and that was it. The girls pulled out gloves and mufflers and leg warmers and hats. Just like that, the three females all started talking at the same time, nonstop. Rosemary carried on two if not three conversations simultaneously…as if she'd always been with them, always been part of the family.

Part of his life.

Maybe she was primarily talking to the girls about mittens versus gloves, who knitted what, what colors looked good with their hair, how both of them desperately needed new jeans, and a bunch about movies he'd never heard of—except, of course *The Princess Bride.*

Somehow, though, she managed to answer a question from him about the lodge in the middle of all that.

"I'm not sure how big the lodge is—I think three thousand square feet or so? My great grandparents built it originally…when families tended to be bigger, and cousins and uncles and spare relatives all wanted a place to get together, so they needed a monster-size place like that..."

Whit wasn't sure where he was going. The gravel road wrapped around the mountaintop like a drunken ribbon, dipping here, climbing there, branches sometimes scraping the sides of the SUV. There was a lot of virgin forest this high, which meant the trees were tall and huge, nothing appropriate for a Christmas tree. Still, trees fell and new growth always emerged. He wasn't looking for perfect trees, just two that had little chance of making it on their own.

In the meantime, she answered another question. "It was kept primitive for a lot of years—no electricity, no hot water. But my brothers and I got into it last year. To start with, we built a solar oven..."

"You're kidding."

"Well, I built most of it. Of course that's not what they'd tell you, because they can't stand it that I'm pretty good with power tools. Tucker put in an on demand water heater, and Ike built the current kitchen table from reclaimed heart pine. Our grandparents never had a generator. I bought that. Once I planned to stay here for quite a while, I needed a way to store food at safe temperatures—not counting needing computers and printers and a phone. Living alone never bothered me, but I definitely needed a way to work and a way to communicate with the outside world."

No matter what he asked, she answered...but that turned into a tit for tat. She had questions of her own. Not over personal subjects, just friendly queries about their lives. Yes, they lived in Charleston, partly be-

cause Zoe adamantly loved city life—and both of them
wanted an area with great schools.

Pepper piped in, just to make sure they knew she
was listening in. "Aw, come on, Dad. You know we
think school is b-o-r-i-n-g. We could move somewhere
else if we wanted to. It's not like there aren't schools
all over the place."

The girls listened just as intently when Rosemary
asked him about his landscaping business. He had a
handful of regular employees and hired temporary help
during the planting and growing seasons. "I really like
doing larger scapes, like for businesses, community
centers, university planning…but overall, I've always
loved working with dirt, more than sitting at a desk
chair. I'm just lucky to have found something I love,
with a lot of variety and something new every day."

"There's nothing like it, is there?" she mused.
"Doing work you love? I went into botany for the same
reasons—I wanted to be outside more than inside, didn't
want to sit in a fancy office all day."

"Mom used to say that nobody could get dirtier than
Dad. She used to say that he walked outside and dirt
flew on him." Lilly provided this information.

Pepper added detail. "My mom wanted white carpeting in the living room. But then she said better not,
because Dad would never be allowed in there."

"But then she said it didn't make any difference, because Dad would rather have a beer at the kitchen table
than wine at a party."

He felt Rosemary glance at him. The girls could
never be trusted to not talk a stranger's ear off, and they
had no sense of boundaries for what was off-limits. But

their mom was okay to talk about. And the white carpet conversation was nothing weird. Still, he felt her gaze on him, a question in the sudden silence that she never asked.

That was okay. He finally found a good spot to stop, where a range of young trees struggled for growth on the shade side of the mountain. As far as Whit was concerned, he'd found the site just in time.

He couldn't remember being more sexually conscious of a woman in a long time. She was so natural. Earthy. Easy. No airs, no high-heel attitudes. Just pure female.

She flooded the front seat with estrogen, something tantalizing, alluring.

So it was a damned good thing he could open the door, pop out and get some bracing cold air in his lungs.

"Okay, here's the deal, ladies. We don't want a perfect tree. We want a hopelessly ugly tree. A tree so weirdly shaped that it probably doesn't have much chance to survive. That way we're cutting down a tree that needs a future in our Christmas, because that's probably the best future it's got. And small." He motioned to his shoulder. "No taller than that. And we need two, one for our place, and one for Rosemary's."

"Honest, guys, I'm happy to do this with you, but I don't really need a tree," Rosemary said.

"Yes she does, Dad. She doesn't have any lights or wreaths or anything at her place. She *really* needs a tree. Even more than us."

"Lilly has spoken," he said apologetically. "Sorry, but you're getting a tree."

The three peeled out of the car before he even had

his door closed. The first tree took the longest to find. It had to be suitably ugly, suitably small. Crooked, not straight, thin in the branches, pitiful. Since Lilly loved every tree, it was tough to make a decision—it was *always* tough for the girls to agree on anything, and when they finally did, the three females deserted him. While he took the tools from the back of the SUV, they went searching for the second tree.

It didn't take long, to cut down the scrawny trunk, wrap a tarp to secure the branches and haul it to the top of the car. By the time he turned around, the girls were nowhere.

They had to be close. He'd heard them all chattering moments before—Lilly saying, "Darn it, it's starting to rain."

And Rosemary correcting her, "Look up, hon. That's not rain—it's white stuff coming down. It's snow."

And then Pepper aiming for high volume, "*Snow!* I haven't seen *snow* in my whole life!"

Truthfully, the sky was barely spitting white than offering a true snowfall, but he had to grin, too, at the soft splash of white crystals drifting down. He ambled in the direction of the last conversation he'd heard. They couldn't have gone far, and he wasn't remotely worried. If there'd been a bear in a five-mile vicinity, it would have to be an awfully dumb bear. The three thrashing and crashing through the woods could have scared an ogre or worse.

Still, when he called out, "Rosemary? Lilly and Pep?" there was no answer.

Seconds later, he found out why. He wove around a cluster of pines, and found a barren patch…where all three were lying on the ground next to each other. All three had closed their eyes. All three had stuck out their tongues.

They were all trying to catch the taste of a snowflake.

Damned, if his heart didn't suddenly start squeezing tight in his chest.

Zoe, their mom, would never have gone for the tree adventure. She'd have been waiting at home, with the prized ornaments and lights, and the artificial tree she loved so much. Zoe would never have laid on the ground in the woods. She'd never have closed her eyes and stuck out her tongue.

Whit tried to take his eyes off her. Not his daughters. Just Rosemary. The joy on her face, the easy fun in her grin, the way his daughters were bookends to her. So she was a little taller. But her stocking cap and mittens looked as silly as theirs, as fun.

Her lips had a wet cherry hue…and her cheeks already had sharp blush from the wind.

He looked and kept looking and couldn't explain it. But watching her try to taste snowflakes caused an avalanche of sudden emotion he'd never expected.

He could fall in love with this woman. Maybe he was already half falling. And he hadn't even kissed her…. But then, he'd never expected to fall in love with anyone ever again.

Chapter Four

Rosemary had to laugh. The girls poured through her front door and threw themselves on the old leather couches as if they couldn't make it another inch.

"I've never been so tired in my whole life!" Pepper said.

"You're such a wuss. There's nothing to be tired about. But I sure am hungry. *Really* hungry, Rosemary—"

"Well, me, too," she admitted as she hooked her red parka on the hall tree and heeled off her boots. "I wasn't exactly planning for company, but I've got a full freezer. The fastest would probably be chili. I made a batch weeks ago, and froze half of it."

"Is it really spicy?" Lilly asked.

"Afraid not. I didn't have any hot peppers to put in, and I pretty much tend to make it mild anyway."

"*Good.* That sounds *great,* then."

"You don't have to feed us." Whit came in last, because he was carrying the tree. Thankfully he'd brought a bucket to put it in, because Rosemary was pretty sure she'd never find the one they'd used at the lodge. The MacKinnons had spent a zillion holidays here. Both the attic and one whole closet held decorations and tableware for Christmas, but she had no memory of seeing a tree stand.

"It's no trouble," she assured Whit. "I just have to thaw and heat it. Won't take more than a few minutes."

She was humming as she aimed for the kitchen. She'd always loved the old room, with its wide beams and plank floor and rustic wood cupboard—the subzero freezer blended in just fine, as far as she was concerned. Only took two shakes to take the container from the freezer, pop it in the microwave and start herding bowls together from the far cupboard.

As she pulled out the silverware drawer, she was still humming, half dancing around the room. Checked the chili in the microwave, gave it a serious stir, punched it on again. Darned if she could remember the song in her head, but she couldn't stop humming. She even knew why.

She was downright *happy*. What a great morning. All four of them had been laughing and having fun. Maybe the three Cochrans could have done the same thing without her—but she'd loved being part of their group. The girls ganged up with her against Whit, the poor lone guy against the assault of estrogen. Lilly laughed once so much she had to hold her stomach.

Whit had to think she had some dingbat genes when he caught the three lying on their backs on the cold ground—but what difference did it make?

She wasn't trying to lure him. She was just trying to help the three have a happy, carefree holiday, where grieving for their mom was eased a bit.

"On the table," she yelled out a few minutes later, and the three hurtled in the room at Olympic speed. They were hungry. "It's not fancy," she began. "And I'm not used to cooking much—"

Whit squeezed her shoulder. Her head shot up—but he wasn't looking at her, only aiming past her in the crowded space between wall and chairs. Still, she felt the imprint of his big hand, the gentleness of it, the sudden unexpected scissor-sharp awareness.

Immediately she put that thought to bed. There was no reason on earth to think his touch had been anything but kindness or friendly affection or something like that. And the girls dug into the chili as if they hadn't eaten in a year.

"Like pigs at a trough." Whit sighed, which earned him a chorus of *"Dad!"* from his offended daughters.

She chuckled. "If anyone's still hungry after this, I have a few—*very* few—brownies that some fabulous bakers happened to leave me…."

"She's talking about us, Dad."

"No kidding?"

Once they'd leveled all the food in sight, they clustered back in the living room to argue about where she "needed" the tree. Lilly wanted it by the fireplace; Pepper wanted it in front of a window. Whit didn't care, as long as he didn't have to keep carting it around from place to place while the girls made up their minds.

Eventually, it seemed to occur to the twins that possibly Rosemary should get a vote. She struggled to find a solution that wouldn't hurt either girl's feelings. "Well," she said slowly, "I like both your ideas better…but I feel kind of stuck, choosing the far corner by the front window. That place is the traditional tree spot in the MacKinnon family for as far back as I can remember."

"It's totally okay," Lilly immediately assured her. Not for the first time, she noted that Lilly was always the one to watch out for other's feelings, even coming to stand by her in support.

So after much groaning and grunting and pine needles all over the floor, Whit finished securing the tree in the holder, and the girls asked for a white sheet to drape around the bottom. Then they all stood back.

"So what do you think?" Whit asked in a gravely serious voice.

"Words almost fail me," Rosemary said. "But the first ones that come to mind are pitiful. Above and beyond any definition of ugly that I can think of. The poorest excuse for a Christmas tree I've ever seen in my life."

"Don't hold back now," Whit encouraged her.

The tree had branches at the top, but then a half foot where the trunk had either lost its branches or never had any. The bottom quarter was straggly, some branches sticking out like lone strangers. The trunk was not just lopsided, but crooked.

The girls agreed on the awfulness. But Rosemary had to pipe up again. "If ever a tree needed loving, it's this one."

"And besides, Rosemary, it looks half dead and all goofed up already. So it wasn't going to live long." Lilly was obviously serious about trees.

"So we didn't hurt anything but taking it out of the forest."

"And it smells like a good tree."

It smelled like Christmas, Rosemary thought—a smell she'd never thought she'd have a chance to love this year. She felt Whit's eyes on her face…half turned to see a private smile aimed her way. "I'll never look for a perfect tree again," she announced. "Not once I can see how right a tree like this belongs here."

"Ours is even uglier, I'm guessing," Pepper said. "We won't know until we get it home."

"Okay," Whit said. "Let's clean up here and then get out of Rosemary's hair. We've got messes to make at our house."

For the three, she doled out brooms and a container for trash, but aimed for the kitchen herself. She'd rather be cleaning up with the crew, but facing dishes with dried-on chili later just wasn't appealing. Besides, it only took a few minutes to collect the dishes, feed them to the dishwasher and wipe down the counters. From the living room, she heard the front door open and close—Whit taking out tools and debris, she suspected—and the usual sound of the girls' chatter.

She was just hanging up a dish towel when she realized there was suddenly silence coming from the great room. She hung the towel, squeezed a dollop of almond hand cream from the dispenser, and glanced around the corner.

Whit had not only cleaned up the tree mess, but brought in kindling and firewood and started a fire. He was an artist at it, she noticed. The crisscross bed was meticulously created, the poke of kindling spearing through the dry brush, the bed of branches fitting like Lincoln Logs. Yellow wicks of fire had already caught and were snipping and scissoring around the kindling.

Bemused, she looked away from the dancing flames…and immediately spotted the girls. They'd crashed like puppies. Lilly had curled at one end of the biggest leather couch and tugged a throw over herself. Pepper had done a total sprawl, stealing three quarters of the couch space, with an arm flung here, a leg flung there, a what-you-see-is-what-you-get kind of deep, abandoned sleep.

She glanced around, but didn't immediately see Whit. Before going to look for him, she scouted around for a second throw blanket, found one at the top of the hall closet, and quietly draped it over Pepper.

After that, she tiptoed around, finally noticed his silhouette on the back porch. She grabbed a jacket to pull over her shoulders and stepped outside.

He turned, with a smile for her.

"I was just about to grab the girls and take off when I saw they'd fallen asleep on the couch. But you're busy. And I can—"

"They're fine, Whit. I had to crack up a little. They're so like little kids, run a hundred miles an hour nonstop…but when they're tired, they drop like stones."

"They had a terrific time."

"Me, too. Good to have noise and laughter and commotion in the lodge again." She took a couple steps so she could stand next to him, looking out where he was. The promise of snow had disappeared, but there were still pockets of white, confectioner's sugar in the tucks of trees, hidden in branches, clustered on rocks.

A stream wound a silver ribbon, not big, just enough to make a clean, rushing sound over rocks and stony banks.

It was cold enough to freeze her nose, but she didn't move. Standing next to him, she was aware of his greater height, the brawn of him compared to her lean frame.

"This place is magic," he said quietly. "I'd have a hard time leaving it, if I lived here."

"Yeah. I love it, too. For a few years, no one really used it...but when my grandparents were alive, we often had holidays here. I remember so many times, cousins and extra kids running around having a ball. So much space. So many places to explore and enjoy."

"Sounds as if you had an idyllic childhood."

"It mostly was. I think I mentioned before that both my parents are surgeons, part of the Greenville Health System. We had a lot of birthdays and holidays interrupted by emergency calls—but my two brothers spoiled me beyond belief. Still do." She tugged her jacket tighter, not wanting to go inside, just starting to freeze. "I still remember one of the first guys I went out with. My brothers never let him through the interview process—*their* interview process. The guy had this little red sports car. Just adorable. I could have killed Tucker and Ike both."

He chuckled. "Good memories."

"In every way. Both brothers got married just this year. I'd like to think that because of superb sisterly coaching, that they knew how to pick outstanding women. Or I guess it's possible that they just lucked out."

He chuckled again, then gave her a thoughtful look. "But you're alone here over the holidays."

She took a breath. It didn't sound as if he were prying, more like he was trying to make sense out of it, put the pieces together of other things she'd told him.

"It's not as if I wanted to be alone exactly. It just seemed the only choice I had, this particular year." She hesitated. "For my parents, I always tried to be the little girl who wasn't demanding, who didn't want to cause them any worry. And for my brothers, they've always been so darned good to me, that I just didn't want to disappoint them."

"Hard to imagine you could."

"Thanks. But I definitely did. I was engaged last year, was supposed to be married in June. I broke it off. Just weeks before the wedding."

"Ouch. That couldn't have been a happy deal."

"About as painful as you could get. But there were reasons why I couldn't explain the situation completely to family. I wasn't trying to duck the problem. I just felt I didn't have a choice. So I pretended as if I had way too much work to do—which is partly the truth, if I want to finish this grant earlier than expected. And the other part of the truth is that especially my parents understand heavy work schedules."

He glanced out toward the stream again, as if trying to figure out what to say. "So this grant...you're aiming for a Ph.D.?"

"It sure seems that way. Truthfully I'd never planned on getting a Ph.D., and I liked the work I was doing before. But I had to do *something* after the breakup, and I knew a certain prof at Duke. He knew about some open grants, mentioned the two-year project on the wild orchids. It just hit me at the perfect time. The money wasn't that great, but good enough to live on. And I loved the project, so it all worked out."

Neither said anything after that. She hadn't spoken to anyone but her ex-fiancé. It wasn't as if she'd spilled the mortifying part of the story…but it felt unexpectedly good just to tell someone, to feel Whit had somehow become enough of a friend to trust him with some personal things about her life.

It was just…suddenly she realized they were standing extremely close.

She assumed they were standing that close so they could talk in whispers, not wanting the girls to hear them.

She assumed that he was looking at her just as a natural way of responding to the conversation.

Only suddenly she couldn't remember the conversation. And he wasn't looking at her like a new acquaintance or a neighbor or the father of two girls. He was looking at her as if she was the only woman in the universe—at least his universe.

She backed up a step. Or half a step. Behind her seemed to be a log wall, nowhere else to go, no place else to move. Of course she had the choice to say something intelligent, like what on earth do you think you're doing?

Only he was already leaning in to her by then. She saw his eyes. Deep blue and getting bluer.

Some instinct sent adrenaline spearing through her pulse. She couldn't imagine why. She'd grown up with brothers, been around men all her life. Of course,

George had demolished her confidence, sabotaged her judgment…but even so, she was absolutely positive she had no reason to fear Whit.

But there it was. That whistle and heat of danger, of warning, that suddenly made her heart pound. And all he was doing was leaning down, his eyes open, on hers, watching, waiting.

When his mouth connected with hers, a switch flipped on in her head, forcing her to close her eyes, to sink back, to feel her bones turn liquid.

It was just a kiss. She told herself that once. Twice. Three times. She even believed it.

Only there was something in Whit. Something that was different to her, for her. Her hormones suddenly jolted awake.

His lips tasted like something…alluring, intoxicating. The kiss started with no pressure, then sneaked down to another level, an earthier level, an exploring secrets, just-let-go level.

His mouth lifted. She opened her eyes, saw his expression, surprise, interest. He could have stopped then, but no, he came back for another kiss, this one involving sound and pressure. He cocked his leg, needing support to lean down to her level for so long…but then she was almost on tiptoe by then; he was damned tall…and she had to wind her arms around his neck. Had to. Because otherwise she would have fallen.

Her fingertips sieved into his hair, then stroked the long muscles of his neck. He was so strong, his upper arms solid as a tree trunk. She'd always been strong and fit in her own right, but Whit was like an oak…where lately she'd felt as fragile as a reed.

She murmured, "The girls."

Mentioning his daughters had no effect. Possibly if the girls showed up, appeared in the doorway, they'd both get a brain. Only the girls were nowhere in sight, and Whit was still kissing her.

He deserted her mouth, sank lips into her throat, her neck. His eyes were closed, as if the only thing in his sphere of attention was her. When he shifted, she felt his arousal graze against her, reminding her that this was no boy playing with flirtation and desire, but a grown man.

Definitely a grown man.

With a grown man's needs…and a grown man's earthy hunger. An appetite he seemed to definitely have….

For her.

"Whit…"

She was pretty sure he heard her this time. A hundred percent certain he'd stop if she asked him. Only he seemed to hear invitation in her voice instead of the warning she had in mind.

"Whit," she tried again, and tipped her head to enable a kiss that started from her. Hell's bells, if he was that determined to get into trouble, she might as well dive in deep water, too.

No one had wanted her—certainly not her ex-fiancé—the way Whit seemed to. She'd always picked good men, believed she had reasonably good taste in men. Only the good guys she'd picked in the past seemed to find her amazingly replaceable.

Not that she was pretending Whit could have serious feelings for her. They'd just met, for heaven's sake.

She'd always been a practical realist. She never thought for an instant that Whit was thinking about her in any kind of serious way. This was just a kiss.

A kiss that kept coming.

That kept building.

A kiss that wouldn't stop, wouldn't quell, wouldn't behave.

Suddenly he lifted his head. His mouth was still damp, half open, and his hair was rumpled—from her hands—his face flushed. But a frown pinched his forehead. The first frown she'd seen on his face.

"Hey," he said.

"That's exactly what I was thinking. Hey."

The frown eased. His gaze never left hers. He searched her face—owned her wet mouth, owned the shaky silvery look in her eyes. "I just wasn't expecting…"

"Neither was I," she said swiftly. "You don't have to tell me. This just isn't a good idea."

Now he tilted his head, as if confused. "It's not a good idea because?"

Her voice was soft, but she said the obvious. "Because your girls are grieving for their mom. Because you are. Because I wouldn't want any of you worried even for a second that I thought I could take her place. Especially on a holiday, when she must be especially on all your minds."

Again he looked perplexed. Then he brushed a rough thumb against the line of her jaw. "Rosemary. I was kissing you, not the wife I lost. I was thinking about you. Not her."

She smiled. It was a nice thing to say. She didn't believe him for a minute, but the kindness in his nature touched her, warmed her.

A loud shriek echoed from the living room, followed by a second one. As far as she could tell, the girls got along like two peas in a pod...until they didn't.

She cast a rueful glance at Whit, and if her heart hadn't been so scrambled, she might have chuckled. He was tucking in his shirt as fast as she was grabbing her jacket from the ground, straightening her sweater, raking a hand through his hair the same way she was trying to smooth down hers. He shot her a quick, stolen smile—how could she help not smiling back?

But then...that was it. One of the girls woke up, then the other; Whit gathered up their gear and in a matter of minutes, they were gone.

She rubbed her arms uneasily. The silence hit her the same way as when they'd left last time. She knew she was independent, comfortable alone...but now the quiet itched on her heart like a mosquito bite. The verdant Christmas tree filled her vision, and the scent of fresh pine brought back every loving Christmas memory she'd ever had.

She wanted family, a yearning so sharp it hurt sometimes. She didn't want a marriage like her parents had—where work dominated both their lives more than family. But she and her brothers loved time together. They laughed, teased, supported and fought together. But more than anything they did, Rosemary felt safe with her brothers the way she'd never felt with outsiders.

That was what she wanted. A man she could be herself with. A man who wanted the kind of family she did—not perfect, not storybook, not pretend—but the real kind of family where you could let down your hair and always know, always, that they'd stand up for you.

From everything she'd seen so far…Whit was that kind of man. He couldn't be the kind of father she'd seen if he weren't that kind of man. But he must have deeply, hugely loved his wife to be that kind of man as well—and a strange woman in the picture of this specific Christmas was just totally wrong.

So there'd been a kiss.

Okay, more than a kiss.

Okay, a whole lot more than a kiss—at least for her.

But she could put it out of her mind. For their sakes.

Whit was on his second mug of coffee when the girls woke up. Typical of a Saturday morning, Lilly sprang awake at gallop speed to greet the day…where Pepper slouched into the kitchen with a yawn and a scowl, daring anyone to speak to her before she'd had her favorite cereal and a banana.

He'd woken before dawn, found himself staring out the window, waiting for the sun to come up, replaying that embrace with Rosemary over and over in his mind.

Maybe he'd liked her on sight, but he'd never expected Armageddon or the Clash of Titans emanating from a first kiss. But it had. It troubled him that Rosemary clearly believed he was pining for his wife…the truth was more complex than that, and probably not a truth that he knew how to share. He'd never tried putting words to his feelings. Certainly not with a woman he barely knew.

But it festered more why she was living like a hermit, what exactly her damn fool fiancé had done that was so profound she'd shut herself away. He assumed the jerk had cheated on her…wasn't that the conclusion most people would leap to? And some guys just had roving eyes, a screw loose that way that nothing seemed to fix.

Still, Whit couldn't fathom how a guy would ever cheat on a woman with so much heart and passion. It didn't make sense.

All he really knew was that she'd obviously been badly hurt. And that he didn't want to add to that hurt.

"Dad?" Lilly poured a heaping bowl of cereal, no milk, and sat on her legs the way she always did. "What are we going to do today?"

"I figured we'd do some tree decorating. At least a little later."

"With what? We didn't bring any ornaments."

"I looked up some old traditions on the Net. We could string popcorn. And cranberries. Decorate with stuff like that. I also thought…how about if we make cookies? Starting with oatmeal raisin, your mom's favorite."

Pepper dropped her spoon and stared at him. Lilly raised the same stricken eyes her sister had.

"I didn't mean we had to do your mom's favorite," Whit said hastily. "I just figured you'd like making cookies. Lilly, you love—"

"Double chocolate chip."

Which he knew. "And Pepper—"

"My favorite's oatmeal raisin. Like Mom's."

Another silence fell with a clunk. No one seemed able to fill it.

Whit tried. "What about those cookies that are just plain? You know where you put the frosting on and sprinkles, like that."

"Those are sugar cookies, Dad." Lilly used her patient voice. The kind both eleven-year-old girls had opted to use with him for some time now. "And yeah, we could make those."

Thank God for Lilly. He wasn't sure if he was going to survive the girls' coming adolescence, but Lilly tended to say an exuberant yes to most ideas.

Pepper played with her cereal. "Are we really not going to do presents this year?"

Whit hated to answer. She hadn't taken off her first-of-the-morning scowl yet. "I thought we all agreed that this year—just this year—we'd do presents in a different way. Just buy some things that we could do together. Like games. Or an ice cream maker. I'd pop for new bikes—"

"What about cell phones?" Pepper piped in.

"No new cell phones. You have a cell phone."

"But we don't *both* have cell phones. And the one we have is boring. It doesn't *do* anything."

"Except call home in an emergency," Whit agreed.

"Dad! That's like what you have when you're six years old. We're way past that now."

"I know you both feel that way." Sometimes Whit had the worrisome feeling of being the mouse cornered by two cats. "But a lot of the new technology that costs a ton…we can't do all of it. So some of the fancy stuff, you have to be old enough to work, to earn some money yourselves, rather than count on me to pay for it."

Pepper opened her mouth to argue—this argument had been building for months now—but Lilly intervened, her voice careful and quiet.

"Dad, I think your idea about an ice cream maker

is way awesome. But still. I don't want to wake up Christmas morning with no presents, no surprises at all. Pepper and I like different things these days. We *need* different things these days."

"If you really need something, just tell me. That doesn't have to be about Christmas. I'm pretty sure we can always find a way to do something you really need."

Lilly's lip started to tremble, which meant her emotions were threatening to get away from her, but she obviously had something she wanted to say. "Even before Mom died, we were talking about redoing our room. Or using the study, so we could both have our own rooms. Pepper still wants purple, but I don't. I want blue. I could paint it myself."

Whit didn't have tics. But sometimes he felt like he could easily develop a few when his daughters tossed him in quicksand and he had no rule book about how to get out. "I don't have a problem with your having separate rooms. I didn't know about that. But that has nothing to do with Christmas."

"But it would have. If Mom were here. Because it'd be about coordinating colors of bedspreads and rugs and stuff on the wall. Figuring it out, then doing it together. And shoes. And my school jacket…it's just gorpy now."

"Gorpy," Whit echoed carefully.

"I'm not mad at you or anything," Lilly said. "But you just don't understand."

"I'm trying, honey—"

Too late. Her face had scrunched up, tight and red, the way it did when she was trying hard—too hard— not to cry. She bolted from the chair and ran upstairs before he could try to talk her down.

Pepper ducked her head, mainlined the cereal.

All he could think was that he was way, way over his head. He'd chosen the holiday away so they wouldn't be so constantly reminded of their mom. But nothing ever seemed simple with the twins. It wasn't just their mom they'd lost. But a woman in their lives. A grownup female's influence.

He could buy fifty ice cream makers and he still couldn't come through the way they needed sometimes. Bedspreads? How was he supposed to make getting a bedspread—a color coordinated bedspread—something he could do with his daughters?

He could probably do it.

Hell, he could probably volunteer for a root canal, if it was something good for his girls.

But hell's bells. Sometimes talking with them was like translating a language from New Guinea.

He needed help.

Chapter Five

Years ago, Rosemary had discovered that one of the best places to hide out was a darkroom—figuratively and literally. She wasn't thinking about Whit when she turned out the lights. Or her ex. Or Christmas. Or anything else but her work.

The photograph slowly clarifying in the tray was never going to make National Geographic quality, but that couldn't be helped. She remembered taking it; she'd been deep in the woods, on her stomach, in a pouring rain last summer when she spotted the orchid.

From the far room, she heard the landline ring. She ignored it. She couldn't answer either her cell phone or the lodge's landline when she was in the darkroom. Months before, she'd rigged up an answering device in the darkroom so she could catch messages, but there was no way she could reply without risking the work.

Muddy-browns gradually cleared. Background

greens gradually sharpened. Raindrops on the camera lens hurt the picture—but still, there she was. A tiny pale yellowish flower, with an even tinier white lip.

The species was the small whorled pogonia—a treasure because she was probably the rarest orchid in the eastern U.S. Finding her had been sheer, wonderful luck. The word *orchid* came from the Greek *orchis,* which meant testicle, not that Rosemary mentioned that particularly often in public. The point, though, was that particular shape was a key to identifying species that had orchid characteristics. Like this bitsy whorled pogonia…

The speaker in the corner of the wall registered the answering machine going on, then a hang up.

She returned to developing her baby. Some people called the plant "little five-fingers." If she hadn't found it flowering in late June, likely she'd never have spotted it ever. She wasn't that pretty, but she was *so* unique, and these days, so close to complete extinction.

The telephone rang again. She ignored it again.

Analyzing the testicle shape as the photograph developed to its clearest potential, was not, perhaps, the best way to keep her mind on serious subjects. Not that she was particularly interested in testicles. Or that she ever spent time thinking about testicles, for that matter.

But they were, after all, boy parts. And analyzing boy parts inevitably made her think of the human kind—not that she'd ever wasted daydreaming hours wondering about men's apparatus. Or that she'd ever spent time thinking about an individual man's apparatus, either.

But Whit, she couldn't help but remember, had expressed an inordinate amount of enthusiasm, pressed against her. That moment kept ripping through her consciousness. Feeling his arousal. The sudden thrill, the sudden sense of danger sending blood shooting up and down her pulse.

And there was his voice on the answering system. "I hung up a moment ago, Rosemary. It's me, Whit. I figured you're busy if you can't answer, and that's all right. Just need to leave a message. Here's the thing."

He cleared his throat.

Then cleared his throat again.

She lifted the soaking photo from the tray, hung it up with clothespins, tried not to breathe. When he said nothing else, she wasn't certain if he'd hung up or if she couldn't hear him—or if something else was wrong.

But he finally spoke again. "Okay, here's the truth. I'm in trouble. I wasn't going to call you this quickly after yesterday. I was afraid I may have overstepped some boundaries. I didn't want to make you uncomfortable. But this is different. I'm not kidding about being in trouble. Terrible trouble."

Again, he cleared his throat.

"It's the girls. It's about trying to have a Christmas and my goofing it all up. And somehow it's become about comforters or bedspreads or color coordinating or something like that. The twins...I'm used to them double-teaming me. But when they both completely confuse me, I just plain don't know how to dig my way out."

She couldn't answer the phone, still couldn't leave the darkroom, but the first smile came on strong, then a chuckle.

"I guess this is about shopping. Look. I won't do anything, won't say anything, won't touch even your hand, nothing. This is nothing about…that. But I'd pay you. A mortgage on your real house? A ruby or emerald or something? If you'd please go to Greenville with us tomorrow. I guess we could go to Traveler's Rest, but the girls seem to think we need to shop where there are more choices. Please. Please, Rosemary. I'm groveling. I'm desperate. I'm scared out of my skull. I can do teen-age bras if and when I have to. But I can't color coordinate. I don't even get what that means. Please don't make me do this alone."

She wasn't sure whether he severed the call or her answering machine quit recording. Either way, he was off the line—and she let out a burst of a laugh.

Maybe if she could quit thinking of him as a lover, she could just enjoy what he had to offer. A friend. A caring dad with two daughters alone on a special holiday. Someone to have fun with. Someone to help him with the girls.

It wasn't as if she didn't have the free time…or didn't enjoy them all.

She just had to be careful about Whit. And she could do that.

Somehow she'd find a way to do that.

When Whit's SUV showed up the next morning, Rosemary dashed out. She opened the door, took one look at the expression on the two girls' faces and quickly glanced at Whit.

"Save me," he mouthed.

She popped into the front seat, and opened a travel

tote that was filled to bursting. "I brought catalogs," she told Lilly and Pepper. "So each of you could look through them, give me some idea about what you like and don't like."

As she latched her seat belt, she added to Whit, "Could you give me a general price range?"

He looked at her with the same trapped expression. "Whatever they want?"

She rolled her eyes, turned to the girls. "Where did your mom usually shop for clothes? Things around the house? Shoes?"

Neither had a problem answering the question, but Pepper came through with the most detail. "Mom liked to go on a shopping trip a couple times of year. She'd go to Atlanta or Dallas or like that. She liked Neiman Marcus. And Saks. Places like that."

She shot a startled look at Whit. She'd never envisioned his wife as being fancy and status-driven that way. "And those kinds of prices are okay with you?" she asked carefully.

"Is there something wrong?"

"No, not at all." Except that he was an earthy guy who worked with his hands and loved diving into projects headfirst. And the girls were describing a mom who was a dry-clean-only type of formal lady. She turned back to the girls. "We don't think we have any of those stores in Greenville, but there are still a ton of places to shop. In the meantime, I painted several rooms in the lodge when I moved there last June. Being me, I couldn't make up my mind, so I collected somewhere around five million paint swatches. So..."

Paint swatches came from the bottomless travel tote and were distributed to the backseat.

"You don't have to pick just one color. Pick, like, four or five. If you like blues, they don't have to be all blue. But I want you to choose colors that…well, that make you happy. Colors that you'd like to wake up to every morning. And then…"

She turned halfway, to include Whit in the conversation. "Then, I had another idea. If no one likes it, no problem. But possibly you might want to put up composite board or peg board or cork or something like that for one wall. That way, they'd have a place where they could hang their favorite rock stars or pictures or phone numbers or whatever they wanted. But they could also take down stuff and put up new without damaging the walls."

"Yeah! That's an awesome idea," Pepper said.

"I like it, too," Lilly agreed. The girls looked at each other as if astonished they'd agreed on anything—at least that day.

When Lilly handed back her choice of paint sample cards, they were all in blues and greens. Rosemary pushed her into a little more brainstorming. "Okay, is there something that you'd like to do with these colors? Such as…well, blues and greens make me think of water. The sea. Or I can imagine patterns of blues and greens—in paisley? Dots? Stripes? Paint swirls?"

When it was Pepper's turn, her choices were all violent oranges and reds. "Hmm, so you're not thinking restful. You like pops of color, right? So, we might find a comforter with red on one side, orange on the other. Or a bedspread with those colors in a pattern. Or…we could do white walls, with massive circles of orange and red…. Or do one wall orange, one red, then have white rugs, a white spread…?"

"Yeah, yeah!" If Pepper wasn't wearing a seat belt, she'd have been bouncing off the roof with excitement.

Rosemary felt Whit shoot her a sudden odd look—she wasn't sure why. So far, the trip seemed to be going far more smoothly than she'd thought at first glance. The girls had started out looking so huffy with each other, but they'd warmed up almost right away. She'd felt…well, not like a playmate with the eleven-year-olds. But not like a mother. More like an aunt—an aunt who didn't have to discipline or set rules or responsibilities. She could just…be with them. Be an adult female in their lives. Not intrude in any way that could hurt anyone.

She just had to be careful not to hurt Whit the same way.

She had no way to say anything private to him for quite a while. All roads were crowded with holiday traffic, and once they were inside the Greenville city limits, the congestion quadrupled.

Downtown Greenville, typically, was decorated within an inch of its life. Charity Santas rang bells at every corner. Lights sparkled in every doorway, on every tree; wreaths with red bows blessed every window. People hustled and bustled, frantic to get their last-minute shopping done. Whit likely found the last parking space in the county, and he'd barely locked the car before the girls cavorted ahead.

Rosemary stuck her hands in her pockets and

snugged next to him—not hip-bumping close—but near enough so he could hear her.

"Okay, before I worry it to death—how much of an apology do I owe you?" she asked.

"Apology? For what?" He did a good job of looking confused.

"I can go overboard. I know it. The thing is, I spent so much time with my two brothers that when I finally get around female company...well, I just really love some plain old girl time."

"You mean, like when the three of you were all talking at once and asking and answering questions at the same time?"

She grinned. "Yeah. Exactly that. And what a great definition for girl talk. But...honestly, I didn't mean to get carried away. I know you didn't want a commercial type of Christmas...."

"Are you kidding? Rosemary, I don't care what kind of Christmas we have, as long as the girls do something that doesn't make them sad. Besides, this whole business of redoing their bedrooms...I couldn't be happier you're doing this. For the past year, they stopped wearing the same clothes, stopped brushing their hair exactly the same way. I think it's a good thing, that they want their own sense of identity. I just didn't have a clue how to do the room thing. It just started coming up last year, around when their mom died."

"Still..."

"Still?"

"Well, I bumbled right into trouble—completely forgot to ask you ahead what you might want to budget for this, or how far you wanted me to go. When the girls mentioned Saks, I almost had a stroke."

"Because?"

She lifted her shoulders. "My parents made good money, even what most people would call darned good money. We never wanted for anything. But my mom used to say that if you wanted sheets more expensive than Penney's, you needed your head examined. We were a really busy family. Too busy to be dedicated consumers, I guess. But if your girls are used to shopping by brand, or by what's an 'awesome' brand...I probably won't know names like that."

He stopped dead, which she didn't realize until she glanced up and found him several steps behind her. He was staring at her so intently that she felt a flush— not outside, but inside—warm from her toes on up. "What?" she asked.

"Their mother was all about brands. Status. Appearance. Those things were important to her. I never put down Zoe in front of them, and never intend to. They loved her. She was devoted to them." He hesitated, and just as he started to say something else, the girls abruptly turned around and galloped back to them.

They spotted the first store they wanted to shop in.

The shopping adventure only took three hours... really, they all wanted to continue a little longer, but Whit started looking glassy-eyed and a little bit shell-shocked. Weak pulse, gray, lack of ability to focus. Rosemary may not have chosen a medical profession, but she'd seen men walking in malls before. The symptoms of an impending panic attack were unmistakable.

"Can we go home now? Are we done?" he asked

after the last purchase, which happened to be a quilt that Pepper fell for hook, line and sinker.

"I love it, I love it, I love it!" Pepper crowed. "It's way better than a comforter or a bedspread. It's all the colors I totally love—!"

"Can we drive home now?" Whit repeated, his voice the weakest of the four exchanging conversation.

She patted his hand, which couldn't conceivably be construed as a sexual gesture. "You did very, very well."

"Why isn't shopping recognized as an Olympic sport? Like triathlons or steeplechasing? You know, the kind of sport where you go through intensive training before you have to compete. The kind where you have to have proven athletic abilities to even survive. You three could all bring home medals." He added, "Could I lay down on the pavement now? I can't make it another step."

"You're so funny, Dad." Lilly crowded him with a massive hug on one side, Pepper on the other.

"Maybe the military could hire you three. The Marines are always looking for a few good men, but I suspect they've never met shoppers of your caliber.

"You could probably overthrow a country or two and still have energy left over."

"You'd better sit in the back with us, Rosemary. Trust us. He won't let up." This was whispered loudly from Pepper.

"Isn't there a medal of honor for surviving something like this?" Whit asked the world—as he dug out the key, unlocked and started heaping the packages in the back. "A purple heart. Or a bronze cross. Or maybe just a subtle *D* for *Dad* in neon lights. Or—"

Once the girls dissolved in giggles—and let loose with a few disgusted *"Daaaad"*s—he upped his pace.

"There must be some kind of training you females go through to build up your strength and endurance. And weight training. The tons in those packages in back is probably going to cost us extra mileage—assuming the tires can carry this much ballast. I'll bet you all do run-in-place exercises. Push-ups. Treadmill…"

Before they hit the second stoplight, the girls fell asleep, still strapped in, but limp as puppies, covered with blankets and jackets and packages. Whit glanced in the rearview mirror, realized why the girls were suddenly so quiet and quit with the teasing.

A few minutes later, he said suddenly, "Rosemary… I should have thought. We weren't far from the hospital complex in Greenville. If you'd wanted to stop to see your parents—"

She gave a wry chuckle. "Thanks, but not to worry. My chances of seeing them were probably around a zillion to one."

"That bad?"

She heard the humor in his voice. "Probably worse," she said, in the same humorous tone. "This is their home hospital. But they divide their time between here and Johns Hopkins—where they're always on call. They're both cardiac surgeons, but my mom specializes in small children. My dad works more with transplants, accident victims. Either way, when they're doing surgery, they're pretty much out of contact for five hours at a time or more. And if they're catching a few minutes shut-eye, no one will wake them. Not for a silly reason like a family member calling."

That silenced him, but not for long. "That was true, even when you were a child? That you couldn't reach them?"

She turned her head. He was watching traffic, not looking at her, but there'd been concern in his voice. Sympathy. "I don't think it hurt any of us, that our parents had important work…more important than thinking about us all the time. Besides, there were advantages to not having parents around much."

"Like?"

"Like…the three of us grew up self-reliant. If no one was around for dinner, I'd make a peanut butter and marshmallow sandwich."

He winced.

"Yeah, that's what my brothers thought, too. Ice cream in cereal was another one of my specialties. Sometimes with chocolate topping. Sometimes not."

"Chocolate topping. In the morning?"

"Hey, I'm talking about when I was eight or nine."

He shot her an amused look. She put her head back, and relaxed. Really relaxed, she realized. Shopping with the girls had been total fun, and shopping with Whit playing his suffering-guy act had been hysterical. They were so easy to be with.

Once out of Greenville, traffic lightened up, cars thinned out. Even though it was still afternoon, the sun had already started a fast slide toward the horizon.

"It gets dark so fast this time of year," she murmured, and glanced in the backseat again. "They're still sleeping."

It seemed only minutes later that the highway lights disappeared, and Whit reached the mountain turn-off. He slowed down, and that quickly, they were surrounded by the lush green forests and winding around the road's slithering curves. "Rosemary?"

When she turned her head at his curious tone, he said, "Before we get to your place, I just want to say… those were my daughters you met today. This is the happiest I've seen them in a year. They were rowdy and laughing and arguing and teasing each other, and just…being *alive* again. Thanks. I mean it."

A lump clogged her throat. "I didn't do anything—"

"Yeah, you did. They lightened up with you. They let loose. They even stopped being so darned good all the time and came through with some serious sass. It was all your doing."

The lump in her throat thickened. She couldn't help it, any more than she could help feeling a wave of tenderness toward him. He seemed to see himself as a father, a widower, an ordinary guy.

She saw the rough jaw, the mesmerizing eyes, the hard-honed muscled shoulders. She saw a man who loved his kids deeply, beyond deeply. She saw a man who was steadfast, who valued family, who seemed to have no ego or awareness about his good looks. She got it—that he was a good guy. But that wasn't what rang her chimes.

Lust was.

Near him, she didn't feel a little tingle. She felt fire. She heard sirens.

She heard herself yearning for him like a teenager with a mortifying crush. And it had to stop. It was completely inappropriate and she knew it.

When he pulled up to her place, the girls were still

sleeping hard. Rosemary unbuckled her seat belt, grabbed her bag. Determined to act—to be—as normal around him as possible, she offered, "I'm not sure what I've got, but I could probably scare up some dinner."

"That's okay. I need to get home, get this car unpacked, get the girls settled in. They're scheduled for a Skype call to their grandparents still tonight."

"Your parents, or maternal grandparents?"

"Mine." He pushed the car into Park, then half turned to her. "I mean it, about thanking you. I don't want to embarrass you. I just want you to know how much today meant—for my girls, for us."

"Okay. That does it." She dropped her bag and swiveled toward him on one knee. "I've had it with you." He looked startled, then started to grin. Trying to maneuver over the console with its cupholders and gloves and debris was beyond awkward, but she managed it, managed to balance on one knee and pop a kiss on his mouth. She wanted to ham it up. Hoped she came across as silly and funny—anything to diminish those red-hot feelings for him, to reduce his effect on her down to a normal, livable level.

And she did.

Sort of.

Her lips smacked his then immediately lifted. She only caught a millisecond of his taste, his scent, those butter-soft lips of his. She avoided his eyes, grabbed her purse again, and then reared back to grab the door handle. "Quit with the thank-yous, or you'll be sorry," she said in her crossest voice. "I love spending time with your daughters. Loved spending your money. Loved getting out to do some Christmasy things instead of working."

"I'm sorry I thanked you," he said humbly.

"You should be."

"Are you going to kiss me if I do it again?"

Well, hell. She wanted a lighter feeling between them. Instead there was a glitter in his eyes that hadn't been there before. He had an expression, something like a rooster who just found the key to the henhouse—and she was the hen.

"No," she said. "Next time I'll whack you upside the head. You can count on it."

"And you can count on there being a next time, Rosemary."

She heard him say good-night as she closed the door and headed for the house. She didn't look back—not until she was inside and her jacket and bag had been thrown on the chair. Then she glanced out, watched until the headlights turned around, until he started downhill, until the last wink of his tail lights disappeared.

Then she took a long, deep breath.

There was no way she would hurt that vulnerable family.

No way she would hurt Whit. Which meant—lust or no lust—she would find some way to cool her jets around him, whatever it took.

Chapter Six

"Got to get you into my life...." Whit couldn't remember where the song came from, who sang it, what the rest of the words were. And he didn't care. That title showed up in his head, and like a guest at a party, refused to leave.

He felt that song was his plan for Rosemary. About the woman who kicked up his juices from here to Poughkeepsie. About the woman who engaged him, fascinated him, in ways his wife never had. Rosemary was like him. She liked natural things, no labels, no pretenses, no tickets to the opera. He knew she'd like a wandering hike on a fall-bitten day, knew she'd stop to love the sunshine dancing on a creek. Life with her would be fewer dinners with antique china, more picnics in the shade of an oak. Less ballet tickets and more lying outside and counting stars.

"*Daaad!* Would you quit humming that stupid tune?"

"I didn't know I was doing it," Whit defended.

Lilly said kindly, "We *know* you don't know what you're doing. Look at this mess."

He quit humming and looked. The afternoon project was supposed to be stringing popcorn to decorate the tree. His job, he figured, was making the popcorn. So he'd made it. And made some more. And then more— enough to fill every bowl, every plate, every pitcher in the place, and then to just kind of lay down newspaper to heap the rest.

"You think we have enough?" Whit asked Lilly.

His daughters exchanged glances. When the twins shared that kind of look, it made him terrified of their teenage years. One child was a child. Two children, especially twins, were a pack.

"Dad," Lilly said tactfully, "we have enough popcorn to decorate our tree, Rosemary's tree and probably every tree in Charleston. The problem is that now we have to string it."

"Well, of course. That's the idea."

"Uh-huh. Well, if you didn't pack some needles and thread, we sure didn't," Pepper informed him. "We didn't know we were going to do this."

Whit hadn't either…but normally he had an IQ higher than ten. Obviously they couldn't string garlands of popcorn without needle and thread—unless there was some unknown other way. "Maybe we could try glue?"

"Dad," Lilly said, again using her Be-Patient-With-Dad voice, "we don't have glue, either. We're not home. We don't have the stuff we have around home."

"And glue wouldn't work anyway," Pepper said. "I know what would, though."

"Me, too," Lilly agreed.

"What?" Whit was all ears.

"What we need to make this work is…" Both girls finished the sentence in unison. *"Rosemary."*

"Well, darn," Whit said in a tone of complete meek astonishment. "You two just might be right."

"So could we call her, Dad? Could we?"

"She could come over, help us string the popcorn. Maybe watch a movie with us? Like why *not,* Dad?"

"Well…I don't know. Maybe if you two called her—"

"Yeah! We'll call her right now!"

He did his best to be talked into the plan. Then he did his best to heave himself in the overstuffed chair and look helpless, as he watched the girls grabbing the phone from each other, bouncing around as they talked to Rosemary. Pepper knocked over a glass with drops of milk still left in it. Lilly punched her when Pepper refused to give over the phone.

He wasn't sure what Rosemary was saying…but he was positive the girls could talk her into coming over if anyone in the universe could.

He noted the spilled milk, the knocked over glass, the array of blankets on the couch from where the girls had curled up watching TV the night before, the splash of shoes and scarves strewn in the general vicinity of the back door.

He couldn't help but think of Zoe's reaction. She would have hated everything about this place, would see it as a household out of control—a sin on a par with murder or grand theft, and a lack of manners.

Twenty minutes later, Rosemary came through the front door with her arms full of bags. She heeled off her boots, held her car key between her teeth so she could divest herself of parcels and get her jacket off. Instead of her usual cherry parka, she wore a soft, fuzzy jacket in the girls' favorite purple.

The girls rushed her with the exuberance of defense after the opening kick. Both tried on her jacket—with her permission—the whole time they nonstop chattered. From the parcels and bags, she produced a plastic bag of thread, a container of sewing needles, two bottles of whole cloves, a bag of fresh oranges, fresh lemons, a linen bag of herbs he could smell from the door and a gallon—no, two gallons—of cider.

Whit suddenly suspected that he'd been demoted from manager of the day's events to unpaid flunky.

When she had everything—but the kitchen sink—*on* the kitchen sink, she finally had both hands free. She smooched Lilly on the cheek, then Pepper on the forehead, then loped over, went up on tiptoe, and gave him a fast smooch on the chin.

A kiss like she gave the kids.

Like he was another kid.

He'd never guessed before that she had a cruel side.

"Whit, can you bring in the big pot from my car? Oh, and there's a giant spoon ladle thing on the seat. And there might be another grocery sack...."

The day turned into a marathon honey-do list. Outside, a thready drizzle turned into a window-drumming downpour. The girls turned on a chick flick for background—something about knights and that kind of junk. He was given sets of instructions. Slice lemons and oranges. Put the pot on the stove, pour in the cider, add the linen bag of herbs, start stirring, don't let it boil, keep stirring, add the lemons and oranges, keep stirring.

The girls got the stringing popcorn job. Actually, he offered, but the three females pounced on him when they caught him—it was only one time!—nibbling on the popcorn instead of stringing it. They gave him another god-awful chore after that. He was supposed to stick cloves in oranges. Like cover up the orange completely with cloves. That was interesting for almost three or four minutes, but then his fingertips started hurting from all the clove stabbing, and he couldn't get them in straight anyway.

He complained that his hands were too big for this particular job.

No one paid him any attention.

He continued killing his fingers on the cloves. Continued stirring the wassail. And in the meantime, watched her listen to his girls, really listen, even for answers to the simplest questions she asked them.

She started out by asking what their mom used to like for Christmas—like what kind of presents. Did they ever make things by hand, or did their mom give them ideas, or how did they all work it?

"Well, Mom always made it easy for us. She'd ask for a Dior lipstick or something like that, that Pepper and I could afford by splitting."

"Yeah," Pepper agreed. "But with Dad, she'd give him a whole list. Like a new Coach purse or a Movado watch or two days at a fancy spa—Mom loved that kind of thing."

"And jewelry. She loved jewelry. But she always said men couldn't buy jewelry because they didn't understand what a woman wanted, so she'd pick that out for herself. Just put it on Dad's card."

Pepper added, "So she made it easy on everybody. She could get exactly what she wanted, but nobody had to do anything hard. Dad hates shopping, so he really liked it that way."

Rosemary's back was turned away from his view, so Whit couldn't see her face or read her expression, but her voice took on a different tone. "Okay…so how do you know what to pick out for your dad?"

"Oh, Dad's *really* easy. He always wants tools and stuff like that. And besides, he likes surprises. Like I got him a polka-dotted flashlight one year. Cracked him up. But it was a good light, you know? He used it all the time."

Lilly piped in, "And I got him a big bowl one time. It was for his popcorn. He always said that Mom's china was too darned fancy for a football popcorn afternoon, and there wasn't a big bowl in the whole house. He used that all the time, too."

"And we both made him ties one year in school. I can't remember what they were made of, but we dunked them in this swirl of dye. So everybody's was different. I mean, all the ties were made the same way. But each one had different colors, different swirls."

Lilly jumped in again. "The thing is, Dad doesn't like ties. He never wore ties for anything unless Mom made him. But he liked the ones *we* made. If he picked us up from school or was going to teachers' meetings or something, he *always* wore one of our ties."

"He said we saved him from all the god-awful ties out there in the stores."

"And then Mom'd yell at him for saying god-awful. But we knew what he meant. Ties are pretty boring."

"Father's Day was different, though," Pepper interrupted. "Dad always said he didn't want a present. So we'd try to think of something to do with him. Like we cooked him breakfast even when we were *really* little. Like sometimes adding a maraschino cherry to scrambled eggs. With maybe some peanut butter. And he *ate* it."

"And one Father's Day we said we'd mow the lawn for him. But we couldn't really use the riding mower by ourselves. So Dad mowed while we just hung on. That was fun."

"And sometimes we'd sneak out to get McDonald's or Burger King for Father's Day. Because Mom didn't like that kind of food. And he loves it."

Okay, they had to be boring her ears off. Whit quit listening...but he couldn't seem to stop watching.

The girls glommed on to Rosemary as if she was the rose and they were the bees. They never stopped talking. She'd got them talking about Christmas—when he'd been afraid to do that—but they didn't get upset, mentioning their mom. Not with Rosemary. She just made it...natural somehow.

The three females had claimed the couch, all sewing strings of popcorn. Three pairs of loose socks were perched on the coffee table, not much different in size. All three had blond hair, although the girls had thicker, longer styles, where Rosemary's was short. Still, scooched down, heads against the couch back, the three looked as if they belonged together. Belonged like a family. Free to be yourself—that kind of comfortable. That kind of belonging.

The house filled up with smells. Pine, cloves, oranges. Outside the rain stopped, leaving a glistening cold afternoon. He brought out sandwiches and mugs of wassail. The group weaved their garlands of popcorn on the tree, then strung his cloved-oranges from wherever they could find a hook—lamp arms, window latches, wooden chandeliers.

More smells showed up after that—almond and cinnamon. The girls destroyed the kitchen, leaving flour and crusty bowls everywhere, and eventually sheets of snickerdoodles emerged from the oven, finally cooled enough to devour. After that came a couple batches of sugar almond cookies.

The females claimed they were too tired to clean up—naturally, when the kitchen was in such bad shape the health department would likely have condemned it. He let them get away with it. It wasn't that hard to hurl stuff in the dishwasher, swipe down counters, wrap up cookies.

When he finished, he ambled to the doorway. They'd all moved to the floor by the Christmas tree. Rosemary was lying on her side, the curve of her hip a fabulous view for a man who was already fiercely, helplessly smitten. The conversation had turned mighty serious, seemed to be about the icky boys in their class, the unfair teachers.

He strolled forward, making enough noise so they

knew they were being interrupted, and gave each a slight whip with the dish towel. "We've been inside all day. Time for a walk."

The young ones took out their usual bag of complaints. It was too wet. Too cold. They were too tired. They were happy right where they were.

"Did I just do the dishes for you all? Did I sample your cookies so you could be sure they weren't poisoned? Did I make the wassail? Did I carry the trees in?"

They conceded to a *short* walk. *Very* short. The agreement only came after hard-won union negotiations—their union consisting of the two of them, and no one in the universe could out-negotiate his twins. They wanted to watch some chick flick the following Tuesday that was just coming out. They wanted a sleepover after the first of the year.

They were still tacking on demands as he coaxed them toward their jackets and gloves and shoes—still fine-tuning the details, when he opened the door and delicately pushed them all out. It was like herding cats. They could do spin moves. Evasive tactics. He resorted to carrying Pepper upside down, which was guaranteed to make them both shriek nonstop.

When he finally had all three outside, he turned a beleaguered sigh on Rosemary. "They're monsters. You'd think they'd been raised by wolves."

She was no help. Her cheeks were already pink from laughing so hard. He obviously wasn't going to get any sympathy from her, but damn…she was gorgeous when she laughed. Her eyes picked up sparkle, her skin seemed to glow.

"You have so much fun with them!"

He raised his eyebrows. "Of course I have fun with them. What's the point of having kids if you can't torment them now and then?"

"That's not every parent's attitude."

"I know. But I never understood it. Why people have kids if they don't want to spend time with them."

Talk came easily, nothing demanding or heavy. Outside was a shine-soaked afternoon. The chill had a bite, but raindrops hung on branches like teardrops. Pine needles carpeted the old woods, all washed clean from the midday rain. The house smells had been fabulous, enticing.... The fresh oxygen outside was also enticing, just in a different way. Whit needed that blast of sharp air to clear his head.

Although he already knew what he wanted to do.

The girls pranced on ahead. The gravel path down the mountain was easy to follow, trails just as easily marked. The woods up here were virgin, old, big-trunk trees shadowing out any smaller growth—which made it ideally easy to suddenly, carefully grab Rosemary's hand. A little twist, beyond a tree or two, then a dance behind pines, and he had her alone. Maybe only for seconds, and not far from the girls. But he still had her alone.

He took her mouth. Right then. Fast. Before she had a clue what was coming.

He did. He'd known all day, maybe knew from the minute he'd met her, that something was there between them. Maybe it had to be uncovered, searched for, worked for—but he had an absolutely clear vision

about what he wanted to do with and for and to Rosemary MacKinnon.

He was going for treasure.

At first, she went tense in his arms.

At first.

The wind picked up a sudden bit. So many scents
surrounded them—the tang of pine, the rich scent of
wet earth and stinging fresh air. And her. Covered in
that fluffy purple jacket of hers, all zipped up…but her
lips suddenly parted for his. Her headed tilted back,
and she lifted up, lifted into him, her arms swooping
around his neck.

Aw, man.

She didn't kiss like a good girl. She kissed like
maybe this was her last chance, the last chocolate in
the box, and she was going to savor the best damned
kiss with everything she had. She made a sound. A soft
sweet sound of yearning, a sound so vulnerable and
naked that he felt a silver streak of need.

She wasn't any woman. This wasn't any kiss. It was a
connection. The kind that made him want to own her—
and to be owned right back. To have lusty, wild, sweaty
sex…and then take all night, making tortuously tender
love. He desperately wanted to hold her through the
night. He fiercely needed to protect her through a life.

His hands slid around her, down her back, down
to her butt…felt a fierce resentment at all the darned
clothes between them. He needed to feel her. All of her.
He was too old to invite this kind of frustration, even if
it was a hurt-so-good kind of pain. He just didn't want
to let her go.

A sudden rustling sound broke through his closed-eyes concentrated exploring of her mouth.

The sound didn't immediately stop him. It wasn't some alien wild animal rustling…it was eleven-year-old girls type of rustling. His twins were close—but they hadn't discovered them yet. He still had a few more seconds. He didn't want to give up even a millisecond of these kisses, these touches. With her.

But Rosemary heard Pepper's voice and suddenly sprang back, her eyes glazed and startled. For an instant he saw an unguarded look on her face, in her eyes. She wanted him. Maybe it took a stolen, breathless kiss to unlock that truth from the closet, but he wasn't the only one with feelings. He wasn't the only one who'd never expected an avalanche of emotion and need out of the complete blue.

"Whit," she started to say. From unguarded vulnerability, she turned on the repression button, snapped that attitude into her voice.

But the girls suddenly showed up in sight, and galloped toward them, chattering and yelling the whole way. "Da-ad! You said a *short* walk! And now we did it and we're starving. And exhausted. And Lilly lost a mitten."

"I did not."

"It was *my* mitten and you took it and now it's disappeared!"

"Because you dropped it in the woods, you numbskull!"

He interjected carefully, "If you don't scare off Rosemary with your arguing, I was thinking about asking her to come back home with us, have dinner."

"We're not arguing anymore." Pepper elbowed her sister in the ribs. Lilly elbowed her right back and added a hair pull. Both gleamed beatific smiles at Rosemary.

She opened her mouth as if to say no to the dinner, then shot a quick careful glance at him. "Okay," she said, but she was still looking at him.

She wasn't coming back because of food. She was coming back, he strongly suspected, because she planned on straightening him out about a few things.

Rosemary wasn't one to duck or deny a problem.

But then, neither was he.

Once home, the girls—led by Rosemary, of course—threw him out of the kitchen and insisted they were making dinner...and "he'd better not complain."

A brilliant way to avoid any one-on-one time with him, Whit figured. But it wasn't as if he minded getting a chance to put his feet up in the recliner, catch some news, and half listen to the clatter of pots and splash of water and nonstop giggling from the kitchen. He'd known, when he pushed this holiday week in the mountains on the girls, that it wouldn't be easy. They "played" with him. They had fun with him. But it wasn't the same as having friends or female company around.

He'd fiercely not wanted them to have a grieving, sad Christmas, not have Zoe on their minds all the time, not get swallowed up by that kind of sadness. No matter what issues came up here, he'd been pretty sure anything would be better than staying at home. And it was.

But having Rosemary around brightened up the twins more than a cache of gold. She wasn't like their mom. She was just...herself. But if he could have bought a present that really mattered for his daughters this holiday, it'd be her. Rosemary.

"Dinner, Dad!" Pepper announced, carrying a platter in from the kitchen. Apparently they weren't eating at the table. The menu started with raw carrots, cut in curls. Peanut butter and banana sandwiches. Chips. A plate of cheese, each piece cut in squares or triangles or circles. And, of course, three kinds of cookies.

The biggest plate was the cookies.

The kids ate like vultures. So did Rosemary. The three of them took credit for putting together a totally junk food meal, but Rosemary couldn't look at him with a straight face when she claimed that. After dinner, the paper plates disappeared, the kitchen got wiped down, and when Rosemary said she really needed to get back home, the girls swooped on her for hugs... after which Pepper claimed she was going to wash her hair and Lilly was disappearing upstairs to check her email and Facebook.

Rosemary said she was getting her jacket, but she was gone for a bit. Whit figured she'd run into the bathroom. Whatever, he crouched down, started building a Boy Scout fire, the laying of the kindling just so, striking the flame, blowing just a little to help it catch. The fruitwood he'd brought in did a perfect burn, adding to the great scents in the house already.

"What a perfect end to a great day...a warm fire. Especially next to the tree that's *almost* starting to look like a real Christmas tree," Rosemary suddenly said, striding in from the back hall with her purple jacket on and already zipped to the throat.

He didn't need a crystal ball to get the message—

she was making a run for the nearest exit. No way she was staying. No way she was risking any more kisses with him today.

Zoe had always told him that he wasn't the brightest. But when it came to basic communication, Whit always figured he got an A plus. The worry in Rosemary's eyes told a complete story that started with *n* and ended with *o*.

He lurched to his feet, dusted his hands on the seat of his jeans. "I'll walk you out to your car."

"No need!"

"That's okay. I need a second of fresh air." He kept his hands in his pockets, just so Rosemary could see he was behaving himself. He trailed her out the door, latched it, and then jailed his hands in pockets again. The sky was black and silent as a promise. She dug in her bag for her car key.

"Rosemary, I can't thank you enough for the day. You don't need me to tell you how much fun the girls had with you. You're beyond great with kids."

"Thanks." She shot him a grin. "It's not hard to be great with great kids. Especially when I don't have to be the disciplinarian."

"You'd probably be great with that, too." He scuffed a heel in the gravel drive. "Any plans for kids of your own down the pike?"

The grin on her face froze. "Not likely." Her tone stayed light and easy, but something was there, in that glued-on grin, in her eyes. "It seems I have skinny tubes. Found out in a physical last year. It's not impossible for me to get pregnant, but the chances are around one in a zillion, or so they tell me."

Now it was his turn to freeze up. He'd never guessed he was putting a foot in it. Hell. He'd never have asked her a hurtful question if he'd known. "I'm sorry."

"Me, too. No point in lying about it. I took it hard. On the other hand, being an aunt gives me lots of kid time. My one brother's due his first baby in a couple months…and my other brother has boys, two, just about Pepper and Lilly's age. My theory is that an aunt should be able to spoil kids, give them noisy presents like drums and percussion instruments, take them places their parents never would. It's all payback for my brothers. And the older I get, the more involved I can get. I'd like to take them on the Appalachian Trail. Maybe Alaska. Maybe a hike in Europe. When they get older anyway…."

She was easy to talk to. He liked hearing it all. But he couldn't get it out of his head, that she couldn't have kids. That she'd found out not long ago. He'd known there was a heavy secret related to the bozo, because he couldn't imagine Rosemary dumping a guy right before the wedding on a whim. So…he never wanted to pry, never intended to, but somehow the question blurted out before he could stop it. "Rosemary…was that it? Why you broke off the relationship with the man you were engaged to? Because he wanted kids and you couldn't have them?"

She'd opened the driver's door, tossed her bag inside, was a pinch away from climbing in and turning the key. But now she stopped. Said nothing for a breadth of a second.

"Hell," he mumbled. "I'm sorry, Rosemary. None of that's any of my business. I just…"

"It's all right. Really." She climbed in and latched the seat belt before looking at him again. Her face was in shadow. "You know what's funny? That's exactly what I'd been afraid of, when I told George—that he'd be really upset if we couldn't naturally have kids. But his response was the total opposite. He didn't care. At all. In fact, I realized pretty quickly that he was actually happy about it. Now it seems obvious to me that was a clue."

"A clue?"

She hesitated, and then shook her head. "Whit, I don't mind talking about this sometime, but not tonight. We've had such a good day. So did your girls. And it's just two days until Christmas Eve now…so if you're all not tied up tomorrow, I have an idea for you three."

"We're not remotely tied up."

"I have some work I really want to do, but could I stop over after lunch? I was thinking…the girls might like to make a manger. You know. Like…create a shelter out of boughs, use things we find in the woods to make a crèche, a Nativity scene. Not buy anything. Just work with things we find in nature?"

"Wonderful idea. I love it."

But as she drove away, he thought what he loved… was her. He kept telling himself that he'd only known her for days, but every minute with her, every second, seemed richer than the last. His life seemed bigger than before he met her. Bigger with possibilities. With hope. With excitement over what could be.

When her taillights disappeared, he turned back to the house.

The mystery of her broken engagement was more

troubling than ever. That she was unlikely to have a
baby was impossibly sad for a child lover like her…
but that information only made Whit more concerned
at what the son of a sea dog had done that so devastated her.

He wasn't sure he had a chance…unless she was
past that hurt.

Chapter Seven

Rosemary had glued her behind to the desk chair, determined to get some work done before going over to Whit's—and for darned sure, before allowing herself to think about the man. Outside, the sun poured down, not a puff of cloud in the whole darned sky—a perfect day to be outside, tromping around, breathing in the sweet mountain air.

Instead she was working on ovaries.

Photographs were spread out over a door—literally a door. No table was large enough to display the photographs, not when she needed to see the whole kit and caboodle to determine the proper order. Whether each orchid was beautiful or plain, huge or tiny, each one needed to be identified as either male or female. Often enough, finding the ovary required a serious magnifying glass.

She'd discovered something unexpected in her research. The girl orchids who did the best job of hiding or protecting their ovaries seemed to be the strongest survivors.

Maybe that was why she had skinny tubes? Because she didn't have what it took to be a good survivor? At least after George had kicked her in the emotional teeth, and made her feel like less than a woman.

Would you quit? Stop thinking about men and life and get your mind back on sex.

She was trying. Studying a photograph of the Zygopetalum, she tucked a leg under her and measured the darling's ovaries…and the big lip designed to attract a lusty insect. Measuring the size of the ovaries in proportion to the lip size was taking many hours of painstaking work. The results were fascinating—at least to her. It just took so many exacting, grueling hours that she was starting to fear she'd get blisters on the brain.

When she heard her cell phone sing, she sprang up faster than a criminal let loose from jail.

"Hey, Rose. How's my favorite hermit doing?"

Tucker, God love him, only insulted her when he was too far away to be whacked upside the head. "Doing good. How's marriage? How're my nephews?"

"That's partly why I'm calling. To tell you that UPS seemed to deliver a truckload of Christmas presents here for my monsters. And also to tell you that you might need a bigger truck next year."

"Oh, wow, oh, wow. You mean Garnet's expecting? I'm so excited! Boy or girl, do you know? And when's it due? And how's Garnet feeling? And—"

"Wait a minute. I need to get in a word, too." She heard Ike's voice, which meant the brothers were conference calling her. They only did that when they wanted to gang up on her about something. She carried the phone into the kitchen, where she found the stupid coffeepot was empty and the maid hadn't shown up to refill it.

Oh. She didn't have a maid. Sometimes she forgot.

Ike said, "I've got a little one in the oven, too, you know. And a bride who's going to have Christmas with the MacKinnons for the first time. Rosemary, come on. You could help her like no one else."

"I can smell guilt in the air." Rosemary measured the coffee—more or less. Then added cold water and set the machine to brew. "Both of you might as well pour it on."

"Well, I'm in the same situation. Garnet's met the parents. But her parents are pretty terrifying, so Christmas overall is going to be an extra test of nerves for her. If you could just come for one afternoon. Christmas Day. We'd all be there."

"And we'd miss you. Not just the wives. Us. We're your only brothers, remember? And I know you've been nonstop badgered by the parents." Tucker always went straight to the point. "But we'd be there as buffers. And the idea of you spending a holiday alone just plain sucks—"

"I won't be alone."

There. Silence. "Say that again," Ike insisted.

She glanced at the clock. Whit wouldn't expect her until after lunch, and it was only ten-thirty. She had more than enough time to change into extra warm clothes, fix herself a sandwich, maybe see if she could remember where she'd buried her makeup from six months ago. Not that she was thinking about Whit. Or that she cared what she looked like when the four of them were doing nothing but tromping around the woods.

"Are you talking about the guy you mentioned the other day? The one renting the place down the mountain?" Tucker didn't like to waste time in between questions.

"Yes. The same one. The one who has twins, daughters. They lost their mom last year just before Christmas—"

"Yeah, I remember your telling me."

"Well, no one told me," Ike complained. "So…this guy is obviously single, then?"

"It's not like that," she said firmly. "It's just…we hit it off. All of us. Started doing holiday things together. I feel like…well, like I have the chance to make a good Christmas for them."

"Hey, that's all cool. So…what's he doing for a job? Making any kind of good living? Is he ugly as a rock? Good-looking?—"

"Ike!" God, having two brothers was sometimes a test of faith. Or patience. Or both. "He has two vulnerable kids."

"Yeah, well Garnet and I had two vulnerable kids, and you know how that worked for us." Tucker had a certain tone in his voice. The kind of tone a dog got when someone tried to take his bone. He wasn't going to give up on this easily.

She poured coffee. Added sugar. Then remembered that she didn't take sugar, and turned to face the window.

"Guys. I'll be part of the family again after the holiday. I love you both. I'm going to miss you more than you can imagine—and the kids. And even Mom and

Dad. But I just need this time to myself, okay? And finding a family that needed help is just what the doctor ordered—no pun intended about the doctor metaphor."

"You haven't slept with him, have you?"

"Let's tone that down," Ike chided his brother, only then proceeded to attack from the same side of the fence. "Has he kissed you? Got to first base? Second? How far as this gone?"

"I've only known him less than a week!"

"She isn't answering the question," Ike said to Tucker. "You want me to go up there?"

"We could both—"

"No. No, no, no. Would you quit it? I don't need babysitting or big brother advice. I'll see all of you after the holiday. That's a matter of days, not years. I need to be here. Would you try to believe me?"

Neither spoke for a moment, which told Rosemary she was finally winning the argument.

Tucker said finally, "Here's the thing, Rosemary. The longer you won't talk to the parents about George, the more they worry that something unforgettably traumatic happened to you. I only see one way that's going to change, and that's for you to spend some time with them, let them see that you're okay and doing fine. The holiday's the easiest time to do that, because the rest of us will all be there."

Rosemary pinched her nose. Man, she was sick of keeping the damned secret. If it was just for her sake, she'd have spilled the reason for the broken engagement eons ago. Unfortunately, it was for her parents' sake that she'd kept quiet. They didn't know she was protecting them. How could they?

"Guys," she said carefully. "I need you to trust me. I'd walk on water for you two. I already know you'd do the same for me. But I can't participate in a regular holiday this year. Please just let it go."

They both said "sure," but Rosemary knew perfectly well they didn't mean it. She had to find a better answer than silence, but so far she couldn't think of a way to explain what happened with George without embarrassing and troubling a whole lot of people.

Once she'd severed the call, she put it out of her mind. She wasn't the only one who had reasons to feel vulnerable this holiday. Pepper and Lilly mattered a whole lot more than her problems. Her trouble was just an "issue." The girls had lost their mom.

And Whit had lost his wife.

With another quick glance at a clock, she charged into action. She grabbed a cheese sandwich while she chased down hiking boots, exchanged a sweatshirt for a blue alpaca sweater, brushed her hair, slapped on gloss, filled a thermos with coffee and grabbed her keys. Naturally she had to run back in the house to turn off the coffeepot. Then back again to grab some serious gloves.

The drive to Whit's place took less than five minutes…but it was enough time to give herself a stern mental talking-to. She'd been making too much over those kisses in the woods yesterday.

Twice now, he'd taken her by surprise. Twice now—she admitted it—he'd taken her breath away. And twice now, she could have gone with those stupendous emotions and made love with him. It wouldn't be that hard to put aside morals and hurts and life issues—even Pepper and Lilly, because they didn't have to know. And yeah, there were other major things, like that he lived in Charleston—and she didn't. For sure her life was more flexible than his; down the pike she could relocate to all kinds of places. But none of those were the most serious reason she needed to get a grip and behave herself.

He was a wounded, grieving husband.

She saw two heads in the window when she turned the knob, saw both girls bob around, as if yelling to their dad that "she's here!"

Next thing she knew, the three of them tumbled out with a chorus of greetings. She met Whit's eyes over the kids—and yeah, she felt the *whoop* in her pulse. But sharing a smile with him was about more than that whoop factor. He loved it that his girls were so excited, so happy. He was on her team; she was on his. The look he gave her was a heartwarmer, not just a lustwarmer.

He steered them toward the Gator. His jacket was eons old, a serious outside work jacket, well loved, and as brawny as he was. "Has anyone even asked Rosemary her plan on how to make our manger?"

Since she'd thought up the idea on the spur of the moment, she wasn't exactly prepared with a complex plan. She said, "Well, first, we should pick a site close to your house, so you can see it from the windows. And we need to be careful that the project isn't too complex—we don't want to have a nightmare to take apart after the holiday."

She got two thumbs up, then had to grapple for more plan ideas. "Well…I was just thinking that we'd start gathering twigs and sticks. We'd start building them in a crisscross pattern, the way Boy Scouts are taught to make a fire? Only in our case, we want to make the shape of a cradle."

Yup. Everybody agreed they could do that. Only the three of them were still looking at her, and she was fresh out of ideas. "And after that," she said brightly, "your dad will figure out how to make the shelter around it."

She got her hair ruffled for that, which made the girls laugh. She pretended to slug Whit in retaliation, but that made them laugh even harder. There was something in Whit's eyes that had nothing to do with horseplay and teasing…something hot enough to take the chill out of the brisk, windy day.

But she didn't trust her judgment about Whit, not anymore, and besides that the girls were happy. That's what the whole outing was about, something fun for them, something about the holiday—and hopefully about doing something they'd never done before, so there was no chance the project would remind them of sad memories.

And it worked so well. The temperature tried to warm up, and the winter sun valiantly tried to shine. Leaves crackled and squirrels scattered, shocked by all the human noise and silliness. Rosemary participated, but she watched, too, loving how Whit razzed the girls, how they teased him in return.

The girls kept running back to the house, because they "needed things." And Whit had the toughest job, creating a "shed" with boughs draped over long sticks. Eventually Rosemary and the girls finished the crèche. Sort of. The cradle looked like a cradle, as Lilly put it, if you were standing upside down and were really near-sighted. They'd made the baby from rags and twine, a doll that fit exactly in the twig manger. A kitchen towel worked as a blanket.

But then Lilly fretted that they didn't have a Mary and Joseph or any wise men. She and Pepper charged back in the house, brought back billowing bed sheets, and then more twine and rubber bands, to make them into human characters. Whit said, "Did you guys really bring all the sheets off the bed? What on earth are we going to sleep on tonight?"

But Whit was overruled. The female team already had a new quest. How could you put together a Nativity scene without gifts? Because the wise men—or wise guys, as Pepper put it—had brought "stuff" like frankincense and myrrh.

A long debate ensued over what on earth "myrrh" was. No one was sure—but they were all dead positive they didn't have any, so they had to come up with other gift ideas.

Lilly remembered there were fresh cranberries in the house. Lots of cranberries. More cranberries than they wanted to string for the tree—ever. Pepper had glitter shoes that didn't fit her anymore, even though they were almost new. Both girls had hairpins that sparkled. And they both had glow sticks that lit up when you cracked them. The heap of "gifts" kept building, until they were all tired. Whit called a halt, and they all stood back to assess their masterpiece.

"Magnificent," Rosemary pronounced. "For sure, the most original manger ever created."

"I'm afraid our wise men look a lot more like Halloween ghosts than people. Except for the baby. We did pretty good with the baby."

"Dad, you did the best with the shed. That really looks like a shelter. And now that the sun's going down, our glow lights look really awesome." Lilly said nothing more for a minute, but then from nowhere she came up with, "Man. Mom would really have hated this."

"What?" Rosemary's head whipped around. "Honey, why do you think so?"

Pepper did her classic shrug. "Mom liked things to look just so. And 'just so' pretty much meant like from Nordstrom's or Saks, you know? Tasteful. That was one of Mom's favorite words. *Tasteful. Expensive. Perfect.*"

Rosemary's heart sank. She'd hoped they were doing something they'd never done before…but the last thing she'd wanted was to do something "wrong" on their mom's terms. "But this was a different project than a traditional Christmas thing, don't you think? We weren't trying to do anything perfect. We didn't want to buy anything. We were trying to create something… well, personal…something we did with our own hands, our own effort."

Lilly patted her hand. "Rosemary, chill. It's awesome. We had a great time doing it. We're just saying that Mom wouldn't have liked it, that's all."

Whit came from behind, hooked an arm loosely around her shoulder. "Come on, team. Sun's going down, and the temperature's dropping like a stone. Not even counting that, I'll bet we're all starved."

She glanced up, but he didn't look back at her. His expression was distant, distracted. Perhaps he hadn't heard the girls' comments about their mom. She felt the warmth and weight of his arm around her shoulders, thinking that it felt so darned right to be snugged close to him. To be in touch with him. To feel his warmth, his protectiveness. And yeah, to feel enough sizzle to start a bonfire.

How crazy was that? And when the girls started talking, she felt the glow disappear from the afternoon completely.

They weren't far from the house, but the girls jogged just a bit ahead, bumping shoulders the way they often did when they walked together. Apparently the earlier remark about their mom brought on some memories.

Lilly started it. "Remember that fancy crystal vase thing Dad gave her a couple years ago?"

"I remember you dropping it."

"Yeah, well, when we were in the hospital last year, waiting to see her, waiting to hear if she was all right, I kept thinking about that vase. How upset she was when I broke it. She really loved that thing. And I kept thinking how I'd have given anything not to have dropped it. Because she was so hurt and I was so scared."

"Yeah, well…I keep thinking about Easter dinner. The one where we had an Easter egg hunt in the morning?"

"We had an egg hunt every Easter, doofus."

"But I meant the dinner where she had the yellow tablecloth. And the yellow flowers. And the little yellow bunnies holding the napkins. Everything was just so. Until I threw up."

Lilly nodded. "Oh, I remember that one. You were so gross."

"Everybody jumped up and left the table. Even Grandpa was gagging. And Mom started crying."

Lilly punched her sister in the shoulder. Not hard.

"Yeah, it *was* gross. But you were sick, for Pete's sake. Not like you could help it."

"I *know* that. But when Mom was in the hospital, I kept thinking about that dinner. I didn't want that Easter to be a memory in her head, not when she was so hurt."

Rosemary glanced up at Whit. A quiet frown pleated his forehead, a sign that he was also listening.

And it was Lilly's turn to come through with some memories. "Pep, it's not like you're the only one who did stuff. Remember when we got our two-wheelers? And I fell and skinned my knee and there was blood all over the place and I ran home as fast as I could."

"And Mom had that white cloth all over the living room carpet. She was measuring something. I can't remember what."

"I don't remember, either. I just remember running toward her and blood getting all over that white material and her being so mad."

Pepper punched her sister in the shoulder. Not hard. "She never stayed mad at you for long. Remember how mad she was at *me* when I skipped school in kindergarten?"

"You were such a dolt. How could you think nobody would notice you were gone?"

"You didn't have to tell."

"I wasn't *telling*. Like tattletale. But I didn't know what happened to you!"

"You *told*. And when I got home I sneaked in the back door because I could see a police car out front. The police were there about *me*."

"How was I supposed to know that? You could have been sick or in an accident or something. When you do something dumb, you're supposed to tell me first, remember?"

"All I remember was that Mom wouldn't let me watch television for a whole year."

Lilly rolled her eyes. "It was maybe for a week. Not a year. Besides, remember the first time we went to the dentist. And you didn't want to go. And you ran out as soon as Mom opened the car door and ran right in the street and Mom had to run after you and there were cars honking all over the place—"

"I thought it was funny," Pepper insisted.

"Me, too. It *was* funny. Except to Mom."

They'd almost reached the house. The girls had slowed their pace, and Rosemary not only slowed down, but didn't want to breathe. Everything they said gave her pictures of their mom, of how their family behaved together—at least how Zoe was with her daughters.

Pepper hesitated before they got to the back door. "Mom always said I was a lot of trouble."

"Yeah, well. I wish sometimes that we could have had some do-overs."

"Me, too."

"But you didn't have to worry like I did. You were the good kid. I was the troublemaker. If anything happened, everyone looked at me first, like Mom *knew* I'd been behind it somehow."

Lilly struggled for a second before responding. "When she died, though, Pep, remember how you hit the wall? That's what I wanted to do. Hit things. Hit things hard. The way you did. I wanted to be like you lots of times. In the hospital, I was so sad I was sick. But I couldn't *do* anything."

"Hey."

Whit's quiet voice interrupted the two. Maybe he believed it was a good idea for the girls to talk, get some of those things off their chests. But when he suddenly stepped forward, Rosemary realized what had changed.

The girls had gone from talking to crying. Their faces turned toward their dad, and it got worse. Both of them erupted with tears. Snuffling, nose-dripping tears. And when Whit lifted his arms, both girls hurtled toward him, burying their faces in his chest.

Rosemary sucked in a breath. They'd reached the back door, and he motioned for her to come in with them—and that's what she'd initially planned to do. But not then. Not when the girls were upset, when the three of them were obviously having a private, fragile family moment together.

The girls and Whit had so easily made her feel part of their family group.

But at a time like this, Rosemary thought she needed to remember that she was an outsider, an interloper.

Whit protested about her leaving, but she made hearty noises about seeing them tomorrow, that she had some work she needed to do.... Aw, hell's bells, she had no idea what excuses she came up with. She just got out of there as fast as she could, with a fast kiss for each girl and a squeeze on Whit's arm for a goodbye.

Right then, that was the best she could do.

Unfortunately she was close to crying herself.

Chapter Eight

Whit put together cheese and bacon sandwiches for the girls, which had always been one of their favorites. The best he could do for a vegetable was to plaster some cream cheese in celery, which they usually liked, too. Both only picked at their food.

Truthfully, he didn't immediately notice how quiet they were at first, because he'd felt pensive ever since Rosemary left. On the walk home, when the twins started talking, he'd been startled at the words coming out of their mouths.

Whit knew his marriage to Zoe wasn't the happiest. He remembered, too well, how difficult it was to live in the pristine house she valued so much. And Zoe had been so sure that marrying a landscape architect would add up to a good life, as defined by money and status.

Whit never had a problem bringing in good money, but Zoe hadn't counted on him coming home with muddy feet and dirt under his fingernails. But the girls had seemed devoted to Zoe, and she'd been a very good mother. They'd always been dressed to the nines. They had salon haircuts. She'd made sure they had riding and dancing lessons. That was her version of being a good mom, and Whit had never been sure she was wrong.

But it hurt, this afternoon, listening to his daughters' stories. He hadn't known they experienced some of the same guilt that he had. He could never guess what wrong thing was going to offend her next. Zoe had the textbook on the "right way to live" and he'd never known the rules until he broke them. During most of the marriage, he'd simply shut up and tried to keep the peace. But he never realized that Zoe had made their daughters feel badly—for doing nothing more than being kids.

Rosemary must have formed impressions from hearing Lilly and Pepper—but he wasn't sure what she'd thought...much less why she'd taken off so abruptly.

And temporarily his concerns were tabled because the girls jumped up from the table and carried their dishes to the counter. Every alarm bell in his nerve system went off. They cleared the table, often did dishes—but only after a lot of badgering and bargaining and stalling. Their volunteering to do the chore without any prompt at all warned him that something was going on.

It got worse. After the dishes were stashed in the dishwasher, they wiped down the counters and swept the floor.

Whit wanted to search for antacids in the first aid kit, but he was afraid to leave them.

He first wanted to have an inkling of what was going

on. So he stoked the fire. Picked up a book from the floor.

"Hey, Dad." Predictably when the twins were planning Armageddon, Pepper took the lead. She and Lilly wandered over to the west window, where they could see their handmade crèche. It was dark as pitch, but their glow sticks created a soft light on the scene.

The manger definitely looked better by night than day.

"We had a good time today, didn't we?" Pepper continued. "It was like...unique. We never did anything like that before."

"I liked it, too," Whit said. "Especially liked doing it with you two."

"And Rosemary." Lilly exchanged a quick glance with Pepper. "Both of us have been worried that she was upset."

So this was the topic they'd been brewing on? "Because she left before dinner?"

"Yeah. We were thinking...maybe we shouldn't have talked about Mom so much."

"Yeah," Pepper chimed in. "I mean, she's done all this great stuff with us. And she's alone this Christmas, too. And then we started talking about Mom and feeling sad."

"Hmm," Whit said.

"What if we hurt her feelings? Like maybe she thought we weren't thinking about *her* being alone. And tomorrow's Christmas Eve. And we want her to come over on Christmas Day, too. And she said she would."

Lilly added, "Tomorrow she said we could go over to her place and make a bunch of stuff. Like a coconut cake for dessert on Christmas. And a blueberry coffee cake for Christmas morning. And like black cherry Jell-O in a mold, you know, like we both liked since probably before we were born. And she said we could have cocoa with marshmallows while we're making everything."

"But we're worried that won't happen if she's upset with us," Pepper said urgently.

"All right. I don't think that's the case, but if you're worried about, I think you should call her."

"No. We can't do it." Pepper and Lilly exchanged glances again, then looked at him. "We think the only answer that'll work is if you go over to her place, Dad."

"Me? Now?"

"Listen, Dad." Pepper pushed Lilly ahead, the way she always did when she thought Lilly could present the most persuasive argument. "First off, it's not very late. And you could talk to her the way a grown-up talks. So if we did something to upset her, you could explain it or fix it. She probably wouldn't say anything to us— not the truthful, *real* thing—because she's nice. And she wouldn't want to hurt our feelings. So if we asked her, we still might never know why she left so fast."

"And tonight, besides, Lilly and I were just gonna watch a movie. *The Hunger Games.*"

"You already saw it," Whit reminded them.

"Exactly. The first time we saw it with you. Because you said we either saw it with you or we didn't get to go. But now we've seen it, and you did, too, so you know it isn't terrible or too old for us or anything. And we want to see it again and you don't. So it's easy, you know? You can go over and talk to Rosemary, and you don't want to be here anyway while we're watching a movie you don't even like."

Whit scratched his head. He was positive a shoe was going to drop. The kids were offering him a chance to do the one thing he really wanted to do—even though they didn't know it. Surely fate was going to show up and drop a shoe on his head. This was just too easy.

"I don't like leaving you at night."

"Like you think we're babies? That's just dumb. If something happened, we could call you and you could be back here in less than ten minutes. What could happen? Even if another bear showed up, we could hide and call you. For Pete's sake, you'd just be a little way up the mountain."

Whit looked up. There had to be a cloud in this sky. There just had to be. "Well, maybe Rosemary's not up for company. For sure I should call her first—"

"No, no! No calling first! That'd just give her a chance to say she's tired or she's working. And then we still won't know if something's wrong. You have to just show up." Pepper frowned. "Like…take something. A glove. Say we thought she dropped it."

"That won't work, dolt," Lilly interrupted. "Dad can't lie. He's no good at it."

Wilt wanted to pursue that unexpected character judgment, but just then he didn't want to look a gift horse in the mouth and risk it disappearing. "Well, if you two are sure you think it's a good idea…" He said grudgingly.

"We do. We both do. And like we can call you or you can call us if there's any problem. We can't go get you. Unless you'd let me drive the Gator—"

"No."

"Worth a try," Pepper muttered to Lilly.

Whit was out the door before he let a bark of a chuckle escape. The girls were so sure they'd outwitted him.

Of course they often did outwit him. Both were smarter than he was, and together, they were formidable.

But right now there was nothing on his mind but Rosemary. All afternoon, he'd watched her with the kids. She wasn't just a natural mom; she was a natural nurturer. Full of fun. Full of zesty energy and up for anything. So easy, so natural to be with. And not just for the girls.

He'd never been comfortable with Zoe. He'd been in love with her, the way a young man could be crazy in lust, and what could possibly matter more than sex when you're a kid? Sex mattered then. And later. And probably forever, Whit figured, since he hadn't noticed any lessening in drive or need.

But the urge had paled in the past years with Zoe. She wasn't any less beautiful. Any different than she'd ever been. But he hadn't noticed, for so long, how critical she was of everyone and everything. He could go weeks without doing anything right. Weeks where he didn't want to go home—except to see the girls. Where dinner and breakfast and weekends were an effort, to be careful about what he said, what he did, how he did pretty much anything.

Rosemary was like…a fresh rose.

Complex. Way smart. But no undercurrents other than pure sweet female, a woman who loved life and loved others and loved every adventure a day could bring.

He wanted to call it smitten. Wanted to call it a major lust attack. Wanted to call it all kinds of things—because it seemed too damn soon to be so sure. But he was sure, like it or not. That he'd fallen in love with her.

Real love.

The SUV already knew its way to her house, even on a pitch-black night, on the unlit mountain road. It was only when he saw the lamp shine in a downstairs window that his stomach suddenly clutched.

Out of nowhere, he suddenly remembered that she'd left faster than a bat out of hell that afternoon. She'd been stressed. He'd guessed a zillion reasons why—starting with her being horrified at the images of Zoe she must have formed—or because the girls' crying had hit her in some unforeseen way—or, or, or. He could guess reasons forever, but the fact was…he didn't know.

And he really had no idea what kind of reception he might get when he knocked on her door.

When Rosemary left Whit and the girls, she felt as unsettled as a cat in the rain. While she put away her jacket, her gaze flew to the fragrant tree, and the crazy, wonderful decorations the girls had made for it.

Somehow the tree made her feel another naggy restlessness.

Christmas should be about kids. And family.

She felt so badly that the girls had broken down into such a serious cry fest. It wasn't that she thought crying was bad. And bringing up memories of their mom wasn't a bad thing, either. But she hadn't wanted to provoke painful memories for the kids…or for Whit.

The whole afternoon had relentlessly reminded her of what she already knew. Whit and his girls' memories of Zoe were still very much part of their lives.

As much as she cared, as much as she'd even come to love them, she was inarguably an outsider. They needed each other, needed to be with each other that night. She understood that.

But she still felt mighty lonely in the big old lodge. She wasn't up for working. Wasn't up for settling in front of a movie or TV show. She couldn't concentrate enough to read.

So…she poured a glass of wine and carted a vanilla candle upstairs to the bathroom. It wasn't often she had a total pamper session, but tonight seemed the time for it.

An hour later, she'd finished half the wine and peeled off a green facial mud mask. She stepped into the shower for the rest of the spa treatment. There wasn't much she could do with her hair, except give it an extra dose of conditioning. Then came shaving her legs—with real shaving cream, because she loved the foam.

It had been months since she'd given herself the whole female indulgence thing, and she wasn't humming by the time she stepped out of the shower and reached for a plump red towel. But she was *almost* humming.

A happier mood was trying to sneak back, and part of that was remembering some of the great things that day. How all four of them had laughed. How they'd all taken the manger idea seriously. How Whit was such a total sucker for anything that made his twins smile. How Lilly was so thoughtful and caring. How Pepper needed someone to help her believe she wasn't just a screw-up.

When it came down to what mattered…she'd laughed more in the past week than she'd laughed in months and months.

The sound of someone pounding on her front door startled her—and made her catch her breath. People occasionally got lost on the mountain…but December 23 was an unusual time for hikers and campers. She'd never been afraid up here. She'd learned young to be self-reliant, and she knew every nook and cranny of her mountaintop. Still, it was dead dark and almost nine at night.

When she failed to answer immediately, someone pounded on her door again. She grabbed jeans and a sweatshirt from her bedroom, yanked them on over still wet skin, used her fingers to comb her damp hair and yelled, "I'm coming!" when the door pounding continued.

She ran downstairs barefoot, her heart starting to pound, instinctively grabbed her gun from the closet top shelf, ran to the door, looked out…

And there was Whit.

He looked cold, his shoulders hunched, his hands stuck in a buffalo plaid shirt jacket, his head bowed. His face appeared blue-white in the yard light.

She immediately opened the door. "You didn't have to stand in the cold, you could have just come in! You know I don't lock the door!"

"I was afraid I'd scare you."

"You did. How come you didn't call first?"

"Because the girls insisted I come over without calling. I'm here on their very specific orders."

"Really," she said quietly. She was pretty sure he hadn't made up fibs before...but the way he looked at her as he pulled off his flannel jacket and tossed it on the couch had no resemblance to a mild-mannered dad. He looked like a lone wolf hungry for firelight. Hungry for her.

"They wanted me to apologize."

"For what?"

"You were terrific with them, Rosemary. The girls—and me—we couldn't have had a better afternoon. And even if it sounds odd, that includes the girls doing some crying near the end. I mean—I don't want you feeling bad about their getting a little upset. I've never been sure if they're supposed to talk about their mom all the time or not. I think it was good, their letting out those memories. And for me, it just felt better because you were there. Because—"

"Whit, it's okay to take a breath." Her tone turned gentle. She'd never seen him talk nonstop before. Never seen him remotely nervous. Once his jacket was off, his hand scraped through his hair. He pivoted around and saw that the fire needed tending, so he hunched down, opened the screen and grabbed the poker.

"They're counting on coming over here tomorrow. Apparently you offered to let them cook with you? Or bake, I guess they said. Stuff that would be part of dinner for the next day. And I forgot to ask you what time we should come for Christmas dinner, mostly because

I don't have a clue. I've got a twelve-pound ham. Not sure how long that takes to cook. I was hoping you could tell me—"

"Whit."

"They're watching one of those *Hunger Games* movies. I'm opposed to kids seeing violence and sex in movies, and even though they think they're old enough, they're only eleven. I went with them the first time, which mortified them to death—which they've told me over and over. Thank God I knew some other dads who insisted on going, too, so I wasn't the only one embarrassing my daughters into an early grave, which they still bring up at every opportunity—"

"Whit. You didn't come here for the girls."

Finally. He stopped talking. Stopped stoking the fire and adding logs and poking it and being busy. He looked at her. "What do you mean?"

"You came for me," she said softly.

"I know. I—"

"You came for me," she repeated, even more softly.

The fire cracked and popped, shooting sparks up the chimney. She flipped off the overhead light—the only glaring light in the room—and then came toward him. She saw his head tilt, expressing a question about what she was doing, but she couldn't have answered him.

She didn't know what she was doing. At least not exactly. For sure she wasn't seducing him, because George had scrubbed any aggressive sexual ideas out of her head with a Brillo pad. But Whit…

She'd seen how he looked at her.

He'd been celibate since Zoe's death—she'd have bet the farm on it.

So he had to be horny. Probably horny times a million. And the girls still dominated his heart, his emotions, so that's how it would likely be for a while yet.

But when she came close—close enough—to lift her arms around his neck, to lift up, to lift her lips to his…a low groan came out of him that was more primal than a wolf's cry.

Just like that, she knew what Whit wanted for Christmas. And that she was likely the only one who could possibly give it to him.

It was easy, so easy, to love him. The first touch of her lips and he folded faster than a house of cards. His arms roped around her, his big hands sliding around her ribs, her waist, pulling her to him. Closer. Then closer yet, until she was leaning against him, her breasts crushed against his chest, her pelvis cradled between his hips. He was erect. In those two seconds, he'd already gone harder than rock, as if she had the precise key for his ignition switch.

His mouth took her invitation and made it into a party. A private party, involving intoxicants and sweets and music and firelight. He was the intoxicant. She was his sweet taste. The fire glowed on his face, on his harshly intent expression, on his closed eyes.

Then her eyes closed, too, taking in the rush of his wanting her, of his touch, the feel of him, the warmth and power of him. The need.

Her need, too.

For so long, she'd needed…without a name for what it was. Needed a man she could trust. Needed to love. To feel loved. Needed to express….

This.

Heat like a fire.

Need like a force. Delicious need. Luxurious, wicked need. Labor intensive need.

And yeah, she worked to provoke, to incite, to please. It was hard work, touching Whit. Yanking off his henley sweater, laying her cheek against his heartbeat as she slowed down, letting her fingers tickle through chest hair, discover the slope of his chest and ribs, find the iron in his shoulders and upper arms.

She tried a kiss on his chest after that, an eyes-closed, petal-soft trail of kisses from his Adam's apple down, down…

Courage came easily. He was so responsive—the sounds he made, the way his body heated for her touch, tensed for her touch, so readily conveyed that he was starting to burn, hot and bright. Maybe he wasn't thinking about her…but for certain he wasn't thinking about Zoe and loss, about kids and loneliness, about life.

He was just…living. Not thinking, not analyzing.

He was just heart-beating alive. Heart-thundering alive.

With her. For her.

Even as those thoughts raced through her head in flashes, she was touching, stroking, learning him. A little fear seeped in there. Not fear of him. Not exactly anyway. It was just…he was so much bigger, so much stronger, so…much. The hammer in his jeans strained the zipper. Strained against her leg to free him, to uncage the tiger.

And that was when that unexpected worried quiver showed up again. She'd never teased a tiger before.

Back when, she'd thought George was. It had been

more than startling to discover George had no more prowess than an alley cat.

And that was the thing she never let surface, didn't want to ever surface, and for damn sure, she didn't want to think about him now. But her history proved that she hadn't been enough for George. Hadn't been enough for a stupid, immoral alley cat.

So it was pretty darned hard to feel safe with a tiger.

Particularly when she abruptly found herself on her back, on the hearth rug, and the look in Whit's eyes was a whole lot hotter than the fire. "So," he said, in a slow voice as if he had all the time in the world to spend on that one syllable, "we know you're a hard-core giver."

"Not necessarily," she began, annoyed as the devil when some of those worried quivers showed up in her voice.

"Yeah. Necessarily. You're a hard-core giver all the time. And as I keep discovering, you're a relentless giver, as well."

"That's not—"

"Yeah, it is true. But the question is, the really serious question, is how good are you at taking?"

"Tak—?" She was utterly confused at the whole conversation, partly because her tongue was so thick, her mind so discombobulated, that she couldn't follow much of anything. At least anything verbal.

The kiss that leveled her flat to the ground...her entire body comprehended that right off. Whit was a bully. Who knew? There were massive holes in his character she hadn't been exposed to before. His bully side. His demanding side. His earthy, no limit to his bad ideas side. His...

She couldn't breathe.... She sucked in a lungful of oxygen when he finally lifted his mouth. His mouth was wet from hers. Bruised from hers. He wasn't breathing all that easily, either. But he looked at her hard again, with that same fire glow in his eyes.

"So...you're not just a giver. You get an A for amazing in the giving category. But we're going to have to work on the taking thing. Think selfish.

"Think greedy. Think 'I want.' Can you do that for me?"

He was talking gibberish. Not making any sense she could comprehend. But she heard the low, throaty tone in his voice. He was talking love words. He was talking coaxing. Wooing. Wanting.

And then he quit talking. Peeled off her sweatshirt, then fought and won her jeans, found bare skin.

Oh, man. He was deep trouble anywhere near bare skin. He sucked in a breath at the look of her, bare, in firelight, vulnerable like she'd never felt vulnerable. By the time he met her eyes again, she considered shrinking. All that concentrated danger in his gaze was downright scary.... At least for a woman who already knew she couldn't make a man happy, not sexually, even when she thought she was pretty naturally comfortable with herself that way. Whit was just different.

Whit was more man.

More man times a million or so.

He changed gears, from high speed to a torturous crawl. Every little thing seemed to slow him down. Her tongue, her lips, her throat. He washed her navel with his tongue, flipped her over...made an adventure trail down her spine with his kisses, took a small, careful nip of her fanny…then flipped her over again.

The man was more powerful than a Hummer. She couldn't catch her breath, couldn't think. He wasn't giving her a chance to do what she needed to do, knew how to do. She wanted to stroke him the right way, the kind of touch that made him feel wanted, desired. She wanted to remember to make the right sounds, the sounds that made a man believe she was enthralled, hot for him.

She knew what to do.

He just wouldn't give her a chance to do it.

The fire hissed and crackled. Shadows danced on the wall, a slow dance of profiles, his, hers, always in motion. A coffee table pushed away. Couch pillows scattered. The dance of fire turned into a glossy sheen on his skin…on hers.

Every nerve in her body turned tense, fraught as wire stretched too tight. All the sensations that had been deliriously, wonderfully changed. Nothing was right. Her pulse picked up edgy, restless beats. Her heart picked up an unhappy thrum. She felt a confused myriad of feelings—thrills like skydiving, wild like running naked in the rain, restless that this would never stop, never get where she needed to go.

She wanted to tell him…something…but then his greedy hands claimed another forbidden spot. The inside of her thigh, behind her knee. Then his fingers found the nest of blond hair, combed through it, found the core of her, forced her to gasp.

He took that gasp seriously. Really seriously, as if world peace were at stake. Worked at winning another gasp out of her.

Then another.

She considered pounding on his head, but he studied the expression on her face and let out a throaty chuckle. "I think one of us is ready."

"Did you get a degree in torture?"

"Thanks. I wanted to do better, but it's been a while. I'm way, way out of practice."

"Are you still talking?"

But then she couldn't talk, either. He moved his hands under her hips, pulled her legs up and around him, climbed on and then in. She sucked in her breath at the sensation of him filling her, her being stretched to the maximum. The torture he'd inflicted before was nothing like this. This was misery at the most exhilarating level, need that took her over and under. Need for him. Need for fulfillment. Need she wanted to scream for.

She didn't scream. But she called out. His name. Furiously, fiercely. Over and over. He was calling hers as well, not in a scream but in a soft, urgent hiss of a whisper. The hot, wild ride headed for a cliff, tipped over.

He collapsed on top of her, then seemed to realize that his weight could crush her and immediately flipped her on top of him. He tried collapsing again, then seemed to realize that she could be cold, so he lifted up, tugged off a throw from the couch, draped it over her, then crashed for the third time.

This time he was out for the count, breathing hard, eyes closed. Recovery wasn't about to come fast.

Recovery was never going to happen for her. Rosemary figured she wouldn't survive making love with him a second time. She was beyond sated. A stupid smile had become glued on her mouth; she still hadn't caught her breath; and her heart was still slamming like a jackhammer. If there was an earthquake, an avalanche, a tornado all at once, she still couldn't have moved. Not then.

Her skin was slick, against his sweat dampened skin. Her cheek rested right in the curve of his shoulder. Her ear pressed against the wild pulse in his throat. She felt his arm around her, his big hand still securing the blanket over her. She tried to grasp a little reality again.

Couldn't.

There was nowhere else she wanted to be than right there, hot and naked in his arms. She didn't want to think about it. Didn't need to think about it. Ten minutes from now, the world might well crash on her head. But not at this second.

Nothing was wrong. Everything was right. For the first time in months. Maybe for the first time in forever.

Days passed. Maybe months.

Maybe just minutes.

She felt the stroke of his hand, his fingers combing into her short hair. "I need to tell you something."

Instinctively she braced. "Sure."

"I meant to tell you before."

"It's all right. Just say it." Whatever it was, she was positive she wouldn't want to hear it.

"The first time I saw you, I thought you were extraordinarily beautiful. The kind of beauty that I couldn't get out of my mind. Special beautiful. Uniquely beautiful. Your heart shows up in your eyes."

"Pardon?"

"I didn't know this was going to happen. But I'd

thought about it." Again, his palm stroked her hair, her neck. "I wanted this. Wanted you. The more time I was around you, the more I was...drawn."

"You'll get over it," she assured him. "I'm feeling delusional right now, too. But then, I've never made love with that much energy. It probably blew out most of my common sense brain cells."

"You're funny. But you're still beautiful. Even if you don't want to hear it. And I'm confused."

"I know you are," she said sympathetically.

"Rosemary. You don't have to fake it. And if you felt you needed to fake it with that ex-fiancé of yours, then he had to be damned stupid and a jerk you're well rid of."

"Fake it?" Now she propped herself up on her elbows, using his chest as a table, and the look she leveled on him wasn't sweet.

"Okay. I'm sorry I brought it up. Not a time to be blunt. I've been accused before of having the finesse of a junkyard dog."

"I never faked it."

"I'm sure you didn't. I was way off base. And I shouldn't have said anything anyway."

"You're right. You shouldn't have." She repeated, "I never faked anything."

"I'd be willing to offer diamonds or rubies or a Mercedes to get out of trouble."

"And furthermore, you have plenty of finesse. Loads. Heaps."

"Um, was that a compliment or a complaint?"

"A compliment, you idiot."

He was still stroking her hair. Still looking into her eyes…as a lover. Possessively. Greedily. Intimately.

"I'm thinking this would be a great time for the phone to ring. Anything to get me out of hock until I figure out how to get my foot out of my mouth." Abruptly a cell phone went off from the pocket of his jacket across the room. "Damn. I didn't mean it. I swear."

"It could be your girls."

"It has to be my girls. At this hour. At this time of night before Christmas Eve tomorrow. Do I have to answer it?" he asked her plaintively.

"Afraid so."

"But I don't want to leave you."

A minute before he'd been so aggravating she wanted to strangle him. Then he said that, and she remembered they were both still naked, still glued together, and maybe her fresh arousal wasn't as public as his, but she wanted him again. Right then. As hard and wild and scary as the first time had been.

The cell peeled out a rap beat again. She said what he already knew. "You have to take the call."

And he uncurled and stood up to do just that, but as he connected the call and pressed the speaker button, Pepper's plaintive voice started up. "Dad. Lilly's already asleep but not me. But she was worried, too. We just wanted to be sure Rosemary wasn't mad at us."

Rosemary had to smile, both at Whit walking naked across the room to dive for his cell phone—the firelight incredibly illuminating his tight little ass. And it was little, compared to those big brawny shoulders and muscular thighs. Sexy. Head to toe.

But even more, lovably, when he scraped a hand

through his hair and talked to his daughter. "Rosemary was never mad at you. She liked it, that you were willing to talk about your mom with her." He glanced back.

She gave him an enthusiastic thumbs-up.

He turned around, so he could look at her even as he talked to his daughter. "And yeah, she's totally still on for the cooking thing tomorrow...."

She sent him another thumbs-up.

"So she wants you to come over around, say..." He waited.

She held up both hands, fingers splayed.

"Around ten o'clock, she says. So you'd better get to sleep, cookie. I'll be home in two shakes."

The instant he clicked off, he scowled and said, "I don't want to be home in two shakes."

She laughed, and draping the couch throw around her shoulders, started scooping up his clothes. He dressed. Unwillingly. Stopped to kiss her. And then return to scowling as he yanked on boots, and finally his jacket. Then kissed her again.

"So do I get to come over tomorrow or is it just the girls who get to come?"

"You can come over midafternoon. We need to do the baking stuff on our own. Unless...well...the only job we have open before midafternoon is washing dishes."

"That's just cruel," he said.

"Uh-huh." She opened the door, then wrapped the throw seriously tight around her. Outside, the night was black velvet, not a star or moon in sight—but toe-stinging cold. "Whit?"

"What?"

"I need to tell you something."

His head shot up, and his eyes lost all that teasing silly nonsense. "So tell me."

"I wanted to say it before."

His expression changed, as if he were bracing for a hurt. She'd felt the same way when he'd started a conversation with those same words. Nothing good ever seemed to follow "I need to tell you something."

She said softly, "I'm really, really glad we did this."

He waited, as if assuming an ax was going to fall on his foot after that announcement.

But there was no ax. She smiled softly, bravely. "Before you go home...I just want you to know that this whole night was absolutely okay. It's the Christmas season. Everything gets crazy emotional around the holiday—for you and the girls especially this year, because of Zoe. I never wanted to interfere with that. Never wanted any of you to think I wanted or could replace her." He opened his mouth, but she pressed two fingers—two very cold fingers now—against his lips.

"Whit, I really wanted to be here for you. I loved having the chance to be here for you. But after the holiday, I know you three are going back to Charleston. And that's fine. I don't want you to worry even a second about tonight. This was all good."

She lifted up, pressed a kiss on his lips—a fast, fast smooch—and then chuckled. "Go, would you? I need to close the door before I freeze to death."

She didn't give him a chance to answer—or a chance to think up some awkward reply. She just closed the door. Fast. Before he could see how hard it was to hold on to that soft smile.

She hustled to the warmth of the fire and crouched

down to secure the screen for the night, feeling that she needed to lock up her emotions the same way. Whit had made her feel beautiful…. When she'd never felt beautiful before.

But after the holiday, she knew he would have trouble remembering her.

Every man she'd ever known seemed to find it all too easy to forget her.

Chapter Nine

The house was quiet as a cave when Whit woke up. He pulled on clothes as he glanced outside. The moon was still up, the landscape black and glistening and silent. A perfect Christmas Eve day was dawning.

There wasn't a whisper coming from the loft—the girls were still clearly dead to the world. He measured coffee, put it on, did some token cleanups until the percolating finally finished.

He carried the mug to the tree, stared at the lopsided wonder they'd created. From the thrown cranberries to the loopy popcorn strands to the sequin slipper Pepper had donated for the top, it was the best tree he could remember.

Because of her.

Rosemary.

Heaven knew where she'd been hiding all that passion…but he'd never figured, at his age, to be blown away by making love. It was her. All her. She inspired his girls; she inspired him. That huge heart of hers seemed to have no limits. She had an endless capacity to give and understand, a magical intuition and perception about what others needed.

He thought about what she'd looked like, naked in the firelight.

He thought about her standing in the doorway, the couch throw covering her but her feet still bare, her legs, her eyes in that freezing night wind, telling him it was okay, she didn't want or expect more from him.

She had the right to expect the moon and the stars from a man. She deserved the best of guys. She deserved to be cherished and appreciated. To be loved.

And he wanted to be the guy to love her. To be loved by her.

Only they'd barely made love before she was kicking him out.

"Hey, Dad." Lilly, loudly yawning, ambled downstairs, wearing her lion floppy slippers and her Christmas jammies, her hair all atumble. "Is it time to go to Rosemary's yet?"

"It's not even eight, lovebug."

"We're gonna have a *great* day." She yawned again. He lifted an arm, and she scooched next to his side, curling up the way she had since she was a little girl. "You're bringing the ham to Rosemary's house, right?"

"Right."

"And the pop."

"And the pop."

"And the ice cream Christmas trees."

"And the trees."

"So we won't have anything to do but love Christmas."

"That's the plan I heard," Whit agreed. "I was told I couldn't come over to her house today, though, until midafternoon. Unless I was willing to shut up and do dishes all morning."

"We're doing girl talk, Dad. You'd be bored anyway. Or you'd be holding your hands over your ears so you didn't have to hear embarrassing stuff. Besides…don't you want to get something for Rosemary for Christmas?"

He hesitated. "You're right. I could pick up something this morning. Do you think it'd be a good idea if it was from all of us?"

Pepper showed up in the doorway. "I think Lilly and me should get her something that isn't, like, a *thing*. We could put a present in an envelope. Like that we'll do all the dishes tomorrow. Or we could vacuum or something. Or fold clothes. You know. Some dumb chore so she wouldn't have to do it."

Lilly considered that idea. "Yeah. That's good. She's not so much about stuff from stores. But still. We could write it on a piece of paper, and in an envelope, and then in a box, and then in a bigger box, and then wrap it up so she couldn't guess what it was."

"And Dad could get us some boxes and wrapping paper if he's going out anyway." Pepper elbowed her way to his right side, where she curled up next to him.

"I wasn't planning a long shopping trip," Whit said.

Lilly shot him a frown. "But you need to take your time, Dad. You need to get something neat for Rosemary."

"Like what do you think is a good idea?"

"I don't know. Just something special and nice and that's a good surprise for her. Like that."

Acid starting churning in his stomach. He wasn't an anxiety-ridden kind of guy, never had been. It was just…well, he'd rather wrestle with a nest of rattlers than shop for a woman. Nothing he'd ever gotten Zoe had pleased her. No matter how hard he tried. And he'd tried. "Like what kind of nice?"

"Dad." Pepper patted his shoulder. "Go to Greenville. Park near downtown. Then just walk. All the shops will be open. You'll see something just right. You can do this."

"Yeah. You can do this, Dad." Lilly stepped up to reassure him, too. "Just take your cell phone. Call us if you get in trouble."

That was a big help. He was already in trouble. Trouble that had nothing to do with his girls or buying a present.

It had to do with falling in love with a woman he'd only known for a few days. A woman who seemed quite sure he was suffering from holiday madness. A woman who had a secret regarding her ex-fiancé—a secret that put sadness in her eyes, a secret that led her to hiding out as a hermit. And a woman who was under the impression that he was still in mourning for Zoe.

A few more days with her. That's all he had. All he and the girls had.

Whit could rack his brain from here to Poughkeepsie. But he had no idea how he could make all that come together in such a short time.

* * *

When Whit showed up to drop off the girls, he came to the door with them.

She greeted the crew with a big smile. "You want some coffee, Whit?" she asked, and it looked as if he was about to answer, but then he just stood there and looked at her.

And she looked back.

It happened again, just like last night. No one had ever made her feel beautiful—because she wasn't. But Whit made her feel treasured that way.

And no one had ever made her feel unforgettable—because all her life, from parents to boyfriends to George, she'd apparently been easy to forget.

Whit was the only one who evoked entirely different emotions. It was the way he looked at her. The way her life seemed different, the way she felt differently, the way the whole world suddenly, softly hushed, when he was close.

For a few seconds, anyway.

"Dad. What's wrong with you? You're looking weird."

"You're not sick, are you? Because it's Christmas Eve."

"And you're supposed to leave so we can bake stuff with Rosemary."

"So you need to go, Dad."

Whit fought to get a word in. To her. "I'm feeling extremely unwanted."

He shouldn't. She could have thrown herself at him right then and there. "Something tells me you'll survive a few hours of peace and quiet."

"*Go,* Dad," Pepper said with an eleven-year-old's complete lack of interest in his feelings.

"Yeah. We love you, Dad. But go." Lilly swooped up to give him a kiss, then pelted into the living room.

Shoes tumbled near the doorway. Hot pink jackets hurled onto chairs. Scarves snaked en route to the kitchen. Whit shook his head. "You sure you're up for this?"

"You'll come back to save me, won't you?"

"You know I will."

She didn't know any such thing. Growing up, she'd never expected to be saved. As an adult, she'd saved herself. She was no fragile princess, and she never wanted to be…but somehow Whit's words sent a silver tingle up her spine.

Even her most fragile orchids found a way to survive in the wild. She never thought of herself as fragile… but she did think of herself as a survivor. She always had been.

Now, though, watching him drive off in his SUV, she didn't feel so tough. She wasn't sure if anything could be right after he was gone.

"*Rosemary!*"

"I'm coming, I'm coming. And I hope you guys are ready to make a huge mess, because we're about to take out the whole darn kitchen."

"I'm *always* ready to make messes," Pepper promised.

"The first part of this is just to make a plain old white cake. That's easy enough…you two can take that on, right?"

"Yeah. We know how to do cakes. I do the measuring," Lilly said, "and Pepper does the mixing. And we both get a beater to lick. And we usually fight over the bowl, but you can have the bowl this time."

Rosemary chuckled. "I can see where your priorities are. Licking the batter is more important than the finished result." She'd already gotten out bowls and pans and measuring devices. "I don't know where this recipe came from. It just always seemed passed on in the family. We've been doing it so long I could probably do it in my sleep…but it'll be a lot more fun with you two."

It was. Licking the cake batter was all good. Then, when the cake came out and while it was still warm, both girls poked holes in the top of a cake with a fork. Rosemary mixed the cream of coconut with the condensed milk and poured it over the whole cake. "We'll make the frosting in a little bit, but first the cake has to cool. So we're moving on to the Christmas coffee cake."

That recipe was more complicated, including butter and sugar and eggs and orange juice and vanilla and blueberry pie filling and cinnamon and a bunch of other magic ingredients. In no time, the counters were crammed with dripping measuring devices and spoons and various size bowls.

"Wow, Rosemary. You really can make a mess."

"Thank you. That's the nicest thing anyone's said to me in a long time."

The girls giggled.

"Hey, you two. Do you have some grandmas and grandpas? Where are they? Do you ever spend holidays with them?"

'Well," Pepper said, "on Mom's side, she was an only child. That's why she was spoiled, she was always telling us. And she liked being spoiled. Anyway, Grand-father died when I was just a kid."

"I was just a kid, too," Lilly reminded her, in the tone of the long-suffering.

"Anyway, we didn't know him much. But Grand-mother used to be with us all the time. She lived in Charleston, too. But something happened to her. We weren't supposed to know, but Mom was on the phone all the time because there were so many calls about Grandma."

"She walked downtown in Charleston without her clothes on in the middle of the night," Pepper piped in. "And that was the end. She had to go to this place."

"I heard Mom tell Dad that Grandmother was too young to have Alzheimer's. But I guess some people get it younger. Anyway, we have to go see her every once in a while." Lilly added honestly, "It's not like we don't love her. But she's not like herself anymore. And the whole place is scary."

"Scary how?" Rosemary asked.

"Well, she doesn't know us. At all. Or Dad. Or any-one else. Like she was knitting this sweater, only it wasn't a sweater. It just kept getting longer and longer until it was taller than Dad. She didn't know."

"And she'd start singing all of a sudden."

"And she said the f-word. You have to understand, Grandmother would never, ever, *ever* say the f-word. Or use any other bad language. So it's like she's not re-ally our grandmother anymore."

"Dad said we have to visit her sometimes anyway. So we do," Lilly said. "I'm just saying, we both get creeped out when we go there." She raised suddenly stricken eyes. "Does that sound mean, Rosemary?"

"I think it sounds honest. You already know she can't help what's happening to her. It's sad." Rosemary aimed for a more cheerful note. "So how about your dad's mom and dad?"

"Oh, they're *awesome*. They just don't live here. They live around Seattle. They fly to see us a couple times a year. And Dad lets us fly there a couple times of year. Gramps is cool. He has horses and everything, lets us ride whenever we want. And Gram does pet therapy stuff. Like she raises dogs and cats—and sometimes the horses—to help out kids. Not sick kids. More like kids in trouble with the law. Tough kids who are always in trouble. But…oh, no. Oh, no, oh, no. Rosemary, I'm *so* sorry!"

Rosemary saw the pan slipping. Lilly had just poured the pie filling on top of the batter. The whole messy recipe was almost done—but neither girl could stand still for long; they had too much energy. The pan slipped when Pepper darted toward the sink…and down it went, with a crash and a spatter, upside down on the kitchen floor.

To Rosemary's shock, Pepper burst into tears…and Lilly looked ready to. Both lifted stricken faces to her. Both looked more upset than if they'd just lost a best friend.

"Good grief. What's all this? It's just a spill, you guys. So it's a pain to clean up, but that's all. It's nothing to be upset about. Pepper…" She crouched on the floor where Pepper had sunk down. "Honey, there's no reason to cry."

"There is. I ruined it."

"Well, yeah, I don't suspect we'll be able to eat it off the floor. But I'm pretty sure I've got the ingredients to make another one. Or we'll make something else."

"I still ruined Christmas Eve. I always ruin things. I was trying to do everything right. And now I broke the dish and made a mess and—"

"Honey, the glass dish is just a glass dish. Next time I'm there, I'll get a new one at Walmart."

Pepper hiccupped. "It's not like your greatgrandma's or something like that? Like an heirloom or like it cost a zillion dollars or couldn't be replaced?"

Rosemary frowned, disbelieving Pepper's tears and fears both. "Pepper. Lilly. To begin with, this is a cottage. It's a place for people to put their feet up, relax, enjoy nature and life and people and family. There's no dish or plate here that's expensive. Never will be."

"You're positive?" Pepper lifted her face for a second time to have her tears mopped up by Rosemary.

"Absolutely. I'm also positive that I don't even want to own things that I have to worry about. So this is just a big old nothing. Except for cleaning it up. We have to do that."

"I'll do it all," Pepper said immediately.

"That sounds good." Lilly had long quit looking so fearful, although she'd sat down on the kitchen floor with the other two.

"Nah," Rosemary said. "If we all help, the mess'll be cleared away in two shakes."

"That's what Dad always says. Two shakes. He means really fast."

"All right, then." Rosemary looked at both of them,

wondering who was more shook up, her or the girls. The burst of tears had seemed to come from nowhere. So had…fear. "Look. How about a hug to get us all back on track again?"

They glommed on to her faster than spit on an envelope. She'd seen Whit hug them. Hugs were so clearly part of their lives…and part of hers. Her brothers were major rib-busters, especially with her. But this was different. This was two eleven-year-old girls who flew into her arms and took her unconditional loving hug for granted—and offered the same kind back to her.

Hell's bells, the two of them almost brought tears to her eyes.

The mess was cleaned up—or cleaned up good enough. A new coffee cake was made. About then, they claimed they were starving for lunch, and because Rosemary hadn't completely forgotten about being a kid, she made mac and cheese—with extra cheese and French-fried onions.

Whit would likely show up at any time, but he wasn't here yet. "Okay, guys, the last thing we need to do is set the table for tomorrow."

Truthfully she'd never planned any such thing, but after the tear burst, she wanted to do something to boost Pepper's confidence. And Lilly's, too.

It was easy to see she'd made a good choice when the girls immediately shared worried glances.

"Here's the thing," she said calmly. "I'll finish cleaning up the kitchen. You two take charge of the table. We need the obvious—five of everything, plates, silverware, napkins, dessert plates. Oh, and glasses. Sound easy so far?"

"Is any of that good stuff?" Lilly asked bravely. "I mean, I know you said you don't have stuff that can't be replaced. But all the same, if we dropped, say, a glass, would it cost a whole lot?"

"Nope. Not that I'd care if you did. Putting out the dishes is the boring part, anyway. There's a linen closet—I'll show you where. There should be a bunch of holiday place mats. Pick out whatever you like."

"You mean, no matter what's there?"

"Yup. There's no fancy white linen in there…not for that old oak table. But there should be lots of place mats. And then in the middle of the table, we need some kind of decoration."

"Like what?" Pepper said warily.

"Well…I'll give you a bunch of things. Pine boughs. Red ribbon. A strip of red plaid fabric. The oranges poked with cloves. Some old, old salt cellars…that you might fill with almond or vanilla or cinnamon. Whatever you think would smell Christmasy. Just play with it, you know? And you can add anything you can think of."

"Like some pine cones from outside?" Lilly asked.

"Exactly. You're getting the picture. Whatever you two think would look nice. Or fun. Or pretty. Or whatever else rings your chimes."

You'd think she'd given them gold. Pepper dealt out the plates faster than a deck of cards. Lilly set the silverware and napkins just so. Then came the table decoration…and they fussed for more than a half hour, with ribbon and sprigs of pine and salt cellars they filled with spices. Then they took a look, and started all over.

Pepper came first into the kitchen. "Do you have any

marshmallows? Big's better but even little marshmal-lows would be okay."

"I think so. Let me look."

After that, Lilly asked for toothpicks…and pepper-corns. Then they fussed with the table all over again. Lilly climbed on the table in her stocking feet, and used ribbon to tie a handful of the clove-studded oranges from the wagon chandelier.

A bunch of the marshmallows disappeared—Rosemary expected they went directly inside tummies—but the rest were turned into toothpick snowmen with peppercorns for eyes. Lilly was still fussing when Pepper, finally bored, ambled into the kitchen and plopped on a stool.

"This was way fun," she told Rosemary.

"For me, too. You thirsty?"

"Yeah. Dying of thirst."

"Cider?" Lilly wanted some, too, but she wasn't fin-ished with her Christmas table centerpiece. Pepper hung in the kitchen, sipping cider, not saying anything…but there was something in her eyes that Rosemary noticed.

"My dad's due pretty soon, isn't he?"

"Actually, he's overdue. But I think he was afraid of getting stuck with dishes, so he might be deliberately a little on the late side."

She thought Pepper might laugh, but she just propped her elbows on the counter and hooked her chin in her palm. "Rosemary?"

"What, hon?" She tried to make her voice casual.

"Sometimes it really bothers me. That most of my memories of my mom are of her yelling at me. It's not that we didn't have good times, but most of the great times I remember were all with my dad."

Rosemary didn't know what to say or how to react. "Maybe your mom tended to yell when she was under a lot of stress?"

"But she didn't yell at Lilly that I can remember. I think sometimes…" Pepper said hesitantly, "that Mom didn't like me."

Cripes. The kid was breaking her heart. "You know what?" Rosemary said, but the phrase was just a stall.

"What?"

Rosemary gulped. "I think, maybe, that parents try so hard to make their kids safe, to teach them lessons and values that will help them in life. So sometimes it could seem like they're yelling too much. Or being mean. Or being critical. When all they're trying to do is be good parents."

Pepper stewed on that for a while. "So. Did your parents yell at you?"

"My parents weren't around enough to do much yelling," Rosemary said honestly.

"Well. I wish my mom had been more like you," Pepper said, and looked as if she was about to say something else, when Lilly yelled from the other room.

"Dad's back! He's just driving up!"

When Pepper took off for the front door, Rosemary let out a long, uneasy breath. Pepper's words punched every worry button. She never wanted the girls to think she could replace their mom—or that she wanted to take their mother's place.

She just never dreamed that either of the girls could form an attachment to her so quickly.

Or that she could feel a deep love for both of them, just as fast.

The icing on the worry was Whit. They'd made extraordinary love last night. But to presume that intimacy meant love or potential commitment or a future together was downright crazy. And unfair. To him. To his daughters.

Whatever they did together was about Christmas. Nothing else. Just Christmas. She damn well better keep that in mind.

And then she heard his voice in the living room, and felt her heart thump like a foolish puppy dog's tail.

Chapter Ten

Whit pushed off his boots at the door, then shed his jacket. His daughters gamboled toward him as if he were their favorite horse and they could both climb on.

"Where have you *been,* Dad!"

"Hey. You two sent me out with a job to do. It took a while. I'm exhausted."

Both girls giggled. "Dad, when you have to shop, you're exhausted before you even walk in the first store."

The twins couldn't be more bright-eyed and happy, but right off, he could see Rosemary was avoiding his eyes. His naked tigress from last night had disappeared. Her red sweatshirt was Christmasy; her socks had Santas. But she was hanging back in the doorway, her posture careful.

"Wow. Looks like you three have been busy." He said, looking at the pretty table.

"You think? Rosemary let us do it. Make up our own centerpiece and all." Lilly swallowed a gulp. "It wasn't like Mom would have done it—"

"It's terrific. Really pretty." Whit squeezed his daughter's shoulders. "You've got a great eye for balance."

"You think so?"

"I think so, too," Rosemary said immediately. "The girls have been going nonstop. Ask them. I've been working them both to the bone."

"No, she hasn't!" Pepper immediately defended her. "We made coconut cake for dessert tomorrow. And a fancy coffee cake for tomorrow morning."

"As you can tell," Rosemary deadpanned, "we concentrated only on the important food groups."

"I figured that ahead of time. The list you gave me was for all the dull stuff—like the twelve-pound ham in the back of the car."

"Which you get to stud with more cloves, Dad!"

"Not that! Anything but that!"

"And tomorrow," Rosemary added, "if you're really, really good, we'll let you peel potatoes."

Whit looked at his daughters. "I thought you guys loved me."

"We do love you, Dad," Lilly assured him. "But you have to face it. You're outnumbered."

"But I was counting on being popular when I got back. I brought dinner. And candied apples for dessert. And two DVDs to watch. And the ham. And potatoes. And…"

"All right, all right." Rosemary turned to the girls. "We did give him the grunt work. And now he's brought dinner. I think we should let him off the hook. In fact, I think we probably have to give him hero status."

Pepper and Lilly both claimed he needed more time to prove himself. "For one thing," Pepper said, "he hasn't told us what DVDs he brought yet."

"One's *Father Goose*."

"*Yeah!* That's tradition in our family, Rosemary. We always get to watch it over Christmas sometime. It's really old, but it's still pretty awesome."

Lilly wasn't giving up so easily. "What's the other tape?"

"It's a surprise. But it has *'Wedding'* in the title," Whit said, in the tone of the long suffering. As far as he knew, the girls' top ten favorite movies all had to do with brides and bridesmaids and junk like that.

Since they both screamed, he figured he'd scored a good one, but Lilly was quick to move on. "Did you get the other thing we talked about?"

"Yeah, did you, Dad?" Both girls looked at Rosemary.

They were about as subtle as a cattle prod. Rosemary picked up the hint in less than two shakes. "If you got me a present," she told him, "you can just take it right back. I haven't been out. Haven't gotten any of you three presents. You'd make me miserable if you gave me something and I had nothing to give back."

"It's not that kind of gift," Whit promised her, and to his daughters, "we're going to have to take some lessons on how to keep secrets."

Rosemary ambled closer, crossing her arms under her chest. "Listen, you three." She took a breath. "I have an idea. I think it's probably a stupid idea, and there's no problem if any of you say no."

"What? What?" The girls couldn't wait to hear.

"Well…you all came up to Whisper Mountain to have a different kind of Christmas. That's why I'm here, too. And since we've been doing things all day, and it's already almost dark…well, Christmas Eve can be on the lonely side if you're remembering the people who aren't with you. So, maybe…would you all like to sleep over?"

Whit's jaw almost dropped. His lady appeared as wary of looking at him, wary of being close to him, as a fragile doe. But before any of them could answer, she forged on.

"We've already collected all the food here. And there are a half-dozen bedrooms upstairs—you girls could either choose your own or share together. Your dad could pick another, or else sleep down here. I'm just saying, there's lots of choices, lots of ways for everyone to be comfortable."

The girls were all for it, judging from their jumping and hand slapping exuberance. So was he—but Rosemary still hadn't made eye contact with him.

He most definitely hadn't taken his eyes off of her. "I think the idea's brilliant," Whit said.

"It's probably not convenient."

"It couldn't be more convenient. Like you said, the food's already here for tomorrow. And we're not doing the usual Christmas morning big-present thing."

"I understand that…but you three probably want some family time just for yourselves. I don't want to intrude. In fact, that may be just what all three of you really want, a quiet family Christmas."

"Rosemary." Lilly's voice went up three octaves. "You're being *silly.* We're already family. We're together all the *time.*"

"Yeah. We get family time whenever we want it."

"I'm on the girls' side," Whit said meekly—since the girls were already laying on the arguments.

"Well, you girls don't have nightgowns and all that—"

"It'll take me less than ten minutes to head back down the mountain, pick up a few things, get back."

She started to make another objection, then stopped. She looked at him, eyes full of worry and nerves. When he first saw those soft blues, he'd been stunned by the sadness in them. Now...some impulse had encouraged her to suggest the sleepover. Knowing her better now, he suspected she wanted to do something for the girls— some way to make Christmas Eve and Christmas morning less sad for them.

A sleepover would definitely help that. No question the girls loved the idea, and it'd be good for them. Good for him. But not, Whit suspected, so good for her, not if she was trying to back away from intimacy between them.

So he'd just have to find a way to make the sleepover a good thing for her.

Sometimes a man had to do what a man had to do.

Just after eleven that night, Rosemary opened her bedroom door and listened. Like the infamous poem claimed, not a creature was stirring, not even a mouse. The whole household had started yawning after nine, and completely folded around ten-thirty.

Rosemary knew she wouldn't sleep, so there was no point in tossing and turning. She crept downstairs barefoot, leaving lights off until she reached the far hall closet in the back.

Her mood was more than ebullient. She'd known the sleepover idea could turn out disastrous, the instant the suggestion came out of her mouth. Encouraging more closeness was risky and foolhardy—especially for a vulnerable family like those three.

But it had all gone so great. Whit made a fast trip back to their place for night gear—and came back with such a huge load that Rosemary had to hold her stomach from laughing so hard. He just looked so beleaguered as he carted in more and more stuff. The girls could have lived for six months in Europe on the "critical things" they needed to stay overnight. Their own pillows. Their own blankets. Their own "sleeping socks." And both of them claimed to have given up dolls "*ages* ago," but it seemed they both slept with life-size stuffed animals— a lion for Lilly, a panda bear for Pepper.

They all chowed down on the chili Whit had brought for dinner, adding cheese on top and dollops of sour cream, then consuming candied apples as if they'd never tasted sweets before. Then the girls charged off for their "blankies," which were apparently required before curling up with the DVDs Whit had brought.

She'd sat on one end of the couch, with the girls in between and Whit on the far end. Everyone had "blankies" heaped over them, and popcorn bowls on top of that.

Whit kept it together until halfway through *Father Goose*...when she suddenly realized he'd leaned his head back and was looking at her. If she leaned her head back, she could see him over the girls' heads. He made gestures of extreme suffering, of major yawns, of gruesome boredom, then covered his head with the blanket.

Silly. Who would have guessed Whit could be downright silly? And since she couldn't help laughing, she had to cover her head with a blanket, too. Chuckling—downright giggling—until the girls admonished the adults to behave themselves.

Rosemary was still smiling at how easily the evening had gone—and how much simple fun she'd had with them. Now, though, since she was stuck with insomnia, she pulled a footstool into the hall closet. Two weeks ago, she'd planned to forget about Christmas altogether. But now, Whit and the girls had put her in the spirit, in spite of herself.

She tugged down two boxes—neither heavy—and carted them into the living room. Family holidays hadn't always been spent at the lodge, especially not in recent years, but certain decorations had always been stored here. One box held coils of old-fashioned Christmas lights, the kind that looked like candles and clasped onto each branch.

The second box held four very old, giant glass bulbs—one sapphire, one emerald, one gold and the last ruby-red. Every generation of MacKinnon kids had to wait until they were old enough to be trusted with the "sacred" balls.

She lit candles on the mantel, providing just enough light for her to add those decorations to the tree. It didn't take long, and once she'd plugged in the old-fashioned lights, she sank in front of the tree with a blanket draped around her.

Memories whispered through her mind…so many Christmas Eves, just like this. Creeping downstairs to look at the lit-up tree, to hear the hiss of fire, to look out at winter stars, to smell the pine and cherrywood. To just inhale the magic of the night.

She heard a quiet footfall, and turned her head.

Whit, wearing jeans and a fisherman's sweater, was just coming down the stairs. "You couldn't sleep, either?"

"Just had some last-minute things I wanted to do." She noted the boxes in his hands. "You, too?"

"Yeah. The girls think we're not doing presents. And in principle, I don't think it'd kill any of us to have a less material Christmas. I know we bought all that stuff for their bedrooms at home, but that was different. And it's nothing I could wrap up, besides. Anyway…"

He was nattering. Whit was so not a natterer.

"Anyway, I bought them each a gift. A camera. Not too easy, not too complex, or that was the goal when I picked them out."

"They'll love it!"

He nodded. "I hope so. When they were talking about your darkroom, it made the mental wheels spin. They were both entranced. Pepper, I suspect, will want to take people pictures. Lilly will want to go prowl around outside, snap flowers and trees and just things that draw her eye."

"They're both artistic in different ways."

"I think so, too. When they were little, the 'twins thing' was fun for them—dressing alike, talking alike.

But these days I can see them trying to differentiate from each other. So I may have bought them both cameras, but I was hoping it was the nature of gift that they could use to develop something in their own individual style."

"And what's the third gift you just snuck under the tree?"

She caught his grin by firelight. "The nongift for you. Nothing scary. Nothing over the top. Nothing to fret about. Besides which, the kids' mother could have told you, I pretty much never get girl gifts right."

He plunked down next to her, cocked up a leg at the base of the tree. She could feel the heat of his body, see the kindling warmth in his eyes.

Too close. She said quickly, "Would you like a glass of wine? Or a beer?"

"Either one. Whatever you have around."

"I can guarantee I don't have anything fancy."

"Anything you have would be perfect," he said.

But the way he looked at her, he wasn't talking about wine. She uncoiled and aimed for the kitchen, unsure what she'd find. She had an occasional glass of wine, but living alone, a bottle usually turned to vinegar before she could finish it. Still, the lodge had a small wine keeper, just underground, with a mishmash variety of wines people had either liked or left or been gifted in the past. She found a Shiraz, opened it, poured it in two jelly glasses. Her mind whirled a million miles an hour at the same time.

There was a background reason she'd come up with the sleepover idea. The reason was real. But now she had the opportunity to do something about it…well, she sure wanted that glass of wine first.

When she came back, Whit had stoked the fire, added a log and was back on the blanket by the tree, an elbow cocked on his knee.

"That tree looks downright magical. In spite of impossible odds," he said wryly.

She handed him his wine, took a couple serious sips. "All trees look magical on Christmas Eve." She gulped. "Whit?"

He looked at her.

"I would like to tell you something—the reason I broke up with my fiancé. And the reason I've been keeping it a secret."

"I've wondered," he admitted.

She nodded. "Actually, I'd like your opinion. It was never that I was unwilling to talk about this. It was that I believed I had to keep the secret from my family. And after I tell you, maybe you could tell me if my judgment was right to keep it all quiet."

He waited. She sipped some more wine, and then started telling the story.

"I practically grew up with George, even though he was a few years older than me. His parents and mine were all doctors. The adults became close friends, did dinners together, parties, sometimes holidays. I didn't think of George—romantically—until after college. He was a brand-new doctor at the time. I was just starting my first serious job. We were both home after being away for a while, both single." She shrugged. "We started going out. Had fun. We already shared a lot of history. We didn't have to waste time getting to know each other, never suffered from those dating nerves. He was so easy to be with…it was almost like we were already family."

She had to stop for breath—and to finish the last sips of wine. "When he got me the ring, our parents were overjoyed. Beyond overjoyed. They considered it a match of the families. Perfect for everyone. To a point, I felt kind of sucked along by the tide. I loved him. It wasn't such an exciting kind of being in love, but I thought we were solid." Again, she had to stop for a gulp of breath. "Unfortunately, that's when the story gets dicey, so it gets a little tough to tell."

Whit, as if he already guessed that, had shot to his feet and made the trek to the kitchen to bring back the wine bottle. He refilled her glass.

"Well…I went to my doc for a physical. The thing was, if we were going to be married, I wanted the pill or some kind of regular birth control that we could count on. Not that I didn't want kids. I absolutely did. But I just wanted to set up house, get settled in our lives first. But the point is…in that physical, I found out that I was likely to be infertile. Skinny tubes. Wouldn't be impossible, but it was highly, highly unlikely."

"I'm sorry, Rosemary." His rough hand cuffed her neck in a quiet gesture of empathy.

"Yeah, I was, too. Devastated, to be honest. I love kids."

"You don't need to tell me that. I can see it every time you're around my girls."

"Anyway…obviously I had to tell George. Immediately, before the wedding. I didn't know if it could be a marriage stopper for him, but no matter what, I needed to get this out front for both our sakes. I thought he'd be as devastated as I was."

Whit frowned. "Instead…what? It didn't bother him?"

"At first…well, I thought he was amazingly sympathetic. Unselfish. He said he was upset, but he didn't seem to be. And then…for days after that, he kept saying things…like that this could be a cloud with a silver lining. If we couldn't have kids, we could have more freedom. Freedom to travel. To be spontaneous. To go places and do things we'd never done before. To be adventurous. To experiment in whatever we wanted to try in our lifestyles. I thought—he was trying to be kind, to help me see that we could have a good marriage without kids."

Whit's frown became darker. He didn't get it yet. Well, it had sure taken her a blue moon to get it herself. She swallowed. Hard. "Okay, so then a couple weeks before the wedding, he called, said he had a surprise for our usual Friday night date. And there certainly was a surprise waiting for me at his place. Whit, I wish to bits you could guess what it was, because I for sure don't want to tell the rest of this story."

"I'm sorry. I can't guess. And you can't keep me hanging, so just get it out."

That's what she figured she had to do. It just wasn't easy. "There was another couple at his place. A married couple. About our age, maybe a few years older. I thought he was introducing me to friends. But they weren't friends. He'd only met them once before. They were, um, partiers."

"Partiers?"

"You know. Like when four people play poker, using stakes like taking off clothes, or anteing up for some type of…behavior. They wanted to strip. To share each other. Switch off. Girls and girls. Boys and boys. Two boys and a girl. And then—"

"Rosemary, tell me you're kidding."

"I wish." She swallowed two huge gulps of wine. "Call me naive. I guess I was. And honestly, I'm not one to judge other people's choices. It's just that I never guessed in a million years that George had that kind of secret life. And there was just no chance in the universe that I wanted a marriage on those terms."

Whit crashed on his back, put a hand over his eyes. "It's hard to admit this," he said, "but the last time I was this shocked, my dad told me once and for all that a baby didn't come out of his mom's belly button."

Her jaw dropped. She didn't know how she'd expected Whit to react. She just knew she needed the story out in the open. But to hear him make a joke… she hadn't known her shoulders were stiff with tension, until all those knots loosened up. Even her face had felt stiff, because when a bubble of a laugh came out, it sounded downright rusty. "Whit."

"I can't talk now. I'm suffering too much shock."

"You goof. I'm glad I told you. You made it easy. You can't imagine…"

"Oh, yeah, I can imagine. The scene with the other couple. The scene when you told your parents the marriage was off. I'm sure glad it was you, because—even being a guy—I'd have collapsed for sure."

Another bubble of laughter escaped her. "It was so awful."

"*Awful* is too light a word. How about mortifying and upsetting and maybe even a little sickening?"

"Hey, could I hire you to be my support person?" she asked wryly.

"Sure. I'm pretty expensive. But not for you. For you, I'll do it for free."

She sank on the blanket next to him. Once the rest of the tension eased from her system, she felt as strong as a cooked noodle. "Telling George to take a hike wasn't that hard. But when it came to calling off the wedding, talking to my parents, my brothers…and his mother, who came over demanding an exact explanation." She lifted a hand in a helpless gesture. "Whit, I *couldn't* tell them. It would have affected their friendships. It was George's business, but all the parents had professional and personal connections together, thirty years of caring about each other."

"So you didn't tell. You just broke off the engagement and took off for the hills."

"Yup. You think it was cowardly?"

"I think it was damned cowardly for your ex to leave you holding the whole bag. He could have tried talking it out, finding something that both of you could say to family and friends about why the marriage was off. It shouldn't all have been on you."

"I meant, do you think I was cowardly to take off for the hills, as you put it?"

"You? Cowardly? In what universe? You take on bears and twins. You don't have a cowardly bone in your whole body."

"Yes I do."

"Where? Show me."

"Show you what?"

"Show me this cowardly bone."

Chapter Eleven

She clearly assumed he was teasing, about finding her cowardly bone.

But she went along with it, lifting her hand to the firelight, motioning to a specific bone.

"I'm pretty sure I have a lot of cowardly bones, but this has to be one of them," she said deadpan.

"Yeah?" He lifted the hand, examined it, then raised it to his mouth, pressed a soft, soft kiss in her palm.

Clearly startled, she lifted her head. Something had changed. He wasn't sure what…maybe letting the George story loose had eased her fears? Maybe he couldn't be sure of the reason, but the expression on her face was different. Unguarded. Vulnerable. And the way she looked at him was heartrending. Her eyes took him in, as if he were magic for her.

That suited him fine, because Rosemary was definitely magic for him.

He leaned closer, scooping her closer, kissing the palm of her hand again. Then looping her hand around his neck and honing down for another kind of kiss. A lip-lock. A serious mouth-to-mouth resuscitation. A kiss of wooing. A kiss of promise.

He wanted his mind and heart on nothing but her. Still, it took a second before he could completely shake off the story about her ex-fiancé. Life didn't hand out treasures very often. Rosemary was a gift, and if George was too stupid to see it, he was a fool. But he'd hurt her. And trapped her from being able to tell anyone. And in general behaved like lowdown pond scum.

For Whit, the story added even more momentum… to cherish Rosemary. To lavish her with some plain old adoring. She was so beautiful, inside and out—a woman to revere, not a woman to take advantage of. A woman to respect, not a woman who was expendable.

Convenient? No. Easy? No. Simple? No chance of that, either.

He didn't care.

He helped her sweatshirt come off—because he could see she was getting overwarm, beads forming on her forehead. Her eyes looked increasingly dazed.

His weren't. He felt he was seeing more clearly than he ever had in his life. This was the woman he wished he'd known first. Before Zoe. Before anyone else.

Her jeans had to come off, then. There was still far too much fabric separating them. He found the waist button, fought with it, won, found the zipper, eased a hand inside.

Her eyes popped open. "We can't," she whispered. "The girls are sleeping like rocks."

"They could still wake up," she objected, but then she looked at the expression on his face and perched up on a bare elbow. "Okay, you. I have a place."

"Not outside. I'd love to make love with you outside, but right now it's colder than—"

"Not outside."

"Storm cellar?"

Better than that."

"Attic?"

"Better than that. My darkroom. It locks automatically. If the girls came to find us, they could knock, but they wouldn't be able to come in unless or until we—"

"Got it. Perfect."

He had to admit that wasn't his first impression of the room. The space was cluttered from ceiling to floor, full of odd smells and strange shapes, with very little space to maneuver. For darn sure, there was no place to lay down. But that was what he saw when she opened the door and switched on the overhead.

He realized exactly how perfect the room was when she closed the door and all light immediately disappeared.

The space was black as pitch. No way to see anything. No way to see her. But his sense of touch and hearing became fiercely acute.

"The office chair," she whispered. "It swivels and it's strong. And it might be miserably uncomfortable, but I just can't think of another place where—"

"It's perfect," he assured her. And then quit talking.

He heard her pull off her jeans…the whisk of denim, the wink of sound when she tossed them on the floor.

He listened to every sound she made—at the same

time he swiftly peeled off everything he had on. Undressing had never before involved so much adventure or risk. He bumped a shin. An elbow. A shoulder. Partly from speed, and partly because it was tough to maneuver in the small space, much less in the dark.

But he liked the dark. It made inhibitions evaporate. Intensified the other senses. It created a world where only she existed for him. Her breath. Her body. Her sounds. Her scent.

Her.

"Whit…" She was laughing. Or almost laughing. "We're going to kill ourselves."

"Yeah. It's not looking good for our surviving this. But look on the bright side…we'll have a whole lot of fun en route."

She chuckled again, the sound throaty and wicked. He loved his sunlit Rosemary…but he loved bringing out the closet wicked in her, too. "I'm just a little worried this isn't possible."

"Aw, love. You can't issue a challenge like that to a man." He heard her suck in a startled breath, grinned in the darkness. "See? Amazing what's possible when there's motivation."

He'd only gotten one good look at her working chair, but it was one of those mesh things with lumbar support and five castered feet and arm wings. There was ample room for him to sit, even to spread his legs. And it wasn't hard to lift her on his lap—he had the shoulders and muscle to do that with no sweat.

Still. Just that fast, her softest, most erotic parts shifted against his helplessly susceptible guy parts. His hands suddenly felt too rough, too harsh, for her beautiful soft flesh. And there was no possible place to put her legs, except up and over the chair arms.

And that was problematic at an Armageddon scale, because their closeness was kin to a lock and its key. One wrong move and he'd be inside her. One right move and he'd be inside her.

Either way, he had to conjure up control from somewhere or this was going to be over before it started.

And that just couldn't be.

He framed her face in his hands, pulled her closer to him for another kiss. A kiss unlike any they'd shared before. A kiss so new that no one had ever experienced it before. A kiss he created just for her. Just with her. Lips and teeth and tongues, soft and deep, owning deep, claiming deep.

She was precious. From breast to elbow, from throat to ribs, from behind her ear to the ripe swell of her breasts...there was no other woman remotely like her. Ever. Perfect for him. Part of that was her loving character and part was her inner sweetness. Part was her strength. She didn't shrink from anything, just did what was right on her own terms, alone, not expecting or asking for anything from anyone.

He didn't care if she asked for it.

He still wanted to give her the moon and the stars. To show her she was cherished. And yeah, that she was wanted. Fiercely, passionately desired. For herself. For who she was and who she wasn't.

It was a lot to tell her without saying a word. It was a lot to show her in a crowded office chair in a velvet-black room. It was a lot to comprehend, for a man who'd never felt those things, showed those things, imagined he was capable of those things.

She moaned and sighed, at first luxurious female sounds, like a cat with a nonstop purr…a sensuous, sensual kitten, responding to every stroke, every caress.

But then she got impatient. At least he thought she was impatient, judging by the small sharp teeth she dug in his shoulder—which was the precise moment he held her fanny in his hands, was holding her, steadying her, as he filled her up. He closed his eyes from the hot blood roaring in his veins, the pain of entering something so sweet, so tight, so silken.

The purrs turned into something louder. The bite in his shoulder turned into two. Good thing she didn't have nails, because her arms swung around his neck, hands, fingers digging into his skin. Sounds turned into groans. The kitten had turned into a live lioness, with pride in the arch of her spine, elegance in how she teased and enticed. She created an up-and-down stroke, just to let him know who was boss…and it wasn't him.

"Rosemary?"

"Sh."

"I'm so in love with you."

"If you talk and interrupt this moment, Whit, I swear I'll never forgive you."

"No more talking," he agreed, and yeah, he noticed she hadn't responded when he admitted being in love with her. But he didn't need her to return an answer or a feeling. Not then. He needed to give her the gift of it. Love. Free and clear.

Her guttural cry of release triggered his. He lasted long enough to give her a second spin, to revel in her after-spasms, the liquid in her breathing. The deep sighs from both of them seemed to define sated. Neither one could talk for a bit. He couldn't, for sure. Just wanted to hold her for the next hundred years, just like this—or at least until they both regained some lung power.

She was the one who managed to talk first. "I have to be killing you."

"You are. You did."

He couldn't see her smile in the darkness, but he could feel it. "I meant, you have to be uncomfortable. You're holding all my weight."

"Oh, that. It's okay. I lost all circulation a while back. But believe me, I don't mind."

She pressed a chuckle on his throat, a soft, devilish kiss. "You don't think the girls will find it odd if they find us locked together in the morning, unable to move, in this, um, definitely compromising position?"

"That'd be a problem," he agreed. "Which means we definitely need to move before six in the morning. Not that they get up that early. But being Christmas, I suspect they won't sleep in like normal."

"You don't think we need sleep ourselves?"

"I do. Right now I'm desperate for sleep. But I'm even more desperate to keep my arms around you."

"You're a darling, Whit."

"Now where did that come from?"

"From me. I thought this was going to be a terrible holiday. Instead, it's turned into one of the best Christmases I've ever had. Because of you."

He wanted to pursue that thought, but she abruptly shifted, threatened all future generations when she climbed off him. Then she started laughing, because her elbow touched something and they both heard the crash of something lightweight and metal hit the floor.

"We're both crazy!" she said. "What on earth were we thinking?!"

He knew what he was thinking. That he was acting like a lovesick calf. He'd wanted to be her Christmas present...only not exactly. He'd wanted her to want him. To see how they were together. How they could be.

He knew, perfectly well, that they'd only known each other for such a short time. Also that his girls were a critical factor in any relationship he took on—and even though they were nuts for Rosemary, that wasn't a guarantee that they could instantly work well as a family. They lived in different places. He knew all that.

And he'd never believed in anyone who instantly fell in love.

But that's how he felt.

Right or wrong, common sense or not, rational or not...he knew she was the right woman for him. The perfect woman for him. A woman he could love the way he'd never loved before.

But he wasn't sure if he could make Rosemary see it. They were both running out of time.

"Listen, you," he said gently.

"What?"

"If you could stay up a few more minutes, let's pour one more glass of wine and meet under the tree in, say... five minutes or so? I just want to tell you something. I promise, it won't take long."

Rosemary cleaned up in the bathroom, pulled on an old, thick robe—the only one she had at the lodge, and then, unfortunately, caught her expression in the mirror. There was a *fat* smile on her mouth. Her eyes were dreamy, drugged. And her face had this absolutely happy look.

Spending even a second more time with Whit Cochran tonight was completely dumb. She should never have agreed. But…she had.

And when she wandered back into the living room, she felt her tension ease. Whit was sitting on the floor with his back to her. He motioned for her to take the reverse position—so she was sitting with her back to him.

"I'm not sure this will work, but I figured we have a chance of behaving if we can't see each other."

"I figured you'd take one look at this ratty old robe and wonder what you ever saw in me."

He poured the wine—a half glass for each, as if promising they weren't staying up long enough to drink more than that. "I know what I saw in you. And see in you. Trust me, the robe's no deterrent." He rubbed her back with his back, making her smile, and she started to relax.

The night had turned quiet as a hush. The fire had gobbled up logs, and become a thick blanket of glowing orange coals. Her body still felt the lushness of Whit's lovemaking, his tenderness, his care, her impossibly strong response to him…but he didn't mention that.

He leaned his head back against her head, said quietly, "You shared something hard and uncomfortable to talk about, when you brought up your ex-fiancé. I'd like to tell you something the same way. Something that needs to stay between the two of us."

"Sure."

"The girls can't know this, Rosemary."

She wanted to turn, when she heard the gravely tone in his voice. She understood he wanted to talk about something difficult for him. But...he'd chosen the sitting arrangements. Maybe because it was easier to say something when he couldn't see her face.

"Here's the thing," he said. "Zoe and I married straight out of school. I couldn't keep my hands off her, never doubted that it was the real kind of love. Her family put on a big wedding, all the trimmings, she looked like an angel. The honeymoon, though, only lasted about three days."

"Uh-oh."

"She liked to tell her friends that I was a work in progress. She thought marrying a landscape architect meant that I'd have a desk job, make good money, come home and we'd do operas and ballet and attend a lot of fancy functions. Fund-raisers. Charity events. Causes. Black-tie stuff."

"Uh-oh," she murmured again.

"I managed to meet one of her expectations. I made good money. It wasn't that hard, because I love the work. It's just that planning a site is only a small part of the job. I pick the plants, the trees and I want to put them in myself, work with the growth sites, the shape of the land, the contours.... I mean, all that stuff is the joy of it."

"You'd love my oldest brother, Tucker. He can get dirty by just stepping outside."

"Yeah. That's me, too. I'd come home, tired to beat the band, and I couldn't even walk in the door. If she had her way, I'd have stripped outside and gotten hosed down before coming in. We had a white couch. White carpeting. Some magazine did a spread of the place. Not because we were that wealthy. But because she was so full of taste and style. Or that's what the article said."

Whit started to rub against her back again, but then he just let out an earthy sigh, and crashed. He was beat. She understood. She was too darned tired to sit any longer, too. Still, they both choose to lie near the hearth, head to head rather than close enough to hold each other. This wasn't about temptation anymore, she understood. It was about him getting something off his mind.

"Okay," she said. "So how'd the marriage go from there?"

"That's exactly what I wanted to tell you. But it isn't really a fun thing to say."

"You think my telling you about George's sexual escapades was fun?"

"No. I think it was damned tough. And that's why I'd like to own up to something on the tough side for me. I was proud of her, Rosemary. What Zoe did, she did so well. I was the screw-up. I went to the ballet, did my best not to fall asleep. I'd do the tux thing, the charity auction thing. I didn't want to argue with her. I didn't want her to be unhappy. If she wanted quiche and I wanted meatloaf, hey, that was no big sacrifice. But the whole package got harder and harder. I just couldn't be the man she wanted."

"Aw, Whit."

"I don't know who screwed up worse—her or me. Maybe she thought I was someone else when she married me. But I was working more and more hours, just to stay away from the house that wasn't my house, the life that wasn't any kind of life I wanted. Only then... she got pregnant."

"Planned?" Rosemary asked.

"Not exactly. Neither of us believed bringing kids into a bad marriage was a good idea. But...we slept together. Not as often as before, but there were always some nights when we'd turn to each other. When the pregnancy test came back, we were both startled. When further testing revealed she was pregnant with twins, well..."

"You were both scared witless?"

"You said it. But...then the girls were born...and from that moment on, everything was completely different. I took one look at those baby girls and fell like a brick. I always liked kids. But this was like...sunstruck. I never expected a bond that fierce, that powerful, that just plain instinctive. And Zoe...well, we didn't fight anymore. We didn't have time. She had help in the house, but twins are still a lot of work. I may not have had the same parenting ideas that she had...but we got along. I would have stayed in the marriage. Hell, I would have done anything to keep the family together for the girls' sake."

"There's a 'but' in your voice," she said softly.

"I never wished her harm. I swear."

"You don't have to swear. I believe you."

"This whole past year, I've felt so much guilt. I never wanted her to die. Never wanted anything bad to happen to her. But there was this feeling of...relief. Week by week, I felt like I was learning to breathe again. To not live 'tight' all the time. I could laugh out loud.

Come in from work on a hot summer day and pop the top on a beer."

"You felt free," Rosemary said.

"I did. I do. But I know the girls think I'm still grieving for their mom, and I can't—would never—tell them otherwise. They loved her. They miss her.

"Zoe was never evil or bad or anything like that. We just didn't fit. I never put her down in front of them. I never will."

"I understand, Whit."

"Yeah, I think you do. Because you felt you had to keep a secret from family. Different reasons, different situations. But that one aspect is the same. When you love someone, you don't want to hurt them. And if that means you have to lie or keep secrets or whatever, you just do it."

"Whatever you have to do," she agreed.

"I don't like lying. Or to feel like I'm a liar."

"I completely understand, Whit. I never wanted my family to think I'd walk out on a wedding on a whim. But…"

"You felt it'd hurt them more if you told them the truth."

She closed her eyes. It was odd—and maybe amazing—how different their stories were. Yet how much they somehow understood each other.

Whit said nothing for a while. Moments passed. When the old chime clock in the far corner hit twice, she realized he'd fallen asleep. And it was past time both of them got up to their separate bedrooms and knocked off some serious z's.

She meant to get up. Meant to wake Whit. But the

night had been precious in so many ways, that she just didn't want to give in yet. There were still sounds and smells and treasures to inhale. Including Whit.

Especially including Whit.

And that thought was the last thing she remembered.

Chapter Twelve

When Whit opened his eyes, two bright faces loomed over him. He strongly suspected the chances of further sleep wouldn't make bookie odds.

"Dad, did you and Rosemary really sleep down here? On the floor like this? Weren't you cold?"

"Dad, there are presents under the tree. You told us we weren't doing any presents this year. Except that you bought all that stuff for our rooms. But you said that wasn't about Christmas and it was all getting shipped home. So what'd you get us? Can we open them?"

"Dad, we have to call Grandma and Grandpa. You think it's too early?"

"Dad—"

"Dad—"

He swiped the sleep from his eyes, recognized that his entire body had been twisted in a cold, cramped position, and swung to a sitting position. Then, looking at his girls, raised his arms.

They swooped in for a Christmas hug. They both snuggled in close, and both seemed to decide the attire for the morning required red tops with lots of glitter, jeans, and red-and-white socks. They'd brushed their hair, used a red, white and green elastic band to make ponytails, and somewhere, somehow, they'd found some eye makeup.

At least he was pretty sure Lilly's eyelids weren't green—and Pepper's weren't red—when they'd gone to sleep last night.

The questions continued. There was no point in trying to answer any until they'd both run out of steam. In the meantime, he turned a sharp eye on the crumpled mound still on the floor. It didn't look like a body. It looked like someone—such as himself—had half woken in the night, and scooped all the afghans and throws from the couches to cover her up.

She was still covered up, including her head.

She wasn't still sleeping, because that was inconceivable with the girls' racket. But considering how little sleep they'd gotten the night before, he wasn't surprised she was trying to fake it.

That, of course, didn't last long. The girls pounced, peeled the blanket off her face, and discovered a smiling Rosemary—who burst out with a "Happy Christmas, you two!"

They shrieked in return.

"Okay guys, we're going to give Rosemary a chance to run upstairs and change clothes, while I make breakfast."

"He's going to make crepes, Rosemary—but that just means pancakes, don't be worried."

"Hey," Whit objected, trying to sound mightily offended. "I brought my copper pan, the Bisquick, the rum. Not like I don't know how to do this."

Lilly, like always, rushed to reassure her. "Yeah, he uses rum, Rosemary, but it's not like you'll feel funny or get drunk or anything. It just takes a tablespoon. But it has to be good rum."

"Like you'd know good rum from bad," Pepper said, then rolled her eyes.

"Girls…" He took that moment to intervene. "Where'd you find the eye shadow?"

"We already had it."

He had the batter made by the time Rosemary popped downstairs, wearing jeans and a white sweater with Christmas trees. Her eyes met his, with an expression so vulnerable, so fragile…so much worry. And then not. "Hey, I really need to call my parents. Is it too late to do it before breakfast?"

"No, go for it. I need to make a call to the kids' grandparents, too."

They both headed for their cell phones. He called his parents—the time change to Washington was always an issue, but no problem to call them early, because they were always up at the crack of dawn. They loved to talk with the girls.

By the time Whit rang off, he aimed back to the kitchen to finish making breakfast.

Rosemary ambled into the kitchen moments later. "I didn't get my parents yet—their line was busy. But they'll call back any minute. I'll set the table."

Her cell drummed on, just as she scooped up a handful of forks and knives. He poured her coffee, then went back to his flapjacks. Or pancakes. Or crepes. Whatever they were. Since Rosemary'd already made that super coffee cake, it didn't much matter if his pancakes worked out.

He could hear Rosemary from the doorway, as she set the table.

"Dad!" Her voice was bright as sunshine. "Good, good, glad Mom can come on, too. Merry Christmas to you both! When are Ike and Tucker and the kids coming over?"

Some sort of chitchat bantered back and forth. He couldn't hear what her parents said—or guess which parent was talking to her—but from the conversation, it appeared that both her parents poured on guilt with all the enthusiasm of alcohol for an alcoholic.

"I'm sorry, but that's just not going to happen. There's no possibility of any kind that George and I will get back together."

Silence again. He had to flip the first set of crepes, put a fresh dollop of butter in the copper skillet. He missed some of the conversation, but heard her respond to one of her parents.

"That's not really true. I'm doing work up here. For positive, I'm not hiding out at the lodge because I'm afraid to face George or anyone else. I…"

More silence. He couldn't stand it, and took the pot in the dining room to refill her mug. The table was set and she'd plunked down in a chair, her elbow on the table and a hand in her hair.

"Listen, you two. I love you both. I'll be seeing you

in a matter of days. And I'm sorry that you're upset with me. I'm sorry that you feel disappointed. But all I can say is that both of you, by now, should know that you can trust me. Trust my judgment. You should know that I broke up with him for serious reasons. And I really don't want to talk about this again. I hope you both have a super day. Say hi to the gang. And I'll see you in a few days, as soon as I can head down the mountain."

When she clicked off, she tilted her head, saw him in the doorway holding the spatula. Her expression changed, from looking crushed and vulnerable…to a wry smile. "Boy, was that fun."

"That's just what I was thinking. Maybe after breakfast, we could both…I don't know…fall off a cliff. Or go kick up some copperheads. Or put our hands into a beehive."

"Darn it. You're making me laugh."

"You want laughter? Wait until you taste these crepes."

The girls descended on the table. Lilly, thankfully, always ate the burned ones, and Pepper, just as predictably, gobbled them up until she groaned, she was so full. Rosemary expressed shock that they actually tasted good, requiring him to pretend to punch her arm.

Then came the presents. He hung back, tense, watching the girls open their cameras, and all the gear and supplies that came with them. He worried, always, whether he'd picked something age-appropriate…but also something they'd personally like. They were old enough to be into labels and clothes styles that he had no way to cope with.

Rosemary, on the floor near his knee, shot him a glance. "I told you so."

"They do like 'em, don't they."

"Are you kidding? *We love them!*"

Whit got buried in hugs and kisses, but all too soon the girls settled down. Too soon, they noticed the one last present under the tree. For Rosemary. From him.

He'd never run from a problem or a tough challenge, but he had the brief, sick wish that he could just disappear. He hadn't known what to get her. Going into stores and shops, nothing jumped out at him. He had no idea whether to get her something funny, or something traditional, or candles or jewelry or clothes, and every store he'd tried in Greenville, some saleslady took one look at him and started in with the advice. He'd never had a panic attack, but he'd come close.

It mattered. That he do something right. In her eyes, on her terms. It mattered more than he could breathe. He wasn't so good with words, like some men. And God knew, Zoe had told him over and over that he was terrible at choosing presents.

The girls brought the box out from under the tree. They were already rolling their eyes. Okay, so the big box looked a little ragged. He'd had to use a lot of Scotch tape. And he didn't have enough paper, so he'd sort of had to add newspaper to it. And then the bow got crushed when it was upside down in the car.

"What on earth…?" Rosemary asked.

"Listen. It's like I told you before. I get presents all wrong. So don't worry if you don't like it or it's wrong or something. Don't expect anything. Don't—"

"Sh," she told him sternly. Inside the big box was a

smaller box. And then another. And finally, was a manila envelope.

She slit open the envelope, and even before she'd pulled out the sheath of papers, the girls rounded on him.

Lilly was almost beside herself. "*Dad!* You were supposed to get her a real present!"

Pepper was more vocal. "Come on, Dad, what'd you do? Paper isn't a present!"

He couldn't answer them for that instant. His gaze was glued to her profile, as she studied the content on the papers. Finally, she lifted her face to his. She started to say something, stopped. Tried again. Her voice barely reached a whisper.

"Whit. How could you do this to me?"

He saw her eyes well up with tears, felt his heart drop like a stone. The girls got even more upset. "What did you *do* to make Rosemary cry? What's going on, Dad? What did you give her?"

An alien suddenly invaded her body. Rosemary didn't cry. She'd never worn emotions on her sleeve, never lost control in public. But the sting of salty tears in her eyes turned on like a switch that wouldn't shut off. She said quickly to the girls, "I'm not really crying, girls. Honest. I... Something..."

Well, she couldn't finish. She could see the look of alarm and worry on their faces, but she couldn't speak. Her throat suddenly felt as thick as molasses.

Whit carefully, calmly intervened. "You know what? I think holidays get crazy for everyone. Let's give Rosemary a little break, guys. We'll go outside, take your cameras, try 'em out."

She couldn't look at him. She wanted to reassure him, immediately, what his present meant to her. But for at least that moment, her throat was still jammed up, the tears still threatening a hurricane deluge. It was stupid and she was mad at herself, but there it was.

By the time Whit and the girls came back in, she still hadn't figured out what had happened to her, but it was better. Everything was better.

She made a joke to the girls about being an idiot sometimes, and the group congregated in the kitchen. Whit took on breakfast cleanup—and clove-studding the ham. She and the girls put together a cherry sauce, and then a huge batch of the cheesy potatoes the girls wanted.

She tried to catch Whit's eye—wanted and needed to explain why she'd reacted so strongly to his present. But the girls hovered like guardian angels, outside, inside, wherever she was.

She found Pepper waiting outside when she opened the door to the bathroom.

"Listen, Rosemary," Pepper said with a wary eye down the hall as if her sister or dad might appear any minute. "You have to understand about my dad. He doesn't know how to give presents to grown women. My mom said so all the time. She used to say, 'Just give me a check, honey. It'll save you having to shop or buying anything crass. Or trashy.' Or something like that. So it's not like he doesn't try, you know? He gets us. He gets kids. But you're another adult, you know?"

Rosemary opened her mouth, then closed it. When

Whit told her about his marriage last night, all the things the girls had mentioned about their mom suddenly added up. The stories she'd heard about Zoe suddenly all had a different interpretation. Zoe had been a harper. An overcritical badger. Especially of men, but also of her daughters.

That made it all the more important that she catch Whit alone for a few minutes, but she just couldn't make it happen.

Once dinner was in the oven, Whit dragged them all outside again—they'd forgotten to check on their manger, and both girls wanted to take pictures of the crèche. The kids pranced and danced outside, singing off-key renditions of their favorite carols, and coaxing her to sing with them—at least until they arrived at the manger.

Their manger was unrecognizable. The lean-to shelter had leaned over and crashed. The wind had whipped around their sheet people. Some critter had stolen the blanket from the crèche.

"You know what?" Rosemary said, when the kids' exuberance suddenly bottomed out.

"That it was never as great as we thought?" Lilly asked mournfully.

"No. I think what we created was a moment in time. A Christmas Eve moment in time. A moment that no one else was meant to see or hear, exactly the way we did. So we four have the memory of it…but no one else ever will. It's just for us."

Whit looked at her. She felt his gaze, felt the warmth of his eyes. But the girls looked at her as if she'd said something deep and profound and they were trying to figure it out. Finally Lilly stepped forward, and put an arm around her waist.

"Rosemary," she said tactfully, "I think you're really goofy sometimes. But we love you anyway."

"Hey, I love you, too," Pepper said, and took up roost on her other side. Whit came up from behind, and flapped her on the head with a glove...not the most romantic gesture.

"Me, too, on thinking you're goofy," he said gravely. "But also that you probably can't help it."

The twins turned on him, all giggles again. They chased through the woods for a while longer—even though a drizzly rain began—until everyone finally tired. If there was time before dinner, the girls wanted to play a game—something with dice and pretend money, that required a great deal of groaning, moaning and other dramatics. Every time she tried to meet Whit's eye, the girls were engaging him in something or another. Every time she caught him looking at her, and she started to say something—a scream from the girls diverted them both.

Midafternoon, the ham was done. The scramble to the table was akin to heathen wolves who'd been starving in the desert for a half century, and Rosemary told them so.

"Now, Rosemary," Whit said, "I don't think we're *that* bad."

"Well, you wolves have to wait for a minute, because I have something to say."

"Oh, yeah," Pepper said. "We need to say grace."

"Good idea," Whit affirmed.

Rosemary raised her hand. "I agree, too, but first—

I just want to say that I have a sort of present for you girls, but it isn't something I could wrap. I know you're going home to Charleston in a few days. You want to see your friends, get back to school and all that good stuff. But when you get more into your cameras and taking pictures…I'm inviting you to spend a weekend with me up here. You say whenever it works for you. And I'll show you how to develop the pictures yourselves."

"Oh, wow. That's *awesome,* Rosemary!" Pepper skidded around the chairs to give Rosemary a massive hug.

A glass of milk tipped over.

The ham fork clattered to the floor.

Then Whit came up with a toast—a milk toast—before they sliced the ham. "To Rosemary. Who's made this an incredibly special Christmas for all of us."

She lifted her glass. "To all of you," she said, "for making this an incredible Christmas for me."

Out of nowhere, she suffered another massive soft lump in her throat. It had been fun. The whole day. Every bite, every joke, every goofy carol, every witless game and dropped fork. But somehow, by the time she handed out slices of the coconut cake…she felt as if her heart was breaking.

They were leaving her, of course. Not in a matter of weeks, but a matter of a day or two.

If she'd fallen in love—even if she'd fallen out of her mind in crazy love with Whit—he was leaving. He had a job, a life. The girls had their friends, their school, their lives.

A woman would have to be stupid to make something more of the holiday than it was.

Yeah, it was magical. And special. And unique. But it was going to be over, and she needed to toughen up and face it.

She wrapped up the leftover ham and turned toward the kitchen.

"Nope," Whit said. "You did the lion's share of the work. The three of us will do KP. Out. Put your feet up."

"I don't mind—"

"Girls," Whit said, which worked like a trigger on a gun. The girls immediately rushed her, hustled her out of the kitchen, pushed her onto the couch and put a corny Christmas movie on the flat screen.

"Don't move until my dad says," Pepper warned her.

She tried to obey. She meant to obey. But she'd just settled into the dumb movie, when out of the complete blue, a thundering army showed up at her front door.

Bodies hurled inside. Boys. Adults. A howling blood-hound. A very, very pregnant lady. All yelling Merry Christmases and talking at once.

Whit let the girls loose once the dishwasher was filled up, but some baking pans still needed some work. His mind was on Rosemary, not the sink filling up with white soapsuds.

His present idea had been dumb, dumb, dumb. The kind of classic dumb he specialized in with women. He didn't exactly know why it brought tears to her eyes, but he knew the last thing he'd wanted was to stress her. Or upset her. Or hurt her.

She'd seemed fine the rest of the day—and that was true for all of them—but there'd been endless hours without having a single chance to explain about the present. Or discover why it upset her so much in the first place.

He lifted the potato pan into the sudsy water, then looked around for some kind of scrubbing device… when a noisy commotion erupted in the living room. Visitors.

He grabbed a dish towel to wipe his hands and headed for the doorway. Formal introductions were made—none of which could he hear—but he didn't need the introductions anyway.

The men had to be Rosemary's brothers—Tucker and Ike. Both were tall and lean, with Rosemary's eyes. Tucker looked a little more wash-and-wear; Ike more determinedly scruffy. The boys hanging by Tucker were a Mutt and Jeff pair; one athletic and the other a little geeky. They had to be close to his girls' age.

A dog was in the midst of everything—a huge blood-hound, with a tail thwacking anything that moved. He barged through the bodies, climbed on the couch and went into a prompt coma. That is, his eyes immediately drooped, while the tail continued to thump.

Two women were part of the group. A pregnant woman emerged from the crowded bodies—a *very* pregnant woman—who charged in the living room, watermelon-size stomach first, hands behind her back, and galloped straight for the bathroom. The other woman was built on the slight side, but had a smile that filled her face, easy joy in her eyes.

All of them had brought a heap of presents for Rose-mary. And the boys had brought the presents *from* Rosemary, so they could open them with her there.

Apparently—he heard this in someone's high volume voice—they'd had dinner early at the MacKinnon seniors. The MacKinnon mom/grandma predictably got an emergency call from the hospital. So they'd cleared out, decided to pack up their cars and head for the MacKinnon lodge and Rosemary.

Whit shook a half-dozen hands, met everyone even though he couldn't hear over the din, and watched Rosemary nestle in with her obviously loved and loving kin. At some point the bloodhound realized there were two other kids in the house—the twins—and uncrumpled from the couch to meet them, slobber all over them and get hugged. The kids, boys and girls both, took one look at each other and abruptly turned into wall huggers. Ike's wife, Ginger, noticed the kids were gripped by a terrible case of shyness, and came through with a rum cake.

Both the rum cake and last of the white coconut cake were devoured. Xmas cookies were produced. Presents ripped open. Soft drinks were handed out in the living room. And somewhere around an hour or two later, Whit headed for the refrigerator…when he abruptly discovered Rosemary's two brothers right behind him.

Tucker had a bottle of Carolina Peach Shine. The whiskey had a reputation; it was legal moonshine but that hadn't always been the case. There were still stills up and down the mountains in this part of Carolina. Tucker explained that history, while Ike amiably produced three glasses.

So…Whit didn't need a sledgehammer to get the message. Ike and Tucker took their big brother roles seriously—which meant he was about to get a grilling.

* * *

Rosemary knew the instant she saw her brothers' faces that she needed to save Whit, and quickly. When the MacKinnons first showed up, she saw no reason to worry. Whit ambled right in the middle of it all.

Garnet, Tucker's wife, had brought gifts—vanilla— from her own private vanilla stock. Whit caught on that she was the owner of Plain Vanilla, an herb store down-mountain. Garnet tended to hang back from strangers, but not with Whit, who immediately coaxed her into a dialogue about how she grew the vanilla, her techniques and ideas. Once Whit mentioned being a landscape architect, Rosemary doubted even a machete could pry them apart. Fertilizers. Weed killers. Soil pH levels. They buzzed on about stuff that clearly thrilled them both.

Tucker shot her an amused look. He loved to see his new wife open up and blossom.

The boys finally got to open presents from their aunt Rosemary—and naturally, she'd felt duty bound to choose things their parents wouldn't appreciate. Drums. A chemistry set. An ant farm. But a couple things were a little more serious. She'd bought Pete some modest shares of stock in a respected toy manufacturer, because he was born for business, even at his young age. And Will got a rock tumbler, which was another truly horrible noisemaker intended to drive his parents crazy.

Tucker showed his appreciation by bopping her on the head several times. Ike initially gave her a kiss and a shrug-hug, but then he hunkered down with the kids. The girls and boys were still a little frozen with each other, but Ike got them loosened up by telling bear stories.

En route, Rosemary had to catch up with Ginger, Ike's new bride. Ginger had met Ike when she was in a heap of trouble—her so-loved grandfather had developed Alzheimer's; the family tea plantation had been self-destructing; her ne'er-do-well father showed up, assuming she'd be happy to support him…and oh, yeah, she happened to be pregnant by a man she described as a cross between vermin and a louse.

Ginger, unlike her gentler sister-in-law, never had to be coaxed to talk. She was redoing an antique bassinet for the baby…. Her grandfather was doing far better with family in the house…and she was far, far, far too pregnant to handle the crisis of her deadbeat dad, so she'd passed that crisis on to her new husband.

"Everyone who meets Ike," Ginger told her, "thinks he's laid back and easygoing and not one to walk fast in a tornado."

"I know," Rosemary agreed, half an eye on Whit, who was still talking to Garnet, but simultaneously managed to move a dish of cookies away from the bloodhound's mournful eyes. "Ike always claimed to be lazier than a slug. I think he just really didn't want to be work-obsessed like our parents."

"Well, that's the scam he sold himself. Anyway, he met my father, couldn't have been more welcoming or nicer. Next thing, he took my blood pressure and then just said that my dad could always visit, but he wasn't living with us at this time. I told him that was fine. Next thing I know, he's put my father to work, doing lists and inventories of the tea supplies. My dad took off at the speed of light."

Rosemary chuckled, well able to imagine that picture. "Boy or girl, or do you know that?" She noticed Ginger's hand suddenly press on her bulging abdomen.

"The ultrasound claims it's a girl. Which has made Ike over the moon...but I have a nightmare worrying she'll be a redhead with a temper like mine. And my other nightmare is worrying that there are twins in there. How can I possibly be this big if there's only one?"

"You're not *that* big," Rosemary promised her.

"I am. I feel like my name should be synonymous with whales. Elephants. Defunct dinosaurs. I haven't seen my feet in a month. Thank God for Garnet."

Garnet finally disengaged from Whit and moved closer. "I've been giving her herbs and herbal teas. Not medicinally. She doesn't need medicine. But just to boost her spirits."

"How can my spirits get boosted if I'm so fat I can't see my feet?"

Ike showed up from behind her back. "Have you ever seen a sexier, more desirable woman in your life?" He kissed her on the crown of her head.

"You can't mean that. You're delusional." But she looked at him with pure, naked love in her eyes.

Garnet rolled her eyes at Rosemary. "I thought Tucker and I were bad. But these two can't seem to let up on the google-eyes."

"I love seeing my brothers brought low," Rosemary assured them both.

The kids came pouring through the door. She started

cleaning up one mess—all the Christmas wrappings—
only one of the kids spilled a bowl of nuts, and then
dishes and glasses reproduced at the speed of sound
on all surfaces.

By the time she realized the women and children
were all in the living room and the men were alone in
the kitchen, she almost had a heart attack. Her brothers
had cornered Whit, she just knew it. She climbed over
Ginger's knees, weaved past the kids—all of whom
were eating popcorn from the tree—and galloped toward the kitchen doorway.

Ike and Tucker were just exiting—a bottle of moonshine in Ike's hand. Opened bottle of moonshine. Alarm
drummed in her pulse. "What have you done, you two?"
she asked darkly.

"It's okay. We just need to see you for a minute."

"Why. What's wrong. Where's Whit—"

"We were all outside for just a couple minutes."
Tucker, the eldest, had always used his strength to muscle her into doing what he wanted. Of course, that was
how she'd learned to pinch and bite.

"What's going on?"

"We're going to the bathroom."

"Together? Do we have to?"

"We only want two seconds alone with you. It's the
only place where we can't be overheard."

"What if I'd rather have witnesses?"

"This is between the three of us. Besides. If we're
taking over a bathroom, you can be positive we won't
talk for over three minutes. Ginger can barely wait that
long between visits, and she's not about to waddle all
the way upstairs."

"Where's Whit *now?*" she repeated. "How much moonshine did you pour down him?"

"Rosemary, Rosemary. How could you think such thoughts about your brothers? I swear you won't be mad at us. We just want to tell you a couple things in private."

They were evil, both of them. Always had been, always would be. But to give them credit, they were brief. They locked the door, looked at her portentously, gave big slow sighs—but once she punched them, they both started talking.

"Okay, here's the deal." Tucker spoke first. "We approve. We came here, both of us prepared to mop the floor with him if we had to. But I think you've finally met your match, cookie."

That was all he had to say, and Ike took even less time. "I'll never ask you again about George. Don't care. He doesn't matter. You've moved on. And to a better guy than George ever was."

"That's *it?* You're not even going to ask my opinion? You don't know what's happening or not happening. You don't know—"

"We know enough."

"Except…" Tucker stuck his hands in his pockets. "I was wondering if Whit's girls might like to come home with us. Just for the night. The kids were all talking about some game they wanted to play."

Rosemary frowned. "It wouldn't be up to me. It'd be up to Whit. But—"

"It's not like we'd be far away, sis. Just down-mountain. If the girls wanted to come back, I could have them back here in less than twenty minutes. I figured we should ask you before asking Whit. And before bringing it up to the kids."

"Well, I—"

"We could hear the four of them talking about this dumb game they wanted to play. You know how big our place is. It's not as if we don't have a whole wing to separate the genders."

"That never crossed my mind," Rosemary said, unsure why the brothers were sharing meaningful looks, and she got the feeling she was being manipulated. She didn't think it was necessarily a bad idea; she just felt railroaded.

"For that matter, if they just want to play the game and then come back up here with you and Whit, that'd be fine, too. It's no problem either way."

When Tucker was being nice, there was always a reason. She wanted to object on that basis—Tucker's historical record—only she couldn't really think of any real reason why the kids couldn't play a game together if they all wanted to.

"Ask Whit," she said.

They did. The commotion abruptly turned back into a noisy crescendo, with kids running around, collecting hats and mittens or forgetting them and coming back. Shoes were lost. Then found. Ginger, once she stood up, needed a bathroom run. Before she left, ten minutes later, she needed another one. Pansy, the bloodhound, came out of her coma and wove her way between people, especially people who were trying to carry things to and from cars. The girls were talking in shrieks, which, come to think of it, Rosemary had long figured out was their regular speaking voice.

Over and through it all, she kept track of Whit, and outside when the crew was all leaving, she noticed her two brothers aim toward Whit.

She galloped in front of Whit at breakneck speed. Stood in front of him, folded her arms.

Tucker and Ike stopped dead, glanced at Whit, then at her...and then both of them started laughing like hyenas.

"Whether you like it or not, Whit, it looks like she's going to protect you from us."

"If you two don't start being nice to me, I'd hate to tell you what I'll be giving the kids next Christmas. I'm thinking a boa constrictor. In a cage with a loose lock."

That didn't help. They laughed even harder.

To make matters worse, she suddenly felt Whit's hands on her shoulders from behind. "It's okay," he whispered. "I appreciate your protecting me. They're pretty scary."

"You think they're funny, but you weren't their little sister."

"I get that. But I like how they treat their little sister."

"That's only because you can't help it. You have that same twisted Y chromosome. You're not responsible for occasional Neanderthal opinions."

"Whew. I'm relieved you don't find me responsible."

The whole time she was having this insane conversation with him, his hands were still on her shoulders from behind, and the cars were backing up, lights on, disappearing down the mountain. Heaven knew when night had come on, but the sky was muddy black, clouds blustering against each other and occasionally spitting.

Obviously they needed to head inside, but she wasn't

ready. She wasn't ready for nightfall, for all the sudden silence.

And she definitely wasn't ready to face Whit.

Chapter Thirteen

"You realize that your brothers set us up so we could be alone tonight," Whit said.

"I know. They're both as subtle as sledgehammers." Cold rain kept drooling from the sky. Silver drops slid in her hair. In her eyes.

But she was intensely aware that something was different about Whit. He didn't seem to notice the cold, the dark, the rain. He just kept looking at her. There was a calm in his face, in his gaze.

"I told your brothers what I'd given you for Christmas," he mentioned.

"Oh? And what'd they say?"

"Well, once I told them, they stopped trying to pour moonshine down my throat. That peach moonshine…" Whit shook his head. "That's quite a drink. On a par with…"

"Gasoline?"

"That wasn't my first thought, but close enough. Tucker and Ike had been grilling me nonstop. When I confessed about the present, they both stopped talking altogether. They had this crazy idea that you loved the present."

"I did. I do." Blast it. Tears blurred her eyes again. Showing up like they did before, out of the blue, and including a soft thick feeling in her throat. "I more than loved it, Whit."

Slowly, cautiously, he came closer. Used the edge of his thumbs to wipe the spill of tears. "I thought you were crying because I'd disappointed or upset you."

"No. Never that. Just the opposite. It's just…there isn't much that moves me to tears. Not like this." She had to get past that lump in her throat, needed to tell him—wanted to tell him—exactly what his present had meant. "Most of my life, I've thought of myself as kind of invisible. My parents would sometimes forget that they were leaving me alone. My first boyfriend in high school—he was a good guy, no question—but when we broke up, he was with someone else in less than a week. Easy for me to start thinking of myself as forgettable. And then, of course, there was George. George said he loved me. I don't actually doubt that he meant it…but when push came down to shove, apparently he didn't know me at all. Never saw me. Not really."

"You might be giving me a whole lot more credit than I deserve, love. Your brothers just thought you'd like the present."

She laughed, but there was still a lump in her throat. Still the threat of emotional tears. Yet she raised her face to his.

And right there, so easily, his lips were waiting for her. Waiting for the chance to connect, the way Whit connected with her every second since he'd shown up in her life. He offered softness, tenderness.

"It's starting to freeze. And you're cold," he said.

"I don't want to go in yet. I want you to show me… your plan."

He pulled a stocking cap from his jacket pocket. Popped it on her head. Took off his jacket, wrapped it around her…then wrapped an arm around her, as well.

Ignoring dark and chill, snugged tight against him, he explained about the unique gift he'd given her. When she'd opened the envelope, she'd seen the rough sketched drawing of the yard around the lodge…but almost immediately understood what he was giving her and why.

Now, he walked her down to the fork in the road that marked the MacKinnon property, ambled up the drive, motioning and explaining as they went. "It's quite a slope," he said, "and I could see both that the soil tends to be dry, and tends to get a ton of sun. To make the most of both those issues, I'd want to plant into raised beds, do a gravel mulch. The thing about rosemary…"

He looked at her.

"The thing about Rosemary is that she's as close to perfect as anything on earth."

She gulped. "Doggone it, Whit. You're going to make me cry again."

"I don't think so. I'm just telling you the straight truth of the matter. They used to say rosemary was for remembrance. I think that's because she's so unique. No one could forget her. No one would want to forget her. She attracts birds and butterflies, the beautiful and gentle things around her. She's just as pretty in summer as in winter. She's got this fresh, pretty scent that affects everyone and anything around her." He motioned. "I think a hedge type of rosemary would be perfect; she'd greet everyone as they were coming up the drive. Up closer to the house, we could use a ground cover variety, mix up the blue and pink flowers, have a display that welcomes people coming in. Of course, people already know your door is always open to everyone...."

"Whit," she said, but damnation if her eyes weren't watering again.

"Once she's planted, she's extraordinarily self-sustaining. But that isn't to say she wouldn't thrive even more with care and attention. I have this idea about transplanting certain vulnerable plants. You dig the hole, make a nest for the plant, where it's warm and soft and safe. Then you put her in, and kind of 'love her in'—no tools, just your hands. Rosemary isn't a plaining or whining kind of plant, so if she isn't ing, you need to pay attention. She's strong. She ca weather all kinds of trouble. But that's not to say she doesn't need some cherishing, some cosseting, some plain old everyday love. She..."

Okay. He was going to talk all night if she let him. So she swung around in his arms, lifted up, invited a kiss.

Eyes closed, she cherished the mold and meld of his lips on hers. She tasted love. She tasted hope. She tasted the future.

She also stopped for just a second. "Whit. Did I tell you that I love you?"

"Maybe not in exact words."

"I'm glad you figured it out. But I'd still like to use the exact words. I love you, Whit. More and in a different way than I ever expected to love anyone. You know me, the one no one else ever has."

"I need you in my life, the way I've never needed anyone." His eyes had a fierce shine. "Before the new year, I'd like to pick out a ring."

"Before the new year, I would love to wear your ring."

She knew they needed to talk about the girls. About where they would live, and how they could manage and balance their lives. But she wasn't remotely worried that they could come up with solutions, or that they could conquer any and all challenges in front of them.

Right now, all that could wait. She stole another kiss, then took his hand.

"Before we both freeze to death, I'm taking you in the house."

"I'll take you in. Anywhere, anytime," he said. "Merry Christmas, my love."

"And all the Christmases ahead of us."

They both smiled, and aimed for the house.